Praise for *The Vampire Files*

"The story shifts easily between comedy and mystery, and Elrod's treatment of the practical aspects of vampirism is clever and refreshing."
—*Booklist*

"Echoes of Hammett and Chandler abound, but the novel succeeds in its own right as an entertaining exercise in supernatural noir."
—*Publishers Weekly*

"Plenty of action, full of twists and betrayals, and the quirky characters and many touches of period flavor keep things amusing."
—*Locus*

"Very entertaining."
—*Mystery Scene*

"So fast-paced and so involving that you won't put it down."
—*Romantic Times*

"Fast . . . intriguing."
—*The Midwest Book Review*

"An entertaining blend of detective story and the supernatural. . . "
—*Science Fiction Chronicle*

"Elrod's Vampire Files series featuring Jack Fleming may be unique in both mystery and fantasy annals for its consistently high quality and her steadfast refusal to repeat a plot or take the easy way out."
—*Crescent Blues Book Views*

"Four stars . . . a lot of fun."
—*Rave Reviews*

"The pace is fast . . . intriguing . . . an updated version of the old pulp novels."
—*Science Fiction Review*

"Well done . . . original . . . Fleming makes a powerful and charming detective . . . you won't want to miss this series." —*Cemetery Dance*

"Entertaining."
—*Science Fiction Chronicle*

"Builds to a frenzied climax leaving the reader almost gasping for breath. Be prepared to read the last half of the book in one sitting . . . should satisfy even the most demanding adventure-lover's appetite for breathless, nonstop action and excitement."
—*Big Spring Herald*

"The twists and turns of the story are reminiscent of *The Maltese Falcon* or *The Big Sleep* . . . excellent." —*Tarriel Cell*

The Vampire Files

LADY CRYMSYN

P. N. ELROD

ACE BOOKS, NEW YORK

LADY CRYMSYN

An Ace Book / published by arrangement with
the author

PRINTING HISTORY
Ace hardcover edition / November 2000
Ace mass-market edition / October 2001

Visit our website at
www.penguinputnam.com

Check out the Ace Science Fiction & Fantasy newsletter
and much more on the Internet at Club PPI!

ISBN: 0-441-00873-9

ACE®
Ace Books are published by The Berkley Publishing Group
a division of Penguin Putnam Inc.,
375 Hudson Street, New York, New York 10014.
ACE and the "A" design
are trademarks belonging to Penguin Putnam Inc.

PRINTED IN THE UNITED STATES OF AMERICA

10 9 8 7 6 5 4 3 2 1

Thanks to:
Teresa Patterson
Keven Topham
and
Jean Marie Ward

And a special thanks to:
Joe James
Sherry LaBelle
Gardner Pourcio
Ruth Woodring
and Roddy McDowall

1

Chicago, June 1937

I WOKE up in my basement sanctuary to the sound of a man's shoe heel cracking hollow against linoleum three yards over my head. It was exactly sunset so I'd be awake anyway without the alarm call; this was just my partner's way of telling me something was up and to get moving.

Having fallen into my daylight stupor still wearing a bathrobe and slippers, there was no need to don them as I rose from the army cot that was my humble bed. Being completely unconscious while the sun was high meant that comfort wasn't the big concern so much as having a layer of my home earth sandwiched in between two sheets of oilcloth on the thin mattress. No coffins for me; the damned confining things give me the creeps.

Escott thumped the floor again like a flamenco dancer with no rhythm and called down at me. "Jack? Are you there? Jack?"

It was a perfectly reasonable question. Sometimes I slept

the day over at my girlfriend's place. Escott hadn't bothered to lift the hidden trapdoor under the kitchen table to see if I was in.

"Yeah, yeah," I muttered. My bricked-up alcove with its cot, desk, chair, and lamp vanished into a gray nothingness, and I shot upward until encountering the resistance of the ceiling. Like invisible vapor through a grille, I sieved swiftly through the minute spaces and cracks in the barrier until fully clear. How the process worked, I couldn't really explain, it just did, and though tiring, I often took advantage of the gift.

I materialized, annoyed and puzzled, in the bright light of the kitchen. "What is it, a fire?" I asked, squinting.

"A call," Escott said, pointing to the phone on the wall by the pantry.

"Something wrong with Bobbi?" Past events made me more than a little anxious about the welfare of my girlfriend.

"Miss Smythe is perfectly fine, so far as I'm aware. This has to do with that club of yours."

"Oh." A whole different kind of worry for me. I hurried to snag up the earpiece. "Yeah? Fleming here, what is it?"

"Mr. Fleming, we gotta problem." The voice belonged to Leon Kell, the foreman I'd hired to take care of the renovations of the property I'd leased. He sounded tense. "I donno how you wanna handle it, so I told the boys to back off until you got here."

"What's the problem?"

"I don't wanna say over the phone."

I kept my cursing to myself. He'd apparently seen one too many gangster films. "C'mon, Leon, the G-men don't wire phones of honest citizens," I lied. "What's wrong?"

"The boys found something when they started knocking through that last cellar wall you wanted cleared. It happened just before quittin', an' I told them to hang around until you got here to tell us what to do."

Which meant a crew of half a dozen able-bodied men were all standing about with their picks and shovels in hand getting paid extra by me to smoke cigarettes. "Okay, then let them go for the night and—"

"That might not be such a good idea, considerin'."

"Considering what?"

"I don't wanna say, Mr. Fleming, an' if you come down here you'll know *why* I don't wanna say it."

Shit and Shinola. This was a whole new side to Leon's otherwise sensible character that I could have done without. "Okay, I'll be right there." I slammed the earpiece back on its hook with more force than was really required.

"He strikes me as being a cautious soul," Charles Escott commented from his seat at the kitchen table, where he'd heard my end of the conversation. Before him was his modest evening meal, purchased on the way back from his office. A sandwich and spuds tonight, making a change from his usual white cartons packed full of Chinese food. "He gave you no clue to the problem?"

"Leon's crew found something in the cellar. He wouldn't say what."

Escott looked up, his gray eyes and lean face suddenly bright with interest and grim concern. "It must be a body, then."

"Now where the hell do you get that?"

"If they'd ruptured a gas or water main, Mr. Kell would have been much more forthcoming with information. If it had been buried treasure, he'd not have called, period."

It was too early in the evening for me to deal with this kind of thing, I thought.

"I'll accompany you, if you don't mind."

"You need to eat." It wasn't just his face that was lean. When he got busy on a case Escott sometimes forgot about

food unless someone bothered to remind him. He didn't
have a lot of friends, so that job usually fell to me. Besides,
something was going wrong with the most important new
thing in my life, and I didn't want to sit around waiting
for him to finish his feed bag.

And damned if he didn't seem to read my mind. "I'll
have ingested sufficient nourishment by the time you've
finished changing, unless you plan to establish a truly in-
formal atmosphere to the site by appearing in such attire."

I gave him a brief sour smile, then vanished between
one eyeblink and the next to go upstairs for clothes. He
must have expected the move, for I didn't get his usual
comment of "damn" in reaction. Show-off antics like that
nearly always got some kind of rise from him. I only did
it now to divert myself from the gut-sinking idea that he
was probably right.

This was post-Prohibition Chicago and still reeling from
the aftermath of Big Al's near-uncontested reign. The old
building I'd picked to house what would become Lady
Crymsyn had a violent history; it'd be strange if there
wasn't a nasty surprise in the cellar.

The creation of my own swank nightclub represented a lot
more to me than just an interesting way to provide steady
earnings for decades to come. It meant that for once I'd
deliberately chosen a path for myself, not simply stumbled
along on those created for me by the needs of others.

You see, unaware of committing my worst crime against
myself, I'd wasted my first life.

I'd drifted, one year to the next, assuming I was in
charge of my destiny until a murderous beating and a
gangster's bullet put an abrupt stop to such foolish thinking. There it should have ended, my disappearance an open
mystery to my distant family, but of no concern to anyone
else, least of all to the men who'd killed me.

But much to their appalled surprise my weighted carcass didn't stay where they'd dropped it in the cold depths of Lake Michigan. The one good thing that had happened to me during that wasted life wouldn't leave me in such grim peace. I returned to the world of the living, confused and fired by rage, a dark rebirth attended by blood, madness, and, finally, no small amount of revenge. My killers were dead or the next thing to it; I was alive—or the next thing to it—and it was time for me to cease drifting and move forward.

And for once it would be on my own terms.

Not that God or Fate or whatever you believe in is stingy with second chances. Those are all around us, only we're too distracted to notice them. Most of the time they're a lot more mundane than the special one I'd been handed.

Mine had to do with being a card-carrying, dusk-to-dawn, stake-in-the-heart, you're-damn-right-I-drink-blood vampire.

It was a hell of a resurrection, but not so bad once I got used to things.

And since then I'd done rather well for myself.

A few months back, while flattening out a few wrinkles with a local mob, I discovered a hoard of their cash that they didn't know about. Though someone else walked off with the lion's share, the sixty-eight grand I'd stuffed into my coat pockets like a greedy kid in a candy store seemed more than enough to get me set up for good if I went about it the right way. I'd wasted one life; I wasn't going to repeat the mistake.

First I had to clean the money. Flashing around undeclared fistfuls of dough is a fast way to get the attention of the tax man. Capone himself got tossed in the clink on that little detail, but I could avoid landing in the next cell over by playing smart. The government doesn't seem to care *how* you make your money, so long as it gets its cut. Not much different from the mob, only there's usually less gunplay and more paperwork.

Presently, I was Charles Escott's nominal employee in his private detective business. (He preferred the more genteel title of "private agent.") Whenever we shared a case we split the payment fifty-fifty, but the huge amount I'd collected could not be declared as income from the Escott Agency without putting him in a bad spot. Uncle Sam would want to know what sort of work Escott did to justify such a generous payout to his staff, and, oh, by the way, we'd like to check *your* earnings as well . . .

Sure, I could sit on the dough and declare it a little at a time as cash earnings over the years. Escott was doing just that with his half of a ten-grand windfall we'd once gotten hold of by accident, but I was in too much of a hurry to wait. So with the help of a mobster who owed me a few favors I took advantage of a means to make my good fortune safely innocent. All I needed was a racing form and directions to the nearest line of bookies. Hell, all I needed to do was stand still, and they'd come to me. This town had them thicker than grass.

For a month I hung out in such company, going to various joints as soon as the sun was down in Chicago to put bets on horses about to run in California, where it still shone. Not big bets, but lots of them, to show or place, never to win, since that was more of a risk and could drive down the odds.

My mob advisor told me which horses I should play and which bookies to bet with. Not every race was rigged, but there were enough to slowly turn about half my fortune into legitimate-seeming wins. Only I wasn't really winning money so much as breaking even. For every ten dollars I bet, I'd get back twenty—but the bookie would get a twenty from me, not a ten. It was all numbers in a book.

Count the actual cash and you'd tumble to the game, but no cop or treasury agent ever interfered.

The bookies were all in on the scam and took their cut for cleaning services when I purposely lost every fourth or fifth bet to make things look legit. In this way they took between five and ten percent. I could spare it, figuring it to be a fair commission and much better than me trying to explain the real source of the cash to a nosy government accountant.

Duly entering every last dollar in a ledger, I kept careful records of my wins and losses. Declared cash all squeaky clean and financial records square enough for Euclid, I was free to get down to the real business of making my dream of a swank nightclub into a reality.

Location is everything. I soon found a former speakeasy on the North Side once run by a mug named Welsh Lennet. It closed years ago when thugs tossed a couple of grenades through the front doors as part of an ongoing territorial dispute. Lennet and a few others in his group were killed, with no one to take over for him. When Repeal went into effect, there didn't seem much point in trying to rebuild, so the gutted remains of his speak were left to gently rot.

The present owner was mob, of course, and unwilling to sell, but he could be persuaded into making a two-year lease. I knew the catch on that one: I get the club up and running, then discover I can't renew the contract or that the leasing price has suddenly tripled. Just in case I was unaware of the ploy, my mob mentor, Gordy Weems, mentioned it to me, which was damned decent of him. I decided to sign, though. If, at the end of two years the place was a bust, then I could slip out of it easily enough, and if it was a wild success, I had my own way of getting around the owner. Along with vanishing into thin air, I also possessed an innate talent for hypnosis. When the time came he'd think it was his own idea to cut me a break. If

Gordy had figured out what I was planning, he kept it to himself.

Instead, he put the word out I was a friend of his to keep away the inevitable parade of shakedown artists wanting pieces of the club. Like it or not, to open so much as a hot dog stand in this town you had to give certain people their cut. Usually it was added in with the price of the permits or liquor or labor or deliveries. Gordy told me not to worry about it, so I didn't and just got on with the work.

There was a hell of a lot of it. No one had been near the joint for nearly five years. With its violent history, boarded-up windows, and the beginnings of serious dilapidation I couldn't blame people for staying away. It looked like it should be haunted, but I figured fresh paint and some neon lights would fix that, maybe even a fancy canvas awning going out to the curb . . .

As Escott and I pulled up to its redbrick front, he noticed the big sign above the door declaring: "Coming Soon: Lady Crymsyn."

"I thought it was going to be 'Jack Fleming's Club Crymsyn,' " he said.

"It was, until I figured that more than enough people in this town already know me." For fame, I had fond hopes of becoming a writer—hopes thus far not shared by those editors to whom I'd sent stories. Since it looked like I wasn't going to make any bucks in that direction in the near future, I needed the income from the club to keep my wallet filled. "I don't want the notice, just the money," I told him.

"Most wise. It is rather improved from when I was last here." The boards were off, and the broken windows replaced by diamond-shaped panes of red surrounding squares of clear glass in the center. The inside lights shone through them, bright and warm. Not a necessity in the summer, but come winter I hoped it would be an inviting sight to customers.

"You ain't seen nothing yet," I promised. He'd only been to the place once before, and then just after I'd closed the deal. At that time, my future top-of-the-tops club looked like an outhouse pit. Escott had kept diplomatically quiet.

We walked through the wide front doors to the lush lobby area. It was all finished, with pale marble floors, a substantial bar made of the same material, and a few discreet touches of chrome. Empty shelves made of inch-thick glass awaited their future stock of booze bottles and glassware. The lights underneath cast interesting shadow patterns on the walls and ceiling. It looked great, but they shouldn't have been on. I went behind the bar and found the off switch.

"What? No mirror?" Escott questioned, indicating the padded wall behind the glass shelves.

"Patent leather's got more class," I told him with a straight face.

"And safer for you. Are there any mirrors here at all?"

"Only in the public johns and dressing rooms." I'd just avoid them.

A double doorway sporting red velvet curtains led into the main club area. We went through, and Escott stopped cold.

"My God," he said. He was rarely awestruck. I enjoyed the moment.

On the wall opposite the entry was a larger-than-life-size painting of Lady Crymsyn herself, meant to be the symbolic personification of the club. I'd commissioned it from Alex Adrian—yeah, *that* Alex Adrian, the world-famous artist who could pick and choose his work. The Lady had only existed in my head, but his vision of her in oils made me believe her to be real.

A full-length portrait of a woman in a sweeping red gown, she looked down upon all lesser mortals with a sultry, striking face that expressed both mystery and seductive glamour. Yet her eyes sparkled with a kind of not-so-secret humor, making her approachable. The idea was for every man to want her and for every woman to want to be like her. Alex Adrian had outdone himself so far as I was concerned, and I judged the painting to be well worth the bundle I'd spent for it.

"You wouldn't happen to have gotten the model's phone number?" Escott asked after a moment of slack-jawed shock.

"I think Alex made her up, but on opening night I'll have a look-alike dressed exactly the same acting as hostess. You can try your luck with her."

"I shall do so," he solemnly promised.

We pushed on to the main area. What had been a one-story room was now two stories high since I'd had the crew demolish a large section of ceiling. Three broad tiers of deep, half-circle booths rose to fill the space with chrome divider rails between each level. The main color was dark red, of course.

I'd borrowed the idea of a multilevel horseshoe seating arrangement from Gordy's club. But instead of entering at the top tier and walking down to the dance floor, I'd reversed it. When you came in you could look up and see nearly the whole place. Anyone seated at the dozens of booths above also had the advantage of being able to check out new arrivals. I figured this might appeal to a certain type of customer who preferred not to sit with his back to a door. This place could easily seat about three hundred of them, four with the spare tables. A bar on each side of the room would serve them all.

The big dance floor had a fancy pattern of different kinds and colors of wood, and the stage two feet above it sported the same motif. It was thirty feet wide and almost as deep, which would allow space enough for nearly any act I cared to book, from a full band to a solo singer. In the center stood a white baby grand piano, protected for the time being by a canvas dust sheet. I'd already had in a special stage crew to set up the lights and microphone system. Because of it, there wasn't a bad seat in the house.

"My God," Escott repeated. He'd noticed the liberal use of red velvet upholstery, polished white-and-black marble tabletops, crystal chandeliers, and wall sconces. Gordy had also recommended a decorator.

"Class all the way," I said with a grin.

"I had no idea you were taking things this far. Most impressive."

"And this is with the dust still in the air. Wait'll opening night, when everything's all polished."

"I'll mark my calendar. What is Miss Smythe's opinion of it?"

"She's been helping. I let her have her way with the backstage dressing rooms. The performers are gonna think they died and went to heaven. She can't wait to sing here."

"There can't be that much space, though." Escott had been onstage himself once, and had an appreciation for the hardships of show business.

"I've got four good rooms with showers for the headliners up on this level and cellar dressing areas for anyone else. We're still working on getting that cleared out so the plumbing can go in."

"You have thought it through quite nicely."

"Not me. Bobbi. The talent has its own entrance up top, and I've had a door cut in the backstage wall so we can haul in big things like scenery or that piano—"

"Mr. Fleming!" Leon Kell emerged from the service door behind the bar on the far side of the room. Since it was impossible for me to supervise anything during the day, I had to hire people to do it in my stead. Leon seemed the brightest and had the right kind of experience, so he was put in charge of hiring others and making sure things went smoothly. Every night I'd stop by to check the progress as his crew started from the top and worked their way down, giving Lady Crymsyn the works and then some.

"You sure got here fast."

He was right on that. I hadn't stopped to shave. I shifted from being the proud entrepreneur to serious problem-solver. "What's going on?"

"This way." He motioned for us to come over.

I'd asked what, not where, but followed him downstairs.

The harsh glare of the unshaded bulbs strung along the cellar's exposed ceiling rafters showed up the labor yet to be done. Rubble was scattered over the floor, along with shovels and wheelbarrows to carry it away. Dust hung lazily in the close air, and behind me Escott gave in to an enormous sneeze.

The original cellar had been divided up—unnecessarily, I thought—by several thick brick walls, creating a number of tiny rooms and alcoves. At one point in the building's forty-year history those dismal holes were servant quarters. And I thought times were tough now. I replaced the walls with metal columns and cross beams to hold up the building. The basement gained floor space and lost rats' nests and other undesirable leftovers from previous occupants. Once the cleanup work was done, in would go a layer of cement to even out the floor and walls. It would still be a basement, but it wouldn't look like a medieval torture chamber.

Along with the lesser dressing rooms, the area would be used for storage and take deliveries via an alley doorway and ramp at the back. That door was wide-open, and clustered near it were the idle workmen, smoking on my time as I'd expected. They watched us come down the stairs, but didn't bother to move. It must have been a long day—most looked tired—but there was also a wariness to them as they frowned in my direction.

"It's over here," said Leon, guiding us across the room. He was short and wide and moved with a stumping kind of gait, but covered ground fast. His attitude seemed to be halfway between relief and agitation at my arrival, indicating he wasn't sure how I'd take his news.

The rubble got worse at the other end of the room. Leon picked a path to a corner where the last alcove still stood. Part of the divider was torn down, but there was something odd about the back wall it butted up against.

"You see it, Mr. Fleming?" he asked, pointing. "This here outer part goes right to the building's wall about twelve feet, but the room inside only goes back about nine."

"I see it," I said, doing my best to ignore the cold-pit feeling trying to situate itself in my gut.

There was a dank smell in the air I noticed while speaking. I don't breathe regularly and took an experimental sniff. It wasn't unbearable, only a musty mix of decay and dust. I'd known it once before about twenty years ago when I was serving in France. Me and a few of the boys in my unit got a furlough in Paris, and on one of our too-short days instead of getting drunk and enjoying female company as usual we took a tour of some old catacombs. We didn't stay long. The depressing sight of those endless dark tunnels and piles of ancient bones reminded us too much of what we'd seen on the battlefields. We got out fast and spent the rest of the day and night in a roaring alcoholic fog. The memory came back to me all over again here, razor-sharp.

"Jesus Christ," I muttered, not knowing if it was a prayer or a curse. Escott's face was serious, and he shot me an uneasy look. He'd have picked up on the smell, too.

Leon continued. "With all the crap down here and it being so dark and crowded with the other walls up, you wouldn't notice it so much. But after we got the lights in a couple of us wondered why this one wasn't as deep as the others. The bricks are a little different in color, too. Not as old as the rest. When we started this part of the job we found out." He pointed to a black opening in the newer brickwork about a yard above the floor. It was the right height for someone to swing a pick. A couple of courses had been pried loose and now lay with the rest of the rubble. The hole wasn't more than two feet across and half a foot high, and was the source of the musty smell.

Leon unhooked a flashlight from his tool belt and handed it to me, then stood back. From his manner and Escott's morbid suggestion I already knew what would be there, but I'd have to take a look. I was the boss; it was expected of me.

The flashlight beam was faded from use. Leon must have let the other guys have a good view, too. I angled it around, reluctant to get too close. The uncertain light at first revealed only that there was a space beyond the hole that stopped abruptly about an arm's length in. The opposite wall. The real one.

Now I aimed the beam downward and caught a glimpse of naked bones. I was half-prepared to see a grinning skull, but it wasn't visible. After a few seconds I realized I was looking at the regular knobby march of a spine. The body was lying facedown, then. Amid the pale bones was an incongruous glitter and matted twists of what had been bright red fabric.

Dear God. A woman. The glitter came from the sequins clinging to what was left of her evening gown. I stepped back and gave Escott a chance to look. He kept his expression impassive the whole time, but when he turned around all the blood had drained from his face. His eyebrows and the thin line of his mouth stood out against the gray flesh as though they'd been drawn on.

"Damn, but sometimes I hate being right," he said. His voice had a brittleness to it that I rarely heard. Only when he was deeply affected by something did he sound like that.

Couldn't blame him. I got the light and steeled myself for another look. There wasn't much more to see because of the narrowness of the opening, and I didn't care to pull any more bricks out. During my time in New York as a reporter I'd learned the cops get real annoyed when civilians disturb a crime scene.

The one new thing I did find out from this second glimpse turned me cold and sick. I could just see the hands—what was left of them. They'd been secured together behind her with handcuffs. Also, some stuff that looked like electrical cord started at her wrists and went up to the elbows. Whoever had done the job didn't want to risk her getting free, because a heavy chain led from the handcuffs to a thick bolt set into the inside wall.

"You noticed?" Escott was at my shoulder.

"Yeah," I whispered, with hardly enough spit in my mouth to talk. Dear God in heaven.

"I may be speaking without benefit of absolute proof, but from that and the odd positioning of the body—"

"Yeah. When they put her in there . . . she was still alive."

2

As nights go, I've had worse, but I could have easily done without this one.

None of the work crew had much to say about their find, especially the one who'd broken through the wall with his pick. A few were worried about the law, indicating that they probably had records. No surprise there, since I never questioned Leon about whom he hired. So long as the work went without a hitch, he had a free hand. Those men I took aside for a private little interview. I had an ache behind my eyes before finishing, but my hypnotic interrogation only confirmed that they knew nothing about the body. I gave them each five bucks severance and told them to come back to the job when the fuss was over. They thanked me and vanished like smoke.

I told Leon and the others to keep back from the alcove for the time being, then Escott followed me upstairs, where I could call things in to the cops.

He hitched one hip on an old table that served as a temporary desk and let his gaze wander over the plain room that was to be my office. It was big, but empty of nearly everything but the smell of fresh paint and new plaster. Fancy trimmings would come later. Right now the prospect of running a club didn't appeal to me very damn much anymore. Through no fault of my own things had gotten tragically complicated.

"You look like someone just pulled one of your teeth without benefit of an anesthetic," he commented after I hung up.

"That's just about how I feel."

"Yes, that poor woman."

"Yeah. Jeez, what a way to go." I'd seen (and been subjected to) more than my share of horrors in life, but to think of anyone being bricked up like that gave me the cold sweats. Shut away in perfect silence, no one to hear her screams for help . . .

In my own way, I knew exactly what that was like.

"Awful. She must have died of thirst and hunger, rather than lack of air."

"How do you figure that?" The question was out before I realized I really didn't want to know the answer.

"I spoke to the man who cracked through the wall. He said the quality of the air released was distinctive enough to notice, but not poisonous, so there must have been some small amount of circulation going on over the course of time. There certainly had to be openings into that chamber sufficiently large enough to admit—" He broke off with a grimace.

"Admit what?"

He unhitched himself from the desk and paced around, peering out one of the wide uncurtained windows that overlooked the front of the club. This was as uncomfortable as I'd ever seen him. "To admit rodents. I n-noticed some of the bones showed signs of gnawing."

"Charles, I could have lived all the rest of my life without knowing that."

"As I could as well, but it's knowledge, and you never know what might be useful in an investigation."

"You thinking about looking into this?"

"Only if you feel I should." He sounded less than enthusiastic. Because of its gruesome nature I couldn't blame him for being reluctant, but I also knew he was busy with some paying projects. One of them was pretty important and could land him some steady and lucrative work.

"You've got three things going at once, don't you?" I asked.

"Yes, as it happens I do—"

"Then you don't need this on top of 'em. This is cop-work. Let them do their job."

"But who is she, how did she come to be here?" He was a lean silhouette against the window, hands in his pockets, shoulders bunched with tension. I suddenly realized I'd not turned on the room light. He hadn't bothered with it either. Probably so he could better watch the street below. "Are you not curious?"

"I'm still in shock; gimme some time to get over it."

"You'd best do so straightaway. A police car just pulled up."

"That was quick."

"It has a radio antenna. They must have been very close."

We went downstairs. The two uniforms who'd been sent to check things had already pushed their way into the outer lobby and were gaping at the scenery, but covered up their initial awe pretty fast. For the first of several times that night I gave my name, where I lived, my occupation, and told them the problem. Escott did the same, but since he'd just come along for the ride and wasn't the owner of the joint, they weren't as interested in him.

We took the cops down to the basement and showed them what they needed to see, then stood back for the next few hours as things took their course. Eventually some plainclothes detectives and a photographer turned up. Anyone who didn't have a badge was herded upstairs for questioning.

Everyone got a grilling, and I could understand why the other guys had been so anxious to leave. It wasn't to avoid trouble so much as to get away from the aggravation of telling the same story over and over again.

The cops kept an eye on me the whole time and weren't exactly subtle about it. I shrugged it off, unworried since I had an alibi. The murder had taken place long before I decided to come west.

The coroner's wagon arrived, and I started to have hope that the circus would wind down once they carted off the remains. I had to revise my thinking when another big car pulled up behind, and out stepped Lieutenant Nick Blair, a homicide cop who didn't much like me.

He was even more nattily dressed than I'd remembered, this time in a midnight-black double-breasted suit with a matching fedora at a rakish angle. The getup looked to be worth about two months' pay for him. It was reasonable to assume that he was either on the take or had another source of money than his modest paycheck. He had hard brown eyes, slick dark hair, and sported a thick, wide mustache trimmed to give his mouth a kind of perpetual smile. Its confident good humor was entirely superficial when aimed at me. Along with the workmen and Escott, I stood outside watching all the comings and goings. Blair still managed right away to pick me from the crowd. I heard that sharks do the same thing when it comes to finding fish.

"This could be interesting," Escott murmured.

"Aw, you're just trying to make me feel good."

Blair aimed that false smile that didn't reach his eyes my way for a long ten seconds, then walked into the club without saying a word.

"Most interesting, indeed," Escott added out of the side of his mouth. You couldn't see it, because he was good at holding to a poker face, but I knew he was hiding an amused smirk under there somewhere.

The lieutenant and I did not exactly get along. The man was sharp and knew something was off that made me different from anyone he'd ever dealt with. It amused me and annoyed him that he couldn't figure it out. If he ever did, it'd probably annoy him even more.

We waited for Blair. It took him about a quarter hour to see what was in the wall and talk with the other cops, then he sent a uniform out. For Escott, not me. Blair must have decided to save the best for last. I lighted a cigarette and waited some more in the cool, damp evening air and chatted with one of the officers about the moderate summer we were having. He observed that we'd probably have a bad winter to compensate, then cast a watchful eye back toward the street as more cars pulled up and stopped, spewing forth a number of noisy people moving with great purpose. I didn't know their faces, but sure as hell recognized their occupations, having been in it once myself.

I gave an inward groan and hightailed it into the club, but not before one of the photographers managed to blind me with a flashbulb explosion from his Speed Graphic. Hands groping for the door handle, I made it inside just as their first babbling wave of questions struck, and hoped that the cop would keep them out.

Reporters. I'd wanted publicity for the club, but not this kind. The business I was aiming to draw in would not be attracted by lurid stories about corpses walled up in the basement.

The man outside was losing his battle against the tidal

force of the First Amendment. They'd flood in any second. I ducked for cover down behind the lobby bar just as they burst through the door. There seemed to be a lot of them, all talking at once.

"Holy moley, some joint."

"Ah, I seen better."

"Where? Buckingham Palace?"

"Move outta the way, I wanna shot of this." A flashbulb went off, flooding the lobby with miniature lightning. I flinched and dropped lower, my nose just above an incongruous dark stain marring the brand-new tiles. Damn. That shouldn't have been there. It was like finding that first scratch on a new car.

"This place is all right. Wonder who's paying for it?" A woman's voice.

"One of Big Al's leftover cronies," a man told her with wise surity.

"How do you know that?"

"I don't, but that's what I'll write. You know all these joints have to be cleared by the mob before they can open."

"Cleared?"

"Look around you, sugar, this is *owned* by the mob. Who else has that kind of dough these days?"

"I heard that Welsh Lennet was the man who—"

"Tell me how to suck eggs, sugar. I used to come here back when he ran it. It was just a speak-sleazy then, and I mean sleazy. There was stuff going on in this pit to make your hair stand on end."

"Spare me the cliché quotes, I can make up my own. If it was so bad, why'd you hang here?"

"Stories, my dear, I got miles of copy out of it. I remember when the Nevis gang bombed the joint. Welsh was right over there—and then he was over there and there and there and all mixed up with a couple of his muscle boys and some poor lady bartender caught a freak piece of shrapnel and dropped in her tracks behind the bar and bled to death. They still got that in the same place, I see."

"Leave it to you to notice. So," the woman said, and I could imagine her surveying the room, eyebrows slightly raised with disdain, "where's this year's stiff?"

"In my pants, sugar."

"Dream on, darling, it's all you'll ever get from me."

"Lemme tell you about my dreams—"

"Hire a shrink. What's through here?"

Their babble faded as they moved into the main room, and I relaxed a little. Someone had flicked on the bar light again. Without thinking about it I shut it off. Mistake. One of the guys had lingered and noticed.

"Hey, who's there? Come on out and—"

By the time he'd poked his head around the bar I'd vanished. Safe from view, I hung in place while the intruder thoroughly checked the area. He probably wasn't as interested in finding anyone so much as assuring himself that no booze had been accidentally left lying around. I tried to stay out of his way, but he jostled into—or I should say through—me all the same, collecting a fierce shiver. Any contact people make with me while I'm in this form is a noticeably chilling experience for them. He soon went away, muttering his disappointment, and joined the others.

I materialized and drew enough breath for a sigh of relief. It would be impossible to put them off forever, but I wanted to postpone things for as long as possible.

Vanishing cured the ache behind my eyes, but not this ongoing pain in the neck. I had things to do, starting with another phone call. Alone and unwatched for the moment, now seemed the right time. Gordy had been decent to me; I thought I'd return the favor.

The photographer bozo had flipped the bar light on in his search. With mild annoyance I cut it off yet again, then cat-footed over the marble floor to the stairs without getting spotted. I could have gone invisible one more time, but it takes a lot out of me, and I was already starting to feel the first restless whispers of hunger. Better to conserve my energies for the time being since I didn't know how long the show would last now that Blair was running things.

Up in my office I dialed a number, identified myself to the mug who answered, and told him to find his boss. He must have recognized my voice, for he dropped the receiver with a clunk as he hurried to comply.

Gordy came on a few minutes later. " 'Lo?"

"It's me," I said. "Thought I'd warn you about some trouble here at my place."

"The house or the club?"

"Club." I told him about the workmen finding a body in the wall.

"What? Only one?"

I was in no mood for black humor, until it occurred to me he wasn't joking. "One's more than enough." Then I told him how she'd probably died.

"Tough luck."

"And then some. It might also go bad for the guy who had this place before me."

"I get you." He didn't mention Booth Nevis, the mob tough who owned the lease. Gordy's phones were often tapped so he'd gotten into the habit of keeping shut on names or talking in code.

"It's none of my business what was done here five years back. I will be cooperating with the law on this. They're gonna want to know who owns the building, and I'll have to tell them. I'm not taking any chances over getting shut down before it's even open."

"You do what you gotta. The other guy can take care of himself."

"So long as he doesn't get any ideas about taking care of me for talking."

Gordy made an odd, abrupt sound I interpreted as his version of a laugh. "Like that'll ever happen. I'll see what he knows about it. He won't be bothering you, though."

"Thanks." If Booth Nevis had a murder to hide, he'd probably not say anything, even to Gordy, but it was worth a try if it took the heat off of me.

I hung up and thought about calling my girl, Bobbi, but she'd be in the middle of her set at the Red Deuces about now. She was their headline singer this week, and Thursday a local radio station would be broadcasting the show. Maybe the audience wouldn't be as big as some she'd reached, but she held the opinion that every little bit of work that got her name in front of people helped. A couple months back she'd done a successful performance on a national broadcast, which had resulted in a few promising offers. The Red Deuces was a short engagement for her, only a week, but it drew a swank clientele of show folk, the kind who could help her career. Just the sort I wanted to attract to my own place.

Fat chance of that if I didn't handle this disaster with kid gloves.

Someone clumped his way upstairs and marched toward my office, which was the only lighted room along the bare hall. I'd remembered to flick it on this time for appearance's sake. He was yet another cop telling me I was to come with him. I didn't ask why.

As though I couldn't find my own way, he guided me down to the main room. All the lights were on here, with cops and reporters wandering around like they owned the place. I hoped they weren't messing up the red velvet upholstery; that was the job of future paying customers. My entrance stirred up the fourth estaters, and once more I got blinded by a flashbulb going off. Several of them. Jeez, but when I'd been working on that side of the fence I had no idea how irritating the damn things could be. No wonder cursing people used to take swings at us.

The cop hustled me past the mob. I gladly let him. Better to be in a basement with a corpse than have a bunch of half-crazed reporters shouting questions that I couldn't answer. During the rush I didn't see Escott. I wondered if I should worry.

"Mr. Fleming, isn't it?"

At the foot of the steps, my vision still uncertain when I blinked, I came face-to-face with Lieutenant Blair, mustache, smug smile, and all. For all the dust down here his black suit looked quite untouched. And he damn well knew who I was. "Yeah, Lieutenant, how you doing?"

"Quite a bad business, don't you think?" He didn't bother to shake hands. The cop leaned close and muttered something in Blair's ear before moving off. Because of the noise and echoes I didn't catch much of it, just something about me being in my office.

Looking past his shoulder, I could see he'd put my men to work on the wall, Leon and a couple of others. Most of it had been pulled down, revealing the skeleton. Her tattered and stained dress had been a blazing red once. Red sequins still defiantly flashed tiny points of light under the harsh overheads. She'd died on her knees, back bowed and head down as if praying. She'd probably been praying very hard indeed there in the stifling dark. I repressed a shudder.

"Got anything to say about this?" Blair inquired.

"It's bad business all right," I allowed. "And nothing to do with me."

"We'll see." He sounded very pleased with himself.

"Come on, you know I only moved here last August. This case could be at least five years old."

"How do you figure that?" He was good at his job, only asking questions for which he already knew the answers.

"Because that's when this joint was last open. There are records on file with all the dates, and you know where to find them."

"True, but anyone could have broken in here between then and now and put her here."

"That's for you to figure out. I'm just a victim of circumstance."

"You seem to collect them, Mr. Fleming. Let's go over here for a little chat, why don't we?" He motioned me toward a corner away from the hubbub, where we could have some privacy. "Who were you calling?"

"I called someone?"

"The man I sent to get you heard you talking."

The cop hadn't even been near the office by the time I'd hung up. Blair was slipping by making only a guess, but it had been a good one. "He must have ears like an Airedale or a great imagination."

"Who did you phone?"

"No one."

"Gordy Weems, perhaps?"

I tried not to react, but he was looking for the least little betraying twitch. Sometimes it's a sad thing to be born with a streak of telltale honesty.

"Perhaps to warn him of your little trouble here? No need to be too surprised. I've made a point of finding out who your friends are."

"You must have a lot of time on your hands, then."

"I just like to keep track of troublemakers."

He would.

"For instance, just how is it an unemployed reporter can afford to set up a palace like this?"

"I'm not unemployed; I work for the Escott Agency. As for this place, I got lucky at the track this year and decided to invest my winnings."

"I think you've been investing for the mob. Word is

you're one of Gordy's insiders at the Nightcrawler Club."

"My girlfriend sings there sometimes. I just go over to drive her home after work. If I took her to the train station, would you accuse me of being a Pullman porter? Are you even supposed to be here? I thought this far north would be out of your district."

"Listen, wiseass, after that business with Malcolm—"

"Ancient history, Lieutenant."

"It's still an open case, Fleming."

Before he could get himself fully launched down memory lane, I fixed him with a long, concentrated stare. "And past time you closed it," I whispered after a moment. From the profoundly blank expression that dropped over his face I knew he'd heard me. "The guy's no longer your concern. Your best guess is that he's the one who did the Wrigley Building murder, and the guilt drove him crazy. Ain't that so?"

"Yes, that's what happened." Blair's voice was thin and distant.

I kept focused on his empty eyes. "As for the mess you've got here, I don't have anything useful to give you. Believe it."

"Believe . . ."

"That's right. Now everything I've told your men is the truth. I've no reason to lie, so you've got no reason to stall around here any longer. Get whatever you need to help you with your case, then get out."

"I'll do that."

"Oh, and don't forget that you like me. We're old pals, you know."

"I know."

An idea struck me as I anticipated a possible future need. "And the same goes for Charles Escott. If either of us calls you up wanting information on this or any other case, it will be your pleasure to help. Got that?"

"Got it."

"Good." I broke off with the fish-eye work and gave him a chance to recover. There was no telling how long my suggestions would last with him, especially the ones that went against his nature, but they should be solid for a few weeks, maybe even a few months before completely fading. Sooner or later he'd reassert himself and be as annoying as ever. "Is there anything else I can help you with, Lieutenant?" I asked, as Jack Armstrong as I could make it without sounding too asinine.

Blair blinked once or twice, his posture relaxing somewhat, the way you do in a friend's company. "I think that about covers it."

"Your best bet will be to check on the original owners. I got the lease through Greener Pastures Real Estate. Try them."

"Thank you, I will."

"I'd also like you to keep the press off my back."

"Wouldn't we all?" he said, and this time his smile actually reached his eyes. "I'll give a statement and tell them to get lost."

"I'd appreciate that. Your men find out anything about her?" I nodded toward the alcove.

"Not really, only that she was a young, probably pretty brunette, well-off, with a strong need for attention. And the motive wasn't robbery."

"How do you get all that?"

"That dress, cut low in the back and the front as far as I can tell. Not many old, ugly women wear those. There's still some bits of hair left on her head, and she's wearing a gold necklace, matching bracelet, and some rings. They're real, not dime-store. The killer left them behind."

So, Blair was good at his job after all. "Need for attention?"

"Women are funny about what colors they wear. Only

the ones who want to be noticed would go near a red like that."

Now I was impressed. I filed it all away to tell Escott later. Where the hell was he, anyway? "Your people going to be here much longer?"

"A couple hours. I don't want your workmen in the area until we're finished. I'll be sending people in tomorrow for more pictures and to pick up all those bricks."

I didn't mind him cleaning away the rubble, but asked why.

"In case she or her killer left some kind of clue. There might be other hair, fibers, or something else stuck in the mortar that could be useful."

He was starting to sound like my partner. "How long will that hold up my labor?"

"No telling. You'd better work on some other area of the club for the time being."

Damn. I was afraid he'd say something like that. "Look, I have to have at least half the basement finished by the end of the week. Monday I got people coming in to install the heating and air-conditioning and—"

"You're putting in air-conditioning?" He seemed intrigued.

"Yeah, the movie theaters don't do so bad by it, and once I get three hundred people in upstairs it's gonna be hot here even in the winter. The whole shebang goes in on this side of the basement. Will that be all right with you?" I could have made it all right with him, but I didn't want to interfere with the process of an investigation. My only angle was making sure he wasn't throwing his weight around just to show he could do it.

He thought it over. "Let my people check over this end tomorrow, then you should be able to go ahead. Unless they find something, that is." I agreed to that and wished him luck. He'd need it. "You think you'll turn up anything after all this time?"

"Maybe. We'll find out who was a regular when the place was open, and take it from there. Something as ugly as this is going to leave a hell of a messy trail."

"Why do you say that?"

He leveled a long stare at the other end of the room, where a knot of his men lingered around the alcove. "Because anyone who went to the trouble of walling that poor girl up alive did it as an object lesson. Those kinds of lessons are no good unless you tell others about it. We might not find solid proof against the person who did it, but we'll probably get a likely suspect."

"Huh. Well, if it goes that far, gimme a call. I'd like to know who it is."

He shot me a funny look. "Mr. Fleming, that would be a breach of—"

"Blair—" I focused hard on him again. "I said gimme a call if you find your man. Remember, it'll be a pleasure for you to help me or Escott."

He blinked, maybe even felt a little dizziness from the pressure I was putting on him. "Yes, of course I will."

I released him. He couldn't have known I was trying to do him a favor. If he found a suspect, then I could get a confession. That girl had died in a manner so hideous I shied away from even thinking about it. Putting her killer's neck in a noose seemed little enough punishment for the crime, but I'd gladly do it, given the opportunity.

"You know where to find me," I said, hoping to wind things up.

"Yes . . . ah, that's all for now." His departing smile was brief and tinged with puzzlement, but this time he did shake hands before going off to check on his men.

We were old pals, after all.

* * *

For one whole second I debated running the gauntlet with the reporters again, then took the back way out. Leon Kell caught my eye, though, so I went over to hear what he wanted.

"What a job it was," he said. "They had me and the guys tearing that whole thing out one brick at a time by hand with only hammers and chisels to break up the mortar. We coulda done it in a couple of minutes with picks if they'd let us, but they wanted to take pictures."

"It has something to do with preserving the evidence."

"They got plenty of it and then some. The questions they asked—like how old the mortar was. As if I should know such things. It wasn't even good mortar."

"Yeah?"

"Yeah. Had too much sand in it, made it soft. Guess it's just as well, or we'd still be taking it down."

"What else did you think of the workmanship?"

"It was okay, but I seen better. Whoever put it up knew enough about bricklaying to get the job done, but I wouldn't want him working on no house of mine."

"Maybe he didn't have enough light to see by," I said speculatively.

Leon paused to glance uneasily at me. "There's that."

"Suppose whoever did it brought her down here and had only a flashlight or maybe a lantern?"

"He'd have to. There weren't no electric lights strung so far back into the basement until me and the boys put 'em in ourselves. You sure got some kind of wicked thoughts on that, Mr. Fleming."

"Imagination isn't always a happy gift. He must have had her tied and gagged or maybe she was unconscious. He carries her all the way to the back, to a place where he's sure no one will bother to go. He puts her down next to the wall, secures her bonds to a bolt he drives into the bricks there. Then he starts laying the first course along that uneven floor."

"Yeah, I guess." Leon didn't seem comfortable with the picture I'd conjured.

"How long do you think a job like that would take?"

"I donno. Not a lot of time for someone who knows what he's doing. For this guy, more than just a couple of hours, I'd say. I got a good chance to look at the work while we was taking it apart, and I think he got better at it toward the end. You know, as he got it built up to meet the ceiling."

"Practice makes perfect."

That snagged me another uneasy look. "The mortar was a little different, too. Like he run out halfway up and had to mix another batch. Jeez, now you got me thinking like you."

"Did you tell this to the cops?"

"Nah. They was too interested in us just getting the wall down. They didn't ask us nothing except if we knew who she was and none of us could say yes to that."

"Before you leave I think you should mention what you've told me to Lieutenant Blair."

"Okay, if you want me to." Leon didn't seem too cheered at the prospect.

"You think he won't listen?"

"Ah, he's a cop, they only listen to what they wanna hear."

"You just tell him I sent you over."

"Okay, I'll do it. There's just one thing—about taking the wall down? I didn't want you thinking we was going slow so as to make overtime for ourselves."

"I never thought that," I said truthfully. "But I'm glad you mentioned it. I'll make sure the cops pay for the overtime."

"Really? You think they will?"

"Yeah, I can try, anyway." And succeed, if I chose to.

"Believe me, none of us wanted to be back there any longer than we had to with that thing."

"I don't blame you."

"It's creepy enough here without more—" He shut himself up.

"More what?"

"Of that . . . thing." He gestured helplessly to where the cops were still gathered.

"What's so creepy about this joint, Leon? Something else got you worried?"

"Nothing, boss. It's been a hell of a night, and I need to get home to my wife before she sends out a search party. Those guys said we wasn't to go poking around over there tomorrow, so you got something else you want us to do instead?"

I told him he could start the men on finishing the near half of the basement once they got the okay from Blair's people. Tools and bags of cement and wall plaster were piled up under the new stairs all ready to go.

"There's also some kind of stain on the floor tiles behind the lobby bar," I added. "See if you can get that cleaned up, too."

He promised to handle it all, then with his new observations about the mortar, reluctantly approached Blair. I wondered if I should offer Leon a permanent position doing building maintenance. He seemed to know how to do just about every kind of job I could name. The fact that he was concerned about my misinterpreting things on the overtime gave me to think he had a solid share of personal integrity, that, or he didn't want to risk being fired. Either way, it meant he was honest. I thought he worried too much about small stuff, but it did make him good at the work. There wasn't one wall in the whole building where the painters had missed a spot.

Leon eventually left by way of the back entry ramp, and I followed him up, lighting a cigarette. I couldn't really smoke; my body wouldn't allow me to inhale the stuff any farther than my mouth, but it gave me something to do with my hands, as well as an excuse to loiter in the alley, keeping an eye on the cops.

After six superficial puffs it abruptly dawned on me that this was *my* place, and I could loiter wherever the hell I wanted.

Damn it all, but I should be used to the idea by now. I finally had something of my own, something that would matter to people. It was also okay to have pride in what I was accomplishing. Maybe it wasn't the Panama Canal in terms of general importance to the world, but to me specifically this club was the biggest thing I'd ever done for myself.

Not needing it anymore, I dropped the cigarette in a puddle and took a slow stroll around *my* place, and if there was a bit of a swagger in my walk, I didn't think anyone could blame me for it.

The feeling lasted until I rounded the front corner, saw the cars still parked all over the street along with the meat wagon, and remembered why they were there.

As Blair had said, *That poor girl.*

Maybe Leon had felt her hovering presence, and that's why the joint gave him the creeps tonight. I could imagine her for myself as well, but firmly shrugged it off. I had to believe in vampires since I was one, but my internal jury was still out when it came to ghosts.

"So that's where you've gotten to," called Escott, coming up behind me.

"I could say the same. Where've you been?"

"Observing without being observed." It was one of his specialties. He swatted at his clothes, having picked up a layer of sawdust. There were patches of it on his knees and elbows.

"What happened to you?"

"I found a most excellent place to eavesdrop, though it was a trifle dirty."

"Where?"

"Under the booth seating."

If I asked another question, I'd only sound like a parrot. Instead I put on a face of noncomprehension. He was more than happy to explain.

"It occurred to me that there was a quantity of dead space beneath all those raised tiers. I asked Mr. Kell if there was a way under them, and he obligingly told me about a utility door behind one of the bars."

"Why didn't he tell me?"

"He probably thought you already knew."

I usually arrived at the club well after the workers were gone for the day. Leon could hardly hang around every night to give me a guided tour of what they'd done, but I still felt like an idiot. "I didn't know anything like that was there."

"Well, if it was not, then this night I would have suggested the construction of some sort of access. The workmen have used it for tool storage, but nothing more. Perhaps you should put a lock on the door to prevent misuse of the space. Mr. Kell informed me that it would be a 'dandy place to take a girl,' which is probably not the sort of activity you would wish to encourage during your hours of business."

"Yeah, I can see it might be like going under the boardwalk on Coney Island."

"Something else you might also consider is employing a portion of it as an emergency bolt-hole for yourself. It would be very simple to block off a sizable section and put in whatever you might require for your daylight comfort."

He meant another cot with my home earth like the one at home. It was a great idea, but after what happened in the club's basement, not something I wanted to think about for the time being. I said I'd look into it later and changed the subject. "So you did some eavesdropping?"

"Not in the literal sense, and not easily. The supporting framework for the tiers prevented me from getting near anyone in the lower areas, but the middle and upper seats were fairly clear. However, the materials used for construction prevented me from hearing all that much. The padded upholstery over the wood is most efficient at absorbing sound. It was more of an experiment than anything else. I doubt if one could hear much of anything once the place is open to the public, but in this case conditions were fairly—"

"Learn anything?" I had to interrupt him. His discovery had put him in one of those cheerful moods where he could enthuse for hours.

"A bit about the history of the club. Some of the members of your previous profession were only too pleased recalling the lurid past to notice my thumping around under their feet. They were exchanging tales of what they knew about the death of the owner in '32 and the rather explosive manner of his dispatch. There is rampant speculation that the unfortunate woman in the basement might have been one of his victims, but until she is identified they can form no solid conclusions. Their reasoning about there being a connection probably has merit, but they are most unwise to theorize without facts."

"Or do it in the hearing of anyone who'd steal the idea."

"This fanciful improvisation on the part of some of them is worrisome to me. You once said that reporters rarely have the time to commit such intentional distortions."

"Most of 'em don't, but the yellow press boys thrive on the stuff. It comes with the job. If a guy speculates and the public complains, he blames his editor, who blames the publisher, who blames the demands of the public."

"Very tidy."

"We used to think so. You learn anything else?"

"Nothing I did not already know and a great deal I did not wish to know about competing baseball teams."

"Anyone try to corner you for an interview before you went to ground under all that?"

"Yes, and not to worry, I was frustratingly reticent."

"Don't underestimate them, Charles. When they have to fill space for a deadline they can get a story out of a blind turnip."

"And since there is no such thing—"

"Yeah, think about it."

"Point taken. I believe the worst of it is over, though."

"Don't kid yourself. The worst will be the headlines tomorrow."

"I doubt if this will garner much interest. How does a years-old murder compare with the Duke of Windsor getting married?"

"Trust me, a walled-up body in Chicago is going to make more copy in the American press than a former king tying the knot in Europe."

"The sad fact of the matter being that you are likely correct in your assessment concerning the public's preference. You harbor a most valuable talent."

"Thanks."

"In light of that sort of fine judgment I hope you'll not give up on your writing career. I understand that knowing what the public wants is half the battle."

It was damned decent of him to refer to my irregular attempts at scribbling as a "career." "Nah. I'm just putting it aside until I get the club launched."

"That, my friend, might require some additional effort after this." He nodded at the mess out front. The meat wagon pulled away from the curb and turned down the alley. We pressed into a side doorway until it passed, then followed to watch. The driver made use of the basement loading ramp that opened on the street behind the club. In this case it was more of an unloading ramp. A couple of guys went inside with a bundle and soon reappeared carrying a long, flexible wicker basket, which they put into the wagon. It seemed fairly light in weight. The photographers took more pictures, then stood back to let the truck pass through.

Once the remains were gone the reporters also thinned out, and eventually even the cops went away. I locked things up for what was left of the night. When the law came back tomorrow Leon could let them in again.

I told Escott where I planned to go next and asked if he wanted to come along, but he tiredly declined. He'd had a full day at his office already and didn't need more excitement. Sometimes I forgot that his day was winding down just when mine was beginning.

On the way home I repeated to him all that I'd learned from both Leon and Blair and the little mental whammy I'd done on the latter. "If you're interested in keeping up on this case, you'll find he'll be strangely cooperative for the next few weeks."

"What excellent forethought, thank you." He looked like I'd just handed him the winning ticket for the Irish sweepstakes.

"Okay, what gives? You're a little too happy."

"This particular problem is not my only concern. There are other matters I have in hand that might progress more smoothly for having the help of a senior officer in the local force."

"I thought you already had friends there."

"I do, but not all of them will have the same sort of authority your Lieutenant Blair possesses. I shall strive to make use of his cooperation while the beneficent effect of your influence lasts."

"Be my guest."

After dropping him at the house, I continued on to the Nightcrawler Club.

Gordy and I had some serious talking to do.

3

I USED one of the side entries to the Nightcrawler to avoid
the crowds out front. This wasn't a black tie evening, but
I was still unshaved. Besides, if Blair had any stoolies
working the joint, I wanted to avoid them as well. He knew
entirely too much about me for my own good.

The door was locked from the outside, but I didn't let
that slow me and sieved in through the thin cracks around
its edge, then found the back stairs off the casino room.
There was a touch of trudging in my walk. I wasn't nearly
to the point of being physically tired yet, but my mind had
been hopping nonstop for hours, and that could wear me
out the same as anyone.

Gordy's men must have been busy elsewhere; I didn't
spot his bruisers until I pushed open the office door. The
mug who was there to answer the phone and otherwise
keep an eye on things knew me by sight and understood
I had a special pass to the inner sanctum whenever I
wanted. I got an expressionless up and down, but without
a word he left his game of solitaire to find his boss. I

looked the cards over and decided he might win that round. After a minute he came back and told me to follow the man who stood waiting in the hall. This one was dressed like a waiter and had at least a .32 stuffed under one arm. I was used to seeing most of the Nightcrawler's male employees carrying heat. What would surprise me would be finding one who wasn't.

Usually Gordy would make time to see me whenever I dropped in, and we'd sprawl comfortably on his expensive furniture in the office and talk about all kinds of stuff. I'd saved his life once or twice, and that meant something to him. We also had pretty much the same hours. Escott was a hell of a good friend, but couldn't stay up all night just to keep me company, so Gordy filled in that particular gap. It was pretty educational, too. I learned more about who was who in mob politics than should be healthy, but Gordy knew it wouldn't be repeated by me to others. Well . . . maybe to Escott.

This being escorted to another room was different from his regular pattern, so my curiosity perked up. Things got more interesting when I was led down more stairs to the club's basement. I could have done without the feeling this turn inspired. Gordy didn't keep bodies here—that I knew of—but the dim lighting and the scent of dank, uncirculated air annoyed me with its reminder of what I'd just left. I shoved the bout of *déjà vu* away.

We walked past a trapdoor in the floor. That was a relief. It led to a brick-lined tunnel running under the street all the way to another building. I'd had my fill of sinister underground chambers for the next few decades. We stopped. Amid stacks of boxes containing everything from seltzer water to tinsel party favors I took in an interesting little tableau.

Only one forty-watt bulb lighted things in this wood-and-cardboard grotto. The shadows were harsh and sucked color from everything. Gordy, who was large enough and solid enough to give Mount Rushmore some competition, sat on a crate looking at another man I vaguely knew from my time in the bookie joints. The guy's name was Royce Muldan, a handsome specimen possessing a fine appreciation for his own looks. It was said he risked his life every time he passed a mirror because of the way he twisted around to take in all the gorgeous details. One of these days he'd do it too fast and break his neck. He was dressed with an East Coast polish more suited to Boston than New York, which in Chicago made him stand out like a traffic light in a wheat field. Some people claimed to be blinded by the shine on his shoes.

He wore a patient, somewhat amused expression as I came into view. I nodded once at Gordy and kept my mouth shut until I figured out what was going on.

Gordy nearly always avoided involving me directly with mob business. He knew I preferred to remain on the outside. He rarely talked about the seamier things he had to do to stay on top, though if I asked a question he'd give a straight answer. If there was anything really dirty going on here he'd have kept me waiting in the office until he was finished. All I could pick up for the moment was that this was something he wanted me to see.

Muldan took me in with a glance, then went back to Gordy, having apparently dismissed me as a threat. Maybe he'd have been more impressed if I'd shaved.

Gordy didn't bother with introductions, just made a nod to me in return before putting his attention on Muldan. "It would be better for you to lay off," he said in a slow, measured tone. He sounded patient, but firm. "For you and everyone else."

Muldan shrugged. "Not my decision. The girl likes me, and I'm not going to argue with her good taste."

"You should take a vacation. Havana is very nice this time of year."

"Too hot."

"Cooler than here. Her father—"

"Doesn't matter. She wants to see me, so I'll see her right back."

"That would be a very bad thing. For you."

"Or what? Her father has me scragged? That can't happen, and you and he both know it. I'm too important."

"Royce, you are making difficulties. Make too many of them and anything can happen. Even to important guys. And you know it."

"By the time things get to that point she'll be tired of me and looking at someone else. It's not my fault her father can't control her. Look, I'm just going along for the ride. Tell her old man to step back, let her sow her oats, and he won't have any more trouble with her."

Gordy heaved a great, gentle sigh. The sigh of a man about to do an unpleasant, but necessary task. "I'm sorry you won't listen."

Maybe I'd never been on stage like Escott, but I recognized a cue line when I heard one. "Want me to do something with him?"

Muldan gave me a contempt-tinged "what's it to you" look, on guard, ready to meet my challenge.

Gordy said, "Only if you don't mind. I'm thinking this guy needs to take a nap."

I smiled, briefly. "Then have your guys take a break."

He signed to the other mugs hanging around in the background, and they silently moved off. He knew I never cared to have witnesses for certain kinds of work.

Muldan was aware something was up, but his mind would be running along ordinary lines, anticipating ordinary threats. He stood up a little straighter and loosened the buttons on his coat. It was finely tailored, but not to the point where it could completely conceal his shoulder holster. "Just what do you think you're doing, Gordy? Have you forgotten who I am?"

"Nope, but you are not being smart about this. You are making a problem. Though sometimes when you sleep on a problem it clears itself up."

"I'm not the one with the prob—" Muldan began.

But I was already moving in on him.

The lighting was bad, but adequate. I put all my attention on Royce Muldan, catching him with my gaze before he had a chance to draw his gun. A few seconds later he was standing very still, hands relaxed at his sides, eyes shut fast.

What a fate for Mrs. Fleming's youngest—becoming part-time mob muscle. If she ever found out, she'd thump my head with her big mixing spoon, and if she still used the one I remembered, which was made of wood, it would cause me damage.

"Sure a good thing to be able to do stuff like that," said Gordy as he peered at the quiescent and now quite oblivious Muldan. There was a note in his normally deadpan tone that was very close to admiration.

"Yeah. What's the beef with this one?"

"Son of a New York big shot. Thinks he's immune to trouble. Seeing the wrong girl. Thing is, Muldan's right about her. If her pop left her alone, she'd grow out of it, but he don't look at it that way. He's ready to take his shotgun to this chump, which would mean he'd get himself killed, too. This town don't need another war."

"Huh."

"So I told the pop I'd talk to Muldan. It wasn't going so good until you showed up. This bird don't intimidate easy."

Considering the sinister surroundings, that said a lot for Muldan's courage—or stupidity. Hell, I wasn't the one brought down here to be talked to, and I still had to fight off getting the creeps. "What do you want to do with him?"

"Tell him he's changed his mind about the girl. He don't want to see her again, and that he should tell her so."

"How about he says he's not good enough for her, and she can do better?"

"You'd be doing them both a favor."

So I got Muldan in the right frame of mind to listen, planted the suggestions, and told him to go. He went, followed at a distance by a few of the bruisers who'd hung around by the stairs. They'd make sure he'd leave all the way. He'd wake out of his trance sometime during the cab ride to his hotel. He wouldn't remember me at all.

Gordy stood, his looming shadow blotting out a large hunk of the basement. "I owe you again, Fleming."

"No problem; I prefer reason over gunplay."

"You should get into the business, you'd make a fortune."

"I got enough of one to suit me for now."

"If you're ever short, then you come hit the tables here. Anytime." The odds favored the house at the casino games here, but for a select few, the house could be made to lose on demand. I had an edge or two of my own as well, when I was in the mood for it.

"Thanks."

" 'Course, if you put some tables in at your place, you'd be set for life."

"And have to pay for it."

"It don't have to be roulette or the slots. A fancy joint like what you want could get by fine taking a percentage from high-stakes poker."

There was an interesting thought. But I shook my head. "I'd still have to split too much of the profits with certain kinds of cops to keep them off my back—and it would give them something to hold over me."

"They don't have to know. You could make your whole investment back in one month."

I laughed once. "You tell me a way to keep a secret in this town, and I might consider it."

He took the point. "But you got ways around that. Like what you did just now with Muldan."

"I'm going into this club for fun as well as money. If I get myself gummed up with making payoffs, it stops being fun and there's not as much money. As long as I keep my nose clean, the cops got no easy way to hurt me. Anything else makes things too complicated, and I've got enough complications to keep me busy." Like finding a dead woman in the basement wall.

He shrugged, which was a minimal lift of his massive shoulders, then turned, and I followed him up to his lush office. The man who had been there earlier was still there, but gathered up his cards and left when we came in. Gordy made a drink for himself; as far as I could tell it was just tonic water and a shot of lime juice. He didn't ask if I wanted anything, knowing better.

"You getting a cold?" I asked, with a nod at his quinine-laced glass.

"I like the taste."

It kept him sober, too. Yet another way of staying ahead of rivals.

"So . . . what's the story with the body?" he asked.

"It's more of a skeleton by now." I dropped into an oversize chair, stretched my legs, and gave him the short version of the whole sad business at Lady Crymsyn, putting in the part about Blair. "He guessed that I'd called you on it. Is there any link between the body and you that I should know about?"

He shook his head, taking a seat on his vast couch. I could trust him to be telling the truth. He always did with me. "It's probably to do with Welsh Lennet before he got bumped. Walling up broads don't sound like his style, but he had some real bastards working for him that might have done it. Most of them are dead, too, though. The guy who tossed those grenades did the whole town a favor."

"Are any of Lennet's people still around?"

"Shivvey Coker. He was just muscle then; now he's working for Booth Nevis." Gordy let that news sink in. I didn't like it. Nevis was the man who owned Crymsyn's lease.

"What's Coker do for him?"

"Runs errands."

"That's pretty vague."

"Has to be; he covers a lot of different areas. If Booth wants something done, Shivvey's the guy he sends out to make sure it gets done."

"Maybe Shivvey can tell me something about the dead woman."

"Worth a try."

"No idea on who she could be?" I gave him the description Blair gave me.

Gordy thought it through for some moments. He had a memory like a file cabinet. "Nothing comes to mind, but I wasn't in Lennet's crowd back then, so I couldn't say who might have been with him or any of his boys. This burg's full of women. Most guys don't bother to keep track of 'em. There's always another girl coming in while one's going out. I can ask around, but you'd have better luck. And you'd be able to get a straight answer. Try asking Shivvey."

"I plan to. Anyone find out who did the boom on Lennet? The reporters said it was Nevis."

"Some thought it might be him because he hated Lennet and then ended up owning the place, but he never did anything with it, so that didn't make sense when it came to a motive. It was a good-paying speak, too. A shame to let it go to waste."

"Unless he knew about the body in the wall and didn't want to go stirring things up."

Gordy shook his head. "Something like that wouldn't bother him. He'd either leave it as is or get someone to dig it out and sink it in the lake. He knew you'd be redoing the joint and might find it. Makes more sense that he didn't know anything. This is probably one of Lennet's leftovers."

"Why did Nevis hate Lennet?"

"Ever see one junkyard mutt go up against another junkyard mutt? Those two didn't need a reason; that's just how things were."

"Then Shivvey went to work for Lennet's enemy," I stated.

"Welsh Lennet and Booth Nevis didn't get along, but Shivvey's a for-sale kind of mug. After Lennet's funeral he got on Nevis's payroll. He must have figured it to be safer than trying to take his dead boss's place."

"Ever think he had anything to do with arranging the boom?"

A shrug. "He could have. Lots of guys could. The cops never got close to nailing anyone for it and were probably told not to try."

"Who would have told 'em?"

"Back then, Big Al himself. Lennet's speak was the last in a lot of straws. The camel's back broke. After the dust settled, everyone had to get into line and stay that way or else. Al's a mean one with a baseball bat."

I'd heard stories to back up that opinion. "Not much good to him now." Capone was presently doing his time in Atlanta for unpaid taxes.

"Don't kid yourself. Nitti still listens to him. Wanna

meet Frank? He's here tonight with some of the boys."

"No thanks. I've had enough excitement for one evening." I leaned my head back and stared at the ceiling, not fighting the frown that took over my face. "I don't look forward to the papers tomorrow. The morning edition's already out and won't have anything on this mess, but the afternoon's . . ."

"If you play it right, you can turn them in your favor."

"How so?"

"First, you say you knew nothing about the body, be surprised as the next guy about finding it. That's all true, anyway. Second, you say something about crime and criminals being bad. Everyone likes to hear stuff like that. And third, you give the dead dame a good funeral."

I sat up straight, alarmed at this turn. "I couldn't do that!"

"You can afford it."

"It's not the money—I'd be exploiting her death for cheap publicity, and everyone would know it."

"Then do it on the sly. Don't tell anyone. Sooner or later some newshawk'll find out who's footin' the bill. By not talking about it you come out a hero instead. Everyone loves a secret Good Samaritan."

I shook my head. "No."

"Hey, someone's got to bury her. If nobody comes forward to claim her as their long-lost relative, then how good you gonna look if you let her go to potter's field? The papers would really love that one."

I'd been stuck fast in cleft sticks before and hated the squeeze. "All right," I grumbled. "But nobody's going to know about it. I mean that."

"If you want, I can fix things on the quiet, and you can pay in cash. Make it harder to trace."

"That'd be fine."

"You work this right you could take the funeral off your taxes as a business expense."

If I thought I could have gotten away with it, I'd have slugged him, then I saw the crinkle in the corners of his eyes. He'd been joking with that last idea. At least I hoped it was a joke. "Wiseass."

"You'll have to play ball with the sob sisters, though. Get them on your side."

I made grumbling noises.

"You can do it. You won't have to give 'em the eye for it either. Just flirt a little and say you like their hats. Works for me."

Gordy flirting with the sentimental, yet iron-hearted sob sisters of the yellow press. I had difficulty trying to picture that.

He went on. "Tell them what a bad thing this is and how you're helping the cops any way you can. Say you hope it won't spoil the wholesome image for your club."

"Wholesome? With all the liquor I'll be selling?"

"If they like you, they'll write you up as a hero."

"If they like me."

He spread his hands. "Look, you're gonna have a shit-load of headlines off this no matter what. Would you rather let them choose the angle or fix one for yourself? You were in that game, you know the rules. Make 'em work for you."

"I guess I could type up a statement. If I don't say something, they'll put words in my mouth."

Gordy nodded approval. "And the faster you say it for yourself, the faster they'll go away. When do you pick up Bobbi?"

"Around three."

"Then you got plenty of time to write it. There's a typewriter and paper in the desk."

"What are you in such a hurry for?"

"To make sure you do it. And there's a couple of the

crime beat boys from the *Trib* downstairs. They're here watching Nitti having a good time. I can give 'em whatever you want."

"You do have this town sewn up."

He finished his tonic and lime and put the glass on a table. "Just a pocket or two."

"Do they know about this story yet? If they take it away from the other reporters—"

"Not to worry. They'll pass it on if I ask 'em nice."

Pocket or two, my ass. He had the whole damn city in a suit if he had the crime beat boys doing what he asked. Or maybe he was playing them the way he just told me to do. That would explain why some of the stories about cops raiding the Nightcrawler were short, bland, and never mentioned Gordy by name. He had only to invite a select few—or their editors—into the casino and give them a profitable run around the tables for an hour or three. If they won some money, then it was from their own good luck. They were free of the corruption of a bribe and yet full of kindly feelings toward their host, who would probably welcome them back for more, so they had a solid reason to keep the club up and running.

I went to the desk and found the promised typewriter. "You got carbon paper?"

Gordy needed to look in on his business, said good night, and left. I scribbled out a draft of what I wanted to say, then typed it out twice with carbons to make six copies. My old reporting style came back to me like riding a bicycle, so I made short work of the job. Too bad I couldn't yet do fiction as easily. I took a copy with me and left the rest for Gordy to deal with, noting on each page the name of the paper it should go to; the *Trib* was on top. Great, I'd finally get printed in one of the best papers in the country, but as the topic of a story, not as one of its journalists.

*   *   *

I had some time left before going to pick up Bobbi, so I
used it to run home. A freshly shaved face and clean set
of clothes helped my disposition, but there was one other
task I needed to see to, one that I normally left until the
end of an evening because of the potential mess. It had
been dry the last few days, though, so the damage to my
shoes might be lessened if I was careful about where I
stepped. I drove south until the summer air got thick with
farm-smell.

Parking my Buick in the shadow between two streetlights I checked out the territory before going in,
something that was so much a habit for me that I hardly
thought about it anymore. Tonight I was still a bit on edge,
so I sat and looked things over first. Some especially zeal-
ous reporter might have managed to follow me all evening
without getting spotted. That in itself was unlikely, but I've
never regretted being too careful when it came to concealing my condition from the public.

If you read up on the subject like I've done, you find
that people in general nearly always have a bad reaction
when they discover there's a vampire lurking around their
usually sane and otherwise normal world. They'll tolerate
mass murder going on in Spain, believe it when Hitler says
he only wants peace, and even welcome marathon dancing,
but let them know there's a guy on their street drinking
animal blood, and they have a conniption. They don't even
need to believe in the existence of vampires; it's the blood-
drinking that brings on the fit.

Not that I blame them. It took me some time to get used
to the idea myself. And I *like* the stuff.

Now.

Of course, getting to a supply of it could be a little
tricky. Not every bovine I approached in the countless cor-
rals of the Union Stockyards was willing to share. Some

were stirred up by the stink of the place, no doubt sensing their pending demise. By now I'd become an expert at picking out a quiet animal who'd let me get close enough to feed. Then I would use a soothing word and a steady look to calm it even more. It was a variation of the forced hypnosis I'd done on Muldan—just as effective, but more rewarding.

Satisfied the area was clear of inconvenient witnesses, I quit the car. My corner teeth were already budding in anticipation as I strode across the street, and slipped through—and I really mean through—the fence. The noise and smell seemed worse on this side, though that was just my imagination. One thin barrier of wood wouldn't have made all that much difference in controlling the flow of the fetid air. Bad as it was, the reek did not discourage my awakened hunger. The scent of blood, old and new, hung heavy all around me, teasing at my fully wakened hunger.

The Yards covered a vast amount of real estate and never really closed. Depression or no, America had to eat, and this is where most of her beef and bacon came from. Trains constantly arrived full and left full; the cattle and swine cars changed out for refrigerated cars of frozen carcasses headed all over the States. There was a similar yard in my hometown of Cincinnati, chiefly concerned with pork, but nothing like this.

The constant activity often worked in my favor since there were plenty of anonymous men walking about. I was frequently not dressed like the regular workers, but few of them ever bothered to stop a man in a suit, particularly when he acted as though he knew what he was doing. This night I passed unnoticed into the pens as usual and found a likely donor from the dozen or so cattle there. They were new arrivals. It wasn't too muddy for my shoes.

Feeding didn't take all that much time. Most nights it took longer to actually get into the Yards than anything else. A few moments was all I needed to cut through the tough hide with my teeth to reach a surface vein on a leg and draw off my fill. I could drink up to a quart or more of the stuff and usually did. It was enough to keep me going for up to three nights, four in a pinch, but I came in every second night whenever possible. Going without for longer than three in a row is bad. The hunger tears at me from the inside out, and I can't think straight. My reflexes slow and an all-over weakness makes every movement an effort. When that happens it's dangerous for me and could also be so for anyone around me. Not that I've ever lurched out of a dark alley to attack some poor innocent bastard for his blood, but there's a first time for everything when desperation's in charge. I'd taken blood from unwilling human donors, but it's not something I'm proud of; nor was it safe. On one occasion the tainted stuff I drank damn near killed me. Again. For keeps.

The pure heat I drew in now was good. It was always good. The change I'd undergone made it so. Whether or not they like the taste, normal humans can't handle large quantities of blood; it's too much like drinking seawater, but I thrived on it. When that liquid fire hits the back of my throat it's like an electric charge, but without the pain. It wakes me up until I feel ten feet tall and able to do anything. I've heard that drug addicts get the same kind of reaction, only my drug sustains life instead of destroying it. The only odd side effect I have is the way my eyes flush deep red right after feeding, but that passes off pretty quick.

I straightened and quickly dabbed my mouth with a handkerchief. There was hardly a trace to wipe away, but such close contact with a cow's hairy skin wasn't what I'd call pleasant. Maybe I should switch to horses. Shorter, smoother coats. I knew of two people like me on Long

Island who preferred them over cattle for that very reason.

But I'd think about that another night. Now I had to get to the Red Deuces.

It was a roundabout drive to leave the Stockyards, spinning through the Back of the Yards to find a big enough street that would take me north without too many stops. Chicago's composed of a lot of different little towns disguised as neighborhoods, each with its special ethnic group or groups. Sometimes the divisions were from street to street, with Jews or Italians on this side, Poles or Irish or Germans on the other. I'd heard about America being a melting pot, and the description was particularly true here. Much of the time it was less a pot and more of a boiling stew as each group tried to beat the other for supremacy, or lord it over newcomers. Old World rivalries and prejudices didn't stop at Ellis Island. It was mostly the young kids in gangs who made the more violent trouble after being carefully educated by their parents and the hardness of life in general about whom to hate.

Having been raised on a farm just north of Cincinnati, I didn't know what I'd been missing, and it was probably just as well. When your day-to-day focus is on making enough food to get you through the winter, you don't have time to take exception to your neighbor's religion or skin color. Either that, or maybe my parents were a little smarter than most with their seven kids. Real intolerance didn't come up to bite me in the ass until I joined the Army and got labeled as a know-nothing hick, and when that happened I decided I didn't care much for it. Live and let live, I figured. Everyone's got a right to breathe the air, and to hell with anybody who wants to put a price on it.

Crazy opinions like that made me real popular in the barracks. It was the first time I'd been glad to have had older brothers who used to beat on me. Having survived countless behind-the-barn donnybrooks with them, I'd unknowingly learned to fight to win. After I thumped a few thick skulls, the troublemakers took the hint, got more respectful, and left me alone.

I hoped the same thing would happen now. My arrival in this town last August might have gone completely unnoticed by Chicago's mobs if I hadn't offered to help the wrong man at the wrong time. It ended up with me getting killed. I soon got better—and I started throwing my weight around. But I wasn't stirring up grief so much as trying to defend myself. This made a strong impression on a few people, though. Things were quiet at present. Hopefully, with Gordy having put a word or two out in my favor, the mobs would keep clear of me so I could get on with my humble ambitions about Lady Cyrmsyn in peace.

The Red Dueces was close to the Loop and, like any good nightspot, had terrible parking. The street was lined solid with cars, most of them belonging to the people living in the area. At this late hour the club's neon lights were dark. Most of the patrons were staggering off home or in search of another watering hole. They were on foot, though, so nothing opened up for me. I had to park a good long block away and hike back.

Bobbi, all finished with her singing for the night, met me at the halfway point. "I saw your car go past just as I was coming through the front door," she said, a little breathless from hurrying. She had a lovely flush on her cheeks.

I kissed her hello and told her she looked too good to be out walking alone.

"No one's roaming loose this late."

"There's a few who could give you trouble."

She opened her purse and pulled out a couple of pounds of serious-looking blackjack. "Then I give it right back again—but they have to catch me first."

I tried to put most of my worry for her away. She was

a big girl, after all. But next time I'd keep my eyes open for her at the door. Being a knockout blonde with a gorgeous figure, she'd learned to take care of herself, but some guys didn't understand the word "no" unless you tattooed it to their face with a car fender.

We strolled slowly down the block to my buggy, not saying anything, just walking close and holding each other. It was something neither of us had yet gotten tired of doing. The way I felt about her I hoped that time would never come. I'd asked her to marry me more than once, but she always said she liked things just as they were. It had nothing to do with me being dead half the while; she made it clear that she only preferred to keep her independence. I accepted her answer and always backed off . . . until the next time the fit came over me.

Sooner or later in a weak moment she might say yes.

"How did the show go?" I asked after we were in the car. I hit the starter, threw it in gear, and pulled into the empty street.

"Fairly well. One of the guys got too drunk to sing his last set, so I did it for him."

"That's good."

"Not really, since the management said I got paid the same."

"That's bad."

"Not really, because I was able to trot out some fresh songs. They liked me, and that's all that really matters."

They being her audience. "Anyone important see you?"

"A few, maybe. Someone told me there was a Hollywood producer in the house, but it was probably just wishful thinking. Anyway, no one tried to come backstage except for the usual johnnies, and the bouncers take care of them. Someone who was really in show business would send his card first or get the manager to make introductions. Nothing like that happened, so it was quiet."

"Yeah, yeah, sure it was. I know how you light up a stage."

She snuggled closer to me and chuckled. She knew she was good, but liked hearing me say it. "How did your night go?"

"It's a long, grim story with no ending."

"What happened?"

So I told her pretty much what I had told Gordy, but put in more small stuff to fill out the picture. I did not give a detailed description of the body. Bobbi got through the incredulity and shock part pretty fast. She'd been in Chicago a while, and even a murder as terrible as this one was not beyond easy belief. She said how awful it was and fired a dozen questions at me, most of which I couldn't answer.

"And Gordy couldn't guess who it might be?" she asked.

"Not off the top of his head. He said he'd check around, but I don't think anyone's going to own up to something like this. I'll do my own checking, though."

"You sure you want to?"

There was a lot unsaid behind her question. I'd been through some hard times in the last few months. If I poked around in the wrong areas, it could make fresh trouble for me, and she was only reminding me of it. I pushed that aside. "I don't want to, but I have to. Someone walled that poor woman up alive, and if I can drop a noose around the bastard that did it, I will."

She shot a guarded look my way. "Then keep your eyes open, huh? I've seen what it does to you."

"I'll be careful. I'll let Lieutenant Blair take all the heat and get the glory for the arrest. Maybe after that he'll start liking me for real."

But the conversation stalled out. She wasn't happy at

my decision, but neither would she ask me to lay off. It was like her dream about going to Hollywood. I didn't care much for our being separated when the time came, but I wasn't going to stop her. On the other hand, that was something she really wanted to do. This was something I was stuck with.

In her flat on the tenth floor of her residence hotel the atmosphere between us eased slightly and warmed up. She was in her own territory now and better able to relax. Not bothering to turn on the lights, she dropped her purse and hat on a chair by the entry and marched across the living room to one of the big corner windows. She opened it wide and leaned on the sill, letting the breeze pluck at her. It was her favorite spot, giving her a grand view of the city and a slice of the lake. Lights glinted everywhere, even at this hour: starlike shimmers from the water, the steady cold blue of streetlamps, and the whites and reds of slow-moving cars. From this high up everything moved slow.

"Isn't it cold for you?" I asked, standing close. Low temperatures didn't affect me like they used to; I was only aware of them in a distant sort of way.

"I need it after the heat of that stage. The days have been nice and cool, but when that spot hits me it makes up for them. We haven't had much of a summer yet, have we?"

"Not that I've heard."

She turned slightly so her back was to me. She had nice round hips, taut from the muscles she'd built up after hours of dancing practice. Tap, ballroom, jitterbug, she was learning it all to be ready in case she got that phone call to go west. I let my hands wander over them, caressing and giving her an experimental squeeze through the thin fabric of her dress.

"You forgot your underwear," I said.

"No, I didn't. It's all in my bureau drawer."

"Oh."

She bumped against me once and looked over her shoulder, an impish smile flashing briefly over her face.

Well, you don't have to clobber me between the eyes when it comes to certain types of invitations. I reached over to pull the blinds down, but she stopped me.

"I want the air," she said.

"I've read about people like you. They're called exhibitionists."

"That's only if I take my clothes off."

"From the feel of things"—and I did, thoroughly, to make sure—"you're halfway there."

"Less work for you, then."

"Sweetheart, this is *not* work."

She pushed her hips against me, raising all sorts of reactions. God, the power she had over me didn't bear thinking about, so I stopped thinking and just let it take over. She held tight to the sill and laughed and sighed while I explored everything I could get my hands on.

It was times like this that the shedding of interfering clothes took too long. Complicated, too. I wanted to keep touching Bobbi, but had to divide my attention between her and undoing my belt and buttons. Then I had to loosen my tie and shirt, so I could lean forward over her. I lifted her hair up and nibbled the base of her neck.

"That's lovely," she murmured. "Just do . . ."

I next lifted her dress, crumpling it around her waist. She arched herself upward, but I wouldn't let her straighten completely, and pressed her down over the sill again.

"Now, try now," she said, a while later.

I did, and slipped right in, both of us sighing together at the sensation. It was absolutely wonderful. It always was with her. She braced herself against my slow thrusts.

"I think—I think someone's watching us over there," she said, looking out at the view. Her voice soft, breathy with excitement.

"It's two blocks away, let him stare."

"Yes, let . . . him . . . yes."

Then we were past speech. It was all about touching, now, acting and reacting. And when she was just to the edge of things, I pulled her up enough to get to that special spot on her sweet throat where the blood rushed close to the surface.

My corner teeth were out and had been the whole time. I kissed her soft skin, first tasting, then breaking through it as gently as I could to give us that crashing mutual release. From the cries she made and kept on making, I was successful. I drew things out, holding her, taking from her, just a drop or two at a time. When it came to making love it was the quality, not the quantity of blood, and it was the best for me when she was in the midst of her climax. The pleasure looped back upon itself, too, for as long as I kept taking, she lingered in its grasp—as did I.

I'd once been on the receiving side of such kisses. Then it had been beautiful Maureen who'd tasted and supped on my blood for hours at a time. Once you've experienced such an intense union like that anything else is kid's play. It took me years to get over her after her abrupt and, at the time, inexplicable departure. Years, until I met Bobbi Smythe. But by then I was a vampire myself, and ready to discover what loving a woman would be like for me after my change. I soon found out, and it only just kept getting better.

I began supporting more and more of Bobbi's weight. She was still caught in the spell, but tiring. Time to pull back. If we'd been stretched out in her bed, I'd have kept going, but positioned as we were it was a bit awkward to comfortably maintain things.

We gradually sorted ourselves out. She was drowsy, but spared a giggle for the sight of me with my pants tangled around my ankles and still in shoes and socks—with shin garters holding them up, yet. There are few things in all of Western civilization that are more ridiculous-looking than a man in such a state. Comics have known about it for ages and exploited it mercilessly. I snagged up my trousers and tried to restore what little dignity remained. Bobbi merely shook her skirt down and grinned.

"I win," she said. She pecked me on the corner of my mouth while I was only halfway buttoned, then glided past, where she spent a few minutes in the bathroom. Then she spent some more time in the bedroom. When she returned, she wore fancy red silk pajamas with a Chinese collar that covered the marks on her neck.

"Those are new, aren't they? I asked, all eyes for the way the fabric clung to her figure. Through the thin silk I could see she'd again omitted underwear. It was one of the things I loved about her.

She gave an artistic turn, standing on tiptoe in her matching slippers like a fashion mannequin. "Like it? It set me back three bucks, but I couldn't resist the embroidery." There was an oriental-style tree stitched all over the jacket front.

"It's worth it. You make it beautiful."

"That," she said, coming over to bestow another kiss on me, "was the right thing to say."

I followed her to the kitchen, where she poured out a big glass of grape juice. As food goes it was one of those few exceptions, like coffee, that still smelled good to me. Anything else usually drove me off. Even though I don't breathe much, it is necessary for talking, and I wanted to keep her company.

We sat at her little white kitchen table. It had two chairs. Enough.

"You drink a lot of that stuff," I said.

"The magazines say it's good for dieting."

"You don't need to diet."

"I still crave it. And liver. Did you crave those when you were still like me?"

She meant breathing regular and walking around during the day. "I guess. I used to eat steak and hamburg' half-raw when I could, and I'd have greens instead of potatoes. Couldn't get enough of them for some reason. Does that count?"

"I suppose. You'd be getting iron that way. Good for the blood. I've always thought that when you want some special kind of food real bad it means your body's telling you what it needs. Read it in a magazine ad somewhere."

"What do you mean 'crave'? You're not—"

"Don't be silly, you know that can't happen with you." She sipped her juice, watching me over the glass rim. "You ever regret that part of your condition?"

"What part?"

"Not being able to have kids."

I shrugged. My change made me like Maureen; everything worked, but I was no longer fertile in the ordinary way. "It's not something I've thought about much. What about you?"

"I've never wanted any."

"I thought all girls wanted babies."

"Not this one. They're noisy, smelly, expensive, and you're stuck with the responsibility of them for your whole life, and what if you mess up and raise them wrong? They get into trouble and break your heart. I can't imagine why anybody would want one."

I couldn't think of a real reply to that, then wondered what was going on under her words. "Bobbi, this is a very strange conversation."

"Am I shocking you?"

"It's just different. I thought you liked kids."

"I do, but I don't want one of my own. They're not a responsibility I'm able to handle, so it's better for the kid's sake that I avoid it."

"Why are you telling me this?"

She put her glass down. "Because you had that look again, like you're going to ask me to marry you."

"Uh . . ."

"I just thought you should know my turning you down is not just because we couldn't have kids."

"Ah . . ."

"Well, you keep getting the same answer from me, and lately you didn't look like you believed it anymore. You deserved to hear a different one for a change. It's still the truth. Just like the other reasons I've given you."

"What's this 'look' I get?"

"It comes and goes. I can't describe it, but I thought you might propose again tonight."

God damn it, but she'd pegged me square. Again. "Am I that transparent, woman?"

"I guess you are to me. Charles isn't the only detective around here."

"Private agent," I automatically corrected. Hunching over, I clasped my hands together on the table and frowned at them a minute. "Should I just stop asking?"

"I don't know. Does it hurt you when I say no?"

"Some, but I can live with it."

"Then you do what feels right to you. But fair warning, my answer's always going to be no."

"Always?"

"Yes. Getting married would be bad for us."

"I don't see it that way."

"But I do, Jack. I'm happy with the way things are. I don't want some piece of paper with our names on it changing anything."

"Why should anything change?"

"Trust me, it would."

"But we love each other—I mean, don't you—?"

"Of course I love you. I adore you. But I won't marry you."

"You'd rather live in sin?"

"If that's what you want to call it." She put both her hands lightly over mine. "I don't feel particularly sinful when I'm with you."

"That's good to know."

"I like it this way. It's all honeymoon for me and none of the drudgery of a marriage. You'll never have to worry that I get sloppy and let myself go."

"That'll be the day."

"And I don't have to worry about why you're with me. I'll always know that it's because you *want* to be here, not because you *have* to be here. The same goes for why I'm with you."

She did have a point. "Maybe it's because I like the sex."

"If that were the only thing then you'd have left while I was changing clothes."

"Honey, if I ever get that stupid, you tell Charles to stake me."

"Bite your tongue," she said quickly.

"Sorry." I'd forgotten that like a lot of performers she could be superstitious. In this case, though, her alarm was justified. I got the subject back on the track. "There were other guys who were stupid with you, huh?"

"A few. You're the only one smart enough to stick around."

"Get used to it."

"Uh-uh. I'm not about to take a guy like you for granted."

That made me feel better.

She finished her juice and rinsed and dried the glass, tucking it away in a cupboard. She liked things tidy. Including her life. Having me around the house all the time might make a mess. She'd had more than her share of those already. Damn me if I was going to be another.

Bobbi slipped back into her chair, and we talked about other things for a while. It didn't take long to come around to discussing my latest trouble.

"This body at your club," she said, looking serious. "People are going to give you all kinds of grief about it. It's not something that'll go away with time."

"I know. Gordy and I hashed it out. That's why I typed that statement for all the papers."

"I think it's sweet of you to give the poor woman a burial."

"Someone has to if they don't find out who she is."

"You want me to make arrangements?"

"Gordy offered to find—"

She waved her hand, shaking her head. "Oh, no, not Gordy. I've seen his funerals. He always picks out the wrong flowers or something, and his choice of music is horrible."

Funny, I'd never thought of Gordy arranging funerals, but considering that he probably caused more than a few to take place, I shouldn't have been too surprised. "Oh. Well. If you wouldn't mind."

"As a favor, one gal to another. I'll do right by her, the poor, poor thing."

"Okay. Maybe you can make it an evening service so I can come. But this is only if they can't find her family."

"I don't see how they could."

"There's ways: missing person reports, dental records, that kind of thing."

"What about that dress she was in?"

"What, like a label or a laundry mark? They'll run those down, too."

"The color—what kind of red was it? Light, dark?"

"Something in the middle, really bright and rich, like a traffic light. Lots of sequins of the same color. Why?"

"Not many women can wear that shade. I don't think it's ever been popular. If there's a maker's label, lemme know whose."

"The cops can track that down."

"I'd still like to know."

I was getting tired of the subject. God knows I'd have my fill of it later when the papers came out. I wanted to end our evening on a more pleasant note. "I'll have Charles call you tomorrow on it."

She looked at the little clock over the stove. Milkmen were on their rounds by now, and I'd have to leave fairly soon. "It's already tomorrow," she pointed out.

"No it ain't."

She quirked an eye at me. "It ain't?"

"Tomorrow doesn't happen until you've been to bed."

"Oh, really?" She started giggling as I stood and came around the table.

"Yeah, lemme show you how it works . . ."

4

GHASTLY REMAINS FOUND IN NIGHTCLUB CELLAR

I GAVE out with a cross between a sigh and a groan.

Escott shoved another paper at me. "If you think that's bad, try this one."

WOMAN WALLED UP ALIVE IN CLUB CRYMSYN

"Then there's this—"

LADY CRYMSYN'S BLOODY PAST

"And finally, this—"

"JANE POE" FOUND IN NIGHTCLUB WALL
Bizarre reenactment of "The Cask of Amontillado"

The remains of a woman whom police have dubbed "Jane Poe" were discovered sealed up behind a

false wall in the basement of the Lady Crymsyn
nightclub in a case as horrific as the famous story
by . . .

"I think that's quite the best one," he said. "It indicates someone on the staff has a literary background. The other papers seem to have missed that element."

"They know their readers probably wouldn't get it. I once had an editor with a phobia against using words with more than two syllables. I'd fight him tooth and nail over my copy, but most of the time he was right."

"He seems to have had some influence with this other article." He tapped one of the more lurid pages spread over the vast dining table. "Though one could hardly call it that. It's more of a series of photographs with captions than anything else."

"Welcome to the world of journalism," I muttered. I skimmed enough of the stuff to get myself thoroughly annoyed, then paced to the parlor and back to brace for more headlines. The murder had caught, if not the public's imagination yet, then that of the press. It was on the front page of all the city papers and even a few out-of-town rags, usually above the fold. It even beat out the steel workers' strike, the latest atrocities in Spain, and, as I'd predicted, the Duke of Windsor's marriage to Mrs. Simpson. I hated every line of oversize type. "Jeez, why'd they have to use the new name of the club so much? It was a completely different one back when the murder took place."

"I fear that 'Lady Crymsyn' is far too colorful an appellation not to be exploited. At least most of them spelled it correctly. And most of them used your official statement."

As I often did, I'd left a note about it and some other things on the kitchen table for him to find in the morning. "Then they followed it up by saying I was 'strangely' unavailable for further comment. Makes it sound like I was ducking out from guilt."

"Only to be expected. It is a rather good picture of you," he said. "At least we've finally ascertained that you can show up on film, but I always thought you might as it is a light-gathering device, and you are visible in light. When you want to be, that is."

"Yeah, gee, just what I always wanted to know." The photo was the one where I'd been caught just outside the club, and I didn't think it all that good a likeness. My face, which I'd not seen in nearly a year, looked a lot younger than the one I remembered. The skin was tighter, newer, the bones more prominent with restored youth. My eyes seemed the same, though, showing about a decade more experience than the rest of me, or so I imagined. The expression the camera caught was that of wary dismay. The caption got my name right and accused me of being mysteriously elusive. "I don't remember things being like this when I was the one doing the reporting," I groused.

"Well, I'm sure they did endure a certain amount of frustration in not being able to locate you today and decided to retaliate with rampant speculation. Your Mr. Kell called me at the office this morning to report the necessity of taking the club's phone off the hook. The constant ringing was disruptive to his schedule."

"Did he say if the cops were finished?"

"Not at that early hour, no. He did mention that two of the other workers decided not to come back. He found replacements, but one of them turned out to be a reporter in disguise. There was another contingent of them camped on the club's doorstep awaiting your arrival in hopes of an interview. Monetary compensation has been offered for exclusives with the men who broke through the wall—"

"For the love of Pete!" That called for another round of pacing.

Escott lighted and puffed on a cigarette, watching patiently from his chair at the head of the dining table. I was still in pajamas and slippers, having just gotten up. Materializing as usual in the kitchen, I'd seen him in the next room with the drift of newsprint scattered all over and stepped in for a look. Not the best thing to wake to, especially for someone who can't get used to things gradually by first putting a cup of coffee between himself and the world.

There were times when I really hated my condition.

"At least they don't know where I live yet—or do they?"

"If you examine the instrument in the kitchen you'll discover that it is also off the hook. I expect some enterprising newshound had the wit to check the records of the real estate office or those at City Hall about your leasing transaction for the club and traced your address from there. They have not yet connected you to the Escott Agency, for which I am thankful. I've not consulted the neighbors yet, but one can presume that several visitors have already come to our door today seeking fresh statements."

"Where do you get that presumption?"

"It's more of a deduction, really. I noticed a number of smudges on what had once been a clean, polished window inset of the front door, exactly the sort of marks a person leaves behind when he cups his hands around his face to peer inside. The nose prints are unmistakable."

And sometimes I kidded him about being too neat. "Think there's more people out on the street waiting to bushwhack me?"

"I came in this evening via the back way and did not see. If reporters are present, then I suggest you give them what they want and send them on their way. Manage things right, and they won't return."

"Gordy told me pretty much the same. That I should whammy them to make sure of it."

He gave an approving nod. "There you are, then."

"Okay, but not until I'm damn good and ready." I started for the stairs, wishing I could still drink coffee, but Escott had one last thing to add.

"I called Lieutenant Blair about that matter you requested. The dead woman's dress?"

"What about it?"

"He was gratifyingly friendly and cooperative. Quite refreshing, that. He's made no new progress on the case, by the way. I fear he's in for a difficult time with the papers making such a great fuss."

"What about the dress?" I prompted.

"There was a label inside for a shop called La Femme Joeena. It went out of business about three years ago. They specialized in custom-made gowns and the like. Very expensive. I passed this information on to Miss Smythe as you asked. It seems she also patronized the place. She then requested a photograph of the garment. I wasn't sure if Blair would go so far as that under your influence, but he did, sending me two separate views. They're under here somewhere." He shoved papers to one side and pulled out a manila envelope, handing it over.

I turned the flap down and drew forth the photos. One was a front view of the dress spread flat on a table with a long measuring stick next to it to show scale. The other picture was a back view. The lighting was pitiless, showing every tatter, tear, and stain on the delicate fabric, but you could see what it must have looked like when new.

"Miss Smythe requested that you come by the Red Deuces at ten," he said.

"That's a lot earlier than usual. She must have found out something."

"One can but hope."

* * *

As I feared, there was a car out front that didn't belong
on our street, and a couple of reporters rushed from it to
waylay me as soon as I poked my face outside.

"Come on, boys, I got a business to run," I said over
their urgent questions, putting my arm up in time to avoid
a picture. I could have tried tossing them a "no comment,"
but that wouldn't have stopped the frenzied inquisition.
My responding only brought them in closer. As soon as
they were within the glow of the porch light I was able to
give them a nice little talk. On my terms. It was pretty
much a repeat of my earlier statement, but they went away
satisfied—if somewhat dazed. I had a pinching feeling behind my eyes, but those mugs wouldn't be back again. In
fact, they'd make a point of throwing away my address
altogether before moving on to other stories.

There were times when I really loved my condition.

My Buick was free of stowaways, so I put it in gear and
drove to Lady Crymsyn to see what sort of progress Leon
and his crew had made. I'd invited Escott along, but he
was content to rest up from the long day he'd put in after
short sleep rations from the night before.

"You'll tell me anything of interest," he'd said, waving
me out. I figured he was anxious to stack up the papers
and polish that window clean again. When the fit was on
him, he was ferociously tidy.

As at the house, there were several hopeful yellow press
diehards lingering around the club when I arrived. They'd
probably heard from the workers that I usually came by
after hours to check on things. A flashbulb went off, but I
ducked in time, sparing my eyes from a burning and my
face from being displayed in the next afternoon edition.
Before the photographer could fit another bulb to his camera I made a general announcement that I'd give a short,

one-at-a-time interview in the club. This resulted in a minor skirmish as they noisily sorted out their pecking order.

Unlocking the door, I led them up to the office and turned on the lights. With the others waiting impatiently in the hall, I gave them each a minute of my time, except for a guy who'd been drinking—he needed five for me to get through to him—and sent them on their way. They were all happy, and so was I; they were gone for good, though there was a chance the drinker could return. My hypnosis was either unreliable or completely ineffective at getting past alcohol with some people, but if the rest of the papers lost interest in the case, then he had no reason to return, and I'd be in the clear. My last suggestion to them was to pester the cops for answers if they had any more questions. Blair would love me for that. If he ever found out.

But unless the cops turned up something, I didn't think much more copy would come of the case. Most news stories had beginnings, but no endings. Only rarely did John Q. Public hear of a conclusion to any of the endless number of human disasters that filled up the evening papers. Once in a while you might find a snippet about someone being arrested in connection to one crime or other, but it was often long after the case ceased to be of front page interest.

Chances were that mine would die down in such a manner. I hoped it would. I wanted Lady Crymsyn to be notable rather than notorious.

The phone was off the hook just as Leon had left it. I put it on again as an experiment, and it remained satisfyingly silent. Things were looking up.

Leon and the others were gone, signing themselves out at the usual time. I noted the two new names on the clipboard roster he'd left on my desk, one of which was heavily scratched through. There was annoyance in every line of the black ink for the reporter he'd bounced off the payroll. If for nothing else, that decided me about asking Leon to stay on to run the building's maintenance after the renovations were finished.

I went through the mail, discarding the junk—which included requests for exclusive interviews slipped through the slot by reporters—and piling up the real stuff. I had insurance forms, employment applications, and bills to see to, and not for the first time realized I'd soon have to find a general manager and an accountant. I had some paperwork experience from helping my dad when he opened a little hardware store back in Cincinnati, but not enough to cover all this. Once the club was running the load would only get worse. Not being up and around during business hours put a serious handicap on me; I needed someone to take care of such necessities so all I had to do was sign checks and enjoy myself.

Getting through this batch of responsibility as quickly as possible took about an hour, then I stretched and went downstairs to see what kind of progress had been made.

There'd been a general cleaning up of the lobby and club areas, and even Escott would have approved of the thoroughness of the job. Someone left the lobby bar light on again, which irked me. There was no reason to use it yet. During the day there had to be plenty of light from the big overheads and the windows to work by, and no one was around at night but me.

As I went to shut it off I noticed Leon had apparently seen to the stain on the floor tiles. He'd seen to it a little too well. Whoever had done the cleaning had scrubbed the glazing right off the surface. The stain was still there, though, some kind of dark stuff. It was probably a flaw that went all the way through the ceramic square. Damn. That'd have to be replaced. I'd brought another clipboard with me and made a note about it before moving on.

The basement was mostly cleaned up, too. Though I could see adequately by the pale light filtering through the doorway, I turned everything on before descending into its dim depths. Being alone in the building didn't bother me, being alone in the dark did. The string of temporary bulbs went all the way to the back where the alcove had been and illuminated everything enough to stave off my heebie-jeebies.

All the rubble was hauled away, by the cops or my own people, it didn't matter. The alcove was clean except for a dusting of mortar grit on the rough floor.

The rest of the false wall and the dividers that held it were now torn completely away, and it seemed like everything was ready for the new cement to be laid out smooth. In this part of the cellar they'd need to use a lot of it. Right against and along the far wall of the basement the floor dipped down about a foot or more below the level of the rest of the room. It looked like it had been chopped out by picks and was either bad planning on the original builder's part or some kind of intentional drainage construction. The contractor said it was unnecessary and to just fill up the trench.

My imagination was well in hand; I didn't feel one sign of the dead woman's lingering presence tonight . . . but then I didn't want to, either. The changes had helped banish her.

I quit the basement and sat at one of the tables near the stage to scribble fresh orders for Leon. He'd left a few notes for me to consider, like buying more cement to go with the bags already stored under the stairs, and the rental of a cement mixer. I gave him the okay to see to it and called it a night, trotting up to the office long enough to leave the clipboard in its usual place so he could start on things in the morning.

Back in the lobby again and ready to leave, I found that this time it had been my turn to forget to flick off the little light. I must have forgotten to do so while busy muttering over the stain on the tile. As I reached around for the switch I suddenly noticed a shot glass sitting on a coaster left in the middle of the shining marble surface of the bar. The glass contained exactly one finger of amber liquid.

I was absolutely certain the glass had not been there when I'd been down earlier. I'd have *seen* something like that. What the hell was this?

Leaning close, I took a cautious sniff. Whiskey, I decided.

My order for glasses and other items hadn't yet arrived. The storage areas for all three bars in the place were quite clear of supplies.

And there was no liquor on the premises either. This could only have been brought in by someone. What the hell for?

"Hello?" I looked around. All I could figure was that one of the workers must have stayed behind or somebody snuck inside after they left and put it there for a joke while I was busy elsewhere. None of my friends would do such a thing since they knew I wouldn't be able to drink the stuff. "Leon?"

No answer. I listened for all I was worth. If I concentrate hard enough, I can hear a mouse belch, but nothing came to me in this big, hollow building.

I was alone, but needed to be sure of it.

Highly aggravated, I searched the joint, starting at the roof and moving downward. I worked fast, vanishing in one spot to appear in another so as not to make any sound myself, and I looked everywhere, even the dead space under the tiers of seating.

Nothing and no one.

I checked all the doors and windows, found them to be

locked, including the front, where I'd been about to make my exit. Maybe someone had his own key and slipped out before I'd come in, but the point of the joke eluded me. A prank's a lot more fun when you can see the face of the sucker you play it on.

There wasn't anything really valuable in the club yet, so I had no huge qualms about going even if somebody had another key. Leaving a shot of whiskey on a bar isn't exactly in the same league as vandalism or burglary. If it really bothered me, I could always get a locksmith in to change things and debated on writing Leon another note about it.

Too much trouble for the moment. The incident was more irritating than worrisome, and there were other things I had to get to tonight. The perpetrator would probably come forward soon enough to get his laugh. I gave the coaster a quick glance. It was of the plain cork variety, clean, but slightly brittle, as though it'd been left unused on the shelf for a long time and had dried out. Shrugging, I dumped the liquor in the sink behind the bar and left the glass there. If the prankster wanted to try some fun and games with me, he'd be back soon enough.

And I'd be ready.

Parking at the Red Deuces, even on a weeknight, was always a pain. This time I tried a different direction, but still had to hike a block to get there. The doorman gave a friendly nod and ushered me in just on the stroke of ten. The hostess knew my face, too, and spared me from paying out the dollar cover charge. I told her Bobbi had asked me to come backstage, and she got one of the waitresses to escort me there. For all the glitter out front, behind the curtains it was plain and run-down-looking, something I planned to avoid with Crymsyn. My entertainers were to be as happy about their surroundings as the patrons.

Bobbi had a tiny dressing room, but it was all hers, and she'd assured me she'd been in worse. I thanked the waitress so she could leave and cautiously inched my way in. A table with a mirror took most of the space. I sniffed the air and picked up a wealth of greasepaint, talcum powder, and old clothes with Bobbi's rose scent over all.

I didn't have long to wait; a small commotion outside announced her presence there as she spoke with other performers in the narrow hall. A few seconds later she came in, flushed from being under the spotlights, but happily relaxed. She wore the exaggerated makeup required for the stage and a midnight-blue dress that I liked for the way its neckline wasn't anywhere near her neck. Instead of jewelry, she'd wrapped a silky blue scarf around her throat to conceal the small marks I'd left there.

"Hi," she said warmly, and came up for a hello kiss. "How's your night been?"

"Not too bad, considering what was in the papers. Charles thought I should be grateful they spelled my name right."

"I saw some of those stories. It'll blow over."

"Not the stigma on the club, I don't think."

"You can make people forget it."

"I could at that, but will the headache be worth it?"

She sat at her dressing table and checked her makeup for smears. "What's got you so testy? Besides the papers?"

I didn't think I was being testy, but she was just too good at reading me. I told her about the shot glass of whiskey on the bar and how impossible it was for it to have been there.

"Someone must have left it while you were in the basement and snuck out one of the fire exit doors," she suggested, fixing her lip rouge.

"That's what I was thinking, but I would have heard him. Those things make a big racket when they swing shut."

"It was eased closed, then. But that building's kinda old. Ever think there might be a secret passage?"

"You've been hanging around Charles too much." Escott loved that sort of thing. He'd been the one to construct the trick trapdoor in the kitchen for emergency access to my sanctuary. His office also contained a couple of hidden surprises.

"That old speak was a hot spot during Prohibition. They might have made a concealed escape for raids. Lots of places did. You know the Nightcrawler's got one."

"I don't see how Leon or the contractors could have missed it. Or me for that matter. The building's not connected to any others; the basement floor's uneven but solid. That place has been gone over inch by inch; they'd have found something." And they had. That woman's remains.

"So whoever it was used a fire exit to get out, then."

"But why leave a shot of whiskey behind? As a joke it's a lame duck."

She spread her hands and shook her head. She wanted to help, but couldn't.

"Okay, I'll figure it out later. Now what's the big deal having me here so early?"

"You complaining?"

"Nope."

"You're sweet. Did Charles tell you I've tracked down the dress?"

"Not exactly, but he got these from Lieutenant Blair." I gave her the manila envelope. She pulled out the photos and studied them. "He said something about the label inside. That you used to go to the dress shop."

"I sure as hell did, and paid through the nose there, too. Could have knocked me over with a feather when he told me the name of the place. It's shut down now, but," and she looked happily smug, "the former owner should be here any minute."

"You're kidding."

She slipped the photos back and held up her index finger. "Look at that and be grateful. I nearly wore it down to the joint from all the dialing I've done today trying to find him."

"Him?" I had some idea that dress shops were strictly female territory.

"He's a bit festive, but very nice. He's got a real gift for knowing what looks good on a girl—"

A brisk knock on the door interrupted her.

"That'll be him."

"The mirror," I said.

"Just a minute—" she yodeled to her visitor.

She grabbed a kimono from a hook and draped it carelessly over the offending furniture, covering its selective reflection of the room. Selective in that I wasn't included with the inventory.

"All right, come in."

A slender, athletic-looking man in his thirties pushed the door open. He was very handsome and dressed in a light mustard sporting coat with tan trousers and two-toned shoes of buff and white. His reddish hair was puffed rather than slicked back and matched his pencil-thin mustache. Instead of a tie he wore a pale scarf bunched around his open shirt collar, held in place by a gold stickpin. He might have gotten first place in a John Barrymore look-alike contest.

"Roberta, darling! It has been entirely tooooo long!" he said, sailing in, arms wide. As the room was small he didn't have far to go before encountering Bobbi. They wrapped up tight in a hard embrace.

"Joe, you sweetheart! You look wonderful!"

"Oh, you are just too, too kind, my dear. And to have me come backstage at the star's special request. My friends will all be soooo jealous!"

They went on like this for a time while I played chopped liver in the corner. When they finally pried themselves apart Bobbi introduced me to Mr. Joe James, designer of beautiful gowns for lovely ladies. We said the usual things to each other and shook hands.

"Joe used to own La Femme Joeena, the ritziest couturier's west of Paris," she said.

"Own! Darling, I *was* La Femme Joeena! And Paris was the ritziest place east of *me*. I'd still have the shop except for the call to higher things."

"He does costume design work for Hollywood now," she explained.

"Here in Chicago?" I asked. The festive Joe James did seem just a touch out of place on the prairie lands, but he'd fit in perfectly in the movies or New York theater.

"Absolutely!" he said. "They send me pictures of the actress and a script, and I send them *exquisite* works of art in return. Most of the time it's pearls before swine, and they change everything, but so long as those nice big checks clear the bank who cares? Roberta, how did you like that last one I did? The one with Joan Crawford? But the other one with what's-her-name—I swear Adrian was stealing all my work from my last film and taking the credit. And what *is* that rag you're wearing? I've used better things than that to dust my studio. I want you to come by tomorrow and let me do you a favor. That blue is just too purple for you. What you need is something cooler and more saturated to do you justice. I've always said that, haven't I?"

"You're a genius, Joe, that's why I called you."

"And only just in time—"

"But it's not my wardrobe I want to talk about."

"Then your friend here? I suppose I could give him a few sterling snippets of advice, but menswear just isn't my specialty, though I *know* what I like." And he gave me a charming smile with lots of twinkle in his eyes.

Bobbi didn't raise her voice; in fact, she sounded just as cheerfully pleasant. "Back off, bitch, he's mine."

Joe James made a little mewing sound of disappointment in his throat. "Oh, well, you can't blame a fellow for trying. Don't mind me, Mr. Fleming, I'm an unrepentant flirt."

"No problem, Mr. James," I said affably.

He gave a huge sigh and rounded on Bobbi. "All right, darling, what *do* you want done?"

"Have a seat." She indicated that he take her dressing chair while she perched on a spare stool facing him. I stood by and watched the show. She took the photos from the manila envelope and gave them to him.

"What is this?" He looked from one to the other and then at Bobbi. "A traffic accident?"

"Just about. I want you to cast your mind back a few years. What can you tell me about a bright red evening gown with matching sequins for a woman with dark hair?"

"Bright red? I use that a lot. You'll have to be more specific."

"This is special. A deep tone, intense, it stands out."

I wondered if she'd compare it to blood. The dress must have been close to that color when new.

James thought about it a moment. "What you might be describing is something I called Royal Red. I'd use it to make a violent splash here and there, but I've not much need for it now. It photographs on film stock as being sooty black. Throws the whole balance off if I'm not careful."

"Can you remember making such a gown in that shade?"

"I made several." Another glance at the photos. "Oh, dear. You mean one of my masterpieces has been reduced to this?"

"Sadly, yes."

"Oh, the poor thing." He clucked and shook his head at the loss.

"The patterning of the sequins on the skirt is pretty distinct. Can you remember this particular design?

"Every last stitch of it. Custom-tailored jobs at that price I *never* forget."

"Who ordered it?"

"No one you'd know, I hope. Bit of jumped-up trash was that bolt of goods, but she had the money, and who am I to argue with the lovely clink of cold cash in these hard times? She called herself Lena Ashley, but I know she couldn't have had that much class on her birth certificate. One is either born with it or not. *She* was not."

Bobbi shot me a happy smirk, brows arched with triumph. "There you are, Sherlock. Joe just solved it for you."

"Lena Ashley? That's her name?" It seemed too good to be true.

"What did I just solve?" he demanded.

"I gotta have more than this," I said to him. "How can you be so sure this is from your shop?"

Mr. James looked both smug and amused at my ignorance. "How could Michelangelo be sure of the difference between his *David* and the Sistine Chapel? Darling, when I make a work of art I remember it."

Bobbi nodded agreement. "He's got one of those kinds of memory, Jack. Like Gordy."

"Just from a color and some sequins?"

"It's a special shade," he said, "custom-made exclusively for La Femme Joeena. Back then I only used that rich a red for accents in my trims, only rarely as a dress. Lena positively fell in love with it and insisted I do a whole gown for her of the stuff. I will admit that she was right in her choice. She had a certain gold tone to her skin, and the red set it off in a most spectacular way. She loved it, but never came back for another, and she said she would. She still had two hundred dollars owing on her account, too, the bitch. I sent her a dozen bills until they started coming back with 'no forwarding' stamped on them."

"When was that?" I asked.

"The bills or the dress?"

"Lena. When was the last time you saw her?"

"Um, that would be about five years ago now last spring. I'd have to find my old account books to give an exact date. Whatever would you want with the likes of Lena Ashley, anyway? She was a soiled dove and no mistake. She sometimes got her colors right, but she was still dumb as a brick for all her airs and money."

"You're sure it's the only dress you ever made in that design?"

"Positive. I remember laying out the sequin pattern myself, then after doing the outline to the motifs, I gladly turned it over to one of the seamstresses to finish filling it in. She cursed me roundly for it, too, but later admitted it was spectacular."

"What if Lena loaned it to someone else?"

Joe looked shocked. "My ladies swapping their gowns around like a rummage sale? Unthinkable. Even Lena wouldn't do that. All my works are custom-fitted to the individual body. This dress wouldn't hang quite the same way on another woman, and she would know it. She'd just *feel* it! Of course, it was just awful if they gained a pound or three, then there was absolute hell to pay with alterations. Oh, the tales I could tell."

"What about another woman wanting an identical dress with the same kind of sequins?"

"Duplication? Just what kind of a Philistine do you take me for? My reputation would have been ruined in a week if I allowed that sort of thing to happen. No, my dear. I always did one design per customer. That was the main idea about their coming to me in the first place, after all. Lena was the only woman who got that particular pattern." His gaze flipped back and forth between me and Bobbi. "What's all this huge interest on the dress? And Lena?"

"You seen the papers today?" I asked.

Joe James blinked dramatically. "My God, you don't mean it! You're *that* Jack Fleming? And . . . and *she* was the one walled up in your club?"

"My club to be, it's not open yet, and yes, I guess she was if you're right about the dress. That's why I had to be sure you were sure. It's what was on the remains they found." I indicated the photos.

He immediately dropped them on the makeup table as though they were hot. "How utterly awful! That poor girl!"

"I'm surprised the cops haven't contacted you already."

"They have to find me first. I'm overdue on a film deadline and hiding out with friends. Those studio bastards keep phoning to hurry me up, and that interrupts my concentration. I've not checked with my answering service in a couple of days. If dear Roberta hadn't called every fashion store in town trying to find me, I'd still be in happy seclusion working away on my new masterpieces."

I turned to Bobbi, lifting her hand and kissing her dialing finger. "Have I ever told you that you're perfect?"

"Yes, but it bears frequent repeating."

"Ah, young love," said Joe in an approving tone. "I must say he's better than the last one, darling. Now tell me what's going on. Am I to have the police on my doorstep? Do you know what effect that will have on my delivery schedule?"

"You'll hear from the cops, all right," I said. "No way out of it."

"Damn."

"Could you tell us what you know about Lena?"

"Of course, but why?"

"It's my nightclub, and I don't want this hanging over the roof like some thunderbolt waiting to drop. If I can point the cops in the right direction for the killer, then maybe that poor woman can rest in peace."

"How utterly noble. The killer? God, but I never thought of that. She didn't get all walled up by herself, did she? Oh, it gives me the leaping fantods just thinking about it. I don't want my name involved. Suppose he comes after me?"

"I can fix it so your name stays out of the papers. I have an in with the guy in charge of the case."

"You *must* tell me your secret sometime. Well, all right, what do you want to hear?"

"Where did she live, who did she know. If she was on the make, who paid her bills?"

"I'll have to look her address up in my old files, but you'd have better luck talking with that Rita creature, if she's still around after all this while. They were best friends, always in the shop together."

"Rita who?"

"Robillard. Cut out of the same cheap cloth if you ask me. She worked—if one may call it that—for Booth Nevis. So did Lena."

I took a short pause to swallow. "Booth Nevis? You sure?"

"Lena usually paid in cash—she always seemed to have plenty, but when she ran out she'd put it on account. Sometimes she let it go for months, and I'd have to get very cross with her. Then she'd turn up the next day with a two-party check to settle it. Booth Nevis was always the name on the check. For both Lena and Rita, I might add."

Bobbi shot me a look. She knew all about Nevis owning the lease on my club.

Joe noticed our interplay and was instantly alarmed. "What's going on? Is this Nevis a gangster? What have I done? He'll put me in cement overshoes or worse for fingering him. That's it, I'll just have to grit my teeth and move to Hollywood with the rest of the harlots."

Bobbi made a calming gesture. "Joe, it'll be all right. Jack said he had the fix in. We won't let anything happen to you." Bobbi put her hand on his, reassuring.

He wasn't all that reassured. "Roberta, this is *serious* stuff, this is my *life,* for God's sake."

"Jack?" She gave me a glance.

"Mr. James, I've also got reasons for wanting to keep my head low," I said. "When the cops come calling you don't mention me, Nevis, or this conversation, and I'll return the favor."

"I'd appreciate that, but that gangster . . ."

"Just because his girl wore a dress from your place doesn't mean Nevis will know you said anything about him. Give the cops Lena Ashley's name and leave it at that. It was five years ago; they'll believe it if you say you don't remember anything more about her. Let them take it from there. And Nevis won't find out about you from me. You're safe."

"Well, if you're sure." He leaned earnestly toward Bobbi. "Is he sure?"

"Jack knows what he's doing."

"Oh, darling, I've heard *that* one before."

It took a lot more talk from me to get a little more talk from Joe, but he eventually calmed down and spilled what he had. Lena Ashley shared a flat with Rita Robillard back then or so he assumed since he sent the bills to the same address for both. They had expensive tastes and frequently indulged them at his shop, coming in nearly every week for something new, though Lena stopped after picking up the red dress. Rita still turned up regularly, and when Joe asked after her roommate she claimed not to know what happened to her. Soon after that she stopped coming in herself.

"In this light, it's all highly suspicious," Joe intoned. "She acted more angry than worried about Lena's vanishing. She must have known something more than she let on."

"Was she the type to wall up anyone alive?" I asked.

"And ruin her manicure? Don't make me laugh. Rita would have talked someone into doing it for her, but I really don't see her doing it in the first place. They got along very well so far as I could see. Rita was the smarter of the pair—though that's not saying much. She knew all the ropes, and Lena often asked her for advice, at least for dressing well. Lena was the real hell-raiser, she liked parties, was always talking about this one or that and always in need of something new to wear. Happy day for me."

"You sure she and Rita were on the make?"

"I suppose they must have been. How else do pretty girls with no family, no talent, no brains, and no job get the kind of money they spent?"

But I'd never heard Gordy mention anything about Booth Nevis being a pimp. Maybe he'd been a customer instead. Evidently a very satisfied one to judge by the money involved.

Or maybe not.

As Joe James said, *poor Lena.*

After having his brain picked clean James confessed to being parched with thirst and that the least I could do was buy him a drink. It was coming up time for Bobbi to do another song set, anyway, and she wanted to freshen her makeup. We left her to it and went out front to the table she'd reserved for him. It was close to, but not on top of the stage. I bought us a couple of martinis.

"Such a treat it is to get out and dust off the cobwebs," he told me. "I spend so much time over the drawing board I'll end up a hunchback before long." He then went on to say his job wasn't all that glamorous, but he wouldn't want to do anything else. "You do meet the nicest people, though, like Roberta—and yourself, of course."

"Thanks."

"Whatever happened to that frightful man she was with before? His name was Slick. Very pretty, but there was nothing behind his eyes."

"Dead. Shot."

Joe pursed his lips. "Oh." He gave me a long look and finished his drink. I said I'd changed my mind about having mine and if he would take it. He said yes and seemed grateful when the lights dimmed for Bobbi's entrance.

With the spot making her platinum hair shimmer like a halo, she started out with a throaty ballad that drew a few late dancers onto the floor. Instead of a regular small band for music there was just the one piano. The Red Deuces could have had more, and often did, but its focus tonight was for the romantics in the crowd. The ones with lots of money. The martinis I bought were on the high end of the pricing scale for this town. I was paying to see and be seen and for the classy atmosphere of the joint. I tried my best to enjoy it. With Bobbi making the entertainment, it was easy.

Part of me was still putting time in on my own place, though. I was taking mental notes as I always did when in a club now. I watched how the staff here did their work and if they were efficient about it. The people almost seemed to be overdoing themselves in amiability. They had a right to it if the tips were in keeping with the price of the drinks, but I got the impression that they were indeed genuinely cheerful. While off to the side, hanging around the bar between orders, they smiled and joked with each other. At the same time they kept their eyes on the patrons, alert for the least signal for service. One waiter even started toward a table as the customer pulled out his cigarette case, arriving in time to hold a lighter under the smoke, then discreetly withdrew like a helpful ghost.

That was good to see. It was just the sort of thing I wanted for Lady Crymsyn.

After Bobbi finished her set, some of the customers left, and if the next singer on stage was troubled by the thinning ranks, he didn't show it and plowed forward. I wondered if he'd been the one too drunk to go on the night before. Yet another item to worry about once the club opened: entertainers who didn't entertain. Bobbi had filled my head with endless horror stories of drunks, fistfights breaking out, and impromptu backstage sex and even impromptu onstage sex when someone pulled a curtain open at the wrong time. There were other alarming examples, but those were the most common reasons why, at times, the show did not go on.

I had my work cut out for me. The sooner I got an experienced general manager to take the load off the better.

Just shy of midnight Joe James said he had to leave, so I offered him a ride home since he'd cabbed over. He accepted, and I went backstage to let Bobbi know.

"I'll return here at the usual time, though," I promised.

"Then I'll be out front. What'd you think of Joe?"

"You were right on the festive part, but he's okay."

She snuggled close, and I caught the scent of her rose perfume again. It seemed to go right through the top of my skull, but in a nice way. "Good. I'm glad you don't have a problem with him."

"He's a friend of yours, so he's all right by me."

She went out front so she could give him a kiss on the cheek good-bye, and they promised each other to get together to talk clothes later that week.

James liked to chat about himself and filled my ear with Hollywood gossip on the drive to his home, or rather to where he was staying. The house was dark, meaning his hosts were asleep and it was too late for the one-for-the-road drink he'd wanted to give me. Just as well, with my condition. I was good at pretending to imbibe, but it didn't always work. At parties I'd just carry a full glass around and keep moving, but it's hard to get away with the trick when it's just me and one other person.

He expressed his regrets, said it had been a pleasure to meet me, shook my hand good-bye, then strode easily up the walkway, happy in his two-toned shoes. I wished him well and pulled back into traffic again.

Between what I'd just learned from him and my talk with Gordy the night before, I had plenty to think about, and right now my thoughts were on Booth Nevis.

Either by accident or on purpose, every single one of the papers failed to include Nevis's name in their many stories, though it was well-known that he'd had a feud with the speak's violently deceased owner, Welsh Lennet. The rank and file reporters seemed to know all about it to judge from what I'd overheard while hidden behind the bar during their invasion last night. If I'd been one of them and trying to work up an interesting angle, it would have only been natural to include at least a line or two on the club's dark history. This strange lack spoke volumes.

I'd have to run by Nevis's place and ask a few questions.

I had a feeling he wouldn't like them much.

5

NOT too far from the west side of the Loop, Booth Nevis ran a place with a good bar, a small band, and a dance floor. That was all pretense; anyone interested who'd been in town for more than a day knew it to be only thin cover for the gambling in the back and upstairs rooms. The Nightcrawler Club had the same thing going, but could cater better to a more respectable, less informed crowd with its fancy shows and singers. The Flying Ace was strictly for the pros and their marks.

Nevis called it the Flying Ace because he was supposed to have been a pilot during the war, but no one believed that. He'd been too busy running numbers for some uncle in San Francisco, learning the family business. Word had it that he and the uncle got interested in the same woman, and she played one against the other for money and gifts. She got found out, though, and wisely left town before either of them could express his annoyance to her. Nevis was supposedly looking for her when he hit Chicago, learned how to pilot a plane, and began short hops across the Canadian border to bring in booze. He couldn't fly big cargoes, being limited by what his plane could carry, so he smuggled in premium stuff for the rich and discriminating and played the role of the dashing bootlegger to the hilt. The snob crowd ate it up. Or rather drank it up.

Selling the fancy booze and special wines at a five hundred percent profit per bottle, he soon had plenty of dough to flash and invested it in staking out a piece of territory to build his club. The lessons he'd learned by the foggy bay stood him just as well by the windy lake. He prospered with the gambling, and now only flew for his own amusement.

The club was decorated with aviation souvenirs, and behind the bar was a big photo of Nevis decked out in leather flight gear standing next to his plane. There were some medals in a frame next to it, the implication being that he'd won them in service. Anyone who'd been in the war would know at a glance that it was bullshit, since the medals were navy honors he'd probably bought in a pawnshop. No one told him that to his face. It just wasn't worth the trouble.

The gorilla watching the door knew me from my dealings with his boss and nodded when I asked if Nevis was in. I passed through a small, bare lobby. It had no cover charge, no hat check, nothing to prevent a person from quickly going through to the gaming rooms, where bigger change was to be made. Anyway, there was little point in leaving your hat out front if you were forced by a raid to make an exit out the back.

The main room was choked with a week's worth of loser's sweat and stale cigarette smoke. My night vision was no good here, but at least I didn't have to breathe the stuff. I felt my way over to the bar. The bartender, who looked far too clean-cut for the joint, came over. Mindful of the drink that had been left so mysteriously on the bar at Lady Crymsyn, I ordered a shot of whiskey and asked where I could find his boss. He gave me one, told me the other, then I paid him fifty cents and said he could keep the change.

Nevis didn't have a regular table for himself, always sitting in a different spot, and he usually moved several times a night. No one was gunning for him that I knew about; he was just being careful. Gordy was often the same way. I hoped I wouldn't need to follow their example once my place was up and running. I was pretty bulletproof, but details like that I just didn't want to have to think about.

The band was playing loud and hot as I threaded between tables, and some couples were making use of the floor. There were a number of dressed-up women sitting in groups. Some looked bored, others predatory, as they drank and smoked, thickening the atmosphere. None of them made an offer at me, so I politely assumed they were waiting on their men to finish gaming in the back. It might be a while; Nevis usually let things go on around the clock.

I discerned Nevis's outline in the shifting murk. He was at a table away from the crowd, his back to a wall, of course. He had a phone receiver jammed against his ear and, from his gestures, was holding quite an animated conversation. In a short lull between the din of the music and other sounds I just barely picked out his voice.

"No, no, no, I'm telling you, you can't push anyone out of a plane like that. The damn door is too small for that kind of thing. Oh, I gotta go." He'd spotted me and hung up, flashing a big smile my way. "Fleming, long time no see. How's that wreck of mine doing?"

"Not too many hitches." Pretending I'd not heard anything amiss, I stuck out my free hand and we shook. He invited me to sit across from him. If anything interesting snuck up behind me, I'd see it in his eyes first. "You can't call it a wreck anymore. I've put too much work into it."

"So I've heard." He was a long lean man, with thin hair smoothed back over a skull without much meat under the skin. He seemed frail, with the hollow, wasted look of a lunger; only his assured manner and robust confidence belied the initial impression of illness. He had a square jaw and wide mouth full of good humor for himself and the world. Most of the time it was sincere. "Is this a social visit?"

"Not really. I'm opening soon and thought you could help me find people to work there. I need the usual and a general manager to run the place when I'm not around."

"Why not ask Gordy? He knows everyone."

"I did. He said to come to you." This was true. Gordy and I had discussed the intricacies of hiring and firing many times.

Nevis smiled amiably, long, nimble fingers lightly touching a sweating glass in front of him. He turned it clockwise slowly, a quarter inch at a time. His drink was down to melting ice.

I wondered how much alcohol he'd had tonight. That would affect my ability to get reliable information from him. "I figured you could put the word out for me."

"Sure, no trouble."

"Especially for the general manager spot. I need a guy who knows how to do books and keep them straight."

"Not asking for a lot in this town, are you? All the people who come here have an angle—their own. Maybe you should advertise for some college kid who's never been hungry."

I let that one pass as the joke it was. "I'll be at my club between nine and midnight for anyone who wants to see me."

"Why so late?"

"So I know they can work the hours."

"What if they're working someplace else at that time?"

"Then they don't need a job." I pretended to taste my whiskey. It was like bringing gasoline to my mouth, but I managed without any face-twisting to wet my lips. Next time I'd just ask for water. "Doing a good business to-night?"

"Good enough on both sides of the door." He jerked his pointed nose toward a discreet opening that I might have seen had there been less smoke. On the other side of it were the gambling rooms. He'd taken me through once, but I'd turned out to be disappointingly immune to the offered temptations. When I wanted to gamble it was always blackjack at the Nightcrawler, where I had a chance to win.

The horse racing bets I didn't count as gambling. Those were a sure thing, after all.

Nevis and I talked a bit about this and that, and he offered to buy me another drink when I carelessly knocked my whiskey off the table. I told him I'd be happy with some plain water as obviously more booze would only add to my problems. He laughed at that and signaled a waiter, telling him what was wanted and added another drink on the order for himself.

"You're all right, Fleming," said Nevis. "Most guys would get a double just to prove they could handle it."

A year ago I'd have done so. Not anymore. "Why give myself a worse hangover than I'm already going to get just to make a point?"

"You're not drunk," he stated. "Come morning you're not going to feel a damn thing from tonight."

Truer words and all that.

He wasn't showing it, just a sheen on his face, but I figured he'd already had too much of his own stock for me to be able to make a hypnotic dent in his mind. There were other ways to get a man to talk, though. A waiter brought his order and mine. We listened to the band, watched the dancers, and with a little prompting I got a couple of funny stories out of him about his business. The phone rang twice. His conversations were no more than a minute each, with words of one syllable. No names were spoken.

He'd worked his drink down to the halfway point when the band took a break. He regarded them with a benign smile as they filed out. When he turned it on me, it beamed with happy goodwill. "So. Why haven't you asked me about that body you found?"

"Because you'd want to talk about it yourself when you were ready."

His eyes warmed up. "Not bad, kid."

No need to correct him on my real age. "What do you know about it?"

Nevis shook his head. "I read the papers. That's all. Welsh Lennet could probably tell you more. But he's not around."

"So I heard." As the previous owner of the building, the thoroughly deceased Lennet would have to be mentioned sooner or later. I had just enough apprehension banging around inside to know Nevis was giving me a mild warning to back off. And maybe I was also being tested for a reaction. I tried not to give one. "I heard he kept rough company. Who's still around I could talk to about him?"

"What's it to you?" Nevis smiled, very steadily.

"My place isn't open yet and already has a black mark against it. I want to wipe it away."

He chuckled. "You shouldn't try to play clean in this town. Most of the time it won't let you."

"I heard that, also. This is something I have to do, though." I waited him out as pieces of other conversations floated around us like the stale smoke. A drunken woman laughed, loud and high, across the room. No one paid her much attention.

Nevis sipped from his glass, put it on the table, and began making those quarter-inch turns again. "You wouldn't come here unless you knew more than you're saying. You're thick with Gordy, and he'd have given you an earful about me and Lennet."

"I just heard rumors, is all. No skin off my nose if you bumped him. My only concern is about the dead woman."

His smile dimmed. "Well, I don't know anything about her."

In the middle of his level, brimming-with-honesty gaze, I said, "They found out she was Lena Ashley."

His smile faltered, then faded completely. His open face shut down and went blank, and not from my influence. "What?"

I repeated the name, giving him a long look of my own. A hypnotic prompt might not work, so I had to wait him out. It took him a while. He seemed genuinely surprised. I couldn't tell if it was real or overacting.

Finally: "You sure?"

"Yeah. You knew her pretty well, too."

"No, I didn't."

I didn't believe him. No one would.

He went back to fiddling with his glass. Now he made turns of a full inch. "Lena, huh? Poor kid. Who would have figured it?"

"Exactly. Who had it in for her?"

"How the hell should I know?"

"Because you paid her bills."

He stopped a moment with the glass. "So I did. My problem is I'm too much of a soft touch when it comes to dames. She'd hit me up for a loan whenever things got tight, and I'd give her dough. I really didn't know her that well."

He *was* nervous. With that last sentence he said just

exactly too much. "Oh, yeah?" I made sure he heard doubt in my tone.

No change to his blank expression, but his face flushed, his hand drawing away from the glass to form a white-knuckled fist. I'd hit one hell of a nerve.

He was a thinking man, though, and restrained himself from actually trying to slug me. The flush faded, and he put on a smile that almost looked right. "I don't need to explain the birds and bees to you. She hit a lot of guys up for what she called loans. She was a great gal, good company, so no one minded too much when she didn't pay back. She spent it fast and would call guys for more. She was like a little kid, always wheedling, forgetting what she owed. Maybe she hit the wrong guy, and he got sore and—"

"Walled her up alive for a bum debt?"

"Sure, why not?"

"Because she could find more money and pay him off. You have to come up with a better excuse than that."

Nevis flushed again and went still. When he finally spoke, he kept his voice level, but cold enough to raise the hackles on a marble statue. "I know what you're doing, and it won't work with me. I don't have to come up with a damn thing. Who the hell do you think you are coming into my place with that kind of shit? You're no cop."

"Right. Meaning you can talk to me and it won't come back on you. Why'd you bump her?"

He started to surge forward. "I didn't—" He caught himself and eased down. In slow stages the smile gradually returned, but his eyes were hard. "You're good, Fleming."

"And I thought I was being subtle. Why'd you bump her?"

Nevis took a drink, watching me over the rim of the glass. "First, I didn't bump her, and second, I couldn't say who did. She just stopped turning up. Except for the people she owed money to, no one was all that much bothered. Nobody knew what happened to her. That's the truth."

"Who'd she owe?"

"Uh-uh. I'm not making trouble for others."

I regretted not being able to really question him. He was past the point of me getting him mad enough to talk. For the moment, he'd say nothing or only shoot out lies, but those could be just as useful in their own right. Now I knew he had something interesting to hide. "Come on. You read the papers."

"Yeah. But it's nothing to me."

"You know what was done to her."

He started turning his glass again, watching me with everything behind his face shut down and locked for the night.

"Nobody deserves that kind of death," I said quietly.

A shrug. "You'd be surprised."

"Who are you protecting?" I could hear the beginnings of futility in my own voice and didn't like it.

"No one. I've got nothing to tell you."

"Look, some bastard's walking around having a good laugh on her—"

"Oh, stop or I'm going to cry."

The power of my own sudden anger and frustration took me by surprise. I'd been holding things in, trying to match Nevis for steadiness. It didn't work. Something shifted and broke free inside; the heat of it rushed through me, spilling out.

I made no effort to stop it.

Though his mind was well insulated by alcohol, Nevis rocked back, big bony hands grasping the table edge at the last second to keep his balance. His eyes went wide.

I pressed him. "Who could have killed her, Nevis?"

His jaw sagged, but he made no sound.

"You hear me? Who?"

His mouth flapped; he couldn't speak, only made a small gasping sound like pain.

Too much. I broke eye contact. When I looked again, he was still holding on to the table, dazed and trembling. Damn. I wondered if I'd done him permanent harm. It didn't seem likely, but I'd been careless with my temper once before with disastrous results.

"Nevis?"

He blinked, shook his head like a boxer with one too many punches. His fish-white skin shone with new sweat.

"Nevis. Who killed Lena Ashley?"

All he could do was shake his head, refusing to meet my gaze. I said his name a couple times, fighting off a stab of real worry. To my relief he finally responded with an inarticulate growl. He sounded more confused than annoyed. "You're okay," I told him with more reassurance than I actually felt.

"Wh—wh—at?"

I gave him my water, helping him slop down a few gulps. He didn't look good, and people were staring. I waved through the smoke at the barely visible waiter. He saw and came over with a fresh drink and a concerned expression. "Something wrong?" he asked.

"Your boss ain't feeling so well. I think he should lie down for a minute."

"The office has a couch."

"That'll do."

He stayed to help, though I could have managed on my own. A lot more stares came our way as we each took an arm and helped Nevis along. He walked under his own power, but needed guidance like a blind man. We went through the door leading to the gambling area. There was a bare, dim hall on the other side and more doors, some open to the gaming within. The sounds of risk, triumph, and failure floated from them.

I'd been in the club's big office before to close the deal for Crymsyn and went straight to it. The waiter and I eased Nevis onto a battered leather couch and put his feet up.

"He just got a little dizzy," I explained, straightening.

The waiter looked dubious. "Should I get a doctor?"

"That's okay. Let him rest. I'll keep an eye on him."

Still dubious, he left. Probably to pass on the news. I dropped to one knee and slapped Nevis's face hard enough to sting. "Come on. Wake up. It's not that bad."

I hoped it wasn't that bad. The change in me could be dangerous for others. On one occasion my uncontrolled rage drove a man stark-staring mad, which had taught me one hell of a lesson about self-restraint. But then I'd had him under my complete hypnotic influence, and that contact made him more vulnerable to mental damage.

Nevis's reaction puzzled me. Maybe he was just highly susceptible to suggestion. Being drunk and having to deal with my anger banging around in his head was apparently not a good combination for him. When I'd had need in the past to try questioning others in a similar alcoholic state, they always seemed able to shrug off my influence. I didn't know what had gone wrong this time.

Or maybe I didn't want to admit to myself that I'd been extremely stupid.

Nevis mumbled something. His eyes were partly open, but not focused on anything.

"What's that? Talk to me." I leaned close.

"Ask," he slurred out.

"Ask what? Ask who?"

His hand brushed against my coat as he struggled with the words. His face went red from the effort to speak. "Ask. Rita."

Rita Robillard. On my list of people to see. "What about Rita? You think she killed Lena?"

"Nuh. Knew her. Friend."

"Where do I find her?"

"Nuh . . ." A head shake, then his eyes shut as he dropped back. "I. Hurt."

"Headache? Is that it?"

"Mi—graine. God-damned migraines. Oh, *damn* . . ." Moaning, he writhed over on his side, bringing his arms up to cradle his skull. There was pain all over his face and in every line of his long body. I knew exactly what it was like to feel that bad.

"You want anything? What do you want?"

"Light. *Off*."

I stood, feeling more than a little helpless, and cut the overhead light. A small desk lamp remained on, but he seemed not to object to its vague glow. He relaxed a little and went very still. His tight breathing gradually steadied, but I didn't know whether to take that as a good sign or not. I took a whiff of air, concentrating, and in between the normal smells of booze, the day's sweat, and tobacco, I caught an odd, flat sourness floating up from him. It was the stink of illness. Sometimes I could pick it off a person. Not one of my favorite abilities.

Someone made a commotion in the hall and pushed in. The light crashing through the door from the outside overhead fell across Nevis, but he was too out of things to notice.

"What's the problem? Tom said the boss got sick." The newcomer was Shivvey Coker, a solidly built man of medium height who seemed to take up more space than he should. He also knew me by sight, nodded a perfunctory greeting, and muscled past for a better look at Nevis. "Musta had too much again," he pronounced with mild disgust.

If Coker was unaware of Nevis having a problem with migraines, then it wasn't my place to enlighten him. "He didn't seem drunk."

"He never does. He packs the stuff away without showing it, then—wham—he's out cold. It's kinda early for him, though."

"Maybe he started early. Let's let him sleep it off."

He hesitated, and I couldn't blame him since Nevis was in charge of his daily wage. From the flashy clothes and the thick gold watch on its gold chain, the pay looked to be pretty good.

"C'mon, I'll buy you one," I said, wanting distance from the sickroom. With every breath I seemed to take in more of that sour scent.

Coker let me herd him out, and I left the desk light on. I'd known a few people plagued by migraines, and there wasn't much you could do for them but leave them alone to sweat it out.

"Don't look so worried, kid," said Coker, as we emerged into the club. "He'll bounce back. He always does."

"Sure." With a small twinge of guilt, I hoped Nevis would be all right, seeing how I was most likely the cause of his attack. No way to fix it, either. Better to forget him for the time being. I now had someone else from my private inquisitional list requiring my full concentration.

Coker found a couple openings at the bar, and we eased in. He had a beer. I asked for water again.

"You could do with something stronger," he observed.

"I don't want to end up like Nevis."

He snorted. With a nickname like Shivvey you expected someone good with knives or an ex-prizefighter. But there was a gun under his coat, and his face and knuckles were unmarked by much of anything. He was ordinary enough to vanish into wallpaper, but if you knew what to look for you could see he was down-deep tough. It was in the way he moved and the hard cast to his colorless eyes; you went by those, not the milk-bland, amiable expression. "You're Fleming, ain't you? The guy what bought Welsh's old place? I'm Shivvey Coker; I used to work for him."

We briefly shook hands. "I heard that. Too bad about what happened to your old boss."

Coker shrugged off the sympathy. "He was an asshole."

"Oh, yeah? Is that why he got scragged?"

"Probably. I didn't like him much, but he paid good, and the girls he kept around were friendly."

The bartender, whom Coker called Malone, delivered our drinks. I gave him a quarter and motioned for him to keep the change. A touch surprised at this second tip, he nodded his thanks and moved off to polish glasses, still looking too clean-cut for the joint. He was within earshot, but the band was filing back, and their noise would cover what conversation I had with Shivvey Coker.

He polished off half his beer in a gulp. I banished any thoughts about hypnotizing straight answers out of him. After what happened to Nevis, I was justifiably gun-shy.

"Who do you think threw those grenades at Welsh Lennet?" I asked, pretending to sip water.

Another shrug. "Not my business to think."

"Lotta people say it was Nevis."

"Why you interested? It's old news."

"Just wondering if there was a connection between his death and that woman who was walled up in what used to be his basement."

He didn't flicker an eyelid. I took it to mean he'd long figured out why I'd come around. "Probably not."

"You're pretty sure."

"Walling up dames wasn't Welsh's style. If they got outta line with him, he'd either bust 'em one in the chops till they behaved or send 'em packing. There was always more coming in to replace the troublemakers."

"What if the dame owed him money?"

"Then he'd take it in trade. I don't have to tell you what he'd trade for." Coker sniggered, enjoying his joke, and finished his beer. I signed for Malone to bring him another.

The band started up. The drunk woman squealed with delight and coaxed a man onto the dance floor. She was a tall, frizzy blonde and for a while looked like she was wrestling with him over who was to lead. I didn't watch long enough to see who won.

"Thanks," said Coker, accepting his new beer. "Now, when you gonna try for the real questions? If you think pumping me full of this stuff will get me talking, it won't work. I got more stamina than Nevis."

"Fair enough. I want to know about Lena Ashley."

He paused in mid-lift of his glass. "Who?"

"You heard. She ever touch you for money?"

"She touched everyone. In all kinds of ways." He winked at Malone the bartender. "Maybe not everyone. She was before your time wasn't she, pretty boy?" Malone gave him a nervous tic of a smile and nearly dropped the glass he was polishing. Coker laughed at him, his mouth suddenly thin with distaste, then looked at me. "Let's get a table before pretty boy here falls in love with one of us."

We carried our glasses to a table by the dance floor. The drunk blonde was all over the place, laughing and whooping as her partner swung her around to the fast music. He was smooth and sober, moving with the ease and assurance of much practice. He didn't look hungry enough to be a real lounge lizard, though he was dressed for the part in an expensive tuxedo. You could shave with the crease of his trousers and use his patent leather dancing shoes for mirrors.

"How well did you know Lena?" I asked.

Coker said he couldn't hear me over the band, and I had to repeat the question. "We was friendly, but that's as far as it went."

"How far was that?"

"Just friendly. You know how it is with some skirts.

We'd have some good times, but I didn't send her no valentines or Christmas cards. She was wise. Didn't nag like other dames might. When she got tired of me she'd just find someone else and play with him."

"Ever loan her money?"

"Me and a dozen other guys. She called it loans, we knew better." He gave a short chuckle.

"Who'd she annoy?"

"Annoy?"

"She had to get someone mad enough to kill her. Who'd she run with?"

"It's been too long. Lot of those guys have moved on."

"Who's left? Besides you and Nevis?"

He grinned, showing two straight front teeth and half a dozen crooked ones. "He didn't know her well enough to want to kill her. And I won't play for it, either. Don't slop your mess on me, kid. Get on my bad side and you're just asking for trouble."

"Then point me to someone else."

"There ain't nobody else." He leaned forward, and though he kept to his amiable expression there was a decided change in him. The pleasant facade simply ceased to exist, and I saw without surprise or any sensible shred of fear that I was dealing with an honest-to-God killer. This was indeed a man who would just as soon shoot me as look. "Lemme give you some good advice, kid. Lay off. The broad's dead, and nothing you do will fix it."

I waited long enough to let him understand that I'd heard. "You know something. I want to—"

He cut me off with an abrupt wave of his hand, then pressed it flat on the table between us. "I know you're a friend of Gordy's. I don't want no trouble with him, but some guys in this town ain't so smart. You make them unhappy, and you will get yourself dead, and then Gordy gets unhappy and all hell breaks loose. It's bad for business."

"He'll be glad you hold me in such high regard."

"Then I'm doing us both a favor." He emptied his glass and stood. "Thanks for the beers. I'll see you around."

He strode toward the office, and that was that, until I could corner him when he was more sober or there were fewer witnesses. I'd either have to start earlier in the evening or somehow persuade him to drink a gallon or so of coffee. Fists wouldn't work on him. He was the type to just grin and spit his crooked teeth at me.

I quit the table and went back to the bar with my glass of water. If Coker wasn't in a mood to talk, then I'd try Malone. Bartenders usually knew a little about everything going on in their place. Instead of change, I put a five-dollar bill in front of me. It didn't take him long to notice and come over.

"Yes, sir, what would you like?"

"Shivvey said you could help me."

He glanced past my shoulder, probably looking for Coker to get some confirmation of my statement. Coker was out of sight, though. "I'll do what I can, sir."

"I'm looking for a woman named Rita Robillard."

That quick nervous tic of a smile came and went, and he gave the bill a fleeting look of regret. "Perhaps Mr. Coker was having a little joke on you, sir. She's right over there, with Mr. Upshaw." He indicated the loud, frizzy blonde twirling over the floor with her well-dressed partner.

I felt foolish having been caught out in my lie. "What do you know about her?"

"She comes here a lot. She enjoys dancing."

"Who are her friends?" I slid the five toward him.

He backed away from it. "Perhaps you should talk to Mr. Coker about her, not me."

"Because he's one of her friends? Okay, I don't want you in trouble with Shivvey, but I'd appreciate an introduction to her."

"I don't think you'll need one. Just ask her to dance."

"I will." I pushed the money at him again.

"Oh, sir, that's not necess—"

"Don't worry about it."

The band eased into a slower number and the man called Upshaw slowed his high-stepping accordingly. He held Rita lightly, hands perfectly placed, balance perfectly centered. There was no intimacy of touch between them, though, not like when Bobbi and I danced. Upshaw was apparently just getting in some practice. Rita's eyes were shut, a dreamy expression on her face. When they circled toward my side of the floor I pressed forward and asked if I could cut in.

Upshaw paused at my interruption; Rita opened her baby blues and gave me a quick once-over. She wore a gold dress that clung like paint to her firmly built figure, yet swirled freely around trim ankles.

"Sure, Sport," she said enthusiastically, answering for him. Showing no more expression than a waxwork, Upshaw smoothly bowed out and glided from the floor.

Rita took hold of me—that was the only way to describe it—smiling like a happy shark. I led off, and we did all right for a few measures, then she tried to turn in another direction, reacting on her own to the music. I held fast, insisting on taking her my way. She finally came along.

"I'm Rita," she said, laughing from our brief wrestling match.

"Jack."

"Hello, Jack. You really know what you're doing, don't you?" She lifted her arms slightly to indicate our dancing.

"Most of the time."

"I saw you talking with Shivvey. You a friend of his?"

"Just business." No need to make up any more lies tonight. I had no real talent for it. "After he left I thought I'd like to dance with you."

"Well, it just shows you've got good taste." She didn't look as drunk as before. All the moving around with Upshaw must have helped her work off some of the booze.

Close up, without the smoky air obscuring the details, she wasn't too bad. There were good bones under the skin, by default giving her pretty features. She had height and was slim enough not to need much in the way of restrictive underwear. Her dress represented a month's pay for most men, and she knew what was becoming.

She would also know that every man had his own angle, and while I moved us around, she studied me from under her lashes, trying to determine mine. I figured her to be twenty-five going on fifty. Too many drinks, cigarettes, and late nights were already taking their toll, aging her fast. I didn't want to think of where'd she be in five years, and chances were it wasn't something she wanted to think about much, either.

"You know Shivvey for long?" she asked.

"Just met him tonight. I've seen him around."

"What are you here for?"

"I had to talk business with Nevis, but he went under the weather. Had to take a nap."

"He does that sometimes. What kinda business?"

"I leased some property from him, turning it into a nightclub: Lady Crymsyn."

"Oh, you're *that* guy! I been hearing about that place all over town. Everyone says it's going to really be something. When do you open?"

"In two weeks." Officially. The private, invitation-only party was in one week.

"I gotta come see it. I used to go there all the time. To the old place, I mean."

"Really? I've made a lot of changes. Maybe I'll give you a special tour."

She punched my shoulder. "Yeah, yeah, I know all about those! Though with you it'd be fun, I bet."

"As much fun as you can handle," I murmured. She'd want to hear something like that.

She gave out with a loud laugh. Loud, but with genuine mirth behind it. This was a gal who knew how to enjoy herself.

"I wasn't in town back when Welsh Lennet had the place," I said. "What was it like?"

"Not fancy, but you could whoop it up fine there most nights. Too bad about poor Welsh. He was a jerk, but could show a girl a good time when he wanted."

"Who else used to be there with you? I might know some of 'em."

"Just the usual gang. Shivvey could tell you better. I'm not so good at remembering names."

Or she was just being naturally cautious. "I heard you were friends with a gal named Lena."

Rita lost rhythm for a moment. "Yeah, sure, we whooped it up, but she went away a long time back."

"Went away?"

"Owed some rent, too—we used to share a flat—but that wasn't the big deal. She left behind all her clothes and things. It was pretty strange. Not one word from her, either. I asked all over, too."

I knew exactly how that felt, looking for someone who would never be found. "Where'd she go? Any reason why?"

She shrugged. "Couldn't say. She left enough stuff to hock so I could cover the rent, so that was something."

"You try to find her?"

"Well, of course I did! I even went to the cops and filed one of those missing person reports, but I might as well have tooted in the wind for all the help they were."

"Was she tight with anyone back then? Maybe with Booth Nevis?"

She stopped dancing altogether. "You ask a lot of questions, Mister."

"With good reason. You need to talk with me."

"Oh, yeah? Why?" She took her arms away and planted her feet.

"To find out what happened to Lena."

"What do you know about her if you wasn't in town then?"

"Where's your table?"

Rita glared a moment, then stalked to a place right by the dance floor. The table was just big enough to hold two glasses, an ashtray, a handbag, and one elbow. She dropped heavily into a chair and leaned toward me as I took the opposite seat.

"C'mon, tell me what's what," she demanded.

"You see the papers today?"

"I don't have time for reading."

Probably too busy sleeping off her nightly revels. "Maybe you caught it on the radio, then. The workmen at my club found a body there—"

"Ohmygod," she breathed. "I *heard* that! Walled up they said. You telling me that it was Lena? I don't believe it."

I kept silent. She needed time for the surprise to wear off. It did, eventually, and the loud Miss Robillard started looking more sober by the second.

She canted her head, giving me a sideways eye. "You're serious, aren't you, Sport? About it being her?"

"Very serious."

"W-why do you think it was Lena?"

"She had on some nice pieces of jewelry. Real stuff, not dime-store. Had dark hair . . ."

"That could be anybody."

"The handmade dress she was wearing had a label of an exclusive shop, La Femme Joeena. The fabric was a really bright, deep red, like a traffic light. With a lot of sequins—"

Rita went white. She sat straight in her chair now, not touching its back, hands in her lap, her big shocked blue eyes staring at me and probably not seeing a thing. Dance music flowed over us; couples drifted past, laughing, talking.

"I'm sorry," I said, an inadequate response to her reaction. Anything would be. I don't think she heard.

After a moment, she scrabbled blindly at her handbag and pulled out some cigarettes and a lighter, which she couldn't get to work. I took it from her twitching fingers and did the gentlemanly thing. She sucked that first draw of smoke deep into her lungs. It shuddered out. Around the fourth draw she looked a little less stricken. I remembered what it was like to need one that badly. No such ordinary cravings now.

"You gonna be okay?" Another man might have offered to buy her a steadying drink, but that would have worked against me. I had plans for this gal.

"Not tonight, I'm not. That's the worst thing I ever heard. That poor kid. What a horrible, *awful* . . ." She sucked in more smoke.

"Try not to think about it."

"Easy for you to say, Sport, but Lena was my best friend. About the only friend I ever had, and I haven't had any like her since. My God . . ." More smoke.

"Look, I didn't know her, and I can't imagine what you're going through with this news, but I want to help."

"Help? How help?" Her eyes narrowed. She was suddenly back to figuring angles.

"To find out who killed her."

"Why should you bother?"

I gave her a short line of what I'd told Nevis about clearing up black marks.

Rita finished her cigarette and stabbed it into the ashtray. "How could you find out anything? That's what cops are supposed to do."

"I got a few tricks up my sleeve; one of them is knowing you can be a big help in this."

"I don't know nothing."

"Yes, you do. I want the names of the people Lena ran with."

She bent forward, words hovering on her carmine lips. Then she must have thought better of it. She pulled back, crossing her arms. "Yeah, so maybe one of 'em comes and stuffs me behind a wall, too. No thanks."

"That won't happen."

"Oh, so you're some kinda swami. You gotta crystal ball to see the future? Nuts to that, Sport."

"Lena was your best friend."

"Yeah, and she wouldn't have wanted me in no trouble on her account."

"You won't get into trouble. I just want to hear what you'll say to the cops."

"I ain't talking to no cops. If the lousy bastards had done their job the first time, they might have found her and Lena'd still be alive."

The chances were that Lena had been dead long before Rita filed her report with the authorities, but there was no point in mentioning it. "You'll have to eventually. They've traced the dress, and they'll trace down where she lived, and finally come to you. You just tell me what you'd tell them."

She studied me, narrow and hard. I'd knocked her flat with the news, but getting back on her feet again must

have been an instant reflex for her. "You're really interested in this, ain't you? It's more than just getting your
club all square again."

"It's one of my more aggravating faults. Bothers the hell
out of me all the time."

She made a short, nervous half laugh that reminded me
of Malone's tic. I glanced at the bar and noticed him looking our way. He went back to polishing glasses. Upshaw
was also there, also looking. I couldn't read his face. He
slid from his stool and retreated into the thick atmosphere.
I followed his murky progress toward the back wall.

Sitting at Booth Nevis's table was Shivvey Coker, returned from wherever he'd gone. Upshaw went there. He
didn't bother to sit, just bent low to talk or to listen. Both,
probably.

I turned back to Rita. "That guy you were dancing with.
What's his story?"

"Tony Upshaw," she said. She got another cigarette out.
I lighted it.

"What's he around here?"

"Nobody special. He just decorates the place, keeps the
girls happy while their men are losing money. Looks like
a pansy, but he ain't. Just likes to dance. What about him?
You think he's with me or something? Nah, it's not like
that. We just dance is all."

"What's he do when he's not dancing?"

"Nothing, 'cause that's all there is for him. He teaches
in a studio somewhere. Takes acting lessons, too. Says he's
going to Hollywood soon to give Fred Astaire some grief.
He just might do it. I think he's waiting around to find a
Ginger Rogers to go with him. Fat chance of that in this
crowd."

"He ever work for Nevis?"

"Not that I heard of."

"Why don't you and me get out of here?" I suggested. "Go someplace where we can really talk."

She gave me a long considering look. Working out a few angles of her own, no doubt. "No, I don't think so."

"You pull that kind of shut-face with the cops, and they'll yank you in on suspicion."

For a second she believed me, then decisively shook her head. "You're not scaring me much, Sport. An' even if the cops do something that crazy, I got plenty of friends to spring me."

"Friends like Shivvey? Or Nevis?"

She puffed away and just grinned. It didn't suit her. I couldn't get mad at her, though, not the way I did with Nevis. Part of me could see things from her side. She'd only been about twenty or so when Lena vanished. Combine that with the life she led, and five years would be a very long time to Rita. In her world it didn't pay to be too loyal to live friends, much less a dead one.

I'd get the information I wanted, though. It would just take a while.

And a lot of coffee. "You eaten yet?"

"I don't have time to eat."

"Make it. I'll take you someplace nice."

There was a wavering in her eyes, and I knew I was reading her right. She was a gal with basic appetites, and enjoyed having them filled. A little food, a sympathetic ear, and maybe I wouldn't have to use hypnosis to discover why Booth Nevis had worked so hard to mutter out her name.

"Nothing good's open this late," she protested. Not too forcefully. She only wanted to be talked into it.

"I know a few spots. Come on."

She was right on the edge of saying yes, then gave a little guilty start. I looked where she looked. Gliding toward us, his tux still fresh despite all his dancing, was Tony Upshaw.

6

HE paused close enough so as not be ignored, but far enough away so as not to crowd either of us. Like a perfect diplomat or a well-trained headwaiter. His features were mostly unremarkable, but he did have a lot of poise and presence and was impeccably turned out. He must have used up half a jar of Vaseline to keep his dark wavy hair slicked so firmly in place. He wore a polite expression and gave a slight bow.

"Pardon me," he said in a gravelly voice with a local accent, "but I'd like to finish my dance with Miss Robillard."

"Sure, Tony," she responded with visible relief, rising from her chair before I could object.

I tried not to show irritation at this turn. To judge by the amused glint in Upshaw's eyes, I failed. Rita allowed herself to be swept onto the dance floor. She and Upshaw made quite a show of things as the band swung into a hot rumba. He was the more practiced of the pair, but she did a reasonable job of keeping up with his lead, laughing and squealing with delight the whole time. When the music shifted into another song, he decisively led her away. They went to Coker's table. Upshaw saw to it she was seated, then melted into the background, his errand of separating us as neatly executed as one of his dance steps.

Rita wouldn't be returning, not while I remained, anyway. I waited long enough to see if Upshaw also planned to retrieve her purse. Instead he approached one of the many other women in the joint, inviting her to dance. She happily accepted.

While the opportunity lasted, I snooped. Rita's little beaded handbag held a folded-up wad of a couple hundred in worn tens and twenties, lip rouge, a gold face powder case with her initials on it, a vial of perfume, some keys, an address book, and a driver's license from which I got her address. I flipped through the book. It had only names and phone numbers to some bookie joints I knew about and a few I didn't.

A girl who liked to gamble. If the cash was anything to go by, she did well at it, too.

Leaving the purse, I moved back to lounge at the bar, finding a spot where I could see Rita and Coker. There was little point moving closer; even if I'd been at the next table my improved hearing wouldn't pick much useful conversation out from the constant blaring music and other voices. I wondered if it was too late in life to start learning how to read lips. The idea of getting away for a moment so I could vanish and sneak up on them occurred, but was momentarily impractical. Upon quitting Rita's table, I noticed every gorilla in the place watching me. I couldn't duck into the john without having company, now. Coker had been too thorough passing word to them.

Rita and Coker had their heads close together. Rita shook hers a few times. I could guess he wanted to know what I'd been asking and was getting all the details. He frowned the whole time, which gave me a warm feeling inside. It meshed comfortably with my burning ears. If I had him worried, then I was definitely on to something interesting.

His questions eventually ended, and he started doing all the talking. He was mostly turned away from me, his attention full on Rita. As he spoke, he made little chopping gestures of emphasis. She began frowning herself. Whatever he said was making a hell of an impression, for she looked both grim and uneasy, quite a contrast to her unrestrained laughter only moments earlier.

It'd be nice to know what was going on between them, but I couldn't find out for some while, not until they relaxed their guard. Annoying, for there was no way to tell how long the wait might be. Working with Escott had taught me a little about patience, but I couldn't hang around all night.

Malone came by to ask if I wanted anything. I said no, then he put someone else in charge of the bar. Break time. He made his way toward the gambling entry. I briefly wondered if he spent his tips on the games there, then decided I needed to get off my duff and do something.

The gorillas still giving me the eyeball, I found a pay phone hiding in a curtained-off nook in the bare lobby and called the Red Deuces. Bobbi was busy on stage, so I left a message for her to take a taxi home if I didn't show at the usual time.

Responsibility discharged, I decisively left the club. I had no doubt word would shortly get back to Coker.

The weather was still strangely cool for summer. I welcomed it, consciously breathing the soft night air to flush my lungs clean of the club's choking smoke. With a certain amount of justified smugness, I knew my own place would have decent ventilation. Bobbi said it was good for the singers' throats.

For a day worker the hour was late, so not many people were out and about. The Flying Ace was in the middle of a business area where everything else closed just as it opened, which further cut down on foot and road traffic. Too bad for me; I wouldn't have minded the extra cover. I went right, toward where I'd parked, but strolled past my car. Apparently I wasn't on a tight leash; the bouncers were content to hang around the front, and didn't bother following.

Unless something better occurred to me, I planned to wait around until Rita left, then follow her home. If I worked it right, she'd never be aware of my invasion. Vampires are known for making clandestine visits in the wee hours to see young ladies in their boudoirs; far be it from me to break with tradition.

I'd get back to Booth Nevis when his migraine eased. His reaction to the news of Lena's death struck me all over again as I walked around the block. That he'd cared for her more deeply than he wanted to admit was obvious. There'd been genuine surprise from him at my bad news. Unless he was a better actor than my partner, I was inclined to think Nevis to be uninvolved with her murder. So, why bother to hide how he felt toward her? Probably something to do with his business; it was a smart man who did not admit to weaknesses like having been in love with a murdered woman. The authorities could turn a blind and well-paid eye to his gambling club so long as no other complications forced them to take notice. The sensational "Jane Poe" death might change that delicate balance for Nevis. Or he had a jealous wife hidden somewhere I didn't know about.

Shivvey Coker I figured to be intelligent muscle primarily interested in keeping his job by making sure things ran smoothly for his boss. That'd be sufficient reason for him not to want to talk to me about Lena and see to it Rita was hushed. I knew a little about his background. He could and certainly had been violent when necessary, but was smart to keep from being solidly linked to any specific crime, not even to the death of Welsh Lennet.

I couldn't picture Coker going to all the work of walling up anyone, though. The slow cruelty of the act somehow didn't seem to fit him. He was more the type to just get the job finished, bury it, and move on. And if, as Escott maintained, Lena Ashley's death was meant to be an example or a warning to others, then why hadn't even a hint of it been whispered about in the last five years? In some ways the Chicago underworld was the smallest town on earth. Always knowing what your neighbors and rivals were up to was as much a necessity of the life as turning a profit.

I'd made nearly a full circle of the block and approached one of the club's side entrances. It was in the middle of a wide service alley and used as a back exit for the gamblers should there be a raid. Some of the rollers were hanging around the steps, having a smoke and lying to each other about this and that. Malone, along with two of the waiters, stood around as well, still taking his break. For me, the knot was cover enough from the bouncers, who were presently out of view. I spotted a few people I knew from the Nightcrawler and went over to join their group. They were always good for rumors.

"Fleming! Heard the cops were giving you the works."

"Don't you know enough to leave dead bodies lie?"

"What's the real story, huh?"

"Ya shoulda let Gordy fix it for ya."

"What kinda action you gonna be runnin' once the place is open?"

This last came from a dapper, clean-jawed guy named Gardner Pourcio. He was addicted to most kinds of betting, but unlike others with the malady, actually managed to win a marginal profit. It was enough to keep him coming back for more. He had at least ten wives in as many cities, and they were all gunning for him.

I'd been faintly hoping I'd run into Pourcio or someone like him. From talks with Gordy about my club's dark history I knew of half a dozen guys who'd been there when Lennet died. Gardner Pourcio was one of them.

"No action in my club, just the best booze, good music, and great acts," I said.

"Jeez, what's the point, then?" His sharp features registered supreme disappointment.

"To keep the cops from giving me more works."

"How's that going? I heard the dead dame you found got carried out in pieces."

"I didn't watch. The cops took care of that, and they were welcome to it."

"Think she was one of Welsh Lennet's leftovers?" Pourcio pushed his fedora a little higher on his head, lifting his chin at me. The others listened in as well; Malone and even the jaundiced-looking waiters were clearly interested.

"Could be. Didn't you go to his old place a lot?"

"All the time. In fact, I was there the night of his big boom. You ever hear about that?"

"No, not really. It must have been something."

Pourcio gave a mock shudder and lighted a cigar half as long as his arm. He'd evidently recounted his story many times; he had a well-rehearsed manner about him. "I tell you, I thought the world was coming to an end. I was toward the back, or I'd have bought it for sure."

"What happened?"

With a riveted audience, he took his time, first getting his cigar well started. "It was like this: I was really doing a number on Buster Yeats—remember him, boys? We had a craps game going, an' I was doin' so well with the sevens

he thought I'd switched the dice. Now everyone knows
I'm honest as the day's long—"

Someone gave a derisive laugh.

"—but I had a hard job convincing Buster of it when
he's in the hole for a grand."

"Last time it was only one hundred," the heckler put in.
A couple of the bouncers emerged from the exit, crowding
through the other staffers. One of them unconcernedly el-
bowed Malone aside. He made no protest and moved clear.

"I'd raised the bet by then," said Pourcio smoothly.
"Well, I put a fifty down and was just wishing to lose it
so Buster'll cool off, when I hear glass breaking up front.
I didn't pay no mind, 'cause that thing happened all the
time with the waiters going butterfingers with stuff, so I
made my roll. But before the dice stopped there was one
hell of a bang. Two or three, I think, and the whole place
is suddenly coming down. There was a big guy right behind me who caught some of it, and he falls on me like a
brick, knocking me flat. I was pissed at the time 'cause he
weighs a ton and bleeding all over, ruining my suit, but
later I figure he saved my life. He took a hunk of shrapnel
that would have cut my arm off, but all he needed was a
few stitches."

"Lucky for you, then," I said.

"Luckiest night of my life, except countin' the time I
raked in a pile from that forty-to-one shot. You guys remember that?"

"What happened after the boom?" I asked to keep him
on the right subject.

Shedding some of his storytelling affectation, Pourcio's
face went serious. "It was pretty bad. Blood and screaming
women, and people running around trying to get out. I got
under the craps table, not knowing if there might be
more of the same coming in, but it was finished. Welsh
and three of his goons was all over the front, making most

of the mess. They wasn't nothing to me, but I was sorry about Myra."

"Who was she?"

"This poor schmuck lady bartender who bought it out in the lobby. Throat got tore wide open, she dropped in her tracks and bled to death. I was sorry about her. Whenever I was playing at Lennet's she'd always steer my fourth wife off to some other joint and even make her believe *I* was the one lookin' for *her*. Poor Myra. I'd have married her, but she was too wise to me."

"What about Welsh Lennet?"

"He was an asshole. And then he was dead." Pourcio dismissed him with a cloud of thick blue smoke. Story ended, his audience broke up a bit, some going back inside. The bouncer with the elbow was saying something forceful to Malone, who listened with a pinched and troubled expression, his gaze lowered. I wondered if he was due for an interview with Coker about me. There was damned little he could say.

"I heard Lennet was good with women, though," I said, returning my main focus to Pourcio.

"He had the money for it, ya mean." He smirked. "That's what made him so good."

"Didn't he have a couple of real classy jobs on the payroll? A gal here said there was one called Lena Ashley that he was tight with."

"News to me, Fleming. I remember her, sort of, but she wasn't one of Lennet's string, she was strictly Booth Nevis's property."

"Oh yeah? I didn't know he was in that game."

"He ain't. I meant she was his special girl. She wasn't working, that is to say, not in the usual sense."

"Tight, huh?"

"He looked out for her. They was joined at the hip, if ya know what I mean." That gave him a laugh.

"If she was with Nevis, then why'd she hang at Lennet's place?"

Pourcio snorted. "Who said she ever went there? Not me. I never seen her there, only at the track or the bookie joints. Wouldn't think she was smart enough for it, but she was a humdinger for pickin' winners. Maybe it was women's intuition or something, but she was good. She never made a big noise about it with the bookies to make them wise, so she could keep on bettin' with 'em. Wouldn't think she was smart enough for that either. She had looks, though, which was enough for her to get by fine."

"You knew her pretty good?"

"Nah, just to see her around. She never said two words to me. Probably heard about my wives and got spooked off; that's the only excuse I can think of."

Another round of derisive laughter along with, "Yeah, Gardner, sure."

"In your ear, too. I've had better luck than you guys could ever hope for and don't you know it." Pourcio turned back to me, puffing out a smoke ring. The air was still enough for it to hold its shape for a time. "They're all jealous of me, you know, so I can afford to feel sorry for 'em."

"That's one way of looking at it." I was about to try for more details about Lena and Nevis, when a commotion toward the back exit got my attention. The bouncer with the elbows was laying into Malone like Benny Leonard with a grudge. Malone was lean and small and not putting up much of a fight. Mostly he was trying to duck and run clear, but the second bouncer trundled forward with an ugly grin and grabbed him. He roughly dragged Malone around so his partner could go to work in earnest. Malone caught some hard fists in his face and gut.

No one stepped in to stop things.

Malone didn't make a sound except for pain-driven grunts as he was hit. The second man abruptly laughed and released him. Malone flopped boneless to the pavement. That's when the first man kicked him.

I was over my surprise and moving by then. I didn't know what the beef was, but two on one just isn't right when he's not hitting back. I pushed through the crowd and shoved the first goon hard out of my way. He cannonballed against the building's brick side with an audible thud and dropped. Onlookers tumbled all over themselves to get clear.

The second man paused to grin at me assessingly; he shifted his balance fast and swung. I blocked it easy with one arm, pushed him back, and told him to take a walk.

His response was to inform me of what I could do with myself. He stepped over the prostrate Malone so we could properly square off.

I felt a smile creeping over my face. Maybe it was only an excuse to show my teeth. "You don't want to do this," I warned him, arms out, palms down.

"Sure he does," Gardner Pourcio crowed behind me. "I'm giving four to one on Fleming, who's taking?"

The big bouncer scowled at what to him must have been insulting odds. We were of a height, but I'm also on the lean side. A year ago, he'd have bent me in two the wrong way and not broken a sweat. I'm no fighter, but had one hell of a supernatural edge he didn't know about.

While Pourcio hastily gathered bets, the bouncer made another swing, which I dodged. I once more tried to tell him he should stop, but that just annoyed him.

He'd had some experience in the ring and in old-fashioned street fighting, with no qualms against hitting below the belt or any other place he could plant a fist or a foot. I kept my distance and darted in when an opening presented itself, but he was quick enough to dodge or put up a guard before I could connect. Someone yelled at me to stop dancing with him.

Okay, what the hell. Pourcio had probably collected enough bets by now to last him a while.

I let the bouncer close and felt a solid punch in my belly that should have flattened me for a week. The pure force of it doubled me over, but I didn't feel much in the way of pain. It did put me in a position to return the favor with some very steep interest. I piled in with a right, not as hard as I could have made it—no need to rupture his internal organs—but sufficient for the job. He wheezed in shock, folding. I followed with a quick, solid shot to his chin, and it was all over.

He wasn't the only one shocked to judge by the faces gaping at me when I straightened and brushed my clothes back into place. An odd silence descended upon the gathering. There was one happy man in the crowd: Pourcio, who immediately began calling in markers.

"Hell of a show, Fleming! Hell of a show! I owe you a drink. Hell, I'll even buy you dinner!"

"You owe me ten percent of the take," I corrected him. I trudged over to Malone, who was feebly trying to sit up. The bloodsmell hit me a yard away. His face looked like a bad road, and his once neat white shirt and black vest were stained with gore and torn past repair. "Can you stand?" I asked.

"One—one thing at a time," he panted, his voice thin and distorted by a split lip.

I looked toward the waiters, thinking his friends would come help, but they turned away, not meeting my eyes. "Hey, get a towel or something."

"Our break's over," one of them said, and slipped off with the other man to get into the club.

"Hey!"

"Never mind," Malone whispered. "I'll be all right."

"Yeah, and prosperity is just around the corner." When he was ready, I helped him up. "C'mon, let's get you—"

"No." He waved off my attempt to turn him toward the door. "No. Please. I'd rather not go back there."

"Okay, then where? You can't walk around like that, you'll scare the muggers."

"I'll just go home."

"You got a car?"

"I—no—I take the El. Please, you've been more than kind, but I'll see to myself now, thank you."

Well, if a man doesn't want to be helped, you can't force the issue. I backed off, checking on the bouncers. Neither of them moved. Pourcio was busy with his collections. I went over.

"What made you put the odds on me?" I asked.

He beamed my way, counting his cash. "I hear stories. You may look like a string bean, but that's only looks."

"What stories?"

"Just stuff. Heard you once mopped a floor with Leadfoot Sam and Bruiser Butler. You're gettin' a reputation, kid."

Wonderful. Just what I needed. In lieu of a dinner I'd never be able to eat, I collected over fifty bucks from Pourcio as my part of his take. He didn't seem to mind and got on with the counting of his lion's share, grinning fit to crack his face.

On uncertain legs, Malone stumbled toward the end of the alley, holding his stomach. He clawed at the lid of a trash can, but couldn't get it pried loose. Swaying, holding on to the can for dear life, he bent forward and vomited. He stayed that way for a time, then slowly straightened. His legs wouldn't hold, though. His back to a wall, he sagged all the way to the pavement. His face was gray under the seeping blood.

No one went near him. No one even looked at him.

"What gives?' I said, mostly to myself.

"He's one of them," Pourcio cheerfully informed me.

"What, a leper?"

"*You* know," he added with a twist of distaste, then moved off to count his money. The others drifted elsewhere until it was just me, Malone, and the two out-for-the-count bouncers in the alley.

Damnation. Now I understood the cause of the beating. I went over to Malone. "You're not going to make it to any train ride in the shape you're in, so don't argue with me."

He squinted up, one of his eyes already puffing shut. "You've helped too much already. I can't impose on you further."

"I'm volunteering. Come on."

He allowed himself to be helped up again and hobbled with me to my car. I'd have to deal with Rita Robillard later, which was annoying, but at the moment questioning her was less important than getting Malone someplace safe. If the goons woke up before he could get away, they would kill him. They'd have to get past me first, but I had enough wrinkles in my suit for one night.

Gently bleeding into one of my handkerchiefs throughout the ride, Malone muttered directions, and about half an hour later I set the brake in front of a two-story clapboard on a narrow street lined with similar structures. It housed eight cheap flats to judge by the number of mail slots. Not the Ritz or a fleabag, but somewhere in between on the lower end of things.

"You sure you don't want a doctor?" I asked. "I know a good one who won't ask questions."

"I'll be all right," he said in a near whisper, looking anything but well. "I'm very much in your debt, Mister—"

"Fleming. Forget it."

Before he could insist on trying to do it for himself, I

went around to the passenger side and helped him out. No
protesting this time. I got him up the steps and inside, then
more steps to the next floor. This tired him; he was panting
and white by the time we reached the upper landing.

His flat was in the back. The building was old, worn,
with creaking wood and faded wallpaper saturated with the
smell of decades of boiled cabbage and fish. He shuffled
to his door and unlocked it, found the light switch. The
kitchen was right there as you walked in. It was clean, but
matched the rest of the joint for general shabbiness. He
dragged himself over to a battered table; I pulled a chair
for him to sit. In his case it was more of a collapse.

I opened the top door of his icebox, found an ice pick
in the draining tray, and chipped some pieces off the block.
There was a dish towel by the sink. I wrapped it around
the melting shards and gave it to him.

"Try this over your eye and that lip," I suggested.

He did so, bowing over the table. "I'm sorry."

"For what? A couple of assholes knocking you around
just for fun?"

He made no reply.

"Not the first time for you, is it?"

By degrees, he managed to look up at me. The forty-
watt overhead didn't improve his face. Right now he was
less clean and more cut. The expression in his brown eyes
made me think of a beaten dog, pleading for the punishment to stop, just for a little while. "You know?"

"It's been explained to me."

"And you still helped?"

"Your life's your business, not mine, but I don't like
bullies much."

"You are an exceptional man, then."

"Sometimes. You got anything to drink here?"

"I'm afraid not."

A bartender who didn't drink. What next? "Too bad, you need it. What about aspirin?"

"That cupboard." He gestured, and I searched. I made him take four tablets with a lot of water. It was even odds if he could keep them down after all those gut punches, but maybe enough would get into his blood to take the sting out of the worst of them.

"What about food?" I asked.

"I'm not hungry, but if you want something—"

"I'm fine, thanks." I allowed myself a quick look around. A wide archway led to a living area with three open doors in the opposite wall leading to a bath and two bedrooms. That seemed to be the whole flat. As with the kitchen, the place was well kept, with no trash or stray laundry on the floor. A tidy man, suddenly violated by brutal chaos. "Did those two guys have a long grudge on you?"

"They're new at the club. The others there, they never bothered much with me, just ignored me. The new ones, though . . . it's been building for the last few weeks. A lot of little things. I couldn't exactly complain to the boss about them."

"I guess not."

"No one seems to understand, this is not something I've chosen. It's just the way things are. Who would want to choose my sort of life?" He started to say more, then seemed to realize he might have said too much to a near stranger. "I'm sorry, I don't wish to burden you."

"Sometimes you gotta talk to somebody. I know what it's like."

"But you're not—"

"No, but I know what it's like." Right after my death and change I'd needed to talk to someone. If it hadn't been for Escott just simply sitting and listening, I'd have gone bug-eyed nuts. He didn't have to understand one word of what I was throwing at him, or offer advice; all he did was listen, and that was enough.

"I suppose you do, in a way," Malone admitted. He started to stand, then thought better of it.

"You got a tub? Hot water should help."

"Quite the doctor, aren't you?"

"I've had some knocks. You learn what to do about them."

While he hunched over with the ice and let the aspirin go to work I went to the tiny bathroom and started filling the tub, dropping in half a box of Epsom salts I found in a cupboard. On the way back through the living area I noticed he had a lot of serious-looking books on his shelves. They had the overweight look of college texts. The subjects were accounting and business and a couple on psychology. The latter made me think that perhaps he'd been seeking an answer to his situation. Or maybe a solution. Sometimes there just isn't one.

On a low table were some comic books and in one corner of the floor by the radio someone had set up an elaborate toy fort made of glued-together bits of cardboard. It was very detailed, with roofs that lifted off and working doors with tape hinges; there was even a stable, a watering trough, and a well in the middle. Wooden cowboys, Indians, and horses were scattered around it. Incongruously next to it was a homemade model of the Empire State Building standing about two feet tall. This time the cardboard had been painted gray, with tiny black rectangles marking its many windows. Someone who had seen *King Kong* had placed a small wooden monkey on the eighty-sixth-floor observation deck.

"You got a kid?" I asked, returning.

Malone's expression lifted and softened. He couldn't quite do that nervous tic smile because of his split lip, but came close. "Yes. Norrie. She stays with my neighbor while I'm at work. Oh, God, how do I explain this to her?"

"Get cleaned up first."

"You don't understand, she's—" Malone shut himself down again.

"She's what?"

"It's complicated," he finished, rather lamely. "She's had upsets like this before."

"And you think your face will scare her?"

He nodded.

"Kids are tough, given the chance. Wash off the blood, don't make a big thing of it, and just go on. If she asks a question, answer plain and keep it short. If you show you're not upset by what's happened, then she won't have anything to react to."

"You have children?"

"No, but it just makes sense."

He digested this while I went to turn off the tub water.

"I may have gotten it too hot," I warned him, coming back.

"I'm sure it will be fine."

"You need some help?"

"I can walk. Only not very fast." He levered himself up, moving by slow considered stages, pausing at the archway between the kitchen and living room. "I've no right to ask you, you've done so much already."

"What do you need?"

"I—I was wondering if you'd mind staying until I was finished. Those men. I'm afraid that they might know where I live."

Chances were they wouldn't be in any shape to come after him, and given a choice would be far more interested in me. Malone had been badly shaken, though. His fears were quite real to him. If it'd been me in his place, I'd have wanted some company, too. "No problem. Take your time. I'm a real nighthawk."

He looked pathetically relieved. "Thank you, Mr. Fleming." He finished shuffling to the bath and shut himself in.

I flipped through the comic books, speculating about his family situation. I could imagine when Malone was a very young man he'd tried to cure himself by getting married, then when things didn't work out, the split came, and it had probably been ugly. Usually any children went with the mother, though. That had happened to a man I'd worked with on the paper back in New York. The office gossip had been poisonous. He got fired, then jumped off a roof that same afternoon, the poor bastard.

I hoped Malone wouldn't be similarly tempted after this setback. He didn't seem the type, but you can't always tell.

There was no reason to expect trouble, but I caught a faint noise in the hall. Someone tried the knob, then softly tapped on the door. Out of habit, I'd locked up. More curious than on guard, I opened it. A sleepy-eyed dark-haired kid of about ten or twelve stood barefooted looking up at me. She was enough like Malone for me to figure out her identity. She wore wrinkled pajamas and clutched a well-worn teddy bear. She seemed too old for such a toy, but there was a fragile air about her, a vulnerability that made me wonder if she'd been sick.

"Who're you?" she asked, without fear.

"A friend of your dad's. He needed a ride home from work."

"Oh. Where is he?"

"Taking a bath. I'm Mr. Fleming. Are you Norrie?"

"Uh-huh." She stepped into the kitchen and slipped up onto a chair. She looked at the soggy, bloodied dishcloth left on the table. "Did Daddy get into a fight?"

"Yeah. He's all right, though." I got the cloth to the sink and rinsed it off.

"You sure? Once someone broke his nose."

"Not this time. He's mostly worried about upsetting you."

"He worries a lot." With a dramatic sigh, she flopped the teddy bear facedown on the table.

"He said you stay with the neighbor while he's at work."

"Mrs. Tanenbaum."

"She might worry, too, if she finds you gone."

"She knows I always come here. I heard him talking and woke up. It was too early for him to be home, so I thought something was wrong."

"You thought right, but it's not too bad. He'll be fine."

"Okay. Who are you? Are you a gangster? There's lots of them where he works, you know."

"Afraid not. Just a Good Samaritan."

"Oh." It seemed to disappoint her. "Can I have a glass of water?"

I got her water. "That's quite a fort you've got in there."

"Yeah, I made it an' the other building. Well, Daddy helped. He cut the stuff out for me, but I drew it out."

"So you want to be a cowgirl when you grow up?"

"No, an architect."

That brought me up short. At Norrie's tender age I wouldn't have been able to make even a close guess on the definition of the word. "Sounds pretty ambitious."

"I'm really good at drawing. Wanna see? I gotta real por'folio."

"Sure."

She toddled off to one of the bedrooms, returning with two big sheets of cardboard held together by a taped hinge and tied at the other three edges by strings. With great dignity, she placed it on the table and solemnly undid the ties, opening it out. I grabbed the stuffed bear and moved the water glass out of the way in time to keep it from being knocked over. Inside the makeshift portfolio was a stack of drawings in pencil, crayon, and ink.

"This is our house," she explained of the top one, which was on graph paper. "See, I've got it to scale. Every quarter inch equals a foot, so if it was real size it'd be as big as this building. Daddy showed me how to measure with a yardstick. And here's what the insides look like. See how the rooms here are like ours but turned around. It's Mrs. Tanenbaum's place where I stay, and that's how I know that it's all backwards from our place."

One by one, she flipped through them, her enthusiasm waking her up. She explained pictures of her house, school, and other buildings; even the Chicago Aquarium had been captured by her with some fair accuracy.

"I copied it from a postcard," she confessed. "But Daddy says it's good practice."

"This is really impressive." I wasn't just blowing hot air. The kid had a talent way beyond her years. "It's great your daddy encourages you so much."

"We visit the library a lot." Norrie shut her portfolio and carefully tied the strings. "He says I should go to college."

"I'd recommend it."

"But I know a whole lot already."

"Then you'll be way ahead of everyone when you get there."

"Maybe they'll think I'm a genius or something."

"Maybe. Just don't tell them you are or—" I shut myself off.

Norrie's plaintive dark eyes went right through me. "Or they might beat me up like Daddy?"

I shook my head. "No. It's just more polite to let other people figure out for themselves that you're smart."

"Why does Daddy get into fights?"

"People can be really stupid. Sometimes stupid people hit others for no reason. Like school bullies."

"You talk like him."

"Is that a good thing?"

"I guess. He knows a lot. He went to college."

You can't learn everything in the halls of higher learning, but it was interesting that Malone had been there. There was no sign of a sheepskin displayed on his walls, though. I wondered what had interrupted his education and kept him in bartending. Probably life.

Norrie talked about how she wanted to build the biggest skyscraper ever, waving her arms high. As she raised her chin toward the ceiling I noticed the pale line of an old scar along the base of her jaw, running with uneven breaks from ear to ear. It didn't seem like the kind you got when the docs remove a goiter. It looked chillingly like someone had used the poor kid for throat-cutting practice. Maybe this was what Malone had meant about things being complicated, and I wondered what history was behind the long-healed damage.

The bathroom door creaked open, and Malone reappeared, wrapped in a long, faded blue robe. His face was clean, but an iodine-stained mess, the bruising getting a real foothold, his eye colorful and swollen fully shut now. Norrie ran over to him, clutching him tight around the waist in greeting.

"Daddy! I been showing Mr. Fleming my por'folio. He likes my drawings."

"Hello, sweetheart," he said calmly. He visibly winced from being hugged, but didn't let on about it to the kid.

"You gotta swell black eye."

Malone glanced at me. I gave him a quick thumbs-up sign so he'd know all was well. "Yes, isn't it. I see we woke you."

"I always hear when you come home. You got in a big fight, huh? Did you beat 'em?"

"No, it was—it was Mr. Fleming's turn this time, then he gave me a ride home."

"He said he wasn't a gangster, but he's got on their kinda clothes."

"Ah—" Malone flashed a horrified look my way.

I held my hands out, grinning at his reaction. "Not me, I'm just trying to open a club. Norrie, just how is it you know what gangsters wear?"

"I seen 'em in the movies. Mrs. Tanenbaum takes me. They all got suits like yours."

"Maybe I better find another tailor, then."

"Maybe Mrs. Tanenbaum should take you to some other kinds of movies," Malone added. "It's very late, young lady. Off to bed with you."

"But I wanna hear about the fight."

"Tomorrow. Say good night to Mr. Fleming. I'll tuck you in later."

She gave another dramatic sigh. "Good night, Mr. Fleming."

"Good night." I tossed her teddy bear at her. She caught it clean, then ran to her bedroom. The sudden creak of bedsprings indicated she'd made a successful flying leap.

Malone paced slowly over and shut Norrie's door, then turned toward me. "She doesn't seem upset at all."

"I tried to cushion things," I said.

"Thank you."

"She's got quite a talent." I tapped the portfolio.

"Yes. She is very smart. Sometimes too smart. I'm sorry about that gangster remark."

"Don't worry, I get it a lot. There's nothing in it." *Not much, anyway.*

"It's this town . . . and my job, I suppose. My former job, I should say." He grimaced, which must have been painful with that shiner.

"You're not going back?"

He shook his head, shuffling to an overstuffed chair and easing into it with a small groan. "Not a chance."

"What'll you do?"

"Find another job when my face heals up."

I drifted over to look at the fort and the building again. The kid had a hell of an eye for detail. "Not a lot of those around these days."

"There's always work for a good bartender. I've been at the Flying Ace for such a long time, though, I'd gotten rather used to it. There were jokes about my being a fixture." The unbruised patches on his face were dead white. He wouldn't be able to hold off his fatigue forever, but I needed him to keep talking.

"If you've been there for so long, then Nevis should take you back. He can get rid of the goons."

"Not if he hears their side of the story first."

"I can fix it for you with him."

Malone waved one hand. "No, really, it's for the best. You saw how the others reacted when I was down. They won't tolerate me now, believe me, I know."

I could tell that he did, since this wasn't his first beating and probably not the last. People could be vicious to those who were different from the crowd. Something I had in common with him.

"Besides," he said, "you've done so very much helping me this far. I can never repay you."

"Maybe you can."

"How?"

"Tell me what the setup is between Shivvey, Rita, and Nevis."

He came out of his weariness just enough to give me a blank stare. "I'm not sure what you mean."

"What they are to each other. Nothing you say will get back to them from me."

The blank look relaxed. "Oh, that. Mr. Coker and Miss Robillard are very close friends. Intimate, you might say."

"Are they really gone on each other, though?"

He didn't have to think on that one. "They strike me as being friendly, but not in love. Neither one is the sort to settle down and make a family. I would say that they are . . . convenient to each other."

"And Nevis?"

"He's definitely everyone's boss. Miss Robillard does some work for him, but I don't know what kind. She's in the club nearly every night, always seeing him for a short while in his office. I've never heard her refer to having any job, but she's well supplied with cash."

"You think she has an intimate arrangement with Nevis? Maybe that's what he pays her for?"

"Oh, I don't think that's it at all, or she'd have said something. She's not exactly secretive in regard to her personal activities. I don't eavesdrop, she just talks. Somewhat loudly, after she's had a few. She's often mentioned her very high opinion of Mr. Coker's skills, which is rather more information than I ever wanted to learn about him."

I was close enough to try to hypnotically influence Malone, and, as he was sober, met with no resistance at all. It made a nice change from the rest of the evening. "You sure you don't know what kind of work she does?"

"No, I don't," he responded in that flat voice they get when they're under.

I pulled back so he could come out of it. He did, with no memory of what I'd done. "What about Tony Upshaw?"

"He comes to the club to dance and meet women. More often than not he leaves with them, too. I've noticed he's most careful not to pick those who might be attached to anyone. Except to the ladies, he's a harmless sort. Very polite."

"He was following Coker's orders tonight, though."

"Mr. Upshaw may best be described as a hanger-on to those in Mr. Coker's line of business. I imagine it gives him some sort of a thrill to do a few small favors, but he's not paid for them that I'm aware."

"I know the type." I'd seen dozens like him come and go at the Nightcrawler. They liked the danger of associating with the real killers, but that's as far as it went. I could expect a similar turnout for Lady Crymsyn, but as long as they bought drinks and didn't break the furniture I had no problem with them.

"Mr. Upshaw entertains when he can. Throws big parties in his dance studio," Malone continued. "I've tended bar at a few of them for extra work. I just heard that he's having one tomorrow night, a sort of *bon voyage* for some gangster's son who's leaving the country."

I raised an eyebrow. "You—ah—you wouldn't happen to know his name, would you?"

"Royce Muldan. Most of the club regulars will be there for it; he's popular with them. Perhaps I could ask Mr. Upshaw if he needs a bartender again, though once he sees my face—what is it?"

"Nothing." I shook my head, letting the chuckle run itself out. "Muldan's name came up in conversation not long back. Where's he headed?"

"Havana, I heard. It must be nice to be able to just go anywhere you want on a moment's notice like that."

And nice to know my suggestion had taken such fast root, though it wouldn't last. In a few weeks Muldan would be wondering what the hell he was doing lolling around in Havana in the off-season. "Yeah, some people got all the luck. The club regulars . . . would that include Miss Robillard and Coker?"

"I should think so; they usually turn up at Mr. Upshaw's events. She enjoys dancing with him. And Mr. Coker is friends with Mr. Muldan."

"So Coker's not jealous of Upshaw?"

"As I mentioned, Mr. Upshaw's careful not to involve

himself with attached females. In her case he is always a gentleman. May I ask why you are so interested in them?"

"It has to do with that woman's body they found in my club's basement," I said, unworried about giving anything away. Malone would have heard all about it from either the radio, papers, or gossip at work.

"Oh, my God." If possible, he went a few shades paler under his already blood-drained skin, and I clearly heard his heart rate shoot up.

It's one thing to read about a killing, another to know the people who might be involved, and quite another to have it trotted out in your own living room. I should have remembered Joe James's appalled reaction to my news and softened things. "Hey, don't worry, they'll never find out I've been talking to you."

"Y—you think they had something to do with that . . . crime?" Malone's mouth must have gone dry, for he could barely whisper the last word. I caught a solid whiff of fear scent from him, mingled with the soap, iodine, and dried blood. There wasn't much, if any, threat to him from my investigation, but after tonight's ugly calamity he had every right to feel nervous. Because of the beating, he'd be looking over his shoulder for weeks afterward and certainly didn't need or want my grisly business crowding in on him as well.

"I don't know. That's what I'm looking into."

"Dear God . . ." Malone's alarmed gaze flicked to Norrie's closed door.

"Hey, I said it's okay. You're not anywhere near this." I made a quick motion to include her. "Both of you. I promise."

"But you—"

"You got my word. No one hears a thing about you. You're safe."

"I don't . . . I . . ."

"Look, it's like this: the dead woman—Lena Ashley was her name—was close friends with Rita and was especially tight with Booth Nevis. Neither of them claims to know anything about when Lena disappeared five years ago, and I'm inclined to believe it. Shivvey Coker's another matter, though. He worked at that club just before someone lobbed the grenades and killed his boss. As near as I can estimate, about a month later Lena vanished, to wind up dead in its basement. I don't know if there's a connection, but I need to check things out. If I find something, I call the cops, and they'll take care of the rest."

Dismay came and made a home on his battered mug.

"You don't come into it," I repeated. "You've got enough troubles. I'll make sure no one bothers you."

He took a deep breath, trying to calm himself. "It's just that . . . that these are very dangerous people. You've no idea what they're like. *I've* no idea, but I have heard things."

I grinned, hoping it would relax him a little. "So have I. I'll be fine. I can take care of myself with clowns like Coker, believe me."

He shook his head, unable to believe.

I'd never convince him otherwise, nor was it really necessary to try. My guess was as soon as I was out the door his own concerns would return quick enough. From the look of him, they were already well started. I didn't have much time left before he'd be too tired to think straight.

"Where's this studio of Upshaw's?" I asked.

It took Malone a moment to take in the question, but he eventually provided me with a name and a street. "You're really going to go there?"

"Unfinished business. I was planning to talk to Rita later, but I'll catch up with her there. I got a little sidetracked tonight. Which reminds me—" I pulled out the fifty-odd bucks I'd collected from Pourcio and gave it to

Malone with a short explanation of its source. It probably represented a month's worth of tips plus salary for him.

His jaw sagged. "Oh, no, I couldn't."

"After all the crap you went through you're the one who earned it, not me."

"But I—"

"No arguments. I'm not out anything. Call it the severance pay you'd never get from Nevis. It'll tide you over until your face heals. Now I'm gonna scram outta here so you can get some rest."

I told him good-bye and let myself out, cutting short the embarrassment for us both.

Back in my car, I drove and thought, drove and thought. Escott often did the same, claiming that it helped him sort through stuff. I was picking up some bad habits. Next I'd be trading in my double-breasted suits for his kind of fussy banker clothes.

All the thinking didn't do me much good, though. I couldn't come up with anything new, needing more information to play with. The party tomorrow would give me another chance to dig around and really make a nuisance of myself.

I took a swing by Rita's address. It was a residence hotel similar to the one where Bobbi lived, but much more expensive. According to the address I'd memorized Rita was on the fifth floor. Making a slow circle around the joint, I counted windows, but found no lights showing, nothing to inspire me to make a break-in. Or in my case a sieve-in. Hell, I had no idea which of those windows was hers; chances were she was in the sack with Coker, which would really complicate the situation. Or maybe she was off at his place instead, and I didn't know where he lived.

Yet.

Anyway, I first wanted to test something out.

I'd taken a risk telling Malone so much about my investigation, but it was a calculated one. My openly talking to him was an experiment, an indirect way of perhaps stirring things up. If he decided to trot over to the Flying Ace in the morning and play stoolie to Coker, I could expect some swift and certainly violent retaliation from that quarter. Coker had warned me off in a friendly way, and that may have been all there was to it. But if he or Nevis had a direct stake in Lena's death, then he just might try to do something about me.

If it happened, then I'd have to be ready for the worst.

I liked Malone, though, and didn't think him to be the type to sell anyone out . . . but I'd been drastically wrong about people before.

I'd find out for certain tomorrow. In the meanwhile, I had just enough time to get over to the Red Deuces and save my girl some cab fare.

"I WAS just one minute away from calling up a ride," Bobbi said, sliding across the seat to give me a kiss hello.

"Yeah, but you get much better service from me." I squeezed her in a tender spot, which made her yelp.

She made a pretend swat at my arm. "Stinker. For that you don't get a tip."

"A *what*?"

She swatted again, this time connecting. "Tip—with a 'p,' you caveman."

"Okay, okay, I'll behave myself."

"Don't you dare." She settled next to me with a sigh. "You're in a good mood. What'd you find out? Did Joe's information help?"

"Yeah, I learned some interesting stuff, but not nearly enough."

"Tell me."

"How about over dinner?" I pulled away from the curb.

"I'm not that hungry. Let's just go straight home. I'll make something there."

Fine with me. She wasn't that hungry, but I was. For her. Always.

I filled her in about my evening on the drive to her hotel. She was in a chatty frame of mind with more than a few questions that sidetracked me one way or another, but I eventually got through my story by the time we reached her door.

"You have been busy," she said. She snapped on lights throughout the place, divesting herself of hat and gloves along the way, then kicking off her shoes. "You think Coker will do anything? I mean whether Malone talks to him or not, Coker will find out you're not keeping clear. Guys like him always do."

"I know, but he can't hurt me. You probably won't have anything to worry about from him, either, but promise you'll keep your eyes open and be careful? I don't want you in the line of fire if he decides to get cute."

"I promise."

No need to ask her twice. Being cautious was instinctive with her by now.

"What about you?" she countered. "You sound like you're expecting trouble from Coker."

"Not really."

"You wanna explain that?"

"If he's not involved with Lena's death, nothing happens. If he is involved, and if he's smart, he'll just stay quiet, let me spin my wheels, and still nothing happens. There's no connection between him and Lena Ashley, except for him running around with her onetime best friend, Rita."

"But you're going to stir him up, aren't you?"

"If he's got nothing to hide, whatever I do won't bother him."

"Jack, everyone's got something to hide. You know that better than most."

I just shrugged and grinned.

She flapped her hands once in capitulation. "Never mind. You'll put your foot into it just to see what happens, won't you?"

"It's one of my more interesting faults."

That got me an amused, ladylike snort. "How long has Coker been seeing Rita, anyway? Did he know either of them five years ago?"

I should have found that out. "Next time why don't you come along to ask the questions. Malone might have had a clue on that. As for the rest of them—Jeez, if just once I could catch someone while they were still sober . . ."

"There, there," she said, gliding into the kitchen. "That was such a sweet thing for you to do for him. Just like Robin Hood."

I dropped into my usual chair at the table. "I didn't rob anyone tonight, just took my percentage off the bets."

"In this town, that's close enough."

She pulled a pitcher of grape juice and some butter from the refrigerator, and bread from its box. She cut two slices and dropped them in a toaster, fiddling with the browning lever. I couldn't help comparing the bright, white-painted newness of this place to Malone's humble kitchen with its aging icebox and cracked linoleum, and wondered how he'd ever get his smart little girl to college.

"That business of you giving Nevis a migraine is spooky," Bobbi said, staring intently down at the toaster slots. "What do you think happened?"

"Beats me. Guess I better not press him so hard when I try again; he'll end up with another one. Wouldn't want him breaking a blood vessel."

"I've got a friend who gets migraines something awful, but she went to a doctor who hypnotized her out of them. Maybe you could do the same for Nevis."

"Yeah, maybe." If I kept my temper, and if he stayed sober.

"On the other hand, it was your hypnosis that set him off in the first place. You sure you want to talk to him again?"

"I have to." And it wouldn't be pleasant for either of us.

The toast popped up too soon to brown. She jumped back, scowled at its underdone state, and mashed the lever down again. "I gotta get another one of these that works," she muttered. "It either comes out too soft or like charcoal unless I watch it."

"You make me glad I don't have to worry about such things."

She threw a glance my way, a curl from her platinum crown drooping artistically over one eyebrow. "Don't you ever miss eating? Having different kinds of things to eat?"

"At first I did, but only because that's what I was used to doing for my whole life."

"And now?"

"I'm used to what I do now instead. It's different, but easier."

"How so?"

"When you only have one thing you can consume, and that only every other night or so, it simplifies life. I don't have to think about what I want to have. That's all solved."

"And you never get tired of it?"

"Never." Which was the absolute truth. There was no way I could really express to her how the stuff made me feel, the profound, fulfilling effect it always worked on my body and mind. That would only happen when and if she became like me.

The toast popped up again, this time just a shade on the dark side, but she liked it that way. She gingerly plucked the hot pieces from their slots onto a plate and tried scraping the still cold butter over them. It was not cooperating too well. She grumbled as crumbs scattered across her pristine counter.

"At least with what you do you never have to clean up a mess," she said, brushing them into the sink.

There was no need to mention what shape my shoes were in after a rainy night at the Stockyards. Or all those bloodstained handkerchiefs when I wiped my mouth clean that had my laundry thinking I suffered from chronic nosebleeds.

She gave up on the butter, poured a glass of grape juice, and brought it and the somewhat mangled toast to the table. In the short minutes it had taken to make her little repast I'd have not only drunk my fill of cow's blood, but have walked back to the car and be driving away. By not having to work out how to fill my stomach every few hours, I had a lot of spare time on my hands.

"You sure you don't miss regular food?" she asked, watching me watch her eat.

"What I really miss is sitting around the table and talking."

"You still do that."

"With you and sometimes Charles when he's home, but in public I still have to pretend to drink a cup of coffee or something, just not to draw any attention."

"Who would notice? A waiter maybe."

"It's a good habit to keep. Waiters get upset if they can't bring you something."

"It's that important not to be noticed?"

"With the way I am, yes. That poor crazy guy from New York who was after me . . ."

She twitched her shoulders, grimacing at the unpleasant memory.

". . . there might be more where he came from. I got

lucky that time. The next would-be van Helsing might be smarter than Braxton. More dangerous."

"God forbid that there is a next one," she said fervently.

"Amen. Anyway, I just do what's expected, keep away from opera capes and determined little guys with Dutch accents, and I should be safe enough."

She made a sound that was a cross between a snort and a hiccup. I thought she'd choked on the toast, but it was laughter. When she recovered, her expression went mildly serious. "But drinking cow's blood is it for you? Forever and ever?"

"As far as I know. Why you so interested? Not that I mind talking about it."

"Just wondering what it's like for you night after night. What I might have to deal with if . . . you know."

"There's nothing to be afraid of."

"Oh, I'm not afraid. Of being a vampire, anyway. It's—"

"What?"

She shrugged, making a face. "It's just that I'm kinda chicken. If something happens to me, I don't want it to hurt is all."

I put my hand on hers. "Join the club."

"But it hurt for you, didn't it?"

"Not the change. What hurt were the guys beating the hell out of me before they shot me."

"Did it—?"

This was hard, going back to that memory, but important that I do so. For her sake. "I saw what was coming, and couldn't do anything to stop them. That was the really bad part. But when it happened I didn't feel much of anything. Maybe it was too fast for there to be any pain."

"What about afterward? When you were in the water?"

"That I'm not too clear about. I just remember being . . . unhappy, helpless. Then confused. I didn't know what was happening to me, but I don't remember being afraid."

"Did you feel anything changing inside?"

"How do you mean?"

"Like in that Fredric March movie a few years back. When he turned from Dr. Jekyll into Mr. Hyde he was writhing around and—"

I chuckled and gently waved her down. "No, nothing like that. It was disorienting, but that was only because I was in the water. Looking back, I think that's when I vanished for the first time, which was how I was able to survive the dunking."

"But other than that?"

"No writhing around or groaning in agony. I promise."

She snickered again and chewed more toast, looking thoughtful, no longer anxious. Good. Maybe we could get on to more pleasant subjects than my untimely and singularly temporary demise.

"What's this?" I asked, gesturing at her throat. She'd changed from her elegant stage gown to a regular dress, but still wore its blue silk scarf wrapped under her chin. "Trying to tease me?"

"Just something to hide the marks," she said, taking it off. "You're not the only one who wants to be careful. It's hot, though."

"Looks like I bruised you last night." I tilted her head to better see. "I'm sorry."

"Don't be, it was worth it."

The damage wasn't much to look at, just a slight discoloration and the tiny red flares of broken capillaries around two larger marks, but I took pride in my ability to do what I do without hurting her or leaving needless traces. Next time I'd be a lot more careful while in the throes of passion.

"I'll just dab on extra powder or wear a high collar tomorrow," she said. "They fade pretty fast these days."

"They do?" That was interesting. "You always been a fast healer?"

"I don't know. Why do you ask?"

"Just wondering. I mean you've got my blood in you now. Maybe it's changing things inside. Maybe that's the sign you're searching for."

She gave me a melting look, half longing, half sorrow. "Oh, Jack, I can hope so, but don't hope too much about me for yourself."

"Why shouldn't I?"

"Because it's dangerous to want something too much. You might get it, but not the way you pictured."

"What do you mean?"

"You know once in a while I get these weird feelings. Not in a bad sense, but just—like there are some things that I *know* will be in my life if I want them hard enough, like my going to Hollywood when the time is right."

"Nothing wrong with that."

"Oh, yeah? Not so long ago I was wishing for a rich, handsome man who would help my career. I wished so hard for him and all the time that I was positively demanding for him to happen. And when he did happen, what I got was Slick Morelli—and you know what he was like."

I knew.

"So if I'm changing to be like you, it'll happen because it's supposed to and when it's supposed to. I just don't want you to wish for it so hard. I'm not ready to die yet."

My gut took a sickening swoop. "Jeez, Bobbi, I never meant anything like that for you!"

"I know, but I thought you should know how I feel."

I couldn't just sit there with her looking at me like that. Neither could she. We both hastily got around the table and held each other tight, and I tried not to think of death. Of *real* death. Of *her* death.

For the change to vampire to take place in me I'd had to die, and Maureen had warned me many times that it still might not work. She'd heard stories about others who'd exchanged blood, but when their human lovers died, they stayed dead. She didn't know why it was like that, why some returned and others did not. There was absolutely no way you could tell, she'd said.

Now I understood that hollow look she'd get in her eyes when she spoke of such things.

There were no guarantees for me and Bobbi, supernatural or otherwise. She could live to be a hundred—and I prayed she would—or she could get hit by a car tomorrow. She could return or—as was more likely from what little I knew—she would not. And that thought always stabbed me right down to the soul and beyond, so I tried never to think it.

As with everyone else, better to live our lives one full hour at a time and try not worry about dark futures without each other. Easier said than done. Ever at the edge of my mind, hovered the wondering, the bleak, futile wondering of what lay in store for her.

"If it helps," she said, her lips close to my ear, "when I was with Slick I began wishing for another man to come along."

"And what? Save you?"

"No, I'd learned my lesson with Slick. Only I could save me, but I did wish for a man who would be the best for me."

"Did I make the grade?"

She pulled back far enough to give me a long, thorough look. Thinking before giving an answer, as she always did when it was something really important. "So far . . . so far, so very, very good." Then she drew me toward her, gently insisting on a kiss.

We didn't have a lot to say to each other for the next few hours. You get to a point where words spoil things.

Waking fast and fully alert in my hidden room exactly at sunset, I heard someone descending the basement steps. It was probably Escott, but I dragged on my bathrobe and sieved through the wall to make sure. His house had been invaded too many times for me to take anything for granted.

False alarm, the best kind. Escott was crouched by the wall he'd built up to enclose the dead space under the stairs. It had a hidden door in the bricks concealing a safe. Since the big crash neither of us trusted banks much, and it was a good place to park certain items we weren't yet ready to declare to the world at large. Among other things, it held the bulk of my hard-won mob money and a share of his own honest earnings. He'd drawn one of his envelopes of cash out and was transferring funds into it from his wallet. He must have had a profitable day, then.

"Going somewhere?" I asked, pausing a few feet behind him.

He almost didn't jump. "Damn! Rap on something or call a warning, why don't you?"

"That's against union rules for vampires. You should be used to it by now."

"I forgot the time, or else I'd have been prepared for your evening's emergence."

"What gives?" I motioned to take in his traveling clothes, which was a nondescript dark coat and sober gray suit, not expensive, not cheap. He'd carefully chosen them to be able to blend into nearly any city background. Except for his height and distinctive face—both of which I'd known him to adjust when he wanted—he could make himself into the human equivalent of wallpaper. "Going on a trip?"

"Yes, an overnight train to New York to recover a kidnapped canine."

"You're kidding."

"My client is paying extremely well," he stated with huffy dignity. Sure, he turned down divorce work, but there was damn little else beneath his notice if the money was good.

"What's the story?"

"Nothing terribly exciting. My client's divorce was finalized some time ago, but her ex-husband was not satisfied with the arrangement concerning the family dog. He, or some agent of his, absconded with the creature, so I'm off to fetch it."

"What kind of dog?"

"No specific breed. I was given a photograph. It's small and fluffy and I expect excitable and prone to yapping, but when a client puts a hundred dollars in my hand I will cheerfully assume the guise of Frank Buck and bring the beast back alive."

He finished putting half his hundred in the safe, keeping the other half for what would be more than generous travel expenses. Maybe he planned to take in some shows while he was in New York. After closing the safe and securing the brick opening, he went upstairs. I followed in the normal way rather than vanishing to waft through the ceiling; impressive as it was, there might be a big night ahead, and I wanted to save my strength.

Escott went into the kitchen. He wasn't one to cook, only using the room to make and drink his coffee in the morning or eat directly from the Chinese food cartons he usually brought home at night. Still, out of habit he'd cleaned things enough in anticipation of his trip to make it look like no one lived here. The garbage pail was empty and swabbed out, the counters wiped clear of crumbs and corner dust. His stringent neatness might have annoyed others, but I didn't mind since he was sensible enough to leave my stuff alone. Of course, I was sensible enough to keep my stuff in my own rooms.

He pulled the Chicago book from the shelf under the wall phone and flipped through its flimsy pages.

"When you due back?" I asked, lounging against the fridge.

"A day or so. You can check with the answering service if there's any change in my plans. I'll notify them."

"If you do the same for me."

"Yes, I read about your case." He indicated some pages on the kitchen table where I'd left them just before dawn. What began as a note turned into a near novel. He told me he wanted to be kept up-to-date on things, so I'd not been sparing in the details. Good thing I could type fast or I wouldn't have finished in time to make it to cover before dawn.

"It's not a case," I protested.

"You've a better description for it?"

He had me there. It's just the way he canted his head and arched the one eyebrow was annoying. Having found a number, he put the phone book away and dialed, calling for a cab to take him to the train station. Rather than risking the perils of public parking, Escott preferred leaving his precious Nash safe in his garage when he traveled.

"I could have given you a ride," I said.

"Most kind, but you've some preparations of your own for the evening to see to, unless I'm mistaken."

"Royce Muldan's party, yeah."

"You will be careful, won't you?"

"You know me."

"Indeed. And I share Shoe's opinion: I've no liking for scraping you off sidewalks."

"That was just the one time. It was months ago."

"It was more than sufficient."

For us both. He and his friend Shoe Coldfield had saved my butt more than once, and sometimes took a perverse delight reminding me about it. None of it bothered me much since I could rib them right back. With interest.

"I'll watch myself," I said. "What about today? Anything new?"

"Miss Smythe called and asked you to telephone her at her place of work at five minutes after nine. She'll be on a break then."

"She say what it was about?"

"Something to do with Lena Ashley's funeral service."

Cheering subject.

"As for the rest of the city, the papers are trying to keep things animated, but there's damned little for them to go on about. Whatever you did last night to that swarm of reporters you encountered seems to have worked. The stories are now below the fold and quite a bit shorter except in certain of the more lurid tabloids. Since you persuaded them to lose interest in you, they're now badgering the police for a swift solution to the 'Sensational Jane Poe Mystery.' By it's very nature I suppose it can hardly be anything else. Oh, that was one of the more restrained headlines."

"I guessed."

"Overly dramatic," he sniffed. "As for the others . . ."

"They gotta tempt people to spend their two cents in the right place. What about the cops? Anything from them?"

He crossed his arms and parked his backside against a counter. "Lieutenant Blair was once more most obliging when I called. He has no exact date on the woman's death, but like you, is privately estimating that it took place about a month after the club closed, around May of 1932. That coincides with Miss Ashley's disappearance and the receipt for the sale of the dress. He spoke with the officers who investigated the grenade-tossing murders and none noticed a freshly bricked-up wall in the cellar at that time."

"They might not have bothered to look, but I'll go along with that."

"Do you think the two incidents are linked?"

Hands shoved into my bathrobe pockets, I shrugged. "I'm figuring that whoever killed Lena knew the club was empty and just used it as a quiet spot for his dirty work."

"Nearly everyone in the city at that time knew it was deserted," he pointed out.

"Yeah. Especially Booth Nevis and Shivvey Coker, but why should they shit in their own yard when there's plenty of other places that wouldn't lead right to them?"

Escott shrugged in turn.

"Did Blair trace the dress label?"

"He did, and Miss Smythe also wanted to let you know Mr. Joe James, though somewhat upset by their intrusion, followed your instructions in regard to being spare in the sharing of information with them."

"That's good. He was worried it might come back on him if he talked too much. He didn't want to end up like Lena."

"Quite understandable."

"Has Blair turned up any next of kin for her?"

"Apparently she had none. At least under that name. If it was false, there will be some difficulty tracing her."

"I'll have to see if she left any papers behind that Rita might have kept. Or have the cops gotten as far as her yet?"

"Not that I was told. You know, despite your influence on him, Blair might take exception to your making the rounds before he's had his chance to ply questions. You could put the wind up his suspects, making them less co-operative than they might otherwise have been."

"I doubt that. Unless I can catch someone before they've tied one on for the night, he's got a better shot at it than me to squeeze 'em. In the end, I'm doing him a favor. If I get a solid lead, I'll turn it over to him to play with. I want this can of worms sealed and delivered so I can get back to business as usual."

"It's more than that to you, though." He had his serious face on. "Granted the affair is bad enough, but trying to sort it out is hardly your concern. The police are more than capable. Why is it so essential for you to be involved?"

That question had been banging around my brain from the start. Sure, the body had been found at my club, but, looking at things cold, that was my only connection to it. None of this should have been more important to me than any other mess left behind by the previous occupants. Appalling as it was, this murder was really something for others to clean up, not me.

"Jack?"

"I think it's . . ." I hunched my shoulders. "I *know* it's because I was murdered, too." My talk with Bobbi last night had dredged up some dark memories. They'd not settled back as usual. In the quiet of my sanctuary, while waiting for unconsciousness to take me for the day, they'd pressed close enough to smother.

Escott gave a small grunt. "I see."

"Back then, when I was . . . when they were killing me . . ."

"Jack—"

"It's just that if I'd been a normal man, no one would have ever found my body. No one would have been punished for what they'd done to me. No one would have known. So this business eats at my gut. I think about that poor woman dying the way she did, and I wonder if those same kinds of thoughts went through her mind while she was buried there in the dark, scared out of her wits, waiting and waiting and waiting. Would anyone find her in time? Would anyone get the bastard who put her there? She had to have gone through days of it, same as me. Only she didn't come back."

"And it makes you angry."

"Damn right." There was something more, but what it might be wasn't going to show itself just yet. Best not to force things. I'd figure it out in time.

He nodded once, understanding, then stepped into the dining room. He used the table there for household paperwork like bills and mail. Retrieving a manila envelope from that day's stack, he handed it over.

"What's this?"

"Blair had it sent over at my request. I understand he got the original from Miss Robillard."

I knew what it might be. Folding back the flap, I drew out a photograph. The paper was slick and new, indicating a copy the police had made. It was a studio portrait of a woman, the kind where they pay attention to the lighting and paint out flaws in the skin, creating a flat artificiality in the image. Dark eyes, dark hair, couldn't tell anything about her figure, since it was just a head shot.

"This is Lena Ashley?" I asked.

"Yes."

She was young and pretty, not remarkably so, a pleasant smile with a certain blankness in the eyes, but that could have been the photography. Or me putting it in on my own. Whatever there was about her that had gotten Booth Nevis wound like a clock wasn't evident to me. Nothing of her personality came out of the picture. I saw what she'd looked like, but had no clue as to what she'd been like. Still, she'd lived and loved and had friends, a life to call her own, until someone sadistically took it from her.

Outside, a car horn sharply sounded.

"My cab," said Escott. He cut through the parlor to the hall and got his hat and overnight bag, then paused as he opened the front door. "Look after yourself, won't you?"

I growled. "Get out or you'll miss your damn train."

Reassured, he snorted once in contempt and left.

Not knowing exactly what sort of evening lay ahead, I put on one of my second-best suits. If the situation got complicated, I'd just as soon not ruin anything new. An overly flashy tie, fresh-polished shoes, and pale gray fedora put me in the right social neighborhood for a mob party, and not for the first time did I wish I could see the effect in a mirror.

My first stop was at Lady Crymsyn to see to the day's business. The private opening was coming up fast. Leon and his men would have to work through the weekend, but they probably wouldn't mind the extra money the overtime would bring.

I was going to park out front as usual, but two cars were already blocking the curb, neither of which I recognized. Two equally unfamiliar men hung around the door, talking and smoking and keeping an eye on the street. Reporters. I knew that bored but still hungry look, having been there myself. Careful not to glance their way, I drove past, taking a turn at the next block over to come up to the alley running behind the club.

My headlights picked out another man sitting in the shallow alcove of the backstage service door.

They had me covered.

He shaded his eyes from the glare. Too late to shift to reverse, I resigned myself to inflicting another hypnosis session on some hapless schmuck. It was with no small amount of surprise I abruptly recognized the man to be Malone. What the hell?

Obviously favoring any number of sore spots, he stood up slowly, waiting for me. I set the parking brake and got out.

"Hello, Mr. Fleming." His face looked worse than before. Some of the swelling had gone down, but the bruising had turned black in spots.

"Hello, yourself." I put my hand out, and we shook. His grip was somewhat less than firm, but I put that down to his weakened condition. "What are you doing here?"

He made that nervous tic smile, or something close to it around the bruises. "I—ah—I'm looking for a job."

That explained his plain blue suit and quiet tie. Both looked like they didn't get a lot of use except to decorate hangers. A faint scent of mothballs drifted from him. "I thought you were going to rest up first."

"By the time your club opens I'll be all better."

I checked him up and down and agreed with his estimate. It must have been quite an act of courage for him to come by. "Inside. We'll talk."

He released a soft sigh of relief, and I knew I'd been right on the courage part.

I unlocked the service door, ushered him in, and locked it again. Once shut, we were in total darkness for him, and something close to it for me. Enough outside glow seeped through the red-tinted panes in the opposite windows so I could navigate without walking into things. For Malone's convenience, I found the lighting box and threw a few switches. He gazed around the stage where we stood, then took in the vast audience area and looked suitably impressed.

"Heavens," he said. "I had no idea it would be this elaborate."

"I'm hoping others will think the same. This way."

I led off to the left, not too fast so he could keep up. He openly gaped at the portrait of Lady Crymsyn and, as before when giving Escott the tour, I tasted the sweet flavor of proprietorship mixed with pride. If it was this satisfying now, come opening night I'd be permanently addicted.

For once, the lobby bar light was off, and no one had bothered to leave another solitary shot glass of whiskey out to annoy and mystify. Good.

We went up to the second-floor office. Malone made no comment about its contrasting lack of decor compared to the luxury below. I found a folding chair for him and put it before the old table I used as a desk. As ever, a pile of paperwork waited for me there, including Leon's clipboard with its ever-growing number of notes. A shipment of glassware and other equipment had arrived today. They'd stored the crates in the main room. Leon wanted to know who to contact to install some of the more specialized items like beer dispensers. That was union labor, and I had someone lined up for it, but it would require a daytime call and supervision. Leon could probably take care of it, but he knew construction, not bars and office work.

I looked at Malone and wondered how many miracles I was entitled to in one lifetime.

"What kind of job did you have in mind?" I asked.

"Bartending." His voice was muted and speech blurred because of his split lip. "I'm very good at it."

"I know. Nevis wouldn't have kept you around for long if you weren't. How'd you learn I was hiring? From him?"

"Not directly. The manager at the Flying Ace called to find out why I'd not come in tonight."

"He hadn't heard about your fight?"

"He'd heard, but was told I'd only been pushed around a little. Just some harmless fun." There was a touch of bitterness in his voice, but he was entitled.

"And he got told by the guys who did the pushing?"

"Yes, exactly that. I gave him my side of things and why I had no desire to return for more, then he said it was tough luck."

"But not tough enough for him to fix things for you?"

Malone puffed one gentle laugh. "Hardly. He isn't a bad

sort, just not one to stick his neck out. Not for me, any-way."

"Some guys think it's catching."

That got another, longer laugh. It might have been more audible if he'd been feeling better. Instead, he pressed one hand to his side. Probably had a stitch in the damaged muscle there or maybe a bruised rib. "I think he did want to help me in some way, though, and suggested I try my luck here. The boss had told him to pass the word around that you were looking to hire people."

So Nevis had had some memory of our conversation. I wondered if he'd fully recovered from his migraine. And what else he might have remembered—or learned—about me today. I fixed a long, concentrated stare on Malone until I was sure he was under. "Did Booth Nevis or anyone else send you to spy on me?"

Malone's battered face was relaxed enough to look dead. Especially around his unblinking, unfocused eyes. "No."

"Why are you here?"

"I . . . I need a job."

"Did Nevis or Coker ever talk about me? Or ask you questions?"

"No."

"Did you ever hear them say anything about Lena Ash-ley?"

"No."

"What about Welsh Lennet?"

"No."

I let go my brief hold on him and watched normal an-imation creep back into his expression. He wouldn't recall anything. "You know Nevis has a black reputation in some quarters. Why'd you work for him for so long?"

"I needed a job; he gave me one."

"There's always places for a good bartender in a city this big."

"Times are hard, Mr. Fleming, and the tips at the Flying Ace were better than I might find elsewhere."

"You'd make even more at one of the fancier watering holes on the north side."

"I liked where I was." He made that tic again. It was almost a grimace.

I decided against giving him a hypnotic nudge, keeping quiet and letting the silence stretch.

He seemed to know what I was trying to do and dropped his gaze to the floor. "There was more to it," he finally muttered.

"Like Nevis asking you to do extra work on the side?"

"What?"

"Did he have you running errands like Tony Upshaw?"

There was genuine startlement in his tone. "N-no, certainly not. I just ran the bar, nothing more."

"Then what else was there?"

Malone went red to his roots, which did not combine well with the black of the bruises. "Mr. Nevis . . . he—he knew I'd been in prison."

I snorted, unimpressed. "Oh, is that all?" He started to add more, then choked it off, surprised at my reaction. Leaning back, I put my hands behind my head. "Listen, half the mugs in this town have been on the inside at one time or another. Anyplace else in the world and it'd be considered a rite of passage. Anthropologists could write reports for *National Geographic*, complete with pictures."

"I've not met many people with that sort of opinion on the subject," he said after a moment.

"What'd they put you away for?" I was careful to phrase it just that way rather than ask "what did you do?" Hanging around in Gordy's crowd had given my manners in regard to the mobs a certain diplomatic polish.

"I wrote some bad checks. Did eight months out of a year. They paroled me early for good behavior."

"Bad checks? Sounds pretty tame to me."

"Not to hear others talk. If they think you've been crooked with money once, they assume you will be again."

"What's the whole story, then? If you don't mind my asking."

"I don't, not really. Things are so different for me now it's as though it all happened a long time ago to some other fellow."

"I know what that's like. Go on."

He shrugged. "It's nothing much. I had a store once, dry goods and that sort of thing, and was partners with my brother. David liked to gamble, though, and he'd drain the profits to pay his debts when he lost. It usually wasn't a lot, and sometimes he'd make a big win and pay it all back, so things tended to balance themselves out. Then he hit a long stretch of bad luck and he kept on betting, hoping it would change."

"But it didn't."

"Bad to worse, and more so because he didn't tell me what was going on. He had to make a big payoff and took nearly everything out of the bank. There were some rough types coming around to collect from him. They would have hurt him, maybe killed him."

"Then the boom fell."

Malone nodded. "The store bills had to be paid . . . and I paid them."

"But if you didn't know the checks would be bad—"

"Actually, I did. It was perfectly stupid of me, but my brother persuaded me to believe that his luck would change for the better. He had a sure thing at the track that he *knew* would come in. Only it didn't, and so I was left with the consequences. It was my signature on the checks, not his, after all, and too late to call them back."

"So he left you swinging in the wind? He couldn't have said something to a judge to help you out?"

"He would have, but he was killed in a car accident a week before the trial. It was an unholy mess."

"Didn't any of this come out in court?"

"Yes, but I couldn't afford a decent attorney, and it was an election year for the prosecutor's office. He managed to get an easy and quick conviction to add to his record."

"Your kid know this about you?"

"Not one word—and she never will if I can help it. She was only three and doesn't remember anything about me being away for so long. I'm an honest man, Mr. Fleming. I made a mistake blinding myself to my brother's weakness. It is not something I'll ever repeat."

That was for damn sure. "What about the rest of your family? You get along with them all right?"

"I haven't any real family left except for Norrie. Her mother . . . had a bad heart. She died giving birth."

"I'm sorry."

"Thank you."

"Your little girl—if I'm stepping over the line, lemme know—but I was wondering about that scar on her neck."

He made a deprecating gesture. "People ask about it; most of them aren't as polite as you. I don't want her growing up self-conscious about it, you see, or being teased by others."

"Uh-huh."

"She was in the car with my brother. There was broken glass. Missed killing her by a fraction. I still have nightmares about what might have happened. Silly of me. She's safe now, thank God. And thank God she doesn't remember any of it, either. Not really. Sometimes she has nightmares, too, but I'm hoping she'll grow out of them."

"Is that what you meant last night about things being complicated?"

"I said that? I suppose so, yes." He made a rueful face.

Awkward silence, with me thinking along there-but-for-the-grace-of-God lines. I shook out of it and cleared my throat. "About last night . . ."

Malone straightened, probably sensing and welcoming a change of subject. "Yes?"

"I saw you had some college books on accounting. Those didn't just come with your flat, did they?"

He looked puzzled. Couldn't blame him; it was quite a shift. "They're mine. That's what I studied for a few years."

"Ever get to use any of it?"

"When I ran the store, but not lately."

"You know how things work in a club bar. Is it much different from your store?"

"Not very."

"How'd you get from dry goods to mixing drinks?"

"It was the only place that would hire me once I was released. Mr. Nevis asked if I knew how to draw beer from a tap—which I did—and I picked up the rest watching the other bartenders."

I nodded. "Okay, Malone, it's like this: I need a general manager for this place, and right now you're the only one I've talked to who looks good for the spot."

Tic. Quite a big one, nearly a full twitch that used up his whole battered face. "G-general manager?"

"It'd mean keeping the books, hiring and firing, and making sure the help doesn't guzzle the inventory or sneak from the till. You'd meet and greet special customers when necessary. For some nights you'll need a tuxedo, but the club can pay for that if you don't have one."

He couldn't seem to shut his mouth.

"It's going to use up time and require a man who's reliable and responsible enough to stay at it. I'm only available in the evenings. I need someone to see to the day work, so you'd have to make plenty of decisions on your own. Think you're up to it?" I sat back and let him mull it over. It didn't take him too long.

"What—what sort of hours would be required?" he asked, his face pinched from furious internal calculation.

"As many as it takes to get the job done. A lot at first until the place is opened and a routine is set, then maybe not so much. Is that going to be a problem?"

"I was just thinking about Norrie. I shouldn't like her to be alone too much. Well, not alone, Mrs. Tanenbaum looks after her, but that's not the same as having her daddy around."

"The first month will be the busiest, but after that—" I lifted my hand, palm up. "Look, soon she'll be in school most of the day, right? You can come in while she's there, do what needs doing, take a couple hours off home with her, then come back until I get here in the evenings. You don't live that far away."

"It might work," he admitted.

"You'd open the place for the waiters and set up the cash registers for them, nothing you haven't done before. And you wouldn't have to stay late since I'll be here to close. What d'ya say?"

He made no reply, still looking overwhelmed by the possibilities.

"Malone?"

He blinked, swallowed a few times. "I don't know. You're giving me quite a lot of trust, and you hardly know me."

"If you were dishonest or dumb, Nevis wouldn't have bothered with you. Guys who sneak from his till only do it once—or so I've heard. The same rule applies here, if that's any comfort."

That raised half a smile on him. "I've no argument with it."

"So. You want this job?"

"Y-yes. But what if things don't work out?"

"Then I find someone else, you go ahead and do regular bartending here, and no hard feelings for either of us."

His smile might have been full on except for the lip damage, but most of it still shone out his one good eye. "Yes, yes, absolutely."

He reached across to shake my outstretched hand on the deal. I froze him in place with one of my looks. My conscience tried to give me a twinge about doing this sort of thing to the guy, but I successfully ignored it. I liked him, and my instincts said he'd work out, but business was business, after all.

"You're not going to steal from me, are you, Malone?"

"N-no, sir."

"Or spy on me for anyone?"

"No."

"And you'll let me know if anyone asks you to?"

"Yes."

"Then we'll get along great." By the time I released his grip, he was back to normal and asking where to start.

8

AT five minutes after nine, I broke off trying to explain my half-assed attempts at bookkeeping to a very patient and bemused Malone and phoned the Red Deuces for Bobbi. She answered herself.

"That was fast," I said after saying hello. "Were you sitting on it?"

"Almost. I've been hanging around the office during my break."

"What's going on? Charles mentioned something about the funeral."

"I've got it all arranged, but it's not going to be a real funeral, because the police haven't released that poor woman's remains yet, which is really stupid of them." She sounded huffy about the situation and gave me a thumbnail of her day's trials and tribulations. She'd juggled a truck-load of them. "In the end I had to settle for just a memorial service for Lena at the funeral home."

"Not a church?"

"I tried, but they were all strangely busy with other things."

"They must be allergic to the notoriety. What happens when the cops do release the body?"

Malone, who couldn't help hearing my end of the conversation, looked up from his work, wide of eye for a moment, then wisely bent back over the account books again.

"They'll do some kind of short service at the cemetery," she answered. "But that won't be for a while. I need your help right away."

"Name it."

"You're going to talk to Rita tonight?"

"I hope to."

"Find out from her whether I need a priest, minister, or rabbi to speak tomorrow. If she and Lena were best friends, then she might know."

"Yeah, sure, I guess." I'd picked up an edge to her voice, which meant she was working too hard.

"It's really important, Jack. The guy at the funeral home told me how people are very particular about that sort of thing. I don't want to muddle any of this up."

"Yeah, we wouldn't want her going to the wrong heaven after all this time."

"That's *not* funny."

"Yes, it is, when you think about it. It's not as though you have to wait to be buried first before you take off."

"Jack—"

"Do you really think anyone needs some kind of notarized statement saying 'Dear Saint Peter, here's another stiff, pass him through the gates, signed, Father Mc-Gonnigill.' "

"Jack—"

" 'PS: He once had a hot dog on a Friday, but don't hold that against him.' "

I didn't get much sense out of her then, but that was okay, a little profane release is always good for the soul. "Feel better?" I asked after a few moments of holding the receiver away from my ear.

"How is it you always know what I need most?" she demanded, sounding more relaxed.

"Native talent, my dear. Now what else can I do to you?"

"I can think of something, but you'll have to save it for later; I've still got grim reaper business."

"Shoot away."

She told me how much the services would cost, which included the graveside stuff and price of the coffin and headstone.

"Doesn't seem like a lot," I said. "Not that I'm complaining."

"The guy who runs the home knew me as being one of Gordy's friends, so he cut a good deal."

Fair enough. Over the years he may have gotten a lot of business thrown his way because of Gordy. I kept such grisly speculations to myself, though, since Malone was still in front of me. He already looked like he'd work out fine for the club; I didn't want to scare him off.

Bobbi told me the where of the service and when: tomorrow evening at eight.

"Isn't it unusual to have it at night?" I asked, scribbling it all down.

"Not for a memorial. Anyway, I figured you'd want to be there."

"I don't want to, but I will to see who turns up and why—and to keep you company," I quickly added.

"Smart man," she purred in a dangerously sweet tone.

"I don't need to be the undertaker's next customer. What about your job? Is there any trouble about you taking time off for this?"

"The boss won't short my check as long as I do my two sets that night. I'm swapping my schedule around with one of the other acts. As long as I'm back by ten, everything's jake. Now, it's too late to put an announcement in the papers, so I'll call Gordy to spread the word and you do the same at that going-away party."

"Yeah. Maybe they can break off their boozing long enough to put in an appearance."

"What if no one comes to this?" she fretted.

"You'll get a good turnout, angel; the place will be jammed with reporters."

"No, it won't." She sounded smug.

"How'd you manage that?"

"Not me, Lieutenant Blair."

"Oh, yeah?"

"I had a nice talk with him about all this, and he promised to have plenty of uniforms around to keep things in hand."

"And keep track of who comes and goes."

"Of course."

"I'll just omit that little detail from the invitations, though the smarter mugs will figure it out on their own."

"Which is why I don't expect a crowd."

"No need to worry about it. I'm sure the guest of honor won't notice a damn thing."

"Jack!" Exasperation. "I'm trying to be serious here."

"Don't mind me, sweetheart. I have to be an ass about it now so I can handle it later."

Pause. Then. "This is digging into you too, isn't it?"

"Enough so Charles had to comment."

"Oh. I didn't know. You going to be all right?"

"Yeah." I put in a note of reassurance. Some of it was genuine.

"Will Charles attend?"

"Hard to say. Right now he's on a train to New York, so I wouldn't count on it." I explained about the dognapping errand. Bobbi was disappointed, but because of her own precarious career understood the odd demands of Escott's irregular business.

When I hung up, Malone stopped pretending to work and put down his pencil. "I don't wish to pry, but . . ."

"It's okay. My girlfriend's making arrangements for the body they found in the cellar. There doesn't seem to be any family coming forward, the cops haven't traced them either, so it's sort of left up to us."

"But I thought the city took care of things like that."

No need for me to repeat all the points Gordy had cited on why I should take up the task. "Yeah, well, if I can borrow a phrase, it's complicated. I don't want people finding out we're doing this, either, so if some reporters ask, you don't know who's behind it."

"Reporters?"

"When you arrived, didn't you see a couple guys hanging around the front?"

"Yes, I'd forgotten about them. I thought they also might be here applying for work."

"Why didn't you wait with them?"

"I didn't like their looks. Rather scruffy and desperate."

"You're a good judge of character. I've shooed most of the others away, so you shouldn't have problems, but you might still have to fend off some phone calls until this sideshow settles down."

He didn't look too thrilled at the prospect, and I took it as a sign that he'd be suitably discouraging to members of my former profession.

"The foreman here, Leon, will help out if anyone gets pushy. Which reminds me, I need to let him know about hiring you on."

While Malone went back to making order of my chaos,

I scribbled a note to Leon, explaining things. The phone rang; it was someone wanting a bartending job. Word was getting around, then. I told him what he needed to know and said he could come in tomorrow to talk to the general manager, then caught myself and put a hand over the mouthpiece.

"Can you be here on a Saturday?" I asked Malone.

"When?"

I gauged how battered he looked against the necessity of getting the club ready for its private, invitation-only opening by next Friday night. He had no problem coming in at noon and staying until six. He said he could be earlier, but I shook my head, confirmed the time to the guy on the phone, and hung up. While I was thinking of it, I fished out the keys to the joint and handed them over.

"You can use these until Leon gets your own set made. The one with the red tag is for the front door, the blue is for the back."

"But how will you get in?"

"I've got another set at home," I lied.

Malone held the keys in his hand a moment, looking at them.

"Something wrong?"

Tic. "It's just, well, it's a lot to take in. I didn't expect anything like this when I decided to come over tonight. Are you sure about me? You don't seem to mind about—about certain things."

"Your private life is none of my business. You being able to do the job right is. If it works out, fine. You won't have to worry about the bouncers here, either. For one thing, you'll be the one hiring them. And if anyone gives you trouble, you let me know so I can deal with it. I'm going to run a nice, smooth operation, and back alley brawls are not in my plans."

"You're very confident, aren't you?"

"I guess I am." It wasn't a word I'd have instantly used to describe myself. "Stubborn smart-ass" struck me as being more appropriate, but I'd readily accept his definition as a more genteel alternative.

"That's a rare quality these days," he said. "So many people have none left because of the hard times, you know."

"Can't blame 'em, but I figure you'd have met mugs with plenty of moxie working at Nevis's place."

"Not really. Most of their bravado was from a bottle or a big win at the tables. Once they're sober and the money's spent they go right back to old habits and fears—until the next time."

I recalled he had some psychology books on his shelves. He'd either read them through or was a part-time barroom philosopher. "Check me again a week after we open. If this place is a bust, you may have to alter your opinion."

"I hope not," he said with half a smile, and gently rapped his knuckles twice against the wooden tabletop before going back to the accounts.

Taking Leon's clipboard, I left to make a quick inspection of the day's progress.

The main floor was now all done except for unpacking glassware and installing the bar equipment. The backstage area was finished and waiting for future performers to break it in. The basement was shaping up, but far too slowly, and we'd come to a major hitch. A portable cement mixer wouldn't be available until next Friday, meaning the crew couldn't complete the floor as planned, much less fill in the eyesore trench under the far wall. Times might be tough, but Roosevelt's NRA was doing a lot of public works stuff this summer, which was why we couldn't get a mixer right away. I made a note to Leon to call every company in the whole damned county if he had to find one and to hell with the cost.

In the meantime, he and the crew had improvised, mixing cement one bag at a time in wheelbarrows. They'd started on the near wall and were working their way toward the back entry. It was a good job, smooth and level, but taking too long for my schedule. At this rate we'd have to string curtains to mark off the dressing rooms, and the only plumbing would be upstairs.

Not the grand beginning I wanted. I had to remind myself that the private opening next week was just a special party for a select group, like a dress rehearsal. If things went to hell and gone, it wouldn't matter all that much. Really.

I trudged upstairs again. Malone would have to pick some other word than *confident* to describe me right now.

In the lobby, I rather resignedly noticed that the damned bar light had turned itself on again. I wrote for Leon to take the plate off and check the wiring, then went behind it to shut it off. The toggle was up. I flipped it a few times, thinking the mechanism had some kind of fault that made it snap on by itself, but it seemed to work fine. I gave up and left it on.

The stained floor tile had been replaced. With another equally stained tile. Irked, I scrawled more instructions on the subject.

That done, I went to unlock the front door, checking to see if the reporters were still there. They were. We had an intense little talk that gave me the usual dull twinge behind the eyes, but both men departed for greener pastures without fuss and without a story. Neither would remember why or be back.

My inspection finished, I went up to tell Malone it was time to pack it in.

"I'm almost done sorting this out, another hour—" he began.

"I have to beat it for someplace else. Take it home if

you want, but get some rest. You're still brittle, and to-morrow's going to hurt more than you think."

"But we haven't covered nearly enough details for me to start," he protested.

"You've got my list of things to do, what positions to fill, all the phone numbers, and a budget to work with. You know the bar business better than I; you've been at it longer. You'll do fine. I said I needed someone who can fend for himself; here's a chance to show your stuff without having a boss breathing down your neck all day."

He made a small, deprecating gesture. "I just don't want to botch things. It's possible I could—"

"Jeez, I go out on a limb, take a chance, and it's complaints already. I'm writing to Roosevelt on this."

He froze for a second before comprehending the joke, then relaxed into a brief, relieved chuckle. With a tic.

Given time, he'd get used to me.

As it was on the way, I dropped Malone off at his house, saving him some bus fare, then drove on to the address I had for Tony Upshaw's studio. It was well after ten by the time I found it, too late for any easy, predrink hypnotic interrogations. That had only been a fond and faint hope, anyway. The sort of crowd that was likely to be there would have begun their celebrations hours ago. What the hell, instead of the acquired hypnosis, I could always fall back on my own inborn charm. It could stand some exercising.

There wasn't much fancy about the outside of the building: a couple of stories of red brick, lots of windows, none of them too clean, but no broken panes. They were all open, spilling out a confused mix of light, music, and voices. A sign attached to the front sported an oversize photo of Upshaw in a tuxedo bending some woman in a white ball gown back in a gracefully executed dip. His

name appeared below along with an invitation for new
students to ascend to the second floor for their lessons.

The main door was open to a dim hall serving the street
level businesses and a stairway going up. Both were
clogged with people sitting or standing at their ease with
drinks and cigarettes in hand. Their conversation was loud,
in direct competition with the music blaring from above.
No one was immediately familiar to me, nor did I cause
much stir except while threading my way upstairs, which
was inconvenient to those sprawling on the steps.

I'd harbored a small worry about having to crash the
party for lack of an invitation. By the look of things it
didn't seem to be anything close to that formal.

The hall above was also crowded, the music more intense, the people more active, a few of them already drunk
and verging on disorderly, much to the roaring amusement
of their slightly less tipsy friends. It was an interesting
crew who had shown up to wish Royce Muldan a good
trip. Mugs with bad-road faces and hundred-dollar suits
bumped elbows with what looked to be artistic types wearing threadbare cuffs, untrimmed hair, and berets.

The women were just as mixed, wearing everything
from shimmering evening gowns to country trousers. One
of them had on what seemed to be a gold satin bathing
costume with a matching top hat. The white tap shoes with
big gold buckles she clicked about in declared her to be a
dancer. I wanted to know what show so I could find out
if there were more like her at home.

I pushed a path through a set of open double doors into
the studio itself: a long wide room with a bank of windows
on one wall, the other covered with a continuous line of
mirrors. Any other time I'd have never crossed the threshold since my lack of a reflection would have been instantly
noticed, but it was safe enough with the crowd in the way.
There was so much booze flowing that if anyone did see—

or rather not see—something odd about me, they might put it down to one too many drinks. Or so I hoped.

Folding tables and chairs were set up all over except for a clear spot in the middle reserved for dancing. I moved closer on the window side of the space, searching dozens of bright, flushed faces in the haze of cigarette smoke, hoping to spot Rita Robillard among them.

The band was good; I recognized the piano man and the drummer as being regular performers at the Nightcrawler. They were busy pounding out something fast and hot for Tony Upshaw, who was twirling a redhead across the floor with expert ease. She wore a loose-fitting white dress, strings of multicolored beads, and her waist-long hair flew as she swung around and around. They were the only ones presently within the reserved space. Smiling her enjoyment, the trim woman matched Upshaw move for move, like Rogers to Astaire.

The number surged to a frenetic finish. Upshaw and his limber partner did some kind of complicated in-out, over-under spinning maneuver they'd obviously practiced to the point of making it seem easy, ending it exactly on a last high note from the horn section. He might have had the look of an ambitious lounge lizard, but he did have talent. They were both rewarded with cheers and applause as they made their bows. As soon as the audience noise died down, the music swelled again, but for a slower number this time. Couples trickled onto the floor, soon filling it.

Upshaw fondly kissed his partner's hand, then they parted in different directions. The flared hem of her white dress flowing around her ankles like foam, the woman glided toward me with a quick, firm step. It turned out I happened to be by the table where she'd left her drink. Somewhat breathless, she picked up a glass amid congratulations from the others already there and drained it. Several of the men volunteered to get her a replacement. She nodded a cheerful agreement to this, and two of them hared off to a bar set up against the mirror wall.

"Excuse me," she said.

I was between her and a chair. I moved clear and held it for her. With a glance my way, she seated herself like royalty and nodded thanks, then gave me a second, longer appraisal.

"Nice dancing," I said, just to be polite before moving on.

"So kind." Her sharp gaze flicked over me from head to toe. "I know you from somewhere," she stated in a melodious contralto that made me think of vanilla ice cream, sweet and melting, on a hot day.

This compelled me to also give her a second scrutiny. Delicate elfin features, clear laughing eyes, with a dusting of freckles on her nose and cheeks. Any other woman might have hidden them under a layer of powder, but this one was apparently secure with her looks. The strings of beads and loose dress style were quite different from the gowns other women at the table wore, and none of them had such a fall of rich red hair hanging past her waist. She seemed to be one of the artistic types, which meant she wouldn't give a damn what was fashionable, only what looked good on her. To me, she looked very good indeed.

"I don't think so," I responded, taking off my hat. "You I would remember."

"You've been here before, haven't you?"

Shook my head. "First time. Came to meet a friend."

She extended her hand. "Then you've done that much. I'm Ruth Woodring. I'm half-owner of this place with Mr. Upshaw. That was the fellow who partnered me."

Unlike Escott or even Upshaw, I couldn't get away with kissing a woman's hand and making it look good, so I lightly squeezed her fingers instead. "Jack Fleming."

"Oh!" Sudden recognition. "You're the one with the body in the cellar."

This got the focused attention of everyone at the table. "Ahhh . . ."

"That's where I know you from, the newspaper picture." Ruth looked at a curly-haired brunette across the table. "Did you see it, Darla? People were being walled up alive in Welsh Lennet's old place—"

"Just one," I interrupted before things got out of hand. "More than enough."

Ruth pursed her lips. "Oh, dear, I've embarrassed you, I'm sorry. Please sit down and have a drink."

Her two errand runners were back with filled glasses; she slid one in front of the empty chair next to her.

Mindful of the dirty looks aimed my way by the other men, I sat, putting my fedora on the table. "Just for a minute."

"Ah, but I'm your hostess; you have to stay at least two minutes. Rules of the party. I was frightfully rude just now, so you must let me make it up to you."

"You've got bodies in your cellar?" asked Darla brightly, leaning forward on her elbows, chin resting on her doubled fists.

"Just one body," I repeated. "And it's long gone. The cops took it away."

"How'd it get there?"

"The papers had the whole story," I hedged, wondering how I could escape without actually vanishing.

"Who reads those? *Do* tell us—"

Ruth narrowed her eyes. "Darla, if you chase this scrumptious specimen off, I shall hide your douche bag."

Darla subsided with an impish smirk.

I tried not to let my jaw sag.

Ruth beamed a warm, comforting look at me and patted my arm, leaving her hand in place. "Don't mind her, Mr.

Fleming. She's a born troublemaker. I'd throw her out, but she's too good a dance instructor. Do you dance?"

"Nothing fancy like what you were just doing, but I can keep off my partner's feet."

"Then you must give me a demonstration." She stood. "I'm sure we can both learn something from the experience."

She had a crystal-clear double meaning under that one, but what the hell. It was more appealing than waiting for Darla's next purposely awkward question, and not to accept would peg me for a heel. All that aside, Ruth was quite a dish, and I'd learned a long time ago never to argue with redheads. I took her arm and escorted her onto the floor. The music was slow enough to allow for conversation.

"Quite a gathering," I said once we'd settled together into the rhythm. She was light enough that I didn't feel like I was leading so much as floating with her.

"One of Tony's more successful accomplishments—Mr. Upshaw, that is to say."

"So was this whole clambake all his idea?"

"Actually, it was Royce Muldan's—the guest of honor?"

I nodded to indicate I knew him.

"But Tony made the arrangements. He's very good at that sort of thing."

"Not bad." I wondered how attached Upshaw really was to the silk suit boys. This seemed a pretty elaborate show for a part-time hanger-on to produce on short notice.

Ruth continued. "It's great publicity for the studio. We may get dozens of new students out of this."

So that was the why of the big exhibition number. "You're a friend of Muldan's?"

"Oh, I never mix with that element. I think you must know him, though." She flicked her sharp gaze over my suit, suddenly having a lot in common with little Norrie Malone when it came to making deductions based on a man's taste in clothes.

"I've only just seen him around," I said. "Heard he was going off to Havana. Real sudden."

"And silly. It's far too hot this time of year, but boys will have their whims. At least he's footing the bill for this, which is a relief. Tony's a sweetheart, but spends too much on parties. Never has more than two nickels to rub together afterward."

"You couldn't tell that from the way he was turned out. Looked like he got that tuxedo right off a movie screen."

"Oh, dear, you're not interested in him instead, are you?" She looked more bewildered than distressed at the prospect.

"Not at all."

"Good, I didn't think I could be that wrong about a man."

"How long have you been partners with Tony?" I asked, wanting to shift the subject back.

"About six years now."

"You've known him that long?"

"We go back before that, centuries at least. When did you meet him? He's not said anything of it."

"Just last night at the Flying Ace. He's quite a hoofer."

"He should be, I taught him *everything*." To judge by her expression she'd thoroughly enjoyed having Upshaw for a student.

"Lucky man."

"You know all the right things to say, don't you?"

"I read a lot." Her smile and the spark in her eyes nearly made me miss a step. She wasn't the only one gifted with native charm. If I wasn't so crazy about Bobbi, I might have been tempted to do more than merely dance with the delectable Miss Woodring. I made myself return to business. "Tony was there with a gal named Rita Robillard. You know her?"

"Is *she* the friend you came to meet?" No approval or disapproval in her tone, just curiosity.

"Yeah. I need to talk with her."

"Oh. Is that what they're calling it now?"

I smiled. She could draw her own conclusions.

"How disappointing *pour moi*," said Ruth. "Not to mention for yourself."

"You'll get no arguments from me, but I do need to find her."

"She'll be lurking around the party someplace. I remember her coming in with that Shivvey fellow, but I'm not sure when."

"Shivvey Coker's here, too, huh?" It was good to know that Malone's information had been solid.

"There's no accounting for some people's taste. Is he also a friend of yours?"

"Enough so I wouldn't turn my back on him."

She laughed. "Does this talk with Rita have to do with the woman's body in your cellar?"

"Why do you ask?"

"Because Tony told me they were once best friends. The dead woman's name escapes me . . ."

"No, it doesn't."

"Mm. Clever fellow." She gave a careless one-shoulder shrug of dismissal. "Lena Ashley, then."

"What do you know about her?"

"Not a jot more than her name."

"Which Tony mentioned to you?"

"He may have casually dropped it when we rehearsed today."

"Now why would he do that?"

"Tony likes to impress people, the poor dear. He shouldn't try so hard. If you talk to him about this, then I want to watch. He's so delightfully *cute* when he's squirm-ing."

That was more than I wanted to know about him. "How far back does Tony go with Lena and Rita?"

"A few years."

"How many?"

Ruth ceased to float and came to a decided stop. "What is this? All these questions—"

"I'm just being social, Miss Woodring."

Her pleasant expression did not change, except in the eyes. They went hard. "The hell you are. Tony's one of my best friends, and I know him better than I know myself. There's not a mean bone in his body, and if you think he could have anything to do with what happened to that woman, then get it right out of your head."

"Are you sure you know him all that well?" I stared at her, putting a little pressure on, but uncertain if it would get past her recent drink. "Absolutely sure?"

She didn't react to the hypnosis so much as my question. The way I'd said it would make anyone think twice.

"No matter how close we are to them none of us can ever really know what's going on in another's head."

She was well aware of that to judge by the flash of dislike and anger in her eyes. She kept it in control, though, and didn't belt me one.

"Maybe he's a nice guy now, but what was he like five or six years ago?"

Her lips tightened into a caustic smile. "Thank you, Mr. Fleming, it's been most diverting, but your two minutes are long up. Good-bye."

She swept away, as adept in the art of making a graceful exit as she was at dancing.

I believed that she believed Tony was on the up-and-up. She was on the up-and-up as well, or she'd have stuck around to try getting more information from me. Her pretending not to know Lena's name was odd, but I figured it to be either a ploy to induce me to talk about the murder at the club or part of her flirting game. Which I'd thoroughly spoiled. There would be no more conversation with her until she got over being mad at me, which might not happen for a few decades. But I had learned more from her questions than she had from mine. Until now I'd not considered Tony Upshaw as being even remotely connected to Lena's death. That lounge lizard polish of his was sufficient to divert anyone from taking him seriously.

One of the errand runners from her table sauntered over with my hat. He gave me an insultingly obvious appraisal and made sure I saw that he was unimpressed. He even held the hat out and tried to let it drop to the floor before I could take it. I saw that one coming, though, and plucked it from midair in plenty of time. Anyone else who was sober could have done the same thing; I just did it a whole lot faster and smoother so it seemed like I hardly moved. That, and my friendly grin seemed to unsettle him quite a lot. Then I noticed he was no longer looking right at me, but at some point behind and beyond.

My back was to the mirrors. Oh. So far he was the only one to notice. That was lucky.

"Thanks, pal," I murmured while he goggled. "Tell Miss Woodring for me that I said I'm sorry about upsetting her." I gave him no time to reply and walked off as though nothing was amiss.

I glanced around after putting a crowd of people between us. He was still rooted in place, in the same posture, staring at the mirrors. After nearly a full minute he hurried off to the bar, not hearing the calls coming from his friends at the table. It was better that way.

The tune changed and picked up the tempo as I continued in the opposite direction toward the bank of windows. I thought I'd glimpsed a particularly flashy tuxedo among those seeking a fresh-air respite from the cigarette smoke. Instead, I found more of the theatrical types freely mingling with the mob boys. It seemed a peculiar combination until I recalled how much Capone liked opera. Maybe these guys were also patrons of the arts.

Bunched in the far corner was a small congregation in a rough circle around the guest of honor, Royce Muldan. I moved close enough so he noticed me, but got no sign of recognition from him. Good.

He had a cigar in one hand and a heavy arm draped over a short, lush-figured strawberry blonde with an exaggerated sulky mouth. He was holding forth, gesturing a lot with the cigar, an indication that he was pretty well oiled. Each of his broad movements was conveyed to the pliant girl, her smooth young face showing no reaction as she was wobbled around. Her blue eyes were quite glazed, and I wondered if she'd had more than just alcohol tonight. I'd seen those kinds of eyes during the war when the wounded were given a dose of morphine to keep them quiet.

Muldan laughed heartily to some comment and shook his head. "No, that's not it at all, I just wanna get away for a while. Havana's real nice this time of year."

Jeez, he sounded exactly like Gordy.

"Then you ain't been there at this time a' year," responded a heckler. He was about a third of Muldan's height and reminded me of one of the seven dwarfs from *Snow White*, but I couldn't recall which. "I think your little twist has got you running scared. She wants a ring an' her old man's ready to get a shotgun to—"

"A ring? Hah!" Muldan doubled over, consumed by booze-enhanced hilarity. He lost his grip on the girl, who woke up a little. She blinked, set her sights on a bottle standing on a table next to her, and picked it up, precise fingers delicate on its neck.

"Yeah, a ring," said the heckler. "An' her old man's—"

"Nothing to me. She wants a ring from me like I want another nose," Muldan countered. "Lemme tell you what she really wants . . ."

The girl raised the bottle to her lips, upended it, and drained off what little remained. "Yes?" she asked in a loud clear voice, addressing no one in particular, her gaze fixed on nothing at all.

"What?" echoed Muldan, his attention momentarily snagged.

"You're saying . . . saying you know what I want."

"Yeah, honey-bunch, and it's not a ring. Why don't you tell the nice man what you want from me."

That was a surprise. I'd instructed him not to go near the girl. She must have sought him out, instead. Nothing I could do about that, though maybe I should have anticipated it.

"What I want from you?" she queried blankly, still not looking at anything.

Muldan flashed his handsome idiot's grin toward his audience, inviting them to join in on the pending laugh at her expense. This brought on a few early snickers as they waited for her response.

"You tell them." He pointed. "What you want."

"I'm better at showing," she stated, finally turning her deep blues on Muldan. She leaned hard against him, nearly falling over. He braced her as they swayed, taking the opportunity to squeeze one of her breasts with his free hand.

More laughter, ugly and suggestive. It seemed about time for me to move in and get her out of there.

"Yeah, you sure are. Show us, honey-bunch," Muldan urged.

"We-eell . . . oka-aay. You stand there."

Muldan took a small step to the side as she indicated,

his own arms spread and ready for her. He was half-turned toward me, eyes and face screwed up with barely restrained mirth. It was interesting how he held unchanged to that expression even after she slammed the bottle against his head. She had a powerful arm. She landed a substantial wallop. And she did it lightning fast. The hollow thump of impact was painful to hear. Everyone winced in sudden sympathy.

Muldan dropped instantly, strings cut, and didn't move. Amazingly, the bottle was unbroken in the girl's hand. With great dignity, she placed it back on the table, then addressed the hushed crowd.

"He said to *show* you," she stated, lifting her chin. She made a small shooing-away gesture with both hands, which cleared her a hasty path in their midst, then strolled off. They eventually closed ranks, staring down at the utterly immobile Muldan. A sharp-featured bearded guy in a brown suit bent to check his pulse. Evidently there was still one to be found. He straightened and rubbed the back of his neck, *tsked*, and blew out a long breath from puffed cheeks.

"Son of a bitch," he said with some awe.

"What do we do with him now?" asked the rotund heckler, genuinely puzzled.

"Leave him. His driver'll put him on his train in the morning."

"You sure?"

"That's what he's paid for."

"But Royce is gonna remember this. He's gonna be plenty mad."

"He won't remember a thing."

"How do you know?"

"Because you didn't when she did it to you."

The heckler thought a moment, then nodded with profound understanding. He and the bearded man dispersed with the others to greener pastures.

Muldan remained solidly inert on the scuffed floor, cigar still in hand. I decided to be kind and plucked it clear before it could burn down to his fingers. I was about to toss it out a nearby open window, but one of the seedier artistic types came up and stopped me.

"That's a real two-bit smoke," he said with no small reproach. "Ya don't wanna waste those."

"I don't?" He was string thin with a young, sly face and the lank white hair of an old man. Half-inch-thick hornrims rode low on his pointed nose. The only thing that kept him from being scary to kids was the benign gaze behind them. Right now it was fixed on the cigar.

"You seen Tony Upshaw or Rita Robillard?" I asked without much hope. I held the nearly whole smoke like a biscuit for an eager puppy. It had about the same effect on this guy.

"Tony?"

"The man in the tux who danced with Ruth Woodring a little while ago."

"Oh, him? Behind the band. Maybe. I think."

Good enough. I gave him the cigar. He was happy.

As no one seemed too worried about Muldan, I moved on. It happened to be toward a fresh knot of party nonsense. This one was a lot noisier owing to its proximity to the music, which had turned fast and furious, all drums and horns. A couple had cut away from the main dance floor and were giving an impromptu exhibition of their own.

The chorus girl in tap shoes I'd seen earlier was being thrown around by a short, muscular boy. Literally. They were in step with each other, but their dance required a lot of acrobatic movement. He swung her one way, pulled her another, lifted her high, then dropped her to the floor to slide between his feet, and swung her up again, her legs in the air and kicking. People on the edge of things applauded and cheered them on to more daring stunts.

A distinct, uninhibited laugh in the din caught my instant notice. Rita Robillard was just on the other side of the circle, whooping her delight at the dancers. She didn't see me at all.

I made a beeline toward her, but had to dodge the chorus girl's flying feet as her partner swung her bodily in a wide turn. He pulled her back again, the momentum curling her around his right side, then with a deft spin, she was curled around on his left. I hadn't seen anything like it since my last visit to a circus, and that act had had a safety net.

Rita still missed spotting me, busy in the process of being helped up onto a table by two red-faced men. She flailed her arms, unsteady for a moment, then got her balance and the rhythm. Encouraged by the approving growls from her helpers, she began tattooing her heels against the wood table while they clapped time for her. Caught up in the music, she squealed like a maniac, going into a kind of rumba step, her eyes shut.

Tonight she wore a long black dress which she grabbed by the skirts and hitched up to show her long legs. We were all treated to a damn good look at her stocking tops and garters and—unless I was really mistaken by a trick of light and shadows—the fact that she had absolutely nothing else on above them. The men by the table had a better view of things. From their pleased leers, I'd gotten it right the first time, no mistake at all.

This time avoiding the dancers, I managed to push my way around into the table group. The blood in my veins might not have been all my own, but it was just as red as the next guy's. Why should those tipsy mugs be the only ones to enjoy the view?

Rita let go her skirts, opened her eyes, and did a couple quick spins on her toes. Her hem flared out. Caught up like the others, I whistled and urged her on. Her face was flushed and eyes too bright. She'd had a snoot full and then some. How she maintained her balance was either drunk's luck or a miracle. The music built up louder as it neared the end of the number. She went back to her rumba, faster, more frenzied.

Then in mid-step, she spotted me.

"You!" she bellowed out, but didn't slow down.

I grinned and waved. Maybe she'd forgotten her talk with Shivvey Coker. She looked happy to see me.

"Catch me!" she screeched. It wasn't a question. Nor was it aimed at the other guys, though they eagerly raised their hands toward her. Most of them were in such a state I wouldn't trust them to catch a cold, and Rita must have been aware of it.

Exactly in beat to the music, exactly at the finish when the drummer banged out his loudest roll and cymbal crash, Rita stamped one last time on the shaking table with her heels, then launched herself at me, arms spread like a high diver.

9

SHE was a big girl. She took a lot of catching.

I braced and had the strength for it, but that wasn't nearly enough. She came in at just the right angle to knock me over and down with bruising, breath-stealing force. I tucked my chin in time to keep from cracking my skull on the wood floor, but that was about all I managed as I was engulfed by heavy armfuls of wriggling, giggling Rita. Before I'd quite figured out the where of things and what to do about them she surprised me again by fastening her red mouth on mine. I got the taste of booze, cigarettes, and tongue, lots of enthusiastic tongue.

It certainly made up for all of the rest.

Around and above us people were egging us on. As it would be ill-mannered to curtail their fun—not to mention mine—I played along, embracing Rita hard and kissing her back. As she responded, I shifted, and quickly rolled on top of her, gaining more cheers. When I pulled back, she was full out laughing, eyes shut, arms splayed and relaxed above her head. Her low neckline was lower than it should have been, her full skirts artfully tangled up in my legs. Had we been alone things might have gotten out of hand in one way or another, so I pulled back farther, retrieved my knocked-off hat, and stood.

"Come on, sweetheart," I said, reaching down. I was smiling, but kept my lips together. My corner teeth were having a reaction all their own to her game.

Back to giggling, she let herself be hauled to her feet, then staggered against me so I had to grab her to keep us from going over again. Evidently it was just what she wanted. "Let's dance, cutie."

"How 'bout I buy you a drink instead?" She'd started sometime back to judge by her condition; one more wouldn't worsen things. No hypnosis for us tonight, but there were other tried-and-true ways to get talk out of a person.

"Just what I was gonna say," she declared. "What-cha waitin' for?"

All the grace she'd displayed tapping her heels on the table seemed to have deserted her, and I had to keep an arm around her waist to hold us on course to the bar. I was conscious of the stares and grins aimed our way, but not concerned about the opinions behind them. My chief worry was over that mirror-covered wall ahead of us. Maybe if I pretended not to notice the odd vacancy that was holding the staggering Rita upright no one else would either.

She slurred out her order, and I threw a tip at the barman. She gulped her drink straight down, using the booze to quench her thirst, which is not the way to treat the stuff, but I had reason to keep her happy. I signed for another, picking up the glass before she could and using it to lead her away.

"Aw, be a sport, I need that," she said, reaching.

"You'll get it, but we need a quiet corner first."

"We do?" Her interest shifted from the glass to me. "So it's like that, huh?"

"It's like whatever you want it to be, sugar."

"Oh, yeah? Then you come right over here—uh—there. Right over there, I mean. This way." She altered course. "Come on, don't be bashful, we're practically engaged, now."

She was pretty insistent, and in too good a mood, so I let her lead rather than argue. Trying to calm her down while she was in this state would only work against me. She'd go contrary and get ugly about it.

We headed toward the front entry, but she veered before reaching it, going through a door marked "office" instead. The small room beyond held a desk and the usual clutter. The walls had framed photos of costumed people frozen in dance poses and brittle posters advertising long-past performances. Rita went through to a narrow hall with doors marked "dressing rooms." She picked the women's and didn't bother turning on the lights as she hauled me in.

A long, wide room, the only light seeped pale through a tall window at the far end. Rita seemed to know her way in what to her must have been very dim conditions. She kept a tight grip on my hand as she took me past a row of partitioned cubicles sporting privacy curtains and mirrors, lots of mirrors. The latter didn't matter in the dark as she wove along toward the back. Beyond the dividing wall I heard the muffled music of the band next door. Except for that, we might as well have been in a wholly separate building for all the contact we had with the party.

"Here—this one," she said. It was the last cubicle, twice as large as the rest with more complete walls and a real door attached to raw lumber uprights, but open to the ceiling. Maybe it was for the star of whatever shows or recitals the dance studio hosted. Within was a chair and a chaise lounge and three mirrors in one corner angled outward.

She gave no reaction to my presence not showing in any of them, so I relaxed. For her it was pitch-dark here. She felt her way forward until she found the lounge, then turned toward me.

"How about that other drink?" Her hand went out. I placed the glass in it, but she only sipped. "You, too." She offered it back. In the dark she also couldn't see me cheating. I raised it to my lips and made the right sounds, then returned it.

"That was quite a performance out there," I said.

"Ha, just wait'll I get my second wind. You ain't seen nothing yet."

From where I'd been standing I'd seen quite a lot already. "Great finish, but next time give me a little more warning."

"Ah, I knew you could take it."

"You figure that out for yourself or was it something Shivvey told you?"

"Shivvey?"

"When you ran off to be so thick with him last night at the Ace. I got lonesome waiting for you to come back."

"Wasn't in the mood, then. You . . . you were talking about—about . . ."

"Lena Ashley."

"Yeah, Lena. That poor kid. You telling me that. Hit me like a truck fulla bricks."

"I'm sorry. You said you were pretty close with her."

"Yeah, that's why I wore black tonight. Outta respect for her. Had a drink to her, too."

Lots of those. "I'm sure she'd appreciate the thought. It might help if you talked about her, you know."

"You don't get it, Sport. It ain't talk with you then or now, it's questions. I hear about my bes' friend getting killed, and you just wanna ask a lotta dumb questions that could get *me* killed."

"Is that what Shivvey told you?"

"He din' tell me nothing."

"What does he know about Lena's death?"

"Nothing."

"Except that it could be dangerous for you to talk to me about Lena."

She squinted mightily. "What?"

"Shivvey. You think he killed Lena?"

Head shake. "No, no, nononono. You stop that."

"He scared you about it."

"No. Shivvey's not—he wouldn't."

"He's got to have a reason to want you quiet. What better reason than if he—"

"He din' do anything to her, so stop saying crazy stuff!" She threw a wide punch at me, not meaning to make a serious slug; it was more like a child trying to fend off a much larger bully. Frustration expressed by an ineffectual fist. I swayed out of range and caught her arm on the backswing. She struggled to get free, but I firmly kept hold, waiting until she stopped fighting. Then she glared at me until that ran down. It's hard to freeze anyone with a look when you can't see them.

I gentled my grip, letting her know that she could relax, and she eventually did. When that happened I raised her arm and kissed the inside of her wrist, taking my time. She didn't expect that and started to pull away, then abruptly changed her mind. She relaxed again, waiting to see what would happen next.

I released her. Made a sigh without too much amusement in it. "Okay, sweetheart. Didn't mean to put you on your hind legs. We'll change the subject."

"Yeah, there's other things we can . . . I mean, jeez, Sport, I din' bring you back here to talk about Shivvey." As proof of this she closed in and snaked an arm around my neck. The heat coming from her blazed against me like an oven. She raised her face; I lowered mine. I didn't help her, but didn't hinder either.

It was a satisfying kiss, if somewhat mechanical. All the right things happened for me and probably for her. You go through the motions, do what you know works, do them long enough, and sooner or later get a result. Its satisfaction is short-lived, but sweet enough for most to live on and think themselves happy. Nothing more than that existed here. I could deliver a reasonable performance of what was required of me, up to a point.

Rita stopped for air, stepped back, and finished her drink. "You're all right."

"So are you."

"You don't know that yet. You think you do, but you don't. An' if you don't put some real stuff into it, you never will."

You can't fool women. Whether they're consciously aware of it or not, whether they admit it to themselves or not, they always know when a man isn't honestly trying with them.

"So what's the holdup?" she asked, cheerfully reasonable. "You got another girl, don't you? That's what it usually is unless you're queer, an' you're not. Well, I'm worth ten of her, Sport. You'd find that out if you gave me half a chance."

"I know I would. But I really need to talk wi—"

"Nix to that, not in the mood for a lotta dumb talk. What the hell, I'll just have to help you along."

"Rita . . ."

"Half a chance, Sport," she murmured. She let the empty glass drop with a clunk on the floor and wrapped both arms around me. "What's the harm in it?"

Her mouth hot on mine, her body pressed to mine, me vividly aware of her lack of underclothes. One kiss really wouldn't hurt.

I justified it as being a way to get to her. Feed her appetite, make her happy, and she'd come around and co-operate. But in the back of my mind I knew it was only a thin excuse for my own appetite. To continue would carry me into a place I'd rather not go. I'd have to keep myself in control or live to regret it.

What I hadn't bargained for was the raw energy surging from her as strongly as when she'd been dancing. When I breathed I couldn't help but take in the mix of provoking scents coming from that big, healthy body. Under the sheen of drying sweat and drink was the detectable musk of her arousal. Heady enough, but add to that the sweet-and-salt temptation of her pounding blood, and I couldn't help but respond in kind. She got the kiss from me she'd been wanting and more as I pressed her back and down on the chaise.

A slower song came through the wall, something with a plaintive horn and sentimental piano. Voices and laughter no more than a foot removed from us also came through. The proximity of so many strangers quite unaware of what we were doing acted like an aphrodisiac.

I didn't think about anything for a while. It was all act and react as we took turns leading in this, the most basic dance of all.

Mouth still on mine, she laughed low and deep within. It was triumph. She'd once again proved to herself that she was desirable. This was how she cheered herself up on the desperate nights when she was alone. A long drink to bring on drowsiness, the phantom heat of past lovings to give her a thin smile, and she could fall asleep contemplating her next conquest, maybe even dare to hope it would be the one that would finally satisfy her.

She wouldn't find it with me, though. She couldn't.

But it was good, all the same, to have her under me, her legs parting and coming up to circle my body. Her dress was in the way, as were my pants. Time enough to remove such details later.

Only I could not allow later to happen.

Easier thought of than accomplished. Especially since things had come this far. Stopping now would baffle and anger her. Not that I'd be in such a happy frame of mind, myself.

Her hands were busy, burrowing between our bodies, working away at my waist, undoing buttons, stroking and kneading through the material. She laughed again, finding more proof of her effect on me.

She couldn't see my teeth. Just as well.

With much difficulty, I made myself slow down the pace, drawing away. She didn't like that and made a pouting sound. She'd probably make more of the same in the next few minutes. I had a lot of fast, smooth, diplomatic talking to do and she would not be in a state to listen.

"We shouldn't be here," I said.

"No one knows, come on."

"It's not that. I want it better for you."

"Honey, this is *fine*."

"No it's not. I want to make it good and make it last all night. We can't do that in this dump."

"But I'm ready *now*."

I drew my lips lightly along her damp brow, down the side of her face, down her throat where the veins pulsed strong and fast, down to between her breasts. "I can make you ready again. I can make what you're feeling now seem like nothing."

"But—"

"You don't know how good I can make it for you, Rita. I gave you half a chance, now it's your turn. Don't you want to find out?" I looked up in time to see her eyes widening at the possibilities. I'd gotten through.

"Yeah, I guess I do."

"Then let's get out of here."

"But couldn't we just . . . just a little?"

"You deserve better."

That made her think again. Would I be the one? That was crazy. But maybe . . . maybe. Why else would I bother? She had to find out. When I saw the decision in her eyes, I got off her, straightening my clothes.

None too soon, I thought, torn between relief and regret and violent physical frustration. It would take a while for my highly stirred-up body to catch up with my mind. I could smell her blood running swiftly under that thin layer of skin, hear the heart driving it. One of us had to leave and walk this off. Fast.

She sat up, smoothing her hair, brushing at wrinkles on her dress. "You better be really good, Sport," she muttered ominously.

"Shh," I said, listening.

"What?"

"We got company. Someone just walked in the office out front."

"Yeah?" The impossibility of my hearing being so acute escaped her. "So what? Let 'em get their own date."

"I'm gonna fade. If they spot you, pretend you're alone. Meet me in the downstairs hall."

"Why so secret?"

"Why not? Adds to the fun." I kissed her hard enough so she'd remember it, then slipped out the door.

I hadn't made the company up. I'd heard voices and footsteps during a lull in the music, and from the sound of things, they didn't belong to another couple seeking a little privacy. As soon as I closed the door, the lights sprang on up and down the long room. The painful brightness made me wince, but it instantly melted to soothing gray as I vanished.

The door behind me opened again almost immediately. Rita would be wincing, too, probably with a puzzled look on her face.

"Hey!" she whispered. "Hey, where'd you go?" She moved past the spot I occupied, walking along the line of dressing stalls. I followed so she could guide me toward the entry. "Come on, no games, dammit."

Another woman's voice cut in. "Rita, *what* are you doing here?" It was Ruth Woodring. "All alone?" She made that sound like an unlikely circumstance.

"I had to fix my garters. My seams got all crooked when I was dancing."

"Leaving the lights off? You can do better than that, dear."

"Where's your friend?" A man speaking now. Tony Upshaw.

"What friend?"

Ruth chuckled. "That tall, dark, bed warmer you dragged back here, of course."

"Jack Fleming," added Upshaw, for clarification.

"What's it to you?" Rita wanted to know.

"Maybe you should think 'what's it to Shivvey?' " he said.

"Lissen, you played fetch for him last night, so don't go doing him or me any more favors. I got my own life to run, and he's not big in it."

"He doesn't want you hanging around that guy."

"Then maybe he shouldn't take a girl to a party and run off on her first thing."

"It's bigger than that, Rita."

"Ah, a lot you know. I'm leaving."

Neither made any effort to stop her. I stayed behind.

As soon as Rita was gone, Ruth filled the silence with a grand sigh. "Well, that wasn't too completely awful. She'd be all right if she'd lay off the booze."

"But she won't." Upshaw was a few yards away and walking fast. Checking the little dressing alcoves for me, apparently.

"Her loss," sniffed Ruth. "Now, what's this about things being bigger than they are?"

"Nothing, just thought I'd scare some sense into her. Shivvey said I should look out for her, keep her out of trouble. That Fleming creep is trouble."

"He's more than that, darling."

"Yeah? What more?"

"Your Mr. Fleming was asking me questions about you."

"What'd he want to know?"

"Oh, I can't remember details, but the core of it has to do with that dead woman in his club. He thinks you're involved with it."

"What?" Upshaw sounded genuinely shocked. "He told you that?"

"Not in so many words, but he gave me the impression that you had something to do with it."

"I didn't have—say, wait a darn minute . . . you're not thinking stuff like that about me, are you?"

"Since you've mixed yourself up with rubbish like Shivvey Coker, I don't know what to think these days."

"Aw, Ruth, you know me better than that."

She made no reply.

"Ruth? Come on, talk to me."

"No, you talk to *me*."

"About what?" Exasperation creeping into his tone.

"Your business with Shivvey."

"There is no business. I just go to the Ace to dance, and sometimes he happens to be there."

"And you do him favors. What kind?"

"Nothing much. Just little things like looking after Rita."

"Why should you be so anxious to please him? What do you get out of it?"

"He's a good man to have for a friend, is all."

"Tony, friends like him you do not need, but you must already know that."

"What do you mean?"

"Because you never used to carry a gun, darling. Before meeting Shivvey, you never had to indulge in such Hollywood dramatics."

"Gun? But I don't—"

"Please, Tony, no fibs. I felt it on you during our dance. I was worried the damn thing would fall out of your trousers and go off like a bad joke."

"It's nothing; don't let it bother you."

"I will if I want to."

"This is a rough town. All the smart guys carry around some kinda protection."

"Tony, you're a much better lover than fighter. Get a little smarter and switch back to carrying French letters for protection instead."

He chuckled. "I got one of those in my pocket, too."

"I'm serious, darling. Men like Shivvey and Fleming are dangerous bastards who chew up people like us without a second thought. We don't matter to them. They don't have friends and never will. You're no one's exception to the rule. You get on their wrong side for one second, and you can end up just like Rita's friend. Are you hearing me?"

"Yeah, I guess."

"Do more than guess, sweetheart. This is your life I'm talking about."

"Nothing's gonna happen to me."

"Then prove it. If you want to dance so much, start going to different clubs."

"Aw, Ruth, you know they charge an arm and a leg to get in. Every night it adds up."

"You know ways around that. Or invite me along some-time. We can do a little jig like tonight's show and collect tips like we used to."

"Come on, you don't need to do that kind of thing any-more. You're above taking such a cheap—"

"I can if it keeps you safe." I sensed her moving closer to him. "Darling Tony, please, listen to me on this." She'd gone soft and serious, almost pleading. She didn't strike me as the sort to do that often, only when it mattered.

"Aw, Ruth . . ."

"Besides, you're such a delicious morsel, I want you around for a long, long time to come." I couldn't hear exactly what happened next, but could imagine her wrap-ping him in a lengthy embrace.

He chuckled again. An intimate sound now, with a note of chagrin in it. Couldn't tell if it was real or not. "Okay. If you wanna put it like that. But no more dancing for tips for you. We got a front to hold up. People might think we're on the skids."

"Haven't you heard? It's become fashionable to be des-titute. I heard Vivian Vandersil say so. She hardly wore any diamonds at all tonight."

"Snooty rich bitch."

"Yes, and may she never lose those twin left feet of hers and graduate, but never mind her." Ruth's voice got lower. "You said you had some French letters?"

"Right here."

"Only one? How pessimistic you've gotten. Or maybe you've used the rest up on other women tonight. You'll be too exhausted for me."

"Honey, I'll show you just how wrong you are . . ."

"Not if that bed warmer is lurking about. I'd rather not have any surprises."

"I checked all over. He's gone."

"Are you sure they both came in here?"

"I was sure. He must have ducked out when I came to get you. I figured you wouldn't like Rita making free with the premises any more than me."

"You're right, darling. The nerve of her, just waltzing in like she owned the place. I reserve that privilege for myself. Legitimately, too. But be a dear and check again on the men's side, won't you? Then do lock the office door. I'm sure no one will miss us for the time being. We can always say we're rehearsing . . ."

What they planned to do next would not convey the sort of information I wanted to know about either of them. Well, maybe about Ruth, but for that sort of thing I'd rather be an active participant than an invisible, eavesdropping presence. Rita would be downstairs impatiently— I hoped—looking for me. I had to keep her happy.

This time using him as a guide, I followed Upshaw as he hastened toward the front and waited for him in the hall while he checked the other dressing area. He was pretty quick about it; I was soon sieving under the office door even as he softly turned the inside catch.

Predicament time. Once all of me was fully on the other side of the door and back in the party I had some obstacles to overcome. I was invisible, stuck in a large room crowded with people, and no matter how drunk some of them were, my sudden appearance in their midst would— to put it mildly—be awkward. Some of the mob element here knew me by sight or by name from all the time I'd spent at the Nightcrawler Club. There were enough rumors and questions floating around town about me. I didn't need to add to them.

But trying to navigate through so many shifting bodies to find the exit, negotiate the stairs down, bumble into the street . . . no, that didn't appeal either. Without sight it was too easy for me to lose my way.

I looked over my last mental picture of the room. From where I floated in front of the office the exit for downstairs was on my right, the mirrored wall was on my left. If I followed along that . . .

Easy enough. I rose high so as not to give a chilling brush to anyone, and drifted along, using the line of distinctively flat surfaces to keep my bearings. I kept the pace slow so as not to confuse up from down. In a way it's like swimming with your eyes shut. All too easy to twist things and end up in the wrong direction when it was time to come up for air. I had no need of air, but it can be a hell of a jolt materializing a few feet above the ground.

"Eek," said a woman. She actually did say "eek." She sounded startled, but not scared. "Look at that!"

"What?" Another woman, sounding bored.

"There! That shadow up there."

"What shadow?"

"There! Moving there!"

"Where?"

"Don't tell me you can't see anything that big."

"Okay, then I won't."

"You *gotta* be able to see! It's right there!"

"Jen, really. How much have you—"

"It's there I say. Look in the *mirror*! You can see it *in the mirror*!"

Oh, shit. I didn't know what the hell was going on; it didn't sound good. I needed to be elsewhere fast, but hesitated, wanting to know more.

"See? It's just hovering there. Like a shadow, but there's nothing to cast it. Oh, that's so strange."

"In the mirror?" Skepticism, unmistakable, thank Houdini.

"Yes!"

"Jeez, Jen, are you gonna go all nuts on us with that occultism again? There are no such things as ghosts."

"Yeah, but there are shadows, and that's what I'm looking at right now. Open your eyes."

"I don't see anything."

"Remember when Madame Arcadia told us about how mirrors can reflect stuff we can't see in this world? That's why we can see ghosts in them, but not when we turn around to look behind us."

"Oh, good God. Jen, there are *no* such—"

"It's my gift! My gift has opened my eyes to it! Madame Arcadia *told* me I was psychic."

"So she could get another buck out of you. For cryin' out loud—"

"Oh! Oh, it's moving!"

Damn right I was moving. Maybe to her I was a ghost, but *I* was the one getting spooked.

"Quick, it's shooting off that way! Follow it!"

Behind me, a lot of noisy commotion went on as the psychic Jen began her hot pursuit of whatever the hell she was seeing of me in the mirrors. She must have been trampling people to judge by the language and outrage springing up in our wake. I nearly veered away from the mirrors to dodge her, but thought better of it. I still needed to follow them. If I had had the time to spare, I'd have stayed on and maybe found a way to talk with her and find out more, but not tonight.

I shot forward until I ran out of smooth surface, slowed, and thus avoided slamming my amorphous form into the far wall. It doesn't hurt, but I didn't want to risk losing my way from the disorientation. There. Now, if I went a little to the right, then one of those big open windows should be just about . . . yes, it was.

Over the sill and hurtle down the side of the building. Had to turn again, as I was going headfirst. Not a pleasant experience, especially because I hate heights. Maybe I couldn't see how far down it was, but I could queasily imagine it.

Finally, a solid, reassuring surface came up to meet me. Sidewalk. Cement. Terra-very happy-firma. No chance of long drops or internal vertigo. I pressed flat against the wall, placing what would become my feet on the ground, and slowly eased back to the rest of the world.

Grayness, then darker patches taking form, coalescing into recognizable shapes. The walk, the lights, the street, lines of parked cars taking on solidity even as I did the same. I kept still and held to a mostly transparent form, making a check for witnesses while remaining fairly un-noticeable. There were people gathered at the front of the building and none pointed my way, all absorbed in their own conversations. I completed the materialization process and gulped a deep breath of exhaust-laced air.

Son of a bitch. I'd gotten away with it. I gave in to a relieved self-congratulatory smile.

Then a brief but saturated weariness stole over me, re-action to the exertions, invisible and physical, and with it came a not-unexpected warning curl of hunger. Rita had awakened a lot of demanding desires within, and they would need to be appeased. Soon. I'd stop at the Stock-yards before the night was out and drink my fill there. That would at least remove the edge of blind need. Though a mediocre substitute for making love, it was safer.

Much, much safer.

And as for the psychic Jen spotting me in the mirrors . . . that was one hell of a discovery. Invisible in them while solid, and the reverse when I wasn't. And not readily apparent to everyone. Maybe there was something in that weird stuff after all. I'd have to toss this one at Escott, hear what he has to say. Hopefully, it would help me get over the stupefaction. But delvings into the world of the weird could wait for another night, though it might have been nice to have gotten Madame Arcadia's number.

I looked up at the second-floor window exactly above and behind. It was that feeling of being watched you sometimes get. Damned if some dark-haired girl wasn't looking down at me. Staring, actually. Mouth open. Lots of white showing in her eyes.

Oh, hell. She must have seen my materialization. Couldn't be helped.

When in doubt, bluff. I smiled and gave her a jaunty wave, wondering if she was Jen the psychic.

"Eek!" she said—and she really did say it, giving me my answer—then recoiled back out of sight so quick that it was as though someone had grabbed her from behind.

I got out of there.

Happily, no one paid any attention to my second entrance to the foyer, not even Rita, but then her back was to me as she peered expectantly up the stairs.

"Let's go," I said, moving in next to her.

She whirled, overbalanced, and caught herself, but I put out a steadying hand. "Hey! Where'd you co—"

I pretended to misunderstand. "Sorry I'm late, had to see a man about a dog. My car's this way." Not giving her time to think, I hustled her along through the artistic crowd. She gave a sputter or two, then subsided.

We couldn't walk too fast, her condition wouldn't allow it, but we eventually got to my Buick, and I loaded her in. She sank gratefully back in the seat with a long sigh and shut her eyes. Not a good omen. That last drink had made a difference after all. I'd have to keep her awake.

Once the car was started I asked for directions to keep her talking. She gave them in a sleepy voice.

I made a turn, a sharp one so she had to rouse a little

to brace for it, then was forced to stop and idle in an empty street waiting for a signal change. She relaxed again. I wanted her awake. "Think anyone'll miss us from the party?"

"Nah."

"They might miss you. You made quite a splash back there with that table show."

"S'nothing. Just did it to keep from being bored. 'Cept for the booze, those things are dull as a country cousin."

The signal went green. I worked the gears and pressed forward. "Why'd you come, then?"

"Shivvey wanted someone to hold up his arm, make him look good. I don't even like that Muldan bird. Stuck-up, overdressed jerk. Always high-hatting a girl. One of these days he's gonna get it right between the eyes from one of us." She'd missed the spectacular decking he'd collected from his diminutive ex-girlfriend.

"Shivvey ran off on you." I made it a statement so she wouldn't ask how I knew. "Not too gentlemanly."

"He's a jerk, too. I got myself all fixed up, too, then soon as we're in the door he leaves me high and dry."

"Why would he do a thing like that?"

"He's a jerk. Thought he knew better than to do that to me."

"Why? You got something on him?"

"Him? Ha! Nobody gets anything on Shivvey; he's too slick. I'm just saying he's usually got more brains than to get on my bad side. See if I go out with him again anytime soon."

"Maybe he thinks he can run you like a train."

"Ha!" She puffed a world of contempt into that one. I'd hit a nerve. She sat up a little and turned to face me. "Lemme tell you, Sport, not nobody—and that includes Mr. Shivvey Coker—tells *me* what to do."

"I believe you." She pointed out another turn, and I took it. "What about Booth Nevis?"

"Him neither."

"You see him a lot."

"Don't get any funny ideas, Sport. That's just business."

I put some cynicism in my tone. "Business? Come on."

"Yeah, business. *Clean* business, so you get your mind outta the gutter. I don't do that sort of thing. Don't have to."

"So, how is business with him?"

She squinted at me a moment, thinking, then shifted to face front again. She stared hard at the windshield. "I don't wanna talk about it. Take a left here."

I took a left. Finding out what sort of deal she had going with Nevis could come later. I'd get it from her or maybe from Tony Upshaw, who seemed to know something about it. "Booth was pretty close to Lena, wasn't he?"

"Again with the damn questions. Lay off for cryin' out loud."

"I have to ask them, Rita."

"Why?"

"Because someone killed your friend."

"What's it to you?"

"It's a mark against my club—"

"Ah, that's crap and you know it. What's the real reason?"

I could give her a song and dance, make up something that would serve, but she'd probably spot the lie.

The truth would not serve either. For then I'd have to tell her about my own slow death. I had come back from that darkness; I had delivered bloody justice to my killers.

But poor Lena, alone and forgotten for so long in her own darkness, no such justice for her.

Until now. Maybe.

10

"Hey, Sport." Rita tapped my arm with the back of her hand. "Come on, ante up."

Because of my own murder, I was all too intimately aware of what Lena Ashley had gone through. The horror, the anger I felt on her behalf were understandable. But of all the people in the world, *I* was in a unique position to give her justice.

Rita tapped again. "Come on. What's your payoff in this?"

"Nothing I can talk about."

"Sure you can. Fork over."

"Just think of me as being an advocate for the dead." Pretentious as hell, but if Escott could call himself a private agent and get away with it, then I could pick a title for myself, too.

"A what?"

"Someone who speaks for people like Lena. Can do something for them. Find and give them the justice they deserve."

She shot me a sideways glance. "You're crazy."

I drove sedately, seeing every detail of the passing streets and none of it registering. "Don't you want somebody to nail the guy who killed Lena? Shouldn't he get what's coming to him?"

"Yeah, but some guys know how to duck out on what they got coming. Whoever did that to Lena would be one of them."

"He can't duck out on me."

"Yeah? What makes you so special?"

I flashed her a quick grin and wink, because it was time to go to work on her, and this was the way to go about it. "You already know that one, sweetheart."

She did, or thought she did, and gave a half smile in agreement, not catching on that my answer was no real answer. "You got a cigarette? I'm dying for a smoke."

I carry a pack mostly for others to borrow from and produced it and some matches. She took both from me and lighted up.

"Talk to me about Lena."

"Oh, jeez. I *told* you—"

"None of it'll come back on you. I promise."

"Yeah, sure it won't, Sport."

"My name's Jack." I had the idea she'd forgotten it.

"Okay . . . Jack," she said, grudgingly. "But I can't talk to you about this." She rolled her window down and blew smoke out onto the city.

"Because you're afraid of Shivvey?"

"Him? He doesn't—"

"The truth, Rita."

Her knee-jerk bravado melted. "He doesn't scare me, but I'd be stupid not to listen when he tells me something. An' last night he told me to keep clear of you."

"So why did you jump off the table at me like you did?"

"Seemed like it would get a laugh, and show him up for

taking off on me, and besides . . . you're cute."

"So are you."

"But I didn't think you'd be sweating me with questions all evening. I want another kind of—"

"All in good time, angel. I'll make up for it with you."

She grumbled something under her breath that sounded like "you'd better."

"Tell me about Lena. Those last days. Never mind about what Shivvey said to do. He's not going to come into this."

"But he—"

"He's nothing, and I won't let him hurt you. You're doing this for Lena's sake."

"But it ain't gonna work. I already tried."

"It will. You'll have help this time. Real help."

Dark narrow look from her as she puffed the cigarette down to nothing. Troubled. Puzzled. Not too many minutes ago she'd been ready to take anything I cared to give her and return it with interest, but this was a different kind of intimacy. She wasn't used to dealing with it. I had to get through to her while there was even a hint of a crack in her armor.

"Wouldn't it be nice not to be alone?" I murmured. I fought down an internal twinge for playing on that particular weakness. It was bald-faced manipulation, but until I could hypnotize her, it was my best way in. "You've been by yourself for a long time, haven't you?"

"I got plenty of friends."

"Not friends like Lena. She was a pretty good egg, wasn't she?"

"Yeah, I guess she was."

"You know she was. Listen to me, Rita. I want you to think back about Lena. Remember how it was for her and for you and having her to pal around with. I bet you two had a lot of fun, lots of parties, shopping, eating at the good places, laughing. Was it like that?"

"Yeah." A very faint whisper. "Those were great times."

"And then some bastard took all the great times away from her, from you. Took away her *life*. All that life she could have had. Someone stole it from her, and they put her through a living hell while they did it."

She made a pushing-away gesture and tossed the cigarette out the window. "I don't wanna hear this."

"You have to. That sadistic bastard walled her up alive and left her to die. It had to have taken days, Rita. Days."

"Stop it. I don't wanna hear." Her hand went to the door handle. She wouldn't use it, but she wanted escape.

"Days of poor Lena shut away in the dark, tied up like an animal, thirsty, hungry, scared out of her mind—"

"Shut up!"

"So thirsty, crying the whole time, her throat on fire, but she's still screaming for help and hearing only silence."

"No!"

"And maybe he'd come by and listen outside to hear how far gone she was. Call through the wall to her to make her say something. And she's behind that cold wall in that awful smothering dark, wondering, hoping, praying he'll change his mind. And she pleads with him, makes bargains, promises, anything that comes into her head if he'll let her live. But he just walks away with a laugh. Then she starts screaming again in the blackness until she's too weak to scream anymore—"

"Stop it!"

"Then one day she doesn't make any noise at all and he walks away for the last time, and *he* has a hell of a laugh about it, and he's been laughing and walking free ever since."

"You're a *shit*! You shut the hell up!"

I let it go. Where all that stuff had come from out of me I didn't know, didn't want to know, but it had the desired effect on her. She was weeping and fighting it,

trying to pull herself clear and failing. I had a clean handkerchief, but didn't offer it. That would have distracted her
from the misery and guilt I'd induced. All the dancing,
boozing, and sex were meant to keep such ugly horrors
and their attendant pain at bay. She needed to feel the full
force of that crushing weight, of that coldness before she
could finally open up.

"You think any of it is right?" I asked, speaking soft.
"Is letting him get away something Lena would have
wanted?"

"No." Thick tears in that one tremulous word. She
swiped hard at her eyes. Snuffled.

"I'm the only person who can give any justice to Lena.
She's overdue."

"What's so special about you? Let the cops—"

"No one's gonna talk to the cops. You know that. But
I can do things they can't."

"Like what?"

"Like talk to you and still keep you out of it."

"But I don't *know* anything. I thought and thought and
asked all over for Lena back then and got nothing. I don't
know—"

"You think you don't, but you do."

"Huh?"

Now I offered the handkerchief. She plucked it away
quick as though I might take it back. I waited until she'd
thoroughly blown her nose and sopped up the tear trails.
Hands shaking, she lighted another cigarette, dragging in
the smoke as though it were oxygen.

"What is it you think I know?" she asked.

"Plenty. You just need to hear the right questions to jog
everything loose."

"Questions." Lots of contempt there.

"The ones to put you in the right frame of mind. All
this time you've been thinking of Lena as just running off

for who knows what reason. Maybe before you only sus-
pected the possibility, wouldn't admit it to yourself, but
now you know for certain she was murdered. That makes
everything different. You're going to remember things.
They didn't matter before, but they'll come to you, and
when they do they will mean something."

She snorted, but didn't argue. I should have asked for
directions again to keep up the pretense of not knowing
her address, but didn't want to interrupt as she thought it
over. She was thinking pretty hard. We passed her building
without her noticing. A block later she told me to turn
around and where to park when we got there.

I had to help her out, keeping a firm grip on her arm.
The ride and the talk had sobered her, but only a little.
She was just starting on the long, unsteady slide down
from the booze. She couldn't slip too soon into the early
stages of the coming hangover, or I wouldn't get anything
useful out of her. Chances were she'd have bottles of re-
inforcements in her flat. I'd have to give her enough to
hold her on the edge, but not so much as to make her pass
out.

She kept a latch key on the molding above her door. It
hardly seemed worth the trouble of locking up—anyone
could have found it. She fumbled the key, then pushed in,
flicking on lights. She mumbled "excuse me," and hurried
off to the back. I returned the key to its place and closed
the door.

The flat was big, but had a shut-in feel, the stale air
hanging close with the scent of her perfume mixed with
long-dead cigarettes. Though the rent must have been
steep, the decor did not reflect it. Bland pale walls, cheap,
ordinary secondhand furniture, a thin layer of dust in the
unused corners of the bare floor. No photos, paintings, or
prints broke up the boxlike monotony. She couldn't have
spent much time here. Scattered bits of cast-off clothing

added a little forlorn homeyness. One of the pieces trailing over a sofa arm was a man's tie. I tried to recall if Coker had been wearing it last night, but couldn't be sure. From the look of things it might have been left here weeks ago.

I heard a toilet flush and running water. She returned some minutes later, having dabbed powder on her nose and combed her frizzy blond hair down. The sharp scent of mint-flavored mouth gargle floated over to me, along with a fresh layer of perfume.

"I just," she began. She shook her head and blinked, losing to the booze for a moment. "I just remembered that we came here for some other reason than to talk about Lena."

Sadly, I was not too surprised by her apparent turn-around. She'd had a lot of unpleasant things to face, and after a moment's consideration wanted no part of them. Her first defense would be a return to something familiar and comforting: booze or a man. Or both.

"Ten minutes," I said. "Let's give her ten minutes."

"There ain't ten minutes of anything I can tell you."

"So we finish that much sooner. You got some stuff to grease the wheels?"

"I'm already greased, Sport." She smiled and gave a slow body undulation to show she wasn't referring to what she'd already imbibed. "Come find out for yourself."

"In ten."

With a resigned grimace, Rita pointed to a cabinet with bottles and glasses crowded on a shelf before a rank of dusty books. I did what I was supposed to do while she fired up another smoke. That done, she arranged herself on the sofa, kicking off her shoes and curling her long legs up. She leaned sideways, one arm over the sofa back. The pose made her neckline dip more than was publicly decent, but we weren't in public now. I made myself look her strictly in the eye as I handed over a glass and did not sit down.

"Come on," she said, patting the cushion.

"In ten."

"Only nine left by now."

I ignored that one. "Tell me about Booth Nevis and Lena. When I gave him the news about her last night he took it pretty hard."

"Oh, he would. They were tight as ticks."

"Must have been more than that."

"Yeah, he was sappy for her. Real love, maybe. She thought so."

"Were there marriage plans?"

"She didn't want any of that. Don't know why. They might have been something if they had hitched up."

"Did she work for him like you do?"

Her gaze slipped away from mine. "I guess so."

"Just what is your job?"

"I help out a little is all. Dance at the club, cheer up the customers when they lose, that sort of thing."

"And that pays enough to get a place like this?" Plain as it was, it was still quite a lot, especially for a girl with no discernible means of support who did not charge for entertaining.

"Yeah, it does. You got eight minutes left."

She was counting too fast. I probably had until she finished her cigarette. "Booth and Lena. They ever fight? Run around on each other?"

"Hey, don't you tell me you think Booth's the one, he—"

I waved her down. "I only want a clear picture of how things were with them."

She sipped her drink, her gaze flicking over me. She licked her lips, making sure I saw her tongue. I smiled and eased down next to her, turning to face close enough to really look her in the eye. My normal kind of forced hypnosis wouldn't work through the booze, but it seemed worthwhile to try something more subtle.

"Booth and Lena," I prompted after a moment's concentration. I didn't see much change in her expression, but there was something, a very tiny flicker of response.

"I said he was sappy for her."

"How did he react to her disappearance?"

"He was pretty tore up. Didn't know what to make of it. He was after me with questions for a long time, calling up all hours wanting to know if she'd come back yet. He thought she threw him over for someone else. He turned over every rock he could find trying to get news of her. He kept it on the quiet, but he covered all the bases."

"Why?"

"He's a funny guy that way. He's pretty tough, but has a soft spot he doesn't like his mugs to see, so he keeps it low. Maybe he should have made a stink, but he didn't. Left that to me. I made a stink, but it didn't do any good. Maybe if *he'd* made a stink, it would have made a difference, but he didn't, so I—"

"Yeah, I get the idea. So he didn't find anything?"

"Not nothin'. A couple months went by, and he just gives up. Knocked the stuffin' outta him, but he hid that, too. Sometimes we'd talk about her. Y'know, looking back on it I think maybe that's when *he* figured someone croaked her, only he didn't tell me. You were right about this remembering stuff, Spor—Jack. A lotta this is coming back to me, an' it looks different."

I nodded. "You think he knew who might have done it?"

"Nah. He'd have told me then because then he'd have scragged the bastard with his bare hands. He probably figured she was gone for good and just gave up. No percentage for him, y'know?"

But the news about Lena had been a bad shock to Nevis.
It could have been guilt. But if not, then he'd harbored
some small kernel of hope that she was alive and might
return. I knew what that felt like. "So he was sappy for
her. How'd she feel toward him?"

"She liked him better than the other mugs."

"Who were they?"

"Just guys hanging around the club. Nobody in particular." She stubbed out the cigarette.

"What about Tony Upshaw?"

"He wasn't there much back then, but he'd dance with
her. He danced with all the girls if they wanted it. Mostly
he was with that partner of his, Ruth. She didn't have him
on any leash, but he knew the butter for his bread came
from her. She gave him that half interest in the dance studio, y'know. You wanna know how he earned it?"

"I've an idea how already." I ran a light hand up the
length of Rita's arm, looking at her the whole time. She
took a deeper breath than normal and gooseflesh budded
on her skin. Very good. "Did Tony do more than dance
with Lena?"

"He was too smart for that. They didn't advertise it, but
everyone knew she was pretty much Booth's girl and to
keep away. 'Cept Shivvey. He was always trying to get
her attention."

"But back then he was working for Booth's rival. He
wouldn't be welcome at the Flying Ace."

"Nah, but Shivvey would run into us at the bookies' or
the track, or he'd turn up at other clubs. Always flirting
with her. He thought she was one juicy pippin an' wanted
to pluck her but good, but she didn't see him the same
way. Because he worked for Welsh, she thought he might
try using her to get at Booth. We used to laugh about it."

"You still laugh at him?"

"Why should I? It was Lena's joke and old news. Welsh

is dead, and Shivvey's working for Booth and friends with me now. A good friend—when he's not being a jerk," she added, her voice sharpening briefly.

"You think Lena might have led Shivvey on a bit? Maybe as a way to help Booth? Then if Shivvey figured her out—"

"Ah, Shivvey wouldn't do something like that to her. Too much trouble. He'd just pop her—right here"—Rita pointed a finger at her temple like a gun barrel—"and walk away. Then fix it so he wouldn't get caught. But he'd have to have a damn good reason to do it. He really liked her."

"But if he got fed up with her turning him down all the time he might have been pissed enough to do something special about her. He might also have had some other reason to make her vanish. Maybe so he could go to work for Booth?"

She snorted. "That's cute. So cute you should put lace pants on it."

She was right, but then I was only tossing out stuff to see what happened. I had more trust in Rita's immediate reactions than her words. She was telling the truth so far as she knew it. She was also showing a definite reaction to my touch and the way I was focused on her. Her expression was much softer, her heartbeat a little faster. I continued to concentrate, holding her gaze.

"What about Tony Upshaw? How deep is he in Shivvey's pocket?"

"He's not. They don't pay him for anything. He just hangs around him and Booth to look tough. He likes to think he can be one of the tough guys, but he just doesn't have what it takes. You know what I mean? But you— you got it."

"I do?"

"Oh, yeah, it's all over you, honey. Yer a lil' skinny, but you got the real kind of tough. Inside. The real kind.

But Tony? If he worked his brain as good as his feet, he'd
have figured out what was missing by now and keep clear
of mugs like Shivvey."

More focus, more light caresses. It was taking longer,
and my hold was cobweb thin, but I could sense a change
within her, a relaxation that had not been there before.

"How did Shivvey take her disappearance?"

She frowned mightily. "I'm not sure. I remember him
asking after her with me, and making a long face when I
said she was gone. He asked where, and thought I was
pulling his leg when I said I didn't know. Me and Booth
had our heads together a lot about it and didn't pay much
attention. Jeez, I wish I could remember better."

"You don't think Booth did it? That he could have been
jealous of Shivvey or another man?"

"He's gotta soft spot."

"That doesn't mean anything, especially if a man thinks
his girl's running around on him . . . was she? Shivvey said
as much to me last night."

"Ah, he was just shoveling you a lot of bull."

"He said she was friendly to most any man she could
hit up for a loan."

Rita bristled, and I felt my hold wavering. "That's a
dirty lie. We had our fun, but she stuck with Booth."

"And the stuff about loans?"

"She only needed to ask Booth. He gave her whatever
she wanted if she came up short. He never did that with
me."

"You sure there weren't any other men?"

"No . . . I don't think so."

I'd worked up her arm and now touched the side of her
face with the backs of my fingers. Her skin was very soft.
"You were roommates."

"Yeah . . ." She sighed it out, looking dreamy.

Too much distraction. I broke off eye contact and let

my hand slip down to rest lightly on her shoulder. That helped. "You were roommates," I repeated. "You had to know what she was doing."

"We weren't tied to each other. She maybe *coulda* had someone on the sly that I coulda missed. I donno for sure, but I don't think so. Wouldn't make sense to mess up the sweet spot she had with Booth, would it?"

"Maybe not, but still—"

"I donno. She was a lotta laughs, but she didn't talk much about herself. Knew how to keep a shut mouth. Never said where she came from, who her people were. Wasn't my business, anyway."

"Who else was in Lena's circle at the time?"

Rita faltered out a few names, but none were familiar to me. Those people had long dropped from circulation or moved elsewhere. I got her talking past the ten-minute limit until she went in a circle and started repeating things. Time to try a different angle.

I caught her eye again, holding for a long time until I was fairly sure I had her. "Tell me the truth, Rita. Did you kill Lena?"

She was under enough not to become angered. Instead, she looked very sad, very tired. "No, I didn't."

"Who do you think did?"

"I donno."

Okay, it was done. I had to ask. For the first time since I'd started working on her my head suddenly hurt. The soft sell was a lot less wear and tear, but still took some effort. I pulled back on the concentration and woke her free of it with another question. "You think you'd like to come to Lena's memorial service?"

She blinked some more, fighting a drowsiness that had nothing to do with my influence. "A service?"

I explained what had been planned.

"What a decent thing to do. Mighty, mighty decent.

Yeah, I think I should go to that. Poor Lena, poor, poor kid." She took a big gulp from her glass and hiccuped once.

"Should it be a priest, preacher, or rabbi?"

"Jeez, I don't know. Preacher, I guess. She once told me she thought the Catholic churches were real pretty compared to the others. Made me think she wasn't used to 'em. She never went to church, though."

Telling Rita the when and where wouldn't do any good now, so I found a discarded bill envelope and wrote everything down on the back, leaving the note on a clear space atop the liquor cabinet. The task reminded me of something else I had to check. "You got any of Lena's papers left?"

"Papers?" Rita finished her drink. She was looking too sleepy to last much longer.

"Old letters, birth certificate, insurance—legal stuff."

"She never kept junk like that."

"Driver's license, a passport?"

"Too much bother for her, she said. She'd take a bus or cab or ride around with Booth."

Interesting. "Sounds pretty odd. She must have had some kind of business papers, a bankbook, something."

"Nah, nothing like that. After the crash she didn't hold much with banks."

"How did she write checks for her bills?"

"She paid cash. Me too. Keeps it simple."

"Booth Nevis pays you in cash?"

"Best way to do it."

And cash transactions are near-impossible to trace. "What is it he pays for? What is it you really do for him?"

She hesitated. I repeated the question. She smirked and wagged a playful finger at me, having apparently forgotten the story she'd already given. "None a' yer beeswax."

All right. So the influence I was trying to exert had

limits. She would cooperate only where she wanted. "Did she leave anything behind? Anything at all?"

"I had to sell or hock most of it to make the rent. It was tough times for a while back then. Booth gimme a raise when he foun' out. He looks after you."

A raise or a payoff? Not something I could ask her. Another time, when I could force things. "What about the stuff of Lena's you couldn't sell?"

"I got a box of some of her things inna closet. S'nothing much."

"Show me."

"It's inna bedroom." She drew out the last word in a little girl voice, almost singing it.

"Good. Show me."

She woke up a bit, smiling, but I had to help her off the couch and keep her steady as she walked. She seemed not to notice and held on to me, humming contentedly.

The bedroom was much like the living room, just more mess with discarded clothes. Under white lace curtains she'd tacked a sheet of black oilcloth over the window. The window faced east, and the glare of the rising sun coming in would have kept her from sleeping off a late night.

Her closet looked like an explosion. She wearily knelt and dug through more clothing that had fallen off hangers, tossing aside a dozen or so shoes before finally pulling out a smashed-in shoe box.

"I think this is it. Yeah, here, but make it quick, sugar."

Stale dust smell. Inside more dust and a few paltry oddments: a knot of cheap jewelry, much of it turning color, some old track tickets, a few mismatched keys, a broken watch, and a small amber vial about two inches long. It rattled when I shook it. I took out the cork and spilled the contents into my palm. They were four tiny irregular shapes, the color of ivory and oddly familiar.

"What the hell are these?" I asked.

Rita squinted at them. Turned one over using the tip of her nail. "Teeth," she pronounced.

"Teeth? What kind of teeth?"

"Baby teeth," she said.

"What's she doing with baby teeth?"

"They must be hers. I got some of mine in one of my jewel boxes."

It was grotesque. "Why would she be keeping her baby teeth? Why do you, for that matter?"

She shrugged. "I donno. Just did. Like hanging on to an old doll. No harm in it. Jeez, lookit how eensie they are . . ."

Not wanting to touch a dead woman's baby teeth, I slipped them back in the vial and returned it to the box. There were faint scribbles on the track tickets in light pencil. Numbers that might have stood for dollar amounts. "I want to take all this with me. I'll give it back when I'm done."

"Sure, Sport, nothing there worth squat." She put her hand out and I helped lift her. "Are you done now? You said you were gonna make things better than the best for me. Was that a lot of hooey or are you finally gonna do something?"

In answer, I put the box on a table and pulled her in for a strong kiss.

I shut off the part of my mind that had to do with dead Lena. I shut off the part that had to do with my hunger. God help me, I was even able to shut off the part that had to do with Bobbi. I was like a machine, with a machine's efficiency. I went through the right motions and got the right reactions . . . and this time Rita didn't catch on.

It was different from our dressing room encounter. Then I'd been caught up in the lust of the moment, giving in and shunting aside the many sane reasons to stop things before they went too far. Though I'd eventually called a halt, it hadn't been easy. I didn't like putting myself through such hoops. Rankling to me, demeaning to the woman. Everyone loses.

But this time I was very much in control, knew exactly what needed to be done, and proceeded to do it.

She eventually had to fight to come up for air. She looked startled, but pleased, then stepped backwards, smiling and drawing me toward her bed. I let her take me, let her sit, bent to kiss her, got kissed back, but she had a lot less energy now, was sleepy, more passive. I worked slowly on her, getting her even more relaxed. I rolled her onto her stomach and undid the dress, exposing the pale flesh of her back, running my hands over its smoothness, kneading, keeping the pressure gentle and constant. She rewarded me with a soft, happy sigh.

"You weren't kidding me, were you, Jack?" she murmured. "More. There. I like that."

She wriggled and turned over again, squinting against the bright overhead light we'd left on. I lay next to her, my face close to hers.

"I want you to listen to me, Rita," I whispered. "Look at me and listen." Booze or not clouding her brain, I had her full attention and that was the real core of it. I couldn't forcibly hypnotize her in the usual way, but this was the next best thing. My suggestions would work so long as I kept them in line with her strongest desires. "Do you hear me? Hear my voice?"

She hummed a yes.

"Look at me."

She made an effort, trying to keep her lids up. I caressed the side of her face and whispered some more, a lot more.

And after a time she slipped into sleep, breathing deeply of the dreams I gave her.

* * *

I sat alone on the living room sofa, the crushed shoe box with Lena's pitiful effects next to me and the radio on, the dial paused on some kind of slow-paced symphony. The old longhair stuff doesn't usually appeal to me, but for the time being it was fine for my present thoughtful mood.

Rita would say nothing of our encounter. I'd made certain of that. She'd have no specifics to recall, only remember its sweetness with no regrets that it would never happen again.

When it came down to it, I *liked* Rita. I really had wanted to do right by her . . . so far as I was willing and so much as was necessary to make it work for her. There was a line I wasn't prepared to cross, and it had to do with Bobbi. I *loved* her, and I would respect that for as long as we were together.

But Rita . . .

She put up a tough front for a reason. I didn't know what it might be, but beneath its brittle protection lay a terrible vulnerability that reminded me of Norrie Malone. A hurt child who's forgotten the cause of the hurt though the scars are visible to those who know where to look. The boozing and men and furious dancing and constant parties helped Rita to keep the demons of her past at bay. It was something I could understand. That was how I knew exactly what to say to her.

Eyes shut, I pushed air around my mostly dormant lungs as though I was a normal, living man. I remembered what that was like in occasional vivid flashes, remembered what it felt to have a beating heart or to sweat in the noon sun heat or to taste a cold beer. Such moments came rarely as time distanced me from what I'd been, but no regrets there, either. Not anymore. If a genie from a lamp suddenly appeared and said he could wish me back to ordinary life again, I'd have turned him down. What I had now for life, with all its shortcomings, consequences, and future sor-

rows was better than what I'd had before when I walked
in the day.

The proof of it lay behind me, asleep in that bland bedroom with the blacked-out window. She would sleep long
and well and soundly. I could never have accomplished
that as an ordinary guy. When she awoke, she would be
happy, even if she did not understand why. It was the last
suggestion I'd given her at the end, the only gift I could
give her that was of any worth. She didn't need another
notch in her bedpost; she needed peace in her soul.

Maybe I couldn't impart it permanently, but at least
she'd know what it was like and perhaps find it again herself for well and good.

Or so I hoped.

Exhaling one last time, I shifted gears in my head, stood,
and looked around. Reflections aside, there was more to
do, and I wouldn't have been worth beans to the Escott
Agency if I didn't know how to take the place apart while
the opportunity was available.

I started with the bedroom, working methodically, keeping it quiet. Not that there was much danger of waking
Rita anytime soon, but why take chances?

Since the mess in the closet was such that she wouldn't
notice my invasion, I started there. The clothes were, so
far as I could compare to what Bobbi wore, expensive.
There were lots of them, enough for Rita to treat most like
she'd gotten them at a dime-store sale. I found plenty of
shoes, shoe boxes, dust, and lint, but nothing else looking
like souvenirs of her late roommate. The hatboxes on the
top shelves contained hats, forgotten bits of jewelry, none
of it worth anything.

Her dresser had the usual froth and the real jewels, so I
knew where she'd invested most of her earnings from Nevis. The stuff was carelessly thrown into a red lacquer box
with the cheaper costume pieces. Lying loose at the bottom

in a velvet-lined corner were a couple of irregularly shaped objects: the baby teeth she'd mentioned keeping. Damn weird things to have around, but I suppose to some people they'd be a tangible link to the past, like holding on to old photographs.

I went through the bath, then the living room, then the kitchen. Nothing unusual except that she obviously didn't eat home a lot. There were more bottles of beer and booze than anything else.

Her intellectual life was pretty thin. The only reading matter lying around was comprised of magazines about film stars and their beauty secrets. Lots of pictures. I checked the books that were neatly lined up in the liquor cabinet behind the bottles. None of the titles were familiar to me, and the few I cracked open all proved to be love stories. No interesting notes dropped from the riffled pages, only a five-year-old track ticket stuck halfway through one. Probably a bookmark.

Rita had said she didn't have time to read, and since they were mostly hidden by bottles, she wasn't using them to decorate the place. I checked the publishing date of one I had in hand, which was 1933. I checked the rest. They all either bore that date or that of the previous year. So . . . these had likely belonged to Lena. Rita now used their cabinet to store her booze, the books overlooked and forgotten in the back.

They were too cheap to hock or sell. The glue holding the end papers had long dried out. One of the older-looking volumes crackled, and pages separated from the spine as I tried to shove it back into place. The glue coming away made it all loose. The more I pushed the more it fell apart. I tried to put it together, and discovered something had been inserted between the end papers and the front cover that prevented it from properly closing flat.

Opening it up, I found the something to be ten one-hundred-dollar bills secreted between the end paper and the front cover.

The back cover and its end paper held identical treasure.

Holy moley.

Keeping control of the tremor that was trying to make me drop things, I knelt and removed all the books, piling them on the floor. For most, the glue was intact, for others it had dried out too much to hold. So far as I could tell by peeling those open enough to count, each book carried two grand in circulated nonsequential C-notes. The dates on them were no earlier than five years ago.

Twenty-six books. Fifty-two thousand dollars.

Where in *hell* had Lena gotten this kind of cash?

11

GREAT care had been taken in the hiding of it. A slight wrinkling on the edges indicated that the end papers had been steamed to loosen them. Perhaps she'd used a butter knife to pry them open enough to slip in the bills. Exactly twenty were in each book, front and back, a nice round number, but not so much as to distort the spines. If the glue hadn't failed on the one, I'd have missed them all.

So, apparently, had Rita. I couldn't imagine her leaving such a treasure trove lying unused for five years, especially if she'd been hocking stuff to make the rent after Lena's disappearance. Unless this was the hock money. And I was the king of Sweden. Nope, I'd found what had to be Lena's very private and not so little nest egg. Rita should have tried reading more in her free time. Quite a rewarding thing, reading.

As for what I would do with it . . .

That could wait until I had thoroughly studied the situation. Twice now I'd helped myself to mob money that had come my way, confident that no one would make much of a fuss over its disappearance. I wouldn't mind adding more to my side of Escott's cellar safe, but wasn't that greedy. This pile really should go to Lena's family.

If she had any. It was a good bet that she'd not been born Lena Ashley. Perhaps, like Malone, she'd served time and had tried to put it behind her. The reasons why anyone wants a name change are countless, and few are the result of anything pleasant.

When Escott got back he could start sniffing on her trail if I or the cops came up dry in the next few days. Compared to retrieving kidnapped pooches it was far more worthy of his talents.

Should there be no family . . . well, conscience dictated that I let Rita know about the cash, what with her being Lena's only friend.

Undisturbed for so long, it seemed safe enough to leave it here for the time being, but I decided against that. The cops would come around for a visit sooner or later, and they might take it into their heads to make a real job of searching. I got a flat knife from the kitchen, another shoe box from the bedroom closet, and went to work peeling back all the end papers. In a surprisingly short time I had all the money out and the books back in place on the shelf with the booze bottles in front as before. I set two books aside, arranging the rest to fill in the gap. There was a slim chance that Lieutenant Blair might be able to find some of Lena's fingerprints embedded in the dried glue, which could lead him to her real name. He would not know about the money, though.

Dusting off my knees, I went to look in on Rita. She hadn't moved a muscle since dropping off. I'd tucked her up snug and demure under the covers; many times I'd done the same for Bobbi when she was especially tired. Thinking about her under the present circumstances gave me no noticeable twinge of guilt. In fact, it was rather reassuring.

Rita was a hell of a gal, but Bobbi was the one I wanted to be with. Always.

I made sure the note about the memorial service was still in place. Since my suggestions would keep Rita from talking about tonight's adventure, I had no qualms about seeing her again even if Bobbi was around. I did debate on whether to add more to the note, like a little personal compliment telling her that she was a hell of a gal, which took all of a second to decide against. Never leave behind anything that could be misinterpreted.

Or interpreted for that matter.

To be thorough, I went through the flat one more time, checking all the out-of-the-way spots I'd skipped before, being too busy with the more obvious ones. Good that I did, too. When I tipped her floor model radio to see if anything might be under it something shifted inside. The protective backing was loose. I opened it more, peering into the dim interior. Shoved into the narrow space between the cabinet and the works, standing on edge a bare inch from the nearest glowing tube, was a slim gray accounts book.

It was about a third the usual size, making it easy to hide. Its ruled pages were divided up by neatly written-out dates, the earliest beginning in 1930. Next to the dates were numbers that could only be for dollar amounts. Some days had long lists of numbers, others only a few, and some were altogether skipped. Various shades of ink were used, but not in a way to indicate coding so much as different pens. All dealt with odd sums of cash and substantial amounts of it, sometimes thousands at a time. I identified the outgo column and the income, the latter being slightly less by an average of ten percent.

Off to the side, in a separate column, were what might have been small amounts of cash. No decimals or dollar signs confirmed this, though. The numbers were round, the most frequently occurring one being twenty. Sometimes fifty or one hundred would pop up, but only when there was an especially large chunk of cash involved. These appeared on each and every transaction. A few initials were listed, identifying either places or people. I picked out a set as belonging to one of the larger betting parlors. Only one name was set down: Booth Nevis, and that was at the front of the book.

There was a break in May of 1933. When the record resumed again in July of that year, a different handwriting had taken over the task. The separate column of round numbers was blank. I made a rough total of what had been listed up to that point.

Wow.

Things suddenly fit into place. I knew where Lena's fortune had come from, maybe who killed her, and why.

For all the money packed inside, the shoe box felt remarkably light. I held it and the one with Lena's effects close, slipped under the flat's entry, then rode the elevator down. The one quick parlor trick didn't take that much out of me, but sieving through all those floors would. The hunger was creeping up to take hold as it always did. No escaping it, but easily remedied.

My watch showed just past midnight. I needed to drop this stuff at Lady Crymsyn before going on to the Flying Ace to see Booth Nevis. No telling how long that interview would take, but I wanted it all finished so I could stop at the Stockyards and still be in time to get Bobbi home. My excuse to see Nevis would be to tell him about the memorial service, and once started, I'd get more from him about his real relationship with Lena. Depending how cooperative he was, I'd be able to confirm what I thought she and Rita really did to earn their keep.

I'd returned the accounts book to the radio. The post-

1933 numbers matched up with the jagged uneven writing in Rita's address book, indicating she'd taken over keeping the records for the last five years. The two-month gap told me about when she'd come across the book, figured out the system, and decided to continue with it. I had a whole fresh batch of questions ready, but there'd be no waking her until tomorrow. She didn't know it, but we had a date for right after the service for some more serious talking.

Unless I got everything from Nevis first.

If I was right about him, getting another migraine from me would be the least of his worries.

Lady Crymsyn was as I'd left her, with no lurking reporters and the lobby dark. But as I unlocked and walked through the front doors, the bar light snapped on right in front of me.

And, yes, I jumped. Anyone would have done the same. I damn near dropped the shoe box of cash. My dormant heart tried to leap up my throat, then got stuck there. Nasty feeling, that. No spit to swallow it down again, either.

"Son of a bitch—*stop that!*" The words just popped out of me, propelled by sudden anger. I didn't know who the hell I was yelling at. No one yelled back. No prankster popped out to laugh. Nothing.

The place was absolutely silent. Just me, a faint background whisper from the city outside, and that goddamned light coming on for no reason whatsoever.

So . . . I gave in to it. The idea of a ghost being in the place, that is.

None of us are that far from the cave, so I didn't feel particularly foolish over the lapse. It jittered around my gut for a very short tight moment, the time it took for the scare to wear off and my thinking brain to get back in the saddle again. This would turn out to be an electrical or hardware problem, nothing more. Leon would eventually find and fix it, then I could stop feeling like a fool.

I wasn't sure I even believed in ghosts; being a vampire didn't mean I automatically swallowed all supernatural stuff whole. If ghosts existed, then they weren't the sort of thing that happened to me; they were someone else's problem, like the psychic girl back at the party. If she could see me in a mirror while I was invisible, maybe she saw ghosts, too. She'd be just the type to do so.

If there were such things.

Right now I didn't want to believe in them at all, because if they were real, then I might have one in my club, and I didn't want anything to do with it. Not for one second. They couldn't be real. Not here, anyway.

Though that *could* explain the light going on and off.

And that shot glass of whiskey on the old coaster.

And a couple of things Leon had hinted about.

No. It was stupid. Completely stupid. That's what I thought as I stood frozen just inside the entry staring at the black marble bar with its bright chrome, the clean glass shelves behind, and their patterns of shadows rising toward the high ceiling.

No. Such. Things.

Really.

So I steeled myself, then strode purposefully across the lobby to the master switch. It was with grim resolve that I skeptically turned on every light in the joint.

No, none of us are that far from the cave at all.

I didn't bother investigating again. The toggle would just be up in the ordinary way. Grumbling, I shook off my heebie-jeebies as best I could and passed into the main room, cutting over its expanse to the bar on the far side. Under my instructions, Leon had installed a padlock to the door that gave access to the dead area under the tiered seating. I liked Escott's idea about turning a corner of it into a second sanctuary for myself; only when that time came I'd fix it to lock up from the inside.

Ducking through, I carried the box with all the cash to the most distant darkest corner, hunching down toward the last to keep from banging my head. None of the workers would be likely to intrude this far in; Leon had better things for them to do. I left the box on the dusty floor shoved behind some supporting framework and gladly vacated the area.

Just as I clicked the padlock home, all the lights went out.

Damnation.

I didn't jump quite so much, but felt a quick sympathy for all those times when I'd startled Escott by appearing out of nowhere. Not so funny now.

"Okay, you've made your point," I called, not sure why. "So cut it out."

I did not expect to hear a reply. A man's voice, grunting something that sounded like, "Huh? Whazzat?"

Hackles rippled high on the back of my neck for an instant. A small, sick laugh escaped me.

The lights came on again.

I'd taken a breath and didn't know it. Released it slowly.

Heard other voices. Relaxed slightly as belated recognition—not to mention relief—kicked in as I hurried toward the front. When I reached the curtained entry I could discern them well enough. No ghost, just six very solid, unpleasant men standing uninvited in my lobby.

The one by the front doors was Shivvey Coker. Two others I knew from last night. They were the same mugs I'd slammed around the alley for beating on Malone. Both looked colorfully the worse for wear after my tender ministrations, but still in shape to try for another bout. The remaining four men seemed to be out of the same tough mold. Between the seven of us this part of the club was getting full of suits and shoulders.

"Fleming," said Coker. His bland face was fixed for

poker-playing, eyes blank, but his posture tense. His right hand was in his coat pocket, and the set of his arm and shoulder indicated he was probably holding a gun. I could feel a tickling just in the center of my gut where he'd have the muzzle pointed.

"Guilty as charged," I said. "What's this about? And what's with playing with the lights?"

"Lights?" said the larger of the battered mugs.

I decided I should ignore that. It was pretty obvious to me that this gang followed my car from Rita's flat; I'd not been watching for tails then. Why had he brought along so many friends? Better for me that I talk fast and not make any sudden moves. "C'mon, the club's not open yet. I was just on my way out. Let's go over to the Ace, where I can buy you a beer."

"Huh," said Coker, unmoved. "Think you're funny?"

I looked at him, then down at his pocket, and gave him a neutral smile. "Don't know what your beef is, Shivvey, but shooting me will only ruin two perfectly good coats."

"Then I'll save mine." He took the gun out, a flat little .22 semiauto, lethal with a steady hand and eye behind it, something to pay attention to, but otherwise not a serious weapon to the mob boys. Its advantages were easy concealment and not a lot of noise. Now that the gun was visible, two of his men—the ones I'd clobbered—casually took up posts on either side of me, not close, but close enough. The rest ranged themselves around us.

"What's the problem?" I asked, less worried by the gun or the bouncers than the damage they could do to my place.

"You've been busy," Coker stated.

"I have?" I didn't think he was talking about the transformation of the club since he'd last been in five years ago.

"Rita."

"What about her?"

"You left the party together."

No one should have noticed us especially, but maybe he'd seen her flying leap from the table onto me and come to a conclusion. "She had a little too much of the firewater. Thought I should get her home."

His eyes were blank no longer. Fascinated, I watched the change as his control slipped and fell away. The hot rage blazing in them would melt a battleship. "Yeah, you went there, then came here. What happened in between?"

"Nothing."

"You can't tell me that when her warpaint's all over your face."

Damn. Not being able to use a mirror when cleaning up was a decided disadvantage. "Nothing happened."

"Gris." Coker nodded to the larger of the two. They were both nearly my height, each packing a good forty more pounds of muscle. They acted like they thought they had the advantage. Gris moved in close on my left, but kept his hands to himself. His slightly shorter buddy came up on my right, grinning. He was enjoying this far too much to judge by the wheezing giggles he wasn't holding in. The other men shifted on their feet, indicating they were also ready for some fun and games, Chicago style.

I kept on facing their boss, thinking he must be out of his mind. He was well aware that I'd been given a hands-off from Gordy. Coker had mentioned it himself only the other night. All I could figure was that he liked Rita a hell of a lot more than he'd let on, or maybe he was one of those jealous types.

"Listen, Shivvey, I'll admit I tried some, but she was too drunk. Passed out on me. I don't like 'em when they're passed out." I put disgust in my tone, hoping that would be enough to at least shield Rita from repercussions. Didn't look like I'd be so lucky.

"Maybe you don't like women at all, punk," put in Gris. "Seems to me you were pretty hot for that faggot last night."

"Seems to me you weren't in any condition to notice after I put your face into the bricks."

Gris decided I deserved a gut punch for that one. He didn't hold back. The force of it doubled me over, and that was about all the harm it did. After a three count, I deliberately straightened. No gasping for lost breath, no retching. I fixed him with what I hoped was a cool, hard stare.

Baffled anger from Gris in response.

"He thinks he's tough," said his grinning buddy, who hadn't caught on. "Give 'im another."

Coker stepped forward. "Not yet." He was sharp, but not sharp enough, being too focused in on what he expected to see rather than what was actually happening. Gordy certainly wouldn't have overlooked my lack of reaction to the abuse. That didn't make Coker any less dangerous, just more difficult.

I frowned at him. "You got a beef with me, Shivvey, then let's talk, but lose the hired help. They don't impress."

"We'll talk. They stay."

"Whatever makes you feel safe."

The boys almost made something of that, but Coker signed for them to back down again. They were big dogs on string-thin leashes. I'd have to watch my mouth, or this could go on all night. It could even get painful. He nodded at a table and some chairs off in a corner. "Sit."

Not much I could do to get rid of them without busting the place up. Coker and I walked over and sat at the same time, his crew following. He rested his gun on the tabletop, his hand loosely holding it, a visible dare. I spared it one unworried glimpse and concentrated on him. Rage still burned in his eyes. Too much for me to get through. I pulled back. Time enough for that later. I checked the faces of the other men, all bouncers from the Flying Ace. Why weren't they at their jobs?

"You're not here just about Rita," I said. Gris and his bruised friend were behind me, doing a good job of looming in a threatening manner. "So what is it?"

"Nevis."

"What about him?"

"Cops took him in about that dead broad. Raided the Ace. You're behind it."

Okay, that's why they were here. Out of work for the evening. Shook my head. "Not me."

"You been digging too much. I told you to lay off."

"Give the cops some credit for brains. They backtracked Lena to her old boss. Nothing surprising about that."

"Rita tell you?"

"She was too drunk, but there were plenty of people at the party who talked."

"Who?"

"Doesn't matter. Use your head, Shivvey, I got better things to do than get in bad with my landlord. Nothing's going to come of it, anyway. They'll sweat him a little, he'll make a payoff somewhere, and he's back running the Ace by tomorrow. Next they'll talk to Rita, and then they talk to you. Got a good story ready for them? Hope it's better than the one you fed me."

Coker showed some teeth; it wasn't a smile. "You son of a—you think *I* killed Lena."

"If not you, then who else? Maybe you had a bad case of unrequited love and decided to wall her up for it."

His face went a mottled red, and his eyes blazed hotter, but his voice was oddly quiet when he finally spoke. "Gris."

Gris stepped in, and he had plenty of help. Three others moved at the same time, their tombstone mitts coming down hard on my shoulders and arms to hold me in place.

In reflex, I started to struggle, but quelled it. Now wasn't the right time.

While the rest kept me still, Gris firmly caught up my right arm, grabbed my index and middle fingers and folded them hard the wrong way. I winced at the double crack they made, my hand bucking from his grasp as though stung. The men braced for me to try fighting; I stayed put. When it was clear I wasn't going to move, they pulled away. Gris eyed me, waiting and ready for an answering challenge.

I calmly checked my wrecked hand. My fingers were at an unnatural angle and hurt like hell. Ugly to see and feel, but nothing to get panicked about. Without a lot of hurry, I held my hand up so Coker and the rest had a good view of things, then popped the fingers back into place. They made a dull cracking sound. There was more pain, briefly, the kind that told me I was already healing.

I flexed my fingers, made a fist, and opened it. I looked across at Coker, and said, "Ow."

That jolted him. He seemed fairly flabbergasted. Mouth sagging, the heat gone from his glare. Almost funny.

Similar reaction from a few of the others. One of them in the back muttered, "I *told* you about this guy."

Before Coker's shock could wear off I did a fast move of my own and, quick as a snake, took away his gun. Left-handed. His yelp galvanized his men, but I jabbed the muzzle right between Coker's eyes. He froze, arms out from his body, palms down, caught halfway between lunge and placation. Everyone else froze as well.

"Shivvey," I said, giving him a steady stare, "this is the night you learn not to annoy me."

"Boss . . ." began Gris.

"Shuddup," Coker snapped. His face was dead white. God knows what he saw in mine as I glared down the length of my arm at him.

All the anger he had that would have blocked me was gone, but there was no need to hypnotize him. I had his full attention. "First, lemme tell you what annoys me, Shivvey. You and your goons coming in here is at the top of the list. Trying to push me around is right next to it, along with not believing me when I give you a straight story. Those are the only ones you need to remember because you're not going to repeat 'em again. You got any of that?"

Some sweat forming on his brows. "You goddamn punk. Think I'll let you—"

I poked the muzzle hard enough against his forehead to make him blink. "I asked if you got that."

He gave out with one nearly imperceptible nod, hating me.

"Good. Now, I'm gonna tell you again, and this time believe it. I did not sleep with Rita. I did not turn Nevis in to the cops. Clear?"

Another small nod. Lots more hate.

Time to ease off. I did so, but kept the gun centered.

Disgust from him now as he lowered his arms, probably because I'd not shot him. He certainly would have shot me. The idea of it made him brave. "You think you got the world by the tail, don't you?"

"A piece of it," I admitted.

"Lemme tell you something, punk. I seen your kind come and go. You may think you've got it all with Gordy looking after you, but that ain't gonna last forever."

I canted my head. "You see Gordy around here? You think I run crying to him every time some bozo pokes his head in the door and makes scary faces? Look around, Shivvey. Look at me." Made another fist with my right hand. The pain was mostly gone. Opened it, then snapped my fingers a few times just to show I could and rapped a tattoo on the table. "I may be a punk kid to you, but you know I can take care of myself. Don't give me a reason to start breaking *your* fingers."

He wasn't in a mood to take in what his eyes were telling him. "I oughta—"

"Yeah, I know how it goes. I break your fingers, then you'll come back and break my leg. But I'd just get up and use it to kick your ass. There's no need for any of this. The fact is that we just had a pissing contest, and you lost. Accept it gracefully while I'm still in a good mood. We both gotta live in this town, and neither of us should have to be looking over his shoulder for the other."

A moment of him breathing hard, hating me some more, then a small change in his eyes. It was enough. Not that it would last. He'd had to back down from me in front of his men; he would not let that go unanswered for long, but I'd worry about it later.

"As long as you're here, we might as well settle some other things."

"What things?" he asked, after a moment.

I eased off with the gun. Gris and the rest looked to him for orders. Coker shook his head. We were all back to being nearly civilized again. Nearly. I still kept the gun in hand on the table and wondered how many of them were also heeled. "Give us some room, boys. We gotta talk."

No one moved until Coker showed them the nod. They reluctantly pulled away a few paces, but Gris stayed behind. Hard to tell if it was out of loyalty to his boss or because he hated me, too. I'd have to stay out of the Flying Ace in the future.

"This is private stuff Shiv. You sure you wanna share?"

He barely glanced at Gris. "He can stay. You got the gun, I got him."

And what a sweet couple they made. "All right."

"What private stuff? Punk."

I kept my voice low, the tone casual. "For instance, how

many other laundry girls besides Rita has Nevis got on the payroll?"

No reaction from him right away. That alone told me a lot. "Laundry girls?"

"For his club. Nevis has to wash all that gambling cash coming into the Ace. There's too much to lay off as legit income from selling booze. What better than for girls like Rita and Lena and others to take it to the track for him? Bet often, on sure things they've been told about, and use only cash. The bookies are in on the game, fix the numbers right, take their percentage. The girls come back with what looks like winnings, collect their pay for the service, and Nevis stays in jake with the tax man."

"He knows way too much, Shiv," said Gris.

"Don't give me that," I drawled. "Everyone in town is onto this, including the cops Nevis pays off so he can keep operating." Somewhat of an exaggeration, but believable to insiders like Coker, who only dealt with others of his kind.

He didn't want to give me any points, though. "Rita shot her mouth off too much."

"She didn't tell me squat. Anybody with half a brain can figure out what's going on." So I'd nailed it right. That book I'd found had indeed been a record of all of Lena's gambling transactions for Booth Nevis. It was similar to one I kept myself, only mine fit on a single sheet of paper and was better hidden. "Rita's a pretty useful gal to have around. I bet she runs a lot more errands for Nevis than that pip-squeak Upshaw does for the both of you."

"I'm gonna kill that big-mouth broad—"

"She never said a word. She likes her cushy spot with Nevis and kept shut to hold on to it. But the guest list for Muldan's party was something else again. I talked to plenty of people, and they talked back. The difference be-tween them and Rita was they actually had something to tell me. And more than just about this scam."

"Like what?"

"Like Lena Ashley and Nevis being so tight. He was off the deep end for her—and she didn't run around with everyone borrowing dough like you claimed. What was your angle feeding me that line? Were you trying to protect your job? If you thought it'd take Nevis off the suspect list, think again."

"What list? Who the hell are you to be doing cop work, anyway?"

"I'm the guy whose club she turned up dead in. Don't know about you, but I don't like that sort of thing, especially when it's a woman. If I can serve the killer up to the cops with gravy on the side, I will. If it turns out to be Nevis, then you might have a good shot at taking over his spot. You ever think that over?"

I'd hit a nerve to judge by how fast he shut down his face. He was back to playing poker again, but just a little too late. Since he made no immediate reply, it meant he was not only thinking hard, but unworried about Gris passing this kind of dynamite on to Nevis. My guess was that Coker had hired on this bunch himself, and they were loyal to him, not Nevis.

"What makes you think the boss did her in?" Coker finally asked.

"Just an idea of mine. I've got no proof. He was crazy for her, though. What if she was running around on him after all? He'd have a reason to be sore enough to kill her and to kill her just that way. Now, I know you wanted her, but it don't figure that she threw him over for you . . . or Nevis would have killed you, as well."

Another hit; his eyelids flickered. "How do you figure that?"

"Because of the way Lena died. A couple of minutes walled up in that hole, and she'd confess her life story with all the names. She'd have talked her head off for the hope of Nevis digging her out again. If that's what happened, and you weren't on her dance card, then he had no reason to kill you. You remember anyone else disappearing about that time? No? Well, no matter."

"You're full of it."

"Maybe. I could be wrong. Lemme try another story. You had the hots for her, she doesn't give you the time of day, then you're the one sore enough to kill. But Nevis doesn't find out, of course, or he'd have never hired you on after Welsh Lennet got croaked."

"Now, wait a minute . . ."

I spread my hands. "I'm just throwing out the same stuff the cops'll be thinking when they start sniffing around your leg. You gotta be ready for it. For my money I think they'll try to hang it on Nevis, whether he did it or not. They always favor the boyfriend first. Once they start closing on him they won't miss out on the rest of the works. They can bring in the Treasury boys, track down all the laundry ladies, and within a week the Flying Ace is shot down for good."

He threw a look to his men that told me a lot.

"But . . . there's a way out of that."

He didn't want to ask, but I had him hooked too well. "Yeah?"

I leaned back. "You turn Nevis in as Lena's killer."

Coker's reactions were more subtle than before, but he was interested.

"It's like this," I said. "The cops got no proof, but if you happen to repeat something Nevis mumbled to you one night when he got drunk and maudlin about Lena . . . doesn't matter whether it ever happened, you just repeat it. I'm sure you can find a few people who were around back then to say how crazy he was for her and let the cops do the rest."

He thought it through, then shook his head. "You got some nerve, but it'd never work. No DA is gonna take a chance on that one or on me. I'm not framing the boss, there's no percentage. If I tried, they'd still shut his place down. And if you go to the cops with that load of bullshit, then I'll make sure you won't live to see the morning."

I chuckled, but he didn't know why. "It's good to see a man with so much loyalty, but if they can't get Nevis, they'll be eyeballing you, the spurned would-be lover. Think Nevis will stick his neck out to cover you if he even *begins* to think you're the one who killed her?"

"But I didn't—" He bit off the rest, staring at me with a kind of surprise that made him very vulnerable. That's when I focused on him full force, holding his gaze, hoping he'd not had anything much to drink that would interfere.

Not a cakewalk. He winced, fighting something he didn't understand, had no preparation for, and the silence stretched between us. His heartbeat shot up, and his breath came shallow. Then he abruptly stopped struggling and that dead look came into his eyes.

"Tell me about Nevis and Lena. Did he find out what she was doing with his winnings?"

"What?"

"The winnings—did Nevis find out she was skimming off the top?"

"Skim . . . ?"

Gris shifted closer. "Shivvey?"

"Answer me." A sharp pinching between my eyes made it hard to keep control. "You have to answer."

Coker made a small noise in the back of his throat.

I felt the same way. This hurt. "Answer me."

Something heavy smacked into the side of my skull, making lights flash behind my eyes. When the lights faded, Coker had come back to himself, looking surprised to see me on the floor. I was surprised myself. Didn't know I was that lost in the concentration. The men quickly moved in; someone slammed a foot down to hold my arm while another took the gun away.

"You take chances," Coker said to Gris, who'd apparently been responsible.

"He was doing something to you."

"Doing what?"

He faltered. "Just . . . something. Don't you know?"

"Know what?"

"You gotta re—" Gris cut it, stared down at me, spooked. "What'd you do to him?"

"Do what?" Coker demanded.

Out of his element, Gris shook his head, and backed off a pace. "You saw," he said to the others.

"Saw what?" Coker. Voice rising.

I had to work hard not to grin and didn't quite manage. That was enough for Gris, who instantly stooped, grabbed handfuls of my second-best suit, and hauled me up.

"What ya want us to do with him, boss?"

I motioned toward the still-open front doors. "Gentlemen, it's been great having you over, but it's late and I have to be—"

"Shuddup, punk," said Coker, realizing he was back in charge again. "Gris, teach him about not annoying *me*."

It was just exactly what Gris and the rest were waiting for.

The next few fast dirty seconds were a confusion of fists, gouging fingers, kicks, and curses, with me getting most of it because I really didn't want to kill anyone. Too hard explaining the bodies to the cops. I could take what the mugs were dishing, pick my opening when it came, and use it. There was no reason to make it easy, though. Whenever I threw a fist or foot I connected; they were packed close and in each other's way. When I connected, it made a satisfying thump and cleared things, but only for an instant. Another body would move in. Five at once and all after the same target was a bit much even for me.

Then a general surge took place as three of them organized enough to lift and carry me backwards. I was strong, but they had momentum on their side as they slammed me hard into the marble-topped bar.

My spine cracked against it, and it hurt. Hurt bad. Right up through my skull kind of hurt. I grunted, my legs going to water. Slithered down, but the goons grabbed me up again, lifting bodily. Managed to wrest one arm free and make a swing that was little more than a wave. No strength in it for some reason.

They put some fancy spin in it and flipped me clean over, a high, forceful somersault with a very messy upside-down landing. I slammed back-first into the thick glass shelving behind the bar.

The stuff broke away from the walls as I dropped in a graceless sprawl on the hard tiles. The shelves landed heavily around and on top of me, shattering with a tremendous noise. Something banged against my neck with unexpected force. Too late I tried to cover my head; I was moving half a step behind everything.

A warm flood from my throat, almost familiar. Too much, too fast. This was wrong.

A ferocious burning along my skin there. All wrong, but what . . . ?

Abrupt haze before my eyes. Light-headed. Sick.

Bloodsmell.

Then I understood. Tried to do something to stop it and to hell with who saw.

The haze became more pronounced . . . but too slowly. It should have been faster. I should have vanished.

Weakness washed over me instead. My hand came up, clamping over the wound to stop the flow. The haze never quite turned to soothing, healing gray. I lay utterly still, not daring to move for fear of making it worse.

Heard them above me. Talking.

"Jeez, lookit the mess."

"Boss, I think you better see."

Pause, then Coker's voice. "Right, leave him."

"You sure?"

"We're cuttin' outta here. Now."

Deep within me, a thin dark voice wailed at the unfairness of it.

12

HEARD the hasty shuffle of departure. The slam of doors. Brief echo throughout the building. Silence, until their car rumbled to life and took them away, then silence again.

No movement from me. None. Didn't dare. Kept the pressure hard on my neck and prayed it would work. The broad rip under my palm burned. Couldn't tell if that was good or not. Wanted to vanish. Bleeding too severe.

Back hurt. Hurt a lot. Terrified it might be broken. If so, then there wasn't a damn thing I could do to help myself.

Wouldn't matter if I bled to death first.

Shied away from the panic. Needed to wait it through. The wound would knit up, everything would heal, but the blood loss would interfere, make it take longer. To mark time I counted to a thousand. Or tried. Had to start over and over. Couldn't keep track of the numbers. Pain distracted. And hunger. Hollow inside. God, I was hungry. Waves of it marched through my battered body.

Blood everywhere. Pooling. Smell of it . . . dizzying, maddening.

Corner teeth were out. Nothing to use them on.

Small move. I could risk that much. Just—just a small one.

Shifted. Carefully. My face against the floor. Wet. Blood there, lots of it. I had to take some of it back. No time to be particular.

Pressed my mouth to the hard tiles. Taste of salt. Grit. Sharp things like fish bones. That would be the broken glass. No matter.

Impossible to take in the quantity I needed, but I couldn't stop myself. Lapped it like a dog, spit glass when I found it, and damned Coker to hell and gone.

No good. I needed much more than this. Had to get up. Had to feed.

Cautiously lifted my hand from the wound. No fresh flow. Hopeful. Felt the damage. Found a spongy, irregular furrow in the flesh, very tender and raw. What was left of a deep gash. Long one, too. Seemed to go halfway around my throat. Fleeting thought about Malone's kid, Norrie, then back to my own troubles.

Arm movement dislodged shards of glass. Pieces dropped away. Destructive tinkling music as they hit the stained tiles.

Tried to move my legs. Couldn't tell if they responded or not. The fire in my back suddenly hotted up. Left off and went still again. Had more healing to do.

Very tired. Wanted sleep, but not until dawn, not for hours yet.

Chance of passing out, though. Even a small loss of blood put me in a bad way. If I gave in to it . . . no, that could not be allowed to happen. Once gone I'd not wake again until tomorrow night, if I was lucky. Though safe enough here from the sun, the last thing I needed was Leon

Kell and his crew coming in and finding me like this in the morning. To him I'd look dead. Then it'd be cops, newspapers, radio flashes about another spectacular murder at Lady Crymsyn . . . no, that just could *not* be allowed to happen at all.

Damn Shivvey Coker to hell and gone. Again. Several times again.

Anger for him helped keep me from drifting off. Several plans—none of them even remotely pleasant—of what to do when I caught up with him helped as well. The same went for his goons. I could get very creative when the mood was on me.

Wincing, I moved my arms enough to find out if they would work. They did, but not too well. Felt like a half-squashed bug. Still able to move, but not very coordinated about it. Weak.

After a bit I managed to lift from the spread of broken glass and blood and push clear of it. Arms only. Legs like anchors. My back sparked a hellish protest; ignored it. Pushed, then dragged along. Two yards of progress, then I had to stop and not do anything. The pain crashed in, blinding. An awful fluttering inside warned me I was about to vomit. When I held still it went away.

Rested and thought longingly about vanishing. Before trying again I had to get fresh blood and lots of it, and right now the Stockyards were too far away.

Only option, though. I needed help to get there. Escott out of town, Bobbi probably still onstage and not readily reachable. So was Shoe Coldfield. I wasn't sure if he'd even be at his club. Couldn't afford to leave a message and hope he'd get it before I was too far gone.

Gordy, perhaps? Not that I ran crying to him all the time, but this was an emergency. I didn't want him involved, but he was a friend who knew about me, who knew everything. And he was always at the Nightcrawler.

All I had to do was call him. The phone was upstairs, though. The public one had been installed in the lobby booth, but I didn't know if it'd been hooked up yet.

I spent what seemed like hours inching across the floor, my back screaming every second. Had to go slow. Whenever that fluttering swooped on me I stopped. The frequency increased; the rest periods lengthened. Could not allow myself to get frustrated over the delay, to waste what little strength I had. By the time I made it to the booth I was shuddering uncontrollably from the strain, and praying again, asking that the phone would work. My alternative would be trying the stairs to the office. In the shape I was in, I'd never make it.

Long rest, then crawled into the booth, reached up. Knocked the receiver clear. Damn. Needed a nickel.

More rest, then huge effort to haul up into the seat. Dizziness hit like a brick. Damn near fell out again. Fluttering. Sick. I braced. Falling down at this point would finish me. Waited until it passed.

Found change. Shaking like a drunk. Barely got a nickel into the slot. The dial tone came on. Thank God, the phone company, and Leon Kell for getting things done.

Was very careful about the numbers. No desire to get the wrong one.

Ringing. After a few rings I began counting. After twelve I was losing hope. Someone was *always* in the Nightcrawler office to catch the phone. Maybe I'd misdialed. I could have called a closed business or—

" 'Lo?" Gordy's voice.

Vast relief. Found it hard to speak.

" 'Lo? Who is it?"

" 'S Jack."

"Can't hear you. Who is this?"

I put more breath behind it. "It's Jack. I need help."

"Where?" From his tone I had his undivided attention.

I never asked for help. Not unless it was life or death.

"My club. Come over. Alone."

"You got company?"

Didn't understand the question for a second. Then I figured out he was worried about walking into an ambush. "Had company. Did me over. Gone now, but I'm hurt."

"How can you be hurt?" Sudden doubt in his voice. From personal experience, he was certain that I was indestructible.

"I lost blood. Lost a lot."

"How?"

"Make it fast, Gordy. Please."

"On my way." He hung up.

How long for him to tell one of his people he'd be going out, get to his car, drive across town . . . how long? I wanted him here yesterday.

Not fair, wailed that thin voice again. I told it to shut up.

I wedged into the corner of the booth for the wait. It would be too humiliating for Gordy to walk in and find me on the floor.

Nasty mess there. Long smears marked my progress. I'd have to clean it up before Leon came in. If I got through the night.

Pain knifed up my spine. Nothing new there. Shifted to ease it. A whole new knife dug into me. This time the sharpness ripped along my limbs like an electrical shock. I cursed and groaned. Felt sweat popping. The cold kind. Sick-making sweat. Wiped my brow. My hand came away bloody. Couldn't afford to lose more. Licked it clean. Was that desperate. Hunger hurting worse than my back.

The bar light went off.

I groaned again. Of all the lousy times . . .

On again.

Grimaced toward the bar.

Off.

On.

About a five-second interval in between.

"Okay," I whispered. "Have your fun. I don't give a shit anymore."

Longer pause with the light on. Then off. *All* of them. Every damn light in the place went off.

One-two-three-four-five—

On. All of them. For the count of five, then off.

From my angle I could see the toggles for the main switch. They were all moving at the same time. By themselves. If that wasn't the damnedest thing.

Began to laugh. It made more pain, but I couldn't help myself. The situation was just too ludicrous.

They were on when Gordy pushed through the door, moving like a mountain shook loose from the rest of the range. He had a .45 in his big fist and swung it with surprising speed to cover the lobby. He spotted me, but did not come immediately forward.

This time the lights stayed on. I waited, but the toggles stopped flipping. Damn, but that was weird.

"Fleming?" He was looking around, puzzled as well. "What's the problem?"

"Short in the wires," I muttered.

"We alone?" he asked.

"Yeah."

He grunted acceptance, then hurried over, holstered his gun, and peered in. I could imagine what was before him: drying blood masked my face, clothes soaked with it, the stink of desperation. His usual phlegmatic expression was quite gone. He was worried, and that scared me. "You shot?"

"Cut. Back's messed up, too."

"How bad?"

"Bad. Can't walk."

"You look like hell."

"Feel worse."

"What do you need?"

"Gotta get to Stockyards. Hungry."

"Hungry?"

"Need to put the blood back. Fast."

"Who did it?" He reached in so I could take his arm.

"Shivvey, his boys. They—oh, *shit*!"

When he tried to pull me out everything snapped loose then and there.

Falling sensation, flames shooting up behind my eyes, and a jagged floor in the pit when I hit bottom. Next thing I knew I was looking at a drunkenly spinning ceiling. No need to breathe, but was gasping all the same. It felt like someone was gouging through my back with a white-hot drill bit. A dull one.

Gordy's face came into view. "Jeez kid, you need a doctor."

"Can't."

"You're not gonna make it to the Stockyards."

"Got to."

"And what when you get there? You can't go climbing fences like this."

"What, then?"

"You gotta hang on. Lemme make a call. Can you hang on?"

I didn't have much of a choice. "Yeah."

He bobbed out of view, and I heard him work the phone. Don't know who he called, the name went by too fast, and then he launched into a kind of spoken shorthand that I couldn't follow. I heard "blood" and the address of the club and for them to hurry. He hung up and came over.

"I'm having some brought in," he said, looking relieved

in a tight-faced sort of way. "What can I do? You want water, a blanket?"

"I'm okay."

"No, you're not, kid. What can I do?"

His version of anxious concern really touched me. "Nothing."

"Want I should get Bobbi?"

Shook my head. She did not need to see me like this. "Later. Time?"

" 'Bout one-thirty."

Only that? Pain does things to one's perception. Thought it'd been hours since Coker's invasion. Days.

Was suddenly aware of Gordy's heartbeat. The blood-smell coming from him. It came right through his skin at me. Teasing, taunting.

Oblivious, Gordy followed my smeared trail to check behind the bar. "Hell of a mess here."

No. This man was trying to save my life. I was not traveling that road again. *No.*

He returned. Squatted next to me. Too close. Weak as I was, I could still reach and grasp. The hunger would make it possible.

"Can you talk?" he asked. "What happened?"

I could make myself talk, a little, in fits and starts. Not easy, but any diversion to keep me from thinking about my back. Or anything else. I gave him a short version of Coker's visit, naming names.

"Shivvey went too far," Gordy said when he had the basics.

"Yeah. But my problem." I knew he'd be thinking about reprisals.

"We'll talk about it later."

"No," I whispered. "He's mine."

Gordy seemed to want to argue the point, but finally nodded. "Okay. But I get to watch."

"See what I can arrange."

"How you doing?"

"Same." It was a lie. I was cold, getting colder. Even the drill bit in my spine was icing up.

He must have seen through the lie. "They'll be here soon." He put a hand briefly to my shoulder—from him an incredibly rare gesture of reassurance—then rose and went to the doors, opening them. Warm city air wafted over me.

Waiting. Not something I liked. Less so under these circumstances. Good to have company, though. Helped, not being alone, but I kept picking up the heavy scent of Gordy's blood. He had more than enough life in his veins. Enough to share. To keep me alive. If he came close again . . .

But I could hold off a little longer. A little.

Cold. So damned *cold*.

Footsteps. Gordy crossing the room. Checking the light switches. He turned most of them off. Looked down at me. "They seem okay now. When I drove up the joint was blinking like Christmas. Thought it was you trying to signal for help. A short, you said? Looked more like an SOS."

Maybe that's what it had been. What a helpful ghost it was to be sure. No strength left in me to smile.

"Fleming?"

"Mm?"

"Keep your eyes open."

"Try."

"Do it."

He *was* worried. Forced my lids up. Wanted to ask, just *ask* if he could roll up his sleeve. Better if he wasn't struggling. Just bring his wrist down so I could . . . "Talk to me. How's business?"

Gordy wasn't much for idle chat, being more of a listener. He made an effort, though, filling me in on the do-

ings at the Nightcrawler. I needed the inanity. It might
keep the darkness away. The temptation.

This week the club's show was some kind of Paris revue
with a can-can line. It'd been specially written for his girlfriend, Adelle Taylor, the radio actress. She was a fair
singer, could dance well, and had a good turn for comedy.

Wanted to move, to get out of my body. Escape the
tearing hunger. "Adelle's having a great time. Customers
can tell, too. They like that," he said.

I could get him to come close again. It wouldn't be hard.
Once he was within grasp . . .

"Papers saying good stuff about her. About the club.
An' I didn't even have to pay 'em for it."

But I'd only take what I needed to survive. No more.
Apologize later.

"Likes the applause."

Or make him forget everything. I'd be able to do that.
No need to apologize if he had no memory.

"Really makes her happy," he concluded.

He'd fight me. He might win. Had to take that chance.
Had to live. He'd understand. Maybe. Didn't matter. I was
past having a choice. The hunger wouldn't wait any
longer. "Gordy?"

Canted his head. "Just a sec."

He went to the front. I heard a car motor. Did the mental
equivalent of holding my breath. Let it out when he returned with a small crate. Muffled clinking noises came
from within. He set the crate down next to me and wasted
no time pulling out a medical-type bottle and removing the
seal.

Bloodsmell. The scent of damnation and death, redemp-
tion and life.

I reached toward him. He fitted the bottle into my hands.
My fingers closed convulsively. Pulled it to my lips with
unexpected strength.

Couldn't stop. I drained the stuff away like a drunk on his last binge. Emptied it in seconds. Gordy quickly opened another for me. Then another.

"Jeez," I heard him say.

Human blood. More than I'd ever had at one time before.

Even cold and long separated from its donor, it was glorious. My chill faded, changing to living heat gusting through me. I felt life and strength and the needle sharp focus of nerve returning. An almost painful tingle encompassed my throat. Had to pause until it passed. When it was gone, I made myself sit up. Was able to do so now. Dived into the crate on my own. Fingers were clumsy, but I got the cap off and gulped another pint.

Odd expression on Gordy's face. Never saw that one before. He was a tough guy, but to watch what I was doing would make anyone sick.

"Why don't you go get a smoke?" I suggested.

He made a small nod. "Maybe. How much of this you gonna need? They only had eight pints on hand."

"All of it."

"You gonna need more?"

"Let you know."

He backed slowly away and stood by the doors. He put a cigarette in his mouth but forgot to light it.

He would have fought me. That much was obvious now that the hunger-driven insanity was clearing from my brain. He'd have fought and lost. I'd have snapped his neck to hold him in place, and if that hadn't killed him . . .

I drank every drop from every bottle, then lay down again to savor a massive bout of profound relief. For everything. Waited. Felt the healing taking hold. Restoring, rebuilding. When instinct said it was time, at long last time, I vanished.

Almost as good as the blood.

Release. No pain, no gravity, no barriers; I was awareness and thought freed from the bondage of a frail body. Just me floating, savoring.

Don't know how long I hung there in the gentle gray nothing. Gordy's voice jolted me out of it. He didn't sound happy.

"Fleming? Where the hell are you?"

I melted back, standing. Still covered with my own blood, slightly wobbly, but on both feet once more. Gordy took his unlit cigarette from his mouth and gave me a long stare. He'd seen my vanishings, so it must have been the sudden restoration surprising him.

"That's . . . pretty goddamned amazing," he said. "Thought you broke your back."

"I think I did, too."

"And this fixed it, just like that?" He motioned toward the crate.

"Pretty much."

"How?"

Spread my hands. "I don't know. It works, and I'm glad it does."

"Doesn't that bother your eyes?"

My whites always flushed deep red after feeding. A disturbing sight. "No, they're fine."

Now he lighted his smoke, watching me. I still felt shaky inside, but it was more mental than physical. All the same, I walked slow as I went around the room, testing, stretching, making sure everything was indeed working. The agony in my back was gone, as though I'd never been injured at all. My flesh all knitted up, better than new. Easy to understand Gordy's view on this; I was pretty amazed myself.

Looked at the damage behind the bar. The glass shelves were so much deadly junk. Couldn't tell which of the shards had laid open my throat, not that I really had to know. I wanted to leave the mess for Leon to deal with, but it would be too much trouble trying to explain about the blood. Cleanup could come later, though; I had other things on my mind.

"Where'd you get this?" I asked, motioning toward the crate.

"A doctor friend. He patches people up when I ask and keeps his mouth shut about it."

"Didn't he wonder why you wanted all the blood?"

"He's paid not to be curious. What now?"

I glanced at him. An unlikely friend who had just saved my life. And nearly lost his own. "Now . . . I think it's my turn to buy *you* a drink."

He took us to my house so I could change and phone Bobbi. I made no mention of what had happened, just apologized for not being able to drive her home tonight. She commented that I sounded funny, but I told her I was in a hurry to get somewhere. I didn't like lying to her, but it seemed the best thing to do for the time being. Tomorrow I might be able to let her in on certain dark realities, but not now. I was still dealing with them myself.

I hung up from the kitchen wall phone and went through the dining room to the parlor. Along the way I got some bottles from Escott's liquor cabinet and a glass, taking them in to Gordy, who was using up most of the couch. He wasn't quite as pale as before, but still seemed in need of a restorative.

"What do you favor?" I asked, putting everything on the coffee table in front of him.

"Don't matter. A triple. Neat."

Escott only ever stocked the good stuff, but I was sure he wouldn't mind. I picked Scotch and poured generously. It would take a minute or five to work on Gordy; I went upstairs and peeled out of my thoroughly ruined second-best suit. A quick rinse and toweling got the blood off me. I pulled on clothes and returned to my guest.

Gordy's color had now fully returned, along with his usual deadpan face. That was a relief to see.

"Thanks," I said, sitting across from him.

He knew what I was talking about. "No problem. Why'd you let it happen in the first place?"

"I didn't 'let it,' things rolled at me too fast. I was trying to be careful with them, not cripple or kill anyone, then they hit me with the bar. After that I couldn't do very damn much for myself."

"I seen you take a lot of punishment and come back for more."

Since Gordy had been the one dishing it out, he knew what he was talking about. "Yeah, but I guess a busted back is enough to slow even me down. Not to mention a cut throat."

"Guess so. Probably should avoid those from now on."

"I'll keep that in mind."

He'd worked halfway through his triple and put it down. "Shivvey thinks you're dead, y'know."

"I know. I been mulling it over and honestly don't believe he meant things to go that far. He wanted me roughed up, not dead."

"You defending him?"

"No, just that I see he lost his common sense along with his temper. He was wound like a clock thinking I'd been with Rita. In his right mind he'd have known better than to risk annoying you."

"Too late for that. Even if he'd only roughed you up, I'd have still been annoyed. I give an order in this town it should be respected. If it ain't respected, then I gotta do something about it."

"But I'm dead to him, not roughed up. He knows you'd have no way of finding who'd killed me."

"Not right away," he admitted. "But I got a lot of sources. If you'd been scragged and stayed scragged, I'd have used 'em. Sooner or later one of 'em would have come through. One of his boys would talk. I know 'em. He picked a bunch like himself; they hire on for the money, especially Gris. Flash enough green under their noses, and I'd get all I need about what they done to you. Shivvey'd know that, and he's gonna take off before then. Might be halfway to Havana by now."

"Maybe not. I got a good reason for him to stay in town. You heard about the cops taking Nevis in for questioning?"

"I heard. They raided the Ace from rafters to basement tonight. Took it apart down to the carpet tacks."

And Gordy wondered why I didn't want gambling at Lady Crymsyn. "I thought it'd just been closed."

"Closed but busted apart. It'll take weeks for Nevis to put it back together. Maybe never if the DA pins your Jane Poe murder on him."

"Okay," I said. "Try this on: Shivvey's boss is busy with the cops, so he uses it as a legitimate excuse to pay his goons to get lost indefinitely. Nothing for them to do with the club closed, after all. Besides, they'll want to get away after what they think they did to me tonight. They know you'll be sore with them. Once his boys have disappeared he won't have to worry about you questioning or bribing them to talk. He's gonna feel pretty safe since there's not much to connect me to him so far as you'd be concerned."

"He'd be stupid to stay."

"His coming to my club in the first place was stupid. Anyway, he's got a reason."

"Which is?"

"I think Shivvey's got his eye on running the Ace himself. During our talk I hit home on him with that one. With Nevis out of his way, the Ace is up for grabs. Even busted apart he can fix it back quick enough to being a hell of a moneymaker."

Gordy digested that one with a frown. "He might just try it."

"You've met him, haven't you? Does he strike you as being a shark when the odds are in his favor?"

Gordy nodded.

"So where will Shivvey be tonight? He'll have thought all this through by now and be moving his men out already. My guess is they'll be eager to go."

"Gimme a minute. I'll make some calls." He heaved off the couch and went to the kitchen.

I resisted the urge to follow. There was no need, anyway, since I could hear him well enough. I leaned wearily back in my overstuffed chair, put my feet on the coffee table, and wished I could finish off the drink he'd left.

The blood I'd taken in had saved my life, healing everything, but though it could give me the same kind of initial jolt as the Scotch, the soporific aftermath wasn't there. At times like this, while the tremors of a narrowly missed mortality were still quivering under my skin, I really regretted not being able to get thoroughly crocked to the gills.

Gordy returned and resumed his seat, resumed sipping from his glass. "Nothing on Shivvey, but I found Gris. Think you can sweat him to find the others?"

I briefly showed my teeth. "Watch me."

He drove us to a small men-only hotel leaning close enough to some railroad tracks to punch passenger tickets for the slower trains. Gris lived here when he wasn't beating up bartenders for fun and vampires for a living. We didn't bother trying the hotel, but took stairs down to the pool hall in the basement. According to Gordy's source,

the manager of the joint, Gris was packed and waiting
there for a ride.

You could swim in the thick air with its sweat stink,
stale beer, and staler smoke. The lighting was bad except
for the shaded bulbs hung above the tables. They illumined
only the stained green felt, making the rest of the room all
the more shadowed. I could see well enough, but Gordy
would be hampered. What I saw wasn't encouraging: a lot
of tough mugs with nothing better to do with themselves
but give us a hostile eyeballing. Some shot a quick sly
glance and looked away; others seemed on the edge of
throwing a challenge, and the rest didn't give a damn.

Gordy was big enough not to have to worry about collecting trouble. He was also not unknown. I saw recognition for him in a few faces, and the news traveled around
the room in the time it took for us to cross to the bar.
Every man in the joint was a mind reader when it came
to survival. A few stared hard at me. I was in dockyard
clothes with my collar high, a cloth hat pulled low, and
dark glasses: anonymous muscle for Gordy.

He stepped up to the bar and muttered at the man there,
who muttered a reply. Gordy trundled toward the back
with me following.

A drunk too far gone to know better put himself in front
of me. "Hey, four-eyes, think yer some kinda movie star?
Why'nt you—"

I threw a backhand into his belly, my version of a gentle
swat. While he was doubled over gasping I added a push
that staggered him into four other guys standing by a table.
None of them liked it much, but all declined to make an
issue of it. Hard to tell if it was because they knew Gordy
or if they could see I was in a bone-crunching mood.
Didn't matter to me. I continued on in his wake, not breaking stride.

He went through a door. Storeroom, no frills. Another

door. Another room. Boxes, a card table, mismatched chairs, bad light, two suitcases, and a highly startled Gris just rising from one of the chairs.

"Gordy? Lissen, I don't want no—*JesusGod!*"

This last was aimed in my direction. Gordy had moved aside, and I'd stepped in, taking off the glasses. While I don't enjoy scaring people, for Gris I could make an exception. He was flat-footed only an instant, though. In the next he'd drawn his gun, but I was on him by then and wrested it away, handing it off to Gordy.

Gris didn't bother to pause for more astonishment. A fight to him was as natural as breathing, so he laid into me. It didn't last long. I put a fist just under his breastbone, driving out all the air, then hauled him around, slamming him facedown over the table. End of discussion.

I gave him a moment so he could remember how to breathe again, then bent his arms up and put on a light pressure. He grunted. More pressure and he cried out. If I went far enough he'd have double dislocations. I held him just on the edge of disaster and let him think about it, then leaned close to his ear.

"You hear me, you piece of shit?" I asked.

"Y-yuh."

"You understand what I can do to you?"

"Uhn." An affirmative tone.

"You know why I'm here?"

"Uhn."

"Then you start talking. Don't leave anything out, or I'll knot you like a pretzel."

"Bu-uhh . . ."

"No buts. You're not getting paid enough to go through this. Am I right?"

He made a sort of groaning sound of resignation. Exactly what I wanted.

The next five minutes were highly informative.

Gris was waiting for a ride to the train station, where he would board the first one heading out to Atlanta. Shivvey Coker was fixing up a job for him somewhere in Florida, muscle at a betting parlor. Same thing for the other men who had participated in my—well, I couldn't call it murder since the attempt thankfully failed. They were to stay clear of Chicago until Coker told them it was safe, then return if they felt like it.

"He's not worried you'll talk?" I asked.

"We talk and we hang ourselves," Gris pointed out, somewhat thin of voice. He was in a lot of pain. I made sure of that. "But you're all right. How can—I saw you— how come you're—"

"Never mind. Where are the others? All of them."

"But—"

"Any of them worth you losing an arm over?" I twisted the limb in question.

Apparently not, to judge by the squeal he made.

He gave up their names and location without more fuss. Coker was going to find them a car, provide a bonus of traveling money, and they weren't to stop until they reached Miami. Gris would have gone with them, but opted to buy a seat on the train, thinking it would be faster and more comfortable.

When we had everything from him that mattered, I released my hold and pulled him from the table. A spin and shove and he fell into one of the chairs. He seemed a lot smaller now than when we'd come in. He was a lot more scared.

Gordy, who was better at looming than anyone else I knew, did just that, his big shadow covering Gris. I crouched to be eye level with him.

"You know who that is?" I asked, pointing up at Gordy.

Mute, Gris nodded, rubbing one shoulder.

"You know who I am?"

Nod.

"You ever see either of us again, you are dead. You ever talk about this or what happened at my club tonight, you are dead. You know the kind of connections he's got?"

Nod.

"You say a word, you even *think* a word about tonight, and he will find out, and then I will find you. When I do, I will finish ripping your arms off and ram them down your throat. You got that clear?"

Nod. He was definitely on my side for this. But I couldn't trust him to stay there. Not without a little help.

"You really enjoyed that," Gordy commented as he drove us away from the hotel.

"The last part gave me a headache." I *had* enjoyed it. Maybe too much. The scent of Gris's fear had been sweet.

"And he ain't coming back ever?"

"Probably not. My evil-eye whammy will eventually wear off, but it lasts longer when it goes along with the normal wishes of the person I talk to. That's why I made a point of first scaring the hell out of him before putting him under."

"Looked more like you were disjointing him."

"Logic and reason never work as well as direct pain when it comes to certain kinds of persuasion."

"You shoulda killed him. Just to be sure."

"You could be right."

"I know I am. He helped kill you. Almost. If you weren't the way you are, that would have been it."

"But it wasn't."

"Suppose he gets too rough with some poor schmuck who can't bounce back like you did?"

Gordy had hit a big weak spot in my admittedly flexible principles. "I've got no answer for that. I just know I can't make him the poor schmuck that I get too rough with. Done that before. Don't like it much."

He gave a small shrug. "To each his own. You gonna do the same with these other guys?"

"Yeah. Have to be one at a time. Need you to cover them while I'm busy."

"No problem. But just to let you know . . . any of 'em gets outta line . . ." He opened his hand palm-up in a throwing-away gesture. "That's all she wrote."

"Just like that?"

"I'm a patient man," he said. "But I am not patient with disrespecters. What Shivvey and his mugs did to you was disrespectful to us both. To you because it was uncalled for, to me because he knew better."

I could see where this was leading for Coker, and it would likely involve a long walk and a short pier. Not that I harbored any friendship for him, but I wasn't easy about anyone getting rubbed out just for being stupid.

On the other hand, I could have honest-to-God died tonight. No second chances.

I gave a small shrug. "To each his own, then."

He grunted. It worried me that there was a decided tone of approval in it.

Our destination was a closed barbershop. The block it was in must have been built right after the big fire, having the look of haste and cheap materials. For the first decade it might have been inoffensive, but five more put it long past the point of decay and in need of a decent burial. The darkened shop was squashed into the middle, an afterthought with a crooked pole and a cracked front window. Gris's friends were waiting there for Coker to come by with a car. With any luck, I could take care of them, then bushwhack Coker when he walked in.

That is, if he hadn't already been and gone.

I tried the door just enough to determine it to be unlocked. Good, they hadn't left yet.

"There's a bell inside," I told Gordy. "Lemme go first."

He stood back to give me space but I didn't need any; I just vanished and slipped in under the threshold. He said something that didn't sound too happy. Well, I had warned him.

Within, I went solid and listened. All was quiet. Maybe they were to be found in a basement like Gris. I lifted the bell out of the way. Gordy came in and shut the door softly behind him. He threw me a questioning look, touched a hand to his ear. I shook my head.

By common consent, since I was more bulletproof, I led the way toward the back. Gordy nearly missed a step, staring as I passed a mirror. Jeez, he should have been used to that by now. The joint was cramped: a simple one-chair operation and none too clean. Unswept hair skittered underfoot, and the air smelled of bay rum, mint, wax, and old cigar smoke. All was quiet. No sign of Gris's friends. If he'd steered us wrong, I'd go back and finish the pretzel job I'd begun on his arms.

The door at the rear was partway open, and light showed through. Again, I went first. A dim, dusty room, with furnishings. I went in and stopped. Took an involuntary breath and picked up the bloodsmell along with the stink of cordite and, oddly, burned meat.

"Not good," said Gordy, looking over my shoulder.

"Yeah," I whispered. "I guess Shivvey wanted to save himself some travel expenses."

Two men had guns in their hands. I pointed; he nodded.

"Cops are supposed to think the game went bad and they shot each other," he said.

"That won't hold."

"You'd be surprised what'll hold in this town. Let's go. Wipe down anything you touched." He already had a white silk handkerchief in his mitt and was moving out.

The four of them had supposedly been playing poker. Small cash and cards were all over a rickety table. Some beer bottles, cigarette butts. One man still had a cigarette end in his mouth, and it had smoked itself down there, burning. The other three, slumped over the table or back in a chair or slipped off to the floor with their chests blown open didn't make as deep an impression on me as that one sorry son of a bitch with his scorched lip.

13

For Lena Ashley's memorial service I wore a somber black suit with an expression to match. Since both were appropriate to the surroundings, Bobbi hadn't yet noticed anything off about me. It also helped that she was distracted by the proceedings, busy making sure everything ran smoothly. I was glad, wanting the freedom to think through the previous night's disasters without having to answer a lot of questions on why I was so quiet.

The chapel of the funeral home she'd chosen was a nice one, real fancy. Dark-stained oak was everywhere, elaborately carved, and in some spots covered with gilt, particularly the speaker's podium. Deep red curtains cloaked the walls behind it, and long stained-glass windows depicting lilies and roses protected us from viewing the outside world. As there was no body, a gold-framed picture of Lena stood at the front where the casket would have been. It was the same photo Escott had gotten from Lieutenant Blair. The easel was draped in black ribbon and flowers; dozens of wreaths and bouquets in vases stood around it on tables and on the floor. The afternoon editions had squeezed in a story about the services and John Q. Public had generously responded. Candles burned on either side, and the organist filled the room with a series of well-practiced hymns.

I'd told Bobbi not to worry about attendance and was proved right; the place was packed. Reporters, curiosity seekers, and cops filled all the pews, so latecomers had to stand. Since I was reluctant to get my picture in the papers again, my seat in the chapel was in a screened-off alcove usually reserved for the deceased's family. I had a good view through the loose weave of the curtains, but no one could see in unless they were crass enough to come around and look inside. Of course several members of the press had done just that, only to find it empty. There was a decided advantage about being able to vanish at a second's notice.

Physically, I was recovered from the impromptu floor show Coker and his clown circus had given me in Lady Crymsyn's lobby. I'd made a stop at the Stockyards just before dawn for another long drink, then home for a day's worth of healing oblivion in my basement sanctuary. Though unaware of the passage of time, it still helped put the horrors at a distance. When I awoke, the tremors no longer troubled me. It was just too bad I couldn't as easily rid my mind of the image of that one dead man and his burned-down cigarette.

Gordy and I got ourselves away from the barbershop, returning to the pool hall, but Gris was gone by then. The bartender informed us that Coker had come by. Gris seemed surprised, apparently expecting someone else, but went along with him, suitcase in hand and no questions asked.

"That's all she wrote," said Gordy as we drove off.

"We can't assume Shivvey killed him."

"No, but I wouldn't take any odds against. I know who

runs that Florida betting shop he was supposed to go to. Give 'em a call in a day or so. If Gris doesn't show . . ." he gave a small shrug.

"Drag the river?"

"If you wanna go to all that trouble."

An idea popped into my head. An ugly one. "Take a right here. I need to check on someone."

He made the turn, following my directions without comment, perhaps having come to the same conclusion. My heart clogged itself midway up my throat for the whole time until he braked in front of Rita Robillard's hotel. He cut the motor and waited while I bolted inside.

Thankfully, Rita was exactly as I'd left her hours before. At the sound of her healthy breathing my heart crept back to its normal spot. She was in a deep, sodden sleep and quite unharmed. I wondered how long that might last. Coker had made a lot of threats against her earlier. After what he'd done to his own men I knew she shouldn't be left alone. Gordy could help there.

On my way out, I noticed a small alteration in the general disorder of her living room. The man's tie that had been carelessly discarded on the couch was gone. I looked around, hoping that it'd just fallen on the floor, but nothing doing. As it seemed unlikely anyone else would have business here, it must have been Coker who had come calling to check up on her. He didn't exactly need his own key, since Rita kept one over the outer door. For some reason he'd chosen not to wake her up, chosen not to kill her.

Aside from Rita there was only one thing here besides a discarded tie he might be interested in—providing that he knew about it. I went to the radio, pulled the backing away enough to see in. The little records book was gone.

Huh. So that's how it was.

Gordy had about the same reaction when I told him.

"Think he's gonna use it against Nevis?" I asked.

"It could come in handy to a smart operator. I know I wouldn't want something like that floating loose. The Treasury boys could get real happy over that kind of evidence."

I wondered if Coker also knew about the fifty-two grand. Probably not, or he'd never have left it lying there for Rita to accidentally find as I had. "We gotta find where he lives."

"I already know."

"Oh, yeah?"

"I make a point to spot troublemakers, keep tabs on 'em. Started back when he was still working for Welsh Lennet. But Shivvey ain't gonna be home, not until he's sure of being clear of the heat for what he did back there."

"How about an anonymous call to the cops? Those four in the barbershop—"

"Can wait. Shivvey thinks you're dead. Use it. Give him some slack, then yank the noose."

He made sense, but only so far as I was concerned. A picture of that man with the cigarette floated back into my brain again. I could almost smell the scorched meat and stink of urine. Too bad I couldn't hypnotize myself into losing this particular memory. "Rita needs to get scarce. He could change his mind and come back for her."

"Shivvey would notice. Might make him jumpy. You don't want jumpy."

"Then someone's gotta keep an eye on her. I can't during the day."

"You," he said, fixing me with a frown, "have done enough. There a phone in that hotel?"

"Just left of the entry."

He grunted and heaved out. It was a minor mystery to me whether Gordy carried a book with all his phone numbers in it or if they were all in his head. The latter, I concluded, since he didn't like anything on paper. I waited and watched the street signals change themselves until he returned some ten minutes later.

"All set," he said. "There's a couple guys coming over to play baby-sitter. She won't know about them. I got a 'nother couple going over to his hotel just in case he turns up there. If he does, they scrag him and leave."

"Just like that?" Sometimes his cold-bloodedness got to me. I should have been used to it by now.

"Just like that, but it won't happen. He's got what he wants from her. He's pulled a hole in after him. Not much we can do until he comes up for air."

"I'd rather not kill him, Gordy."

"Then what?"

"I just want to beat him until I get bored." And let him live with the broken bones. Every time it rained he'd remember me.

"We'll see what happens. But if you find him first, I get the leftovers. I can't have a disrespecter running loose. Bad for business."

Coker had used that last phrase himself when referring to Gordy getting involved in matters. Too bad for him he'd forgotten about it.

Another determined-looking man in a dark suit approached my alcove and peered in. I vanished with time to spare. He went away, disappointed like others before him.

Coker didn't show for the service, but Gordy came, sitting well in the back. In the front row sat Tony Upshaw, resplendent in a perfectly tailored masterpiece of solemnity. Next to him was Rita Robillard, in a black dress dusted with matching sequins, the veil on her hat covering her face.

Bobbi, also in black, but without the sequins, was seated in front next to the organist. She caught some signal from the funeral director and stood. A flashbulb went off, the photographer garnering disapproving looks from some. He was too busy changing bulbs to notice. The organist launched into "Rock of Ages," and Bobbi rendered a moving solo of it. Halfway through, Rita pulled out a handkerchief. Upshaw put an arm around her. Neither of them seemed to be acting.

The hymn finished, Bobbi resumed her seat, and a middle-aged minister with thinning blond hair approached the podium. He asked everyone to stand and say the Lord's Prayer with him, then we all sat, and he delivered a eulogy about a woman he'd never met. It struck me—not for the first time, for I'd attended a few funerals over the years— how at best hard or at worst cynical it must be to say something nice about a complete stranger. A murdered stranger at that. This one made a game effort, taking a theme about universal tragedy and how any death diminishes us all. It seemed to work; Rita was audibly crying. The photographer burned up another flashbulb to get that image, kneeling right in front of her.

Instead of a mere dirty look, he got something he couldn't help but notice. Rita lashed out with a velvet purse the size of a satchel and smacked him right on the bean. He tipped backwards, landing square on his ass, holding his camera high to keep it safe. Didn't work. Rita was out of her seat and caught the thing with the kind of kick that would have got her a first string spot at Notre Dame. There followed an expensive-sounding crash and clatter of breakage. The man recovered and came up cursing, but stopped short when he saw Upshaw and a couple other guys standing next to Rita glowering down at him. With a sick, pasted-on smile of apology, he backed off, palms out, and hastily gathered what was left of his equipment.

"Goddamn vultures," Rita snarled. In the shocked silence it carried throughout the room. This sparked a round of suppressed laughter, most of it from the photographer's cronies.

Somewhat wide of eye, the minister cleared his throat and everyone settled and resumed the face and form of proper mourning. The small army of reporters bent over their notepads, scribbling greedily. The sermon continued, we all recited Psalm 23, said *amen,* sang "Amazing Grace" with Bobbi leading, and that was the end of it. A general milling-around process began as some left to file stories and others walked up for a better look at Lena's photograph.

Bobbi got surrounded by a knot of men—nothing startling about that—but they were all reporters hoping for an interview. She managed to graciously ignore them and went over to Rita, who was now hanging on to Tony Upshaw's arm, using him as a shield against her own assault. They exchanged quiet words, then Bobbi detached Rita and led her over toward the alcove. Reporters followed, but I was already out the door in the back. I waited until Bobbi and Rita came through, then shut it fast. A few diehards banged loud protest, calling questions, but I jammed my foot against the base, effectively holding them at bay.

"You?" said Rita, looking at me with no small surprise. "I thought it was the funeral director wanting to talk to me."

"Jack just wanted to keep out the vultures," said Bobbi. "I've got things to see to, so . . ." She whisked off down a long, plain hallway, her heels clacking on the brown tiles.

Rita recovered fast enough. "What's this about? Who's she? And why are you—oh, never mind. I don't give a damn anymore." She dug into her purse and pulled out a fresh handkerchief, then soundly blew her nose.

"I'm sorry about your friend," I said.

"Yeah, me, too. It was a nice service even if she couldn't be here to see. What are you doing here? Why you hiding out?"

"She was found in my club, so it seemed the right thing

to do, but I didn't want a bunch of newsmen all over me again."

She rolled her eyes. "You're telling me."

"If I'd known one of them was gonna try blinding you, I'd have had you seated in the family area."

"Don't worry. I enjoyed kicking the hell outta that asshole. Just wish I'd hit him instead of the camera."

"Trust me, you hurt him more with that than you could ever imagine."

"So what is this? You fishing for another date or something?" She lifted her veil back over her hat.

If I'd never met Bobbi, I'd have been sorely tempted. Rita looked good tonight. Better than last night. Despite the recent fracas, she seemed calmer somehow. For one thing, she hadn't been drinking. Maybe some of the stuff I'd planted in her head was having a good effect on her.

"I just have a couple more questions," I said.

This time she didn't launch into an argument. She just nodded with her new calmness, and a moment later I captured her full attention. It seemed best to put her under. I didn't know how long we had before Upshaw might come looking for her, and wanted to hurry things. I also didn't care to explain to her conscious mind how I'd acquired certain pieces of information.

"Does Shivvey know about that little records book you have hidden in the radio?" I asked.

"Sure he does," she said, without any hesitation. "I showed it to him when I found it in Lena's things."

"Why did you do that?"

"I didn't know what it was at first. We figured it out, though."

"Did he tell you to continue making entries?"

"Yeah. Said it'd be good insurance."

"Insurance? Against Booth Nevis?"

"Yeah. If he should decide he didn't need me working

anymore, then I could use it to make him change his mind. That's what Shivvey said we could do with it."

"Very neat. You get to boss Nevis around, and Shivvey doesn't even come into the picture."

"I never bossed nobody. Don't have to."

Not yet, anyway. Shivvey could call the shots through Rita, and she'd be the one to take the fall if Nevis objected. If Nevis played along, then doubtless Shivvey would get a generous cut of whatever Rita got. That had changed, though. With Nevis in the clink, Shivvey could give the book to the cops and keep him there. "What about those extra numbers that Lena had in one of the columns? All those twenties and fifties?"

Rita, her eyes not focused on much of anything, shook her head. "I donno."

"What about Shivvey? Did he think she was skimming cash?"

"Skimming?"

"Did Shivvey ever ask you to look for money? For Lena's money?"

"Yeah . . . I looked. Shivvey helped me. Din' find squat."

And both of them had missed the treasure trove in the bookcase. But back then the glue on the end papers had been fresh, and Lena had been very, very careful about concealing her work. Five years of drying had made a world of difference.

"Do you think Nevis found out Lena was stealing from him?"

"Stealing?"

"Suppose Nevis caught her stealing and decided to punish her."

Rita didn't like that idea. She began to blink and shake her head, a sleeper trying to wake herself. "No, he loved her. He loved Lena."

My idea for a motive did seem thin and extreme, but if Nevis was in love, then thought himself betrayed, emotions would win out over common sense. I'd seen worse things happen for less. Hell, the night before I'd barely survived such an extreme.

Awareness came back to her eyes, rather quickly. Awareness and agitation. "What were you saying? You think Booth woulda—no. Oh, no."

"Rita, you have to listen . . ."

She pushed away a few steps, and put her back to me. "No, he'd—no, you don't know anything."

I followed. "Rita, look at me and listen a minute."

She made a small moan of frustration and began to turn. Then the alcove door opened, and Tony Upshaw came through. He gave us each a look, his gaze settling on Rita.

"You okay, doll?"

She snuffled into her handkerchief. "I wanna go home."

"Sure thing. He bothering you?"

"No, let's just get outta here."

He gave me another look, one that conveyed his certainty that I was the cause of her distress, and sauntered past to take her arm. He managed to just brush me on the return. It was meant as a challenge. I chose not to take it. Rita had told me all I really needed for the time being. No telling how much she would recall of my questioning, and no way to make sure of it now.

"Rita," I said before they made the door. They paused; she glanced back. "Stay clear of Nevis and Shivvey. It's important."

"What d'ya mean?"

"Things are happening. You don't want to be in the middle of them."

Upshaw frowned at me, very aware of what I wasn't saying. How much did he know?

"You got that?" I said.

"Yeah, sure I got that," she mumbled in a thick voice. Upshaw guided her out, beating a path through the still-present reporters.

I took Bobbi's hall route toward the front and found her standing in the entry next to Gordy. His massive presence was enough to prevent further interview attempts.

"How did it look to you?" she asked, referring to the service. She had her hat on and purse in hand, ready to leave.

"Just great. You sang like an angel."

"But that camera guy—"

"Just a bit of color, don't worry about it. The rest was very tasteful."

She gave a huge sigh of relief.

"Still think you needed a couple hundred chrysanthemums, big orange and brown ones," said Gordy.

She gave him a narrow look, lips pursed tight together.

"Okay, white then, but really big, the size of bowling balls."

She started to respond, then shook her head, giving up. She motioned at the hall I'd just emerged from. "How'd it go with that gal?"

"Well enough. I heard pretty much what I expected. Thanks for helping."

"Fine, you can tell me all about it later. I've got to get back to my job." She bestowed a quick peck on my cheek, then seemed to tow Gordy out. No mean feat considering his size. He raised one hand to indicate he was in a situation beyond his control, and away they went.

A plainclothes cop noted down their departure. He was obvious enough that he might as well have worn a uniform. He made more notes as others filed by. He already had my name. I had a mind to ask after Lieutenant Blair, but a tall, thin mourner in dark glasses and hat tilted low pushed his way through the press, in a hurry to get out.

There was no mistaking that angular jaw, hollow cheeks, and consumptive-looking frame.

I shot after him, a dog chasing a fresh bone. He was moving fast on those long legs, heading for his car. I caught up with him just as he started to get in.

Booth Nevis halted in mid-motion and stared at me over the car door. I assumed it was a stare; he kept the glasses on. "What are you doing here?" he wanted to know.

"Paying my respects, same as you."

He nodded once. "Well, all right then."

"We need to talk."

"Not now."

"We need to talk about Shivvey's next move."

He tilted his head slightly, considering. There was no telling how much he knew about what was going on, but he must have had some clue since he didn't ask for clarification. "Get in."

I got in. "Let's go to Lady Crymsyn. I heard your place was—"

"Yeah, I heard, too."

He took the specs off for the drive, replacing them once he'd parked in front of my club. I unlocked and ushered him in, this time accepting without annoyance that the bar light would be on.

In the wee hours last night I'd returned and cleaned everything. The odd stain originally confined to one tile had flooded to the grout with my additional contribution. No amount of scrubbing would remove it, but at least all other trace of my blood was gone. Only the soapy smell of the cleaner I'd used remained. The broken shelves I'd wrapped in newspaper and packed into the back alley trash cans, well out of sight and speculation. The work sheet on Malone's clipboard had a note instructing him to buy replacements. I gave no explanation on the fate of the originals.

"You believe in ghosts?" I asked Nevis.

"Huh?"

"Forget it. This way."

"Just a minute. Show me."

"Show you what?"

"Where she was."

Not knowing what to say to that, I kept shut. No spook's hand flicked the light toggles; I did it myself and made a follow-me gesture, taking Nevis through to the main room. He'd not been in the place that I knew of since I signed the lease, but was apparently in no frame of mind to admire the new scenery. He trudged along like a man going to the scaffold.

We went down to the basement. The cement mixer had apparently not arrived today; most of the floor toward the back was in the same rough state as when the men had been tearing down the brick dividers. I led him to the nook, which was quite gone. Scars in old cement and mortar showed where the false wall had been built up, but all else had been swept clean.

"Where?" he asked.

I pointed, glad the cops had taken away the eyebolt that had anchored Lena's bonds.

Nevis put his hands in his pockets and brooded a while in the harsh glare of the unshielded bulbs. He then gave the rest of the shadows a look-see, walking over to the yet unfilled-in trench at the foot of the far wall before turning heel.

"Okay, that's enough." There was no expression on what I could see of his face. The sunglasses hid what was important.

We went up to my office.

The window blinds were taken down, leaving yawning black holes punched into the stark white walls. I'd have to get some pictures or something in to ease the monotony.

Leon's crew—according to the report he'd left on the clip-board next to Malone's report—was still waiting for a portable cement mixer. Among other chores, they'd oc-cupied their time today by painting my office, and the air was hardly breathable. Even if I didn't need it, Nevis was addicted to the stuff, so I opened things wide to let out the fumes. Besides, the dark background turned the glass panes into mirrors, with myself quite absent from their view. No need to complicate things.

The street below hosted only an occasional passing car. I expected Gordy to be coming by after he'd dropped off Bobbi, which wouldn't take long.

"What about Shivvey?" asked Nevis, settling into the spare chair. He didn't look like the cautious man on guard as he'd been the last time I'd seen him. His bony shoulders drooped, his hands hung loose over the chair arms. His posture was not so much tired as don't-give-a-damn ex-haustion.

"When did the cops get done with you?"

He took his time answering. "Couple hours ago. And they're not done with me yet. They were all over that place."

"I saw them. They'd have been there anyway." Head-lights turned onto the road half a block down. A green Ford. It parked in a dark patch between the streetlights. Right in front of a hydrant. Because of the distance I only just dis-cerned the driver's general outline, but no details. Couldn't tell if he had company in the back or not. I stepped away from the window and told Nevis. "Think it's Shivvey?"

He gave a resigned snort. "Not his car. That's a cop keeping tabs on me. Why don't they just hang out neon signs?"

"Same reason why they ran you into a door. They want you off-balance so you spill for them."

One corner of his mouth curled, and he ruefully took off the glasses, folding them into the breast pocket of his coat. He had a spectacular shiner framing his left eye, not unlike Malone's.

"I spilled," he said, "but we had a problem. I wasn't giving them what they wanted to hear."

"As in confessing to Lena Ashley's murder?"

He nodded, flapping one long hand dismissively. "I'm here to talk about Shivvey."

"You heard from him today?"

"No, and I should have. Rita told me about the funeral and said she hadn't seen him since last night. Shivvey's up to something. I can see that now, or he'd have been by to spring me yesterday. I don't know how far he'll go, though. Maybe he wants a bigger piece of pie, maybe he wants the whole bakery. Until I learn different, I'll figure he's going for the bakery."

Wise of him.

"What's your angle in this?" he asked.

"Your boy did some unnecessary pushing around of me last night, which I did not appreciate. Thinks I've got eyes for Rita—which I don't. I'd like the chance to straighten him out on a few facts."

Nevis snorted again, amusement this time. "Hard to tell where he is with her. Some guys who chase her he doesn't care about, like Upshaw; others he gets his nose out of joint. You must be one of the lucky ones."

"So I gathered. Where would he be hiding himself?"

"He's got a hotel room someplace."

"A friend of mine checked on that today. Came up empty." The phone had been ringing just as I'd wakened. Gordy had sounded disappointed about his lack of progress. I was just glad to learn Rita was still safe. Two of the men sitting by her at the service were on the Night-crawler payroll. "You know any other place Shivvey might run to if he didn't want to be found?"

"If I did, he wouldn't be there."

"Come on, you gotta know some bolt-hole he'd creep into."

Nevis grimaced, rubbing his good eye, which was very bloodshot. "Listen, I've been getting shit like this from goddamned cops for longer than I can remember. I've had no sleep since the night before last and no food except for about fifty cups of coffee they gave me to keep me jumping. Why the hell should I start answering your questions?"

I decided to risk giving him another migraine. "Nevis . . ." I focused on him carefully, taking things slow. In the next minute I got to know the lines and planes of his face in rare detail and watched them gradually ease and soften as all thought, all worry seeped from his conscious mind. That was reassuring. I didn't care to have another incident with him collapsing on me.

"Tell me everything you know about Lena Ashley," I said.

"She's dead," he murmured in a lost, hollow voice.

"Yes. I want to know why you walled her up."

"Wha . . . no."

"Talk to me, Nevis. Why did you kill her?"

Tension crept back into his body, starting with his shoulders bunching up, then his head bowing. "No."

"You have to tell me. You'll feel better once you do. Why did you kill her?"

Violent shake of his head. "*No!*"

Jeez, he was jolting himself out of it. I was either losing my touch or his headache was going to reappear to screw things up again. "All right, take it easy, Nevis."

But he didn't take it easy and surged awkwardly up from his chair, lurching a few uneven steps across the office. His eyes were unfocused; if he wanted to hit something, he couldn't see it. I waited, then sniffed the paint-laden air for any whiff of illness coming from him. Just ordinary sweat this time, but tinged with the acid bite of anger.

I said his name a few times. His breathing slowed as I gave him soothing, calming words, but his expression remained tense even after he resumed his seat. I frowned and thought glum thoughts, the kind that come to me when I have to admit I'd tripped up somewhere.

"Okay, Nevis, you're not going to get upset anymore. Just answer me straight. Did you know about Lena skimming money from the bets she placed for you?"

The answer took its own sweet time coming, but he finally shrugged. "Yes, but I could afford it."

"Weren't you angry with her for stealing from you?"

"At first. But it didn't mean anything. I could afford it."

I felt a keen sympathy with the cops. This wasn't what I wanted to hear. "Did you kill Lena?"

"*No!* I want . . . want . . ." He was fighting me again, his anger giving him strength. If I pressed too hard, he'd be useless. Even if it wasn't what I wanted, I had what I needed and told him to relax, then waited until he woke from his hypnotic haze. He gradually wilted like a balloon losing air, until he leaned forward, putting his head in his hands. From the sounds he was making—long shuddering sighs—it was from raw grief, not physical pain. It hurt to watch him, so I stared out the window. The green Ford was still there. The driver had gotten out. He had his back against the curbside face of the car, and sent a plume of cigarette smoke into the still night air. Just filling the time until Nevis emerged.

"I didn't want this," he stated. That hollow note was back in his voice. He looked hollow, gouged from the inside out with a dull chisel. "I was hoping she'd just taken the cash and run away, that when it got spent, she'd come back. I didn't want her dead. My God, dead like that."

"What happened the last time you saw her?"

"Nothing. It was just another night at the club. She'd done her usual run to the bookies and brought in the cash

winnings, same as always. We had a drink, and she went
to sit out front while I did the counting. She kept back a
twenty, and I pretended not to notice. Same as always."

"You sure you didn't mind her stealing?"

"In a five-grand bet who cares if I'm short a couple
bucks? I sure as hell didn't. I spend more than that in tips."

"Who else knew she was stealing?"

"No one."

Which isolated him as a man with a motive. But unless
he was hiding a spectacular force of will or cockeyed insanity, he'd given me the truth about his innocence.

"Who'd she see that last night? Who spoke to her?"

He shrugged. "I don't know. Same people as always.
Rita was there."

"What about Tony Upshaw?"

"Yeah."

"And Shivvey?"

"Him, too. I'd just hired him on a week earlier."

"You knew he was after Lena for himself?"

"Didn't matter. She was with me, and he never went
near her. He started going sweet on Rita about then."

A practical man, Mr. Coker. Never mooch on the boss's
territory. If he'd had an inkling of Lena's skimming game,
that would give him a reason to get rough with her. I found
it easier to believe in Coker's greed as a motive than her
rejecting his advances. Except that he couldn't have known
about the money cache until after her disappearance, when
Rita showed him the records book. I didn't see how any
of them could have lied to me, so I'd very obviously
tripped up. Or maybe missed a step.

The only other man even remotely involved was Tony
Upshaw, and if five years ago as a wet-eared kid he'd had
the balls to wall a young woman up alive, I was a monkey's uncle and then some. He'd be the type to boast about
it. I'd talk to him, just to be thorough. There was a slim

chance he'd known about the skimming, in which case things would almost make sense again. I wanted sense, even if it meant adding bananas to my limited diet.

And if Tony was also innocent, then me and the cops were clean out of luck. Lena could have been the victim of some sadist none of us knew about. Unthinkable, but not impossible. If so, then we'd never find him.

"I want the man who killed her," said Nevis. He'd fully woken out of his trance, was thinking again for himself. "I'm going to take him apart."

The way he spoke gave me to understand that he would be literal with his intent and do it with his bare hands. I hitched a hip on my desk corner.

"You've got no idea who it might have been?"

"I've got no ideas left. I need sleep."

"Go get some, then, but watch your back."

"From Shivvey? Of course."

"I mean it, Nevis. You see the papers today?"

"What about them?"

An afternoon edition was on my table under a stack of the day's mail. I fished it out. The story about the barbershop shoot-out had made it above the fold. The names of the victims were being withheld by the cops pending further investigation.

Nevis had a green cast to his already-present pallor. "What is this?"

"You can expect more heat from the law. Since you were in custody, they can't pin this on you, but those four were all bouncers at the Ace."

"You saying Shivvey did this?"

"I'm pretty certain of it. He wanted to cover his tracks."

"Y-you fill me in. What the hell is going on?"

He got a highly edited version of events. ". . . so Shivvey and his boys left me for dead. He didn't want witnesses blabbing, that's why I figure he scragged them. Gris is gone, too, probably."

He shook his head. "No, this is going too far and too fast. I can see Shivvey trying to take over the Ace, but this?"

"Well, you know him better than me. What's he capable of?"

Nevis closed his sagging jaw. Something new in his weary eyes: fear. He wasn't used to it. "No, none of this happened like you're saying. You don't look like he got anywhere near rough. What kind of bull are you trying to feed me?"

I fixed on his gaze again. "It's no bull, Nevis, you can believe me. Think things over. But watch your back while you do. Don't go anywhere he might know about."

Release.

He pinched the bridge of his nose. "God, I gotta get out of here."

On that we were in agreement. If he was sickening for another headache, I didn't want him around. Gordy would be along soon, and I'd prefer not to risk more hypnosis on Nevis. "Okay, come on."

He levered up, walking stiff and slow as I herded him out. We were in the hall when I heard something, a couple of somethings, making loud, sharp *clunks* behind me in the office. I started to turn, but hesitated, then a leftover instinct from my Army days made me give Nevis a violent push forward and throw myself down next to him. He squawked a ripe protest at the treatment, but the two near-simultaneous *bangs* close behind us utterly drowned him out.

14

THE heavy burst of air pressure shock rather than the cracking noise of the explosions made my ears buzz like a bad radio. I shook my head against the static. It didn't help.

"What the hell was *that*?" Nevis wanted to know. He started to rise, but I shoved him down again.

"Crawl," I ordered, pointing at the stairs.

He seemed inclined to argue, but one look at my face changed his mind. He scrambled along, all knees and elbows, with me holding in place listening for further *clunks*. The hall was littered with glass exploded out from the transom. Slivers cascaded from my clothes when I stood, slamming home an ugly *déjà vu* feeling from last night.

I cautiously angled an eye around the door frame, alert to duck at the least sign of movement.

Smoke and the sharp stink of cordite. There was less damage than I'd expected, but it was bad enough: two blackened pits surrounded by uneven star-shaped scorch patterns smoldering in the floor. The walls and ceiling were pierced in a hundred places by shrapnel. As with the transom, the window glass was gone, blown out to the street below. My table was oddly untouched except for some holes and being knocked a foot out of place; only the papers were scattered. Nevis's chair, however, had been converted in an instant to kindling. Splinters were everywhere, one of the legs freakishly embedded next to the doorjamb. I cringed at the thought of those flying shards spearing through my body, the wood as deadly to me as the grenades would have been to Nevis. We'd escaped by scant seconds.

"My God," said Nevis. From the hall he stared past me.

Deciding to risk it, I crossed the room to look out the windows. He followed. The street was still empty—it would have to be clear of witnesses—except for a lone man walking swiftly toward the green Ford.

"That son of a bitch!" Nevis snapped, recognizing him. He shot out the door for the stairs. Too angry to think about the height, I went transparent and shot out the window, dropping swiftly to hit the sidewalk running.

The man glanced back at the sound, froze only a moment, then ran full tilt toward his one hope of escape. I snagged him just as he reached for the door handle. He yelped and struggled, getting in a couple of solid slugs, which didn't affect me. He tried to pull the gun I knew he carried. I slapped him once on the side of his head, which took all the vinegar out of him.

Nevis suddenly charged in, knocking me out of the way. Too angry to wonder how I'd gotten there ahead of him, he breathlessly cursed, hitting hard and connecting each time he said "shit," which was a lot. Our mutual quarry was on the pavement in short order. I dragged Nevis away before he could start kicking. He was red-faced pissed, and I felt the same, but was still sensible to practicalities. We couldn't question Tony Upshaw if Nevis beat him to death.

Nevis was a handful for a few minutes until the momentum of his rage slowed, combining with his weariness to leave him wheezing and sweating and hardly able to stand. Only then did I let him go so I could see about Upshaw.

His gun had fallen clear; I scooped up the little .22 and tucked it into a pocket. As much as he wanted to be thought tough I wondered why he carried such a small caliber, then concluded he didn't care to ruin the lines of his suit. No need to worry about that now—Nevis had done a thorough job of demolishment. Upshaw was curled into a protective posture, his arms blocking my view of his face, though I could smell the blood. I got a good grip and dragged him toward the club, not bothering to look back for Nevis.

I didn't stop until reaching the lobby stairs, when Upshaw's usually nimble feet went clumsy. He stumbled and collapsed on the steps.

"It wasn't me, it wasn't me," he said with the panicked conviction of a kid caught playing with matches rather than a mob killer who'd missed his target. The whine in his voice was almost funny. Almost.

"You little shit—" began Nevis. He'd recovered enough for a second round, and I got between them again.

"You can have him later." I had to shout to make him hear. Maybe his ears were buzzing, too, but more likely it was sheer emotion making him deaf. "Go bolt the doors so we don't get more booms." I repeated variations of this twice over before he got it, then he moved quick enough, his good eye blazing with fury for Upshaw.

I held still, glaring at Upshaw myself while silently counting to twenty, needing the calm. I counted slowly. Nevis scowled, but kept his distance; Upshaw peered out from between his arms, clearly concluding that I was building up to something. When I moved—merely to lean forward—he covered up again, bracing for another beating.

"Not the face," he pleaded.

Nevis snarled, fists ready. "I'll give you face, you little son of a bitch."

I waved him away. "Upshaw, you answer me straight or I let him go to work on you. Once he's done, the only movie part you'll get is playing stand-in for Boris Karloff."

Upshaw moaned agony and tried to all-four it up the stairs. My guess about his greatest fear had been a bull's-eye. I grabbed his feet and hauled him back, the steps bumping the breath out of him. "I didn't do it," he insisted, the whine more pronounced. His nose streamed red, the stain all over his mug and his once perfect clothing. The slicked-down hair was now sticking up comically in all directions. The supreme self-command he showed on the dance floor was quite shattered. Real life, real death can do that to a person.

Now that his arms were down, I fixed him with a look. It was hard getting through all that fear, but soon his mouth sagged, and his struggles ceased. "Who sent you?"

"Sh-Shivvey."

What a surprise. "Okay. You tell us the whole thing, top to bottom."

I had to prompt him, and Nevis's frequent belligerent interruptions didn't help, but the story finally came out.

Shivvey Coker had phoned Upshaw this afternoon to have a private meeting just outside the dance studio. Upshaw was used to such casual calls; it usually meant he was to run a minor errand. Not this time. Coker was quite the artist at persuasion and knew how to play his fish. A bald instruction to kill Nevis would have been refused, but sitting together in his car and sharing a friendly bottle for a couple of hours took the horror out of the task for Upshaw. Coker had worked gradually up to it, making it seem

part-game, part-initiation, part-duty. If Upshaw really
wanted to play with the big boys, he had to prove his
loyalty and willingness to follow orders.

The offer was a cliché straight out of a dime magazine
and shouldn't have swayed anyone with real sense, but
Upshaw's ambitions made him vulnerable. He wanted the
prestige and respect of the tough guys and obviously
hadn't put too much thought into questioning Coker's motive for suddenly making use of him for so important a
job. The deal had also been sweetened with the promise
of enough cash for Upshaw to make a splashy entrance in
Hollywood.

By the time they'd finished the bottle, Upshaw wanted
to prove himself so badly he'd not even asked for half the
money in advance, as was usual in such deals. He hadn't
been reeled in so much as thrown himself bodily into the
boat, ready for gutting.

All Upshaw had to do was find Nevis, wait for the right
moment, and pull a couple of pins on the grenades Coker
happened to have along to give him. Upshaw had put Rita
in a cab and followed Nevis from the services. He had no
astonishment for my still being alive; Coker must not have
informed him.

Upshaw had parked, strolled right up to the club, and
waited under the open, well-lighted windows until the
street was clear for him to make his lethal pitches. He'd
heard nothing of our talk.

"I guess we both know who killed Welsh Lennet way
back when," I said to Nevis. "Not many people keep grenades on hand."

"Who cares?" Nevis rumbled. Through it all he paced
up and down, slowly, too worked up to notice anything
amiss about Upshaw's extraordinary cooperation. He kept
looking at Upshaw, murderous revenge pouring off him
like smoke from a fire.

This I understood perfectly. Upshaw had been willing to smear me, a bystander, all over the room right along with Nevis. I was hard-pressed to keep Nevis from going to work on him. It could not be me. In my own anger I'd have killed Upshaw. Too quickly.

I counted again until I could look at him and not twist his head off. There were still questions needing answers.

"Upshaw . . . did you kill Lena Ashley?"

"What?" This from a startled Nevis. He transferred his focus to me. "What makes you think he—"

"I don't, but I'm asking all the same. Why the hell not?"

He had no reply and subsided, watching Upshaw with new interest.

I repeated my query.

"No, I didn't kill her," Upshaw murmured, his blank eyes looking at nothing. "Not nobody. This was my first . . ."

"He could be lying," said Nevis, but without much conviction.

I shook my head. "He's too wet-eared to lie. I didn't much figure him for it, anyway."

"Then why ask?"

"Just covering all the bases. You never know." And that negative answer took away my last suspect. Unless someone else turned up, Lena's murderer would go unpunished.

But at least we had Shivvey Coker, or would before the night was out.

"Where's Shivvey?" I asked Upshaw.

"Waiting at the Ace."

An exclamation of disgust from Nevis.

I shot him a look. "Can you think of a better place to lie low than one the cops have shut down?" I was ready to kick myself, since I'd not thought of it.

"He'll give me the money there," said Upshaw.

Or more likely give the coroner another corpse. Coker could put one of those. 22 bullets into Upshaw's head, a suicide in a fit of remorse over his murders. Maybe there would be another grenade planted on his body to clench things. The cops would have Nevis's killer, and, on a good day, considering Lady Crymsyn's history, might even blame Upshaw for Welsh Lennet's explosive demise. It would have been a puzzling bonus for Coker: how I'd managed to survive only to be blown up with his boss, but he'd not have worried about it for long. The new responsibilities of running the Ace would have kept him profitably busy.

We'd see about that.

I drove. Nevis was too nerved, and Upshaw was huddled down in the backseat of his green Ford being agreeably unconscious. It cost me a twinge or three behind the eyes to deal with the both of them, but I'd talked Nevis out of doing murder for the time being and put Upshaw out for the count. Neither of them would remember much about tonight except what I'd told them. Upshaw would only know that he'd been asked by Coker to do a minor tailing job—not murder—on Nevis and had fallen asleep while sitting in his car.

Nevis would recall the grenade attack but Shivvey had been the one with the pitching arm. It seemed the best for all concerned. Sparing Upshaw's life didn't mean that I'd forgiven him. The truth was I'd done it for Rita's sake. She seemed to like him and didn't need to attend another memorial service so soon after Lena's.

Once Shivvey was dealt with, things could settle down to business as usual. Upshaw could go back to dancing, and Nevis could run his club. Shivvey, some still-virtuous part of me hoped, would soon turn himself in to the cops with a full confession about the barbershop murders. This would happen with a nudge from me and only after I'd gotten the records book from him. No need to complicate things. My landlord in jail on tax fraud charges was something I could do without.

"Back door?" I asked Nevis as I began a circle around the Flying Ace's block.

"Yeah, he'd leave it open. We usually did for special work."

I didn't bother asking him what that work might be, just filed it away for a future conversation. Since the darkened club—with police department signs posted on the doors and windows—was very visibly closed, parking wasn't the usual problem tonight. I found a spot close to the back and cut the motor.

"Lemme go in first," I said on the walk toward the alley.

"This is my fight," Nevis protested.

I paused him. "The shape you're in you couldn't go two rounds with a drunk hamster."

"It's me he tried to kill; I want to break him in two."

"You won't miss a thing, I promise, but I've got a better chance of getting the drop on him than you. You watch my back, and I'll see to it he's awake when you walk in. Make a good entrance."

That provided him an acceptable out as well as appealed to his vanity, so he gave me the nod and stepped to one side.

I reflected, as I approached the club's door, that I was falling into the role of mob muscle just a little too easily. Maybe I'd been hanging around with guys like Nevis a whole lot too much. Their casual, if practical acceptance of violence to solve most problems was not only rubbing off, I was enjoying it far too much.

My furtive pleasure ground to a quick stop as I rounded the corner and came face-to-face with Rita Robillard standing in the alley. She was still darkly fetching in her mourn-

ing clothes, and in the deep shadows between the buildings
was invisible to everyone but me. She held a good-size
revolver clutched in one gloved hand.

"You!" we said in unison.

I gaped down at the gun. She didn't shift its aim from
my midsection.

"Rita, honey, why the hell are you here?"

"I'm asking you the same."

"I told you—"

She scowled. "Yeah, yeah, a lotta mugs tell me a lotta
things. It don't mean I gotta believe 'em."

"You're trying to find Nevis? Is that it?"

"Uh-huh. Sooner or later he's gotta come back here.
After what you fed me at the services I wanted to see for
myself what he had to do with Lena . . . and I'll know that
when I see his face."

"Know what?" asked Nevis, coming up. The immediate
effect his presence made was to shift the muzzle from my
midsection to his. "Hey, Rita, what is this?"

"A misunderstanding," I said, but didn't get any further.
The lady with the gun was running things for the moment,
particularly when she swung it up to point it right between
his eyes.

Despite this he didn't look very alarmed. "Is this a joke?
Rita—"

"You—" She got that much out. She was visibly trying
to put the words into the right order. "Booth, did you kill
Lena?"

"What?"

"Did you?" Her voice rose and her hand trembled.

"No, I did not. Who put that crazy idea into your head?"
Her gaze touched on me for an instant.

"Covering the bases?" he asked, looking at me with no
little disgust.

I shrugged, having no need to defend myself. "Rita, I've

talked with him since seeing you. He had nothing to do with it. I was wrong. I promise you he's clean." Of Lena's death, anyway.

"You're sure?"

"Scout's honor."

"Really sure?"

Insufficient light to work with to compel her to believe, but whether or not she recalled it I'd forged a very strong bond of trust between us last night. That she so readily turned to me for reassurance was proof of its actuality. My word would be enough for her. "He did not kill Lena."

"Damn!"

"Huh?" Nevis, just a fraction behind things, but then he was tired.

"She was all worked up to shoot you," I informed him after Rita lowered the revolver. "Be glad she's not and let her have her disappointment."

"Well, if he didn't do it, who did?" she demanded. "Shivvey? Jack, was it Shivvey? Is that why you told me to keep clear of him?"

Again, I regretted having been unable to adjust her memory about our last interview. "This is something we can talk about later."

"Why? Why not now?"

Any second she could blurt out something about that damned records book. Nevis didn't need to know about it just now. If ever.

Before I could come up with a reasonable placation, he stepped in. "We're here on business, Rita. And you know what that means."

Another scowl. Thankfully it was one of grudging acceptance. "Yeah, I get it. I just don't want it." She opened her big purse and put the gun inside. If she'd been packing that thing at the service, then it was no wonder she'd walloped the photographer flat. "One of you mugs call me and tell me what's going on." She began to turn away, then paused. "Booth, I'm sorry I did that. Ya believe me?"

"Yeah, I believe you, now beat it."

"Couldn't we have a drink before you start all your business? I could really use a beer."

"I would, doll, but the cops didn't leave anything after the raid. I'll buy you one later."

"Me too," I said, taking her arm and leading her toward the other end of the alley. "You got a ride home?"

"I took the El in. There's a stop just up the—"

"Great. You take it right back again."

"This is a bum's rush, and don't think I don't know it," she said crossly.

"You got that right, honey, but me and your boss have got business. We'll get together afterward and have a drink to Lena."

That promise sat well with her, and she became more cooperative. I walked her to within sight of the El and waved her on, then hurried back to the alley.

Nevis was no longer alone. The door to the club was wide-open, spilling out a fan of faint light from some distant source within. Shivvey Coker stood on the threshold. He had a gun pointed at Nevis. This time Nevis looked worried. He held his hands clear of his body and kept himself very still.

Focused on each other, neither of them noticed me in the dark, and it seemed prudent to leave things as they were. I got fairly close on foot, then vanished and floated the rest of the way, moving quick. Coker could pull the trigger any instant he chose.

I bumped and blundered along until I was exactly behind him, but he was moving now, backing up.

"That's it," he said. "Come on and easy does it."

I wasn't prepared for the surge of rage that flooded me at the sound of Coker's voice. All I wanted to do was go solid and smash his face in. Roaring instinct said kill him, kill the man who'd tried to kill me. Reason, thin and small, said wait, learn more. For the crucial moment I hesitated. It was long enough to hold me in check until curiosity kicked in. I wanted to know what they'd have to say to each other. Things would be more candid between them without my presence.

"Come on. Shut the door. Don't slam it."

Had to remember that Coker was speaking to Nevis, not me. The door closed softly, the latch snicking firmly into place.

"Just what do you think you're doing?" Nevis asked. He sounded more irked than afraid.

"The office," Coker told him.

They walked to the office; another latch snicked.

"Have a seat," he said expansively. "On the couch. Take a night off from the desk work."

"It's not too late to cut a deal, Shivvey. I can be generous."

Coker laughed. "I'm gonna miss your jokes."

"Yeah, well, what have I got to lose?"

"Nothing at all, but you won't win. Not this game."

"You're holding off. What are you waiting for?"

"I got a friend coming in."

"Little Tony the dancer? 'Fraid not. He's been sidetracked." Nevis was taking a chance with that one. I hoped he wasn't speeding up his imminent demise.

Silence for a moment as Coker digested the bad news. I positioned myself next to him. He stood before the desk, the better to face down the couch-seated Nevis. I thought about blanketing Coker. When I touched people while in this form the effect was a profound icy-to-the-bone chill. Coker might have a hair trigger on his gun; it could go off if he shivered too hard. Stranger things had happened.

"What'd you do to Tony?" he asked, sounding casual.

"Nothing. Yet. Sure you don't want to deal?"

"I might change my mind. Where is he?"

"Don't kid a kidder, Shivvey. You don't give a tinker's damn about the little bastard. What you want to know is if he'll rat on you because your game with the grenades didn't work."

Coker gave a snort. "He won't talk."

"He already did. You should have offered to pay him more." Nevis was buying himself time, then, probably hoping I'd come charging in to the rescue, or at least provide a diversion so he could make his own move. Seated on that low couch had him at a disadvantage, which is why Coker put him there.

"So what'd he say?"

"Enough about you to get me in good with the cops. It was stupid to use grenades again, especially at Lennet's old place. What the hell were you thinking? When they start sweating you you're gonna need a friend with influence, not some jumped-up hoofer in a monkey suit. You need me, Shivvey. You need me alive and on your side."

"Lennet's place? What were you doing there?"

Damn. Maybe I shouldn't have altered Nevis's memory. What I'd put there didn't jibe with Coker's talk.

"Don't change the subject," Nevis purred. "You missed me tonight, and I could still kill you for it, but for old time's sake I can let it slide."

"You could kill me? I'm the one with the gun."

"True, but I'm the one with the money. You'll need it to get the Ace up and running again. Taking me out of the picture would complicate everything for you."

"Not really. No one has to know you're dead. With the cops giving you the eye like today, no one'll blame you if you skip town and don't leave an address."

Nevis snorted. "You think with me out of the way you can waltz in here and take over like Gordy did with the

Nightcrawler? That won't happen for you, my friend. You like to play too much. And there's not a lot of time off when you're being boss. When you're running things it means you have to be here all night every night, in good health or on your deathbed. *You* don't have the head for the paperwork, or the patience to deal with every drunken asshole who thinks he's Diamond Jim Brady on a roll. In a month the new would wear off for you along with all the fun, and you'd suddenly realize you're not the owner of the club, the club owns you. It's too late to get away then because you have to have the money like a train needs tracks."

Jeez. And I thought I was good at hypnotizing people. Nevis had me half-convinced.

"Having this club means no more time for skirt-chasing unless you settle down with Rita, and she's too smart to get stuck with you."

"Shut up, Nevis."

"If this annoys you, then that means I pegged it. Face the facts, Shivvey, you want the money, but not the work that goes with it. Believe me, you're much better off with the job you've got. If you want a raise, you can have one; all you had to do was ask."

Somewhere along the way Coker had lost control of the conversation, and I doubted that he was aware of it.

"I see now that's what you tried to do with Lennet way back when. You figured to bump him and I get the blame and you take over running the club, only it didn't work out like you wanted. Lennet's joint gets boarded up and you're out of a job, so you came over to my payroll, liked how I do things, and settled in for a few years. They were pretty good years—until Fleming opens the old joint up again and finds what's in the cellar. Is that what set this off for you, Shivvey? Did his finding Lena set it off?"

Coker didn't answer immediately. I wanted to see his

face. He could be raising the gun right then.

"It did and it didn't," he muttered instead.

"Come on and spill." Nevis sounded more like an understanding big brother than a man seated six feet away from a bullet.

"I figured if the cops put you away for her, then I might as well be here to take over. Just makes sense to make another try when the odds favor."

"Yeah, that does make sense," agreed Nevis. "I might have done the same thing myself. But they're not going to put me away. Not enough evidence."

That's when Coker woke out of Nevis's spell and laughed. "You don't know everything. Boss."

"Fill me in. I'm not going anywhere."

"No, you're not. For one thing, you're sweet little twist Lena was stealing from you."

"Tell me what I don't know."

"Good, Nevis. I didn't think you were that dumb. Why'd you let her get away with it? Were you in love?"

Nevis kept his temper against the inherent contempt. "It didn't bother me is all. Anything else?"

"Oh, yeah. Plenty. Lena kept a record of every bet she made. I think it was some kind of insurance for her in case you decided to fall out of love."

Great. One cat out of the bag. One can of worms opened wide. One pot of beans spilled to hell and gone all over the floor. I suppose I could edit Nevis's memory later. What's a splitting headache or two between friends?

"A record?"

"She had a little book. The only thing in it was your name and a lot of numbers and dates of all the work you had for her with the bookies. Very incriminating. It wouldn't take the cops very long to—"

"You're lying."

I could almost see Coker's shrug. "Doesn't matter. I was

going to give it to them to nail you to the wall, but then they'd close this place down for good. Or make it too expensive for me to pay them off."

"So you forget the book and kill me instead? And who do you think they'd pick as the most likely suspect?"

"Me, of course. Only I'll have plenty of alibi. Same as the other time." He didn't have to add that last bit. It was his way of informing Nevis his end was definitely nigh, just as it'd been for Welsh Lennet.

"The other time it went bust on you."

"Not my fault. I got things better prepared now."

"Sure you have. You think I wouldn't know? Or allowed for it? You bump me, and you won't see one thin dime off this place. I made a will."

"Oh, yeah?"

"Something happens to me, and it all goes to my uncle in San Francisco. I figure it might make up for some bad blood between us."

"Well, you said it yourself, don't kid a kidder."

"You'll find out the truth of it soon enough."

"Maybe so," Coker said after a minute. "But even if it does go to him, he'll need someone local to run things. I still get the club. Why you shaking your head?"

"Because my uncle is anything but stupid, except when it comes to women—which runs in the family if I'm any judge of myself. He may not like me, but he'd get over it once I'm dead. He's funny that way about relatives. He can hit them, but no one else can. He will turn this town inside out, call in every favor to get my killer. You, my old buddy, would lose, because you don't have that many friends willing to keep their yaps shut once he starts waving the cash around. Then, when he closes on you . . ."

"Yeah, what?"

"You'll end up wishing your ma and pa never made eyes

at each other. I've seen Uncle Grim at work." Nevis drew
a breath between his teeth to make a hissing sound. "It's
ugly. You have to have a strong stomach to watch, but
he's kind of an artist about it. The results are impressive.
It's amazing how long he can keep them alive, too. You
wouldn't think—"

"That's good, Nevis. I almost believe you, but if any of
that were true, you'd have said something about it a long
time back. You like to talk too much, but you've never
mentioned any of this before."

"I've never had a man holding a gun on me for this long
before. It's downright inspiring to the memory."

"You're boring me."

"I'm just getting to the good part, though, the part where
we both come up smelling like roses."

This was something I wanted to hear as well.

"The part where I make you a real deal—one we can
both live with."

A pause. "Okay, go ahead. Surprise me."

"I just might. Lena had a practical streak in her. Maybe
that's why she didn't want to hook up with me permanent.
If she'd ever wanted out and I said no, she'd have had that
book to convince me to back off. Something simple and
easy. You can use it the same way."

"Which is . . . ?"

"I run the club, you pull the strings. You get ten percent
of the weekly take after it's cleaned up. You've got the
book to keep me from killing you, and you don't kill me
because I'm doing the work."

"Keep talking."

"All you have to do is fix up a dead man's switch with
the book. If you're ever killed or you disappear, the book
is delivered to the cops with an appropriate note about me.
You can find a lawyer somewhere who'll do it for you.
You will always be safe from me. Actually, I'll have a

vested interest in keeping you safe and healthy for years to come."

"What keeps me from killing you? I forget."

"My business sense. You don't really want to run the club, you just want to be boss. This way you get to be boss, but without the responsibilities."

"And what do you get out of it?"

"I get to live. Which I want more than this club. I could sign the place over to you, but it wouldn't be the same. You wouldn't trust me not to sneak up on you someday, dead man switch or no, and you'd have to bump me. But this way we both win. We both get something."

Coker fell silent. I couldn't tell if he was fuming or thinking. "I want fifty percent."

"Fifteen is as high as I can go. Ten's pushing it as it is. The people I report to will notice a drop in the profits. Fifteen I can blame on hard times; any more, and you risk getting noticed."

I couldn't laugh in this form, but wanted to; I should have been taking notes.

"What's to keep you from bumping me until I get this lawyer thing set up?"

"Nothing, but you're a smart boy, Shivvey, and there's the phone. You can find someone to sit with me until you're squared away."

"Sure, so you talk to them like you did with Tony? Turn them against me?"

"Then tie and gag me for the duration. I'd prefer that to a grenade or bullet."

"You got all the angles figured, don't you?"

"It's what I'm good at. Is it too early to start calling you boss?"

Coker took a long time thinking, probably thinking very hard, then he laughed once. "Hell, why not?"

Something banged and thumped—a door opening violently—and a woman's shrill voice cut in on what might have been their pending handshake.

"You goddamn bastards!"

"Rita?"

Couldn't tell which of them said it; I was too busy hauling ass.

I got to her a fraction too late, a gun went off just as I materialized in the hall next to her.

She gave a loud, full-throated screech of pure outrage as I pummeled against her big body, pushing her out of the doorway. She staggered and fell, cursing. Good. If she could do that, then she'd not been shot.

"Let me *go*!" she bellowed, struggling to rise. I'd planted a foot square between her shoulders and bent to take her gun. Awkward, but I managed to pull it clear without breaking her fingers or having it fire.

The muzzle was hot. I left her. Looked inside the office.

Nevis was on the floor in front of the couch, having apparently ducked. He didn't seem to be injured and was staring at Coker, who stood next to the desk. He had his gun on Nevis, but swung it toward me. Slack-jawed shock rocked him on his heels.

"Fleming? How the hell . . . ?"

Another fast move for me, risking a bullet to melt the few steps between us. I expected Coker to be surprised just long enough for me to turn things in my favor, but he didn't try to shoot. I took his gun without even token resistance.

"You're dead," he whispered, all astonishment as I backed off, covering him. "Dead . . . oh. Oh, shit."

Then Coker settled unsteadily into the chair behind the desk. He'd gone abruptly gray-faced.

"You lemme finish!" shouted Rita, surging in like the marines. I put an arm out and kept her from hitting him.

"Never mind, honey, that's enough for now," I said, for

by then I'd caught the whiff of bloodsmell.

Coker put a hand to his chest. The hole there wasn't big, but colorful. Red pumped down his white shirtfront. "Damn," he said. "That hurts like hell. That—"

He bowed his head and kept bowing until he slipped untidily from the chair. His body struggled with a long ugly spasm and made ugly sounds as it fought against inevitability.

I watched without pity, without any emotion at all, remembering what he and his men had done to me and what he'd done to his men. Maybe now I'd be able to forget about that one mug and his burned-down cigarette.

Nevis was the first to wake out of the spell. He went to Coker and checked him over, slowly straightening. He looked at me, then Rita, who'd gone quiet. He shrugged and sat on the couch. He pulled out a cigarette. His hands were steady.

"Gimme," said Rita. This time I let her push past. She dropped heavily next to Nevis, who gave her one from his pack and a light. I had to turn away. I wasn't beyond feeling after all, but this one was of nausea for a memory, not for what lay on the floor.

"What did you think you were doing?" Nevis asked her. "Were you gonna get me next?"

"No—yes—I don't know. You two were—oh, jeez, Booth, after what he did to Lena how could you hop into bed with him like that?" She got up and came to stand on my right. I put the guns in my coat pockets. Quite a collection I had, including Upshaw's.

"He was making a deal to stay alive," I explained. "He had no intention of turning the club over to Shivvey. He was buying time."

Nevis snorted. "Hell, yes. You stop to ask directions or something? I was running out of ideas."

That'd be the day, I thought.

She looked up at me. "Really? He was just shooting bull?"

"Yeah, really. I was in the next room over, heard the whole thing."

"But I was going to—"

"The less said the better, honey."

She frowned fiercely at the body. "What do I do?"

"Nothing," said Nevis. "It's all figured. You go home."

"Then what?"

"You go home, you forget about it."

"Can you?" There was no reproach in her question; she wanted to know what he intended toward her.

He smiled. It was a death's-head kind of grin on his gaunt face. "You did me a favor. I don't forget favors. Maybe you were gonna plug me, too, but it didn't happen, so get out. Me and Fleming got work to do."

"Work?"

"Cleanup," I said, nodding down at Coker's mortal and quite solid remains. They wouldn't be going anywhere without help.

"Oh."

"You'll be all right?"

She took a heavy draw on her cigarette, and my gaze slipped elsewhere for a second, then returned. "I donno. What's gonna happen to me?"

"Nothing. You go home and have a drink for Lena. You did the right thing for her."

She had to know that, to believe it. Maybe I could help her out with a mental push and nudge later on if it was necessary, but for now she needed to be sure of the rightness of her action. It would make the nights to come easier.

That's what I always told myself when I thought about the people I'd killed.

* * *

This time I made sure that Rita actually boarded the El, then went back to help Nevis. He had a plan, the first part requiring we back Upshaw's car into the alley. We parked it close to the door, then hauled Coker's body out, tucking it into the trunk.

Next I drove us to a diner, where Nevis bought a couple cups of coffee and some sandwiches. All of it was for him, and he did not enjoy the coffee to judge by his expression as he drank. He gave me terse directions between bites as he wolfed the sandwiches.

We ended up at a small airport. It seemed closed for the night, but no one challenged us as we went through the gates and up to a cluster of small buildings where lights still shone. They were surmounted by a tower that vaguely reminded me of a lighthouse. I waited in the car while Nevis bolted out and did whatever business was required. I didn't ask, as it would have made a delay. When you have a body in your trunk, you don't want things like delays.

It took him just under ten minutes.

"Goddamn cops," he grumbled, climbing into the passenger seat. He now wore a fleece-lined leather jacket over his suit and had pulled on another pair of pants made of heavy wool. It looked bulky, but warm.

"Cops?"

"They were here earlier. Told the guy running this place that he should make sure I didn't try to skip off to Canada in my plane. Told him to put it out of commission and call them if I showed up."

"Did he?"

"Of course not." He sounded pained. "We go back a long ways. Besides, the cops don't pay him, I do. Take us over to that hangar that's opening up."

I took us. The hangar was massive, holding several different small planes. The man who had opened the wide doors turned the lights on, gave us a friendly wave, and walked unconcernedly off toward the tall tower. Whether it was on purpose or not, he never once looked back.

Nevis had me park next to one of the planes. I didn't know much about them, only that they were heavier than air. Given that important fact, I knew I would stick to trains, cars, or my own feet when it came to travel. Nevis concentrated on checking his machine over top to bottom. He made a thorough job of it, his engrossment such that even I could see he was probably a very good pilot. I stayed quiet and out of his way until, satisfied, he motioned for me to open the trunk.

The hangar lights recklessly on, we loaded Coker into the passenger seat of the plane. It was a good-size craft, with space for two more seats in the rear; only those had been removed to make room for a small cargo. I wondered if Nevis missed his days as a rumrunner of select, expensive booze.

We belted Coker in. He kept bowing forward until Nevis found a strap to tie him in place.

"That'll hold long enough," he said. "Just until I can get rid of him."

"You'll want some weights so he doesn't float."

"What? I'm not dumping him in the lake. No need." He picked Coker's pockets clean of wallet, keys, and other items—including the little records book.

"Where then?"

"Not sure exactly. They got some good thick woods up in Wisconsin. They'll do fine."

"You're burying him in the woods?"

"No, I'm dropping him."

I wasn't sure that I'd heard him right and said as much.

He closed the passenger door and ducked under it to come up the other side. I followed.

"I just keep flying north," he said. "It's easy at night. You can see where the lights give out. When I find a big enough patch of black below I just push our friend here out. From that height, the body pretty much goes to pieces when it hits the ground. The bears and other animals take care of the rest."

Not a picture I wanted in my head, but I had worse things there. This one at least explained something about that fragment of a phone conversation I'd overheard the other night.

He shot me another grin like death, then opened the book. He flipped through the pages, giving them the same concentration he'd afforded his plane. "That's her writing," he concluded, sounding resigned. "I remember this bet— it was a hell of a payoff, and on my birthday, too. Made me wish I'd placed some real money on that nag. Lena took a fifty from that one."

"You sure you're not sore at her?"

"I'm sure. She wasn't obvious about it, and she never acted guilty. I've had other girls who tried to steal off the top, and they did both. Annoyed the hell outta me. Lena ... well ..." He released a short breath and shut the book. "I don't like to think of her dying like she did. If that's how it happened, then he got off too easy, too quick." He looked toward the plane.

Coker's body was in shadow, but you could tell it was a man sitting there. Sitting a lot too still to be right.

"Maybe ... maybe her heart gave out. I mean she'd have been scared, and bad off, but that's better than—"

"It happened a long time ago, Nevis. She's not hurting now."

A small kind of shift took place in him. "Okay, you're right. I better get in the air before the coffee wears off.

Thanks for the help."

"You're welcome. You mean that about Rita? You going to leave her alone?"

"Like I said, she did me a favor. You don't need to worry about her. We'll get together tomorrow sometime and have that drink to Lena, huh?"

"Sure."

"You seeing Rita tonight?"

"I got a mess of my own to clear up." I nodded at the car, where Upshaw sprawled out of sight in the back.

"Heh, when you sock 'em they stay socked. Looks like some of the stuff I've heard about you is true."

"Maybe." I would have liked to have found out what he'd heard, but this wasn't the time.

I hung around long enough to watch him take off, following the retreating shape of his sleek silver plane against what to me was a pale gray sky. The haze of distance soon blended the silver with the gray until it was quite invisible. After that I returned to the city, satisfied that most of my problems were over, or could be shoved aside for later consideration.

There was one left to me I felt would never be resolved, though. Nevis and Rita thought that Lena's murderer was dead.

Only I knew better.

15

ESCOTT used his pliers to pull out yet another jagged piece of shrapnel from the wall to expertly flip into the wastebasket standing in the middle of my office. He was able to work faster than I and had nearly cleared two walls of the stuff while I smoothed patching plaster into the holes. We both wore overalls and were generously coated with plaster dust, paint, and other remodeling souvenirs. The newly glazed windows were covered by blinds; the broken glass was swept away.

For the last two hours, since we'd arrived at Lady Crymsyn, I'd been telling him all that he'd missed for being in New York tracing a purloined pooch. It shouldn't have taken me so long, but he had questions, and that drew out the process. In exchange for being caught up, he'd offered to help me gradually restore order to the grenade-induced chaos.

"So I came back here," I said, "and found Gordy waiting in the lobby with a regular goon squad of muscle all set to charge San Juan Hill."

"May I take that to mean he understood the significance of the wreckage here?" Escott indicated the walls and holes in the floor, which was presently protected by a stained tarp. I'd bought a thick rug to hide the latter damage until it could be repaired.

"In spades. He didn't know what to think since there was no blood or bodies, but it got him moving. He figured if I came back I might need help, so he brought in plenty. I explained everything." That had taken some doing. In his own laconic way, Gordy had expressed a sincere desire to take Tony Upshaw apart with a dull boning knife and distribute the pieces up and down the Chicago River. I'd eventually convinced him how unnecessary it was since Tony no longer recalled his crime. In fact, he was back giving dance lessons at his studio, his conscience clean, his memory thoroughly scrubbed by yours truly. Before leaving him to wake in his car I'd thought of accounting for his bloodied clothes and bruises and decided against it. Everyone needs some mystery in his life.

"I hope you thanked Gordy for his concern."

"Yeah. I did." It cost me a few rounds of drinks at another bar, but well worth it for the goodwill among us all. Gordy was quietly relieved that I was unharmed, and pleased that Shivvey Coker was no longer running around. "He needed killing," he'd told me. I'd kept the more interesting news like the who and how of his death to just between ourselves. His men were content to drink their beers, used to the fact that—unlike their boss—they didn't need to know all that went on in the city.

"And what about Mr. Nevis?"

"He got back from his wilderness flight, then slept through the next twenty-four hours. Far as the cops know he's never been out of town."

"The police are still interested in him?"

"Not really. Not since I talked to Lieutenant Blair. Shivvey was the next boy they wanted to interview, both about Lena and the barbershop killings. All those guys were known to be his cronies, and suddenly he ups and leaves town without a trace. Pretty suspicious behavior."

"But would that not lead them to conjecture he might also be a victim of foul play?"

"Yeah, but I paid a trip to his hotel and did some packing. I made it look hurried. His car is gone, too. They'll draw the right conclusions."

"I hope you weren't seen."

"Gimme a break." No one could have spotted my very late-night entry into Coker's rooms. They'd been on the fourth floor, but I'd quelled my dislike of heights and floated up the side of the building to sieve in through the window. I'd gone through the place like a dose of salts, stuffing a couple of suitcases full of clothes and such papers and items as he might have taken along for an extended trip. I left behind what he might have left. Later, I got rid of it all at some charity places, making sure no one of them got more than a couple of things each.

Not a good feeling going through a dead man's effects. I kept looking over my shoulder as though expecting to see him hovering in midair with a hole in his chest and wearing an accusatory face. Stupid of me, since I'd not been the one to put it there. I chalked it up to nerves and just got the hell out, my fingers burning inside their gloves.

His car had required a little more effort, that is to say, Gordy's help. Pieces of it were now anonymously distributed in a dozen or more garages, parts shops, and wreckage yards throughout Cook County and beyond. It hadn't taken more than three hours for some mechanics to pull the thing apart, with other men stopping by to carry the pieces away. The whole process reminded me of ants stripping the body of a dead bug.

That's all there was to make a man disappear forever.

He'd left behind a reasonable hole, but it would soon fill up.

"The cops will keep hunting for him," I said. "On the books the Lena Ashley case will remain open, but Lieutenant Blair has privately made up his mind about Coker's guilt, same as Nevis and Rita."

"But you are certain Coker did not kill her?"

"I asked him straight-out while I had him under. I don't see how he could have lied, unless he was nuts or drunk, and I never got that off of him."

"Why not inform the police?"

"Because then they'd go back to questioning Rita and Nevis again, and I know for sure they're in the clear as well. Nothing would be served to keep pushing. All I can figure is Lena was into something over her head, or maybe she ran into some lunatic sadist. We'll never know. I suppose I could question every bookie in town that she had contact with. Sooner or later I might turn something up."

"There is an alternative."

"My ears are flapping, talk to me."

He paused in mid shrapnel-pull, frowning at the pocked wall and probably not seeing it. "I think it's a significant point about Mr. Coker that he persuaded Mr. Upshaw to do his dirty work for him. He wanted Booth Nevis out of the way, but delegated the task of actually throwing the grenades to another fellow. Suppose he did the same thing five years past to get rid of Lena Ashley?"

"Then he could truthfully say he hadn't killed her. When they're under they answer questions pretty literally. I should have thought of that."

"He might well have done the same in removing the previous owner of this place also. *Modus operandi* is a difficult habit to break—particularly when one is unaware of one's own pattern, or if it happens to work especially well."

"Huh. Guess I get to talk to Rita and Nevis again, though I don't think she had anything to do with it. Him neither for that matter, but I wanna cover the bases."

"Of course, one must be thorough. What if you're wrong about either of them?"

"I'll cross that bridge when I come to it," I said with the confidence of a man who knows there will be no bridge on his path. It was only an outside chance of Escott being right, after all, at least concerning them. Maybe Coker had fobbed the job off onto some other mug. Gris was still missing. Had he been around five years ago and up for hire? I'd talk it over with Gordy later.

"Hm." Escott wrestled with a deeply embedded piece and yanked it clear in a shower of plaster. "Oh, dear. There's a nasty mess."

"I'll fix it when I get there." I mashed patch into another hole and smoothed it. Leon Kell would have done a better job, but I had reason to keep the grenade incident from him and his work crew. The private party opening for Lady Crymsyn was only days away; I didn't want to spook them off.

"What about Miss Robillard? How is she doing?"

"Pretty well, as far as I can see."

"You're certain? She had a lengthy relationship with Mr. Coker, and then to be the one to kill him . . . it doesn't strike me that she would recover too quickly from such a shock."

"She'll be all right. She's a tough gal."

She'd been steady enough right after the shooting, but a day of thinking it over had eaten away at her, with predictable results. I'd spent several hours with her the next night, holding her while she sobbed her head off. When the worst of the wave of rage, grief, regret, and guilt subsided, I did a little hypnotic suggestion work, hoping it wouldn't backfire. I couldn't take away what she'd done, but I could make it easier for her to live with it, but had to word everything most carefully. Easing her guilt was one thing, but I couldn't go too far with that lest she come to think it was okay to shoot just anyone who annoyed her.

Helping her seemed to help me, as well. She was able to express what I could not, and the reassurances I gave to her echoed back to me and settled down inside somewhere. Whenever my shoulders started to hunch up from a bad memory I'd hear myself talking to her and listen.

"She sounds a most remarkable young woman."

"I invited her to the opening. I'll introduce you. She'd go for you in a big way."

"Really, now, you were going to introduce me to the model you're hiring to impersonate Lady Crymsyn."

"Her, too, why not?"

"I'm not the sort who can divide his attention in that manner."

"Go on, I've seen you juggling lots of things at one time."

"Things, yes, young ladies, no. I prefer to deal with them one at a time, if you don't mind. It cuts down on mistakes, and where women are concerned one requires a great deal of concentration to avoid making too many errors."

"Too many?"

"It has been my experience that they allow you only a certain number, the exact amount of which is known only to themselves. Once a fellow has exceeded that number he may as well go home to his pipe and paper."

Escott spent a lot of evenings home that way. You'd think with that English accent he'd have women by the truckload, because I'd watched him use it to good effect on them. Maybe he didn't want to get tied down. A lot of women would count that against a man.

He kept at his work, his hands moving while his mind obviously soared elsewhere. I respected that he could do that. "Interesting about you being able to give Mr. Nevis a migraine," he said thoughtfully.

"Spooked the hell out of me. I thought I'd given him a heart attack or something."

"It was most disturbing to see, I'm sure."

"I think it was because I pushed him too hard, and he'd been drinking beforehand."

"I should like to question him about it."

"He won't remember anything. They never do."

"Pity."

Escott had a healthy curiosity about my condition that went beyond reading all the folklore about vampires—which was mostly wrong.

"I wish you would reconsider having yourself checked out by a physician," he said. "It might prove to be most valuable to know the exact nature of your condition in scientific terms. You could always hypnotize the fellow into forgetting about it afterward."

"Okay. I will."

He stopped work to gape at me, for I always turned him down. "You will?"

"Yeah, but first you go out and buy a really good double-breasted suit and wear it to work regularly."

Escott's reply was brief, scaldingly acidic, and not to be repeated in polite company, but the language he chose made me grin.

I'd turn him into an American yet.

The next few nights flew by as I put my full energy into getting the club ready. Though it looked all right, there was an astonishing amount that needed doing, but miracles can happen if you invest enough cash in them. I had to spend more than planned, but knew that I'd get it back. It was all legit business expenses, each one duly recorded in the ledgers by Malone.

He was the best miracle of all, interviewing and hiring the staff, getting them uniforms, and training them as to how things would be done at Lady Crymsyn. Hesitant at first, he gained a tremendous confidence in a very short time, and just as well. I was relying heavily upon him to keep things running during the day, but he was honestly interested in redeeming my trust and worked beyond my expectations.

There was a brief crisis concerning the actress who was to play Lady Crymsyn. Finding a girl who looked the part was less difficult than finding one who also had the presence to get away with it. She had to live up to the promise in the Alex Adrian portrait. Not easy. Such a girl was finally located, then Malone had to find a costume-maker who could reproduce the red gown in time. A ten-dollar bonus for the seamstress worked toward that end.

Bobbi had taken over the direction of the entertainment, having booked a band, several other performers, and arranged their order of presentation. She'd reserved the top billing of the evening for herself, with my wholehearted blessing, as she had more than earned it. Things were on the level, too, since I was paying her just like the rest. It felt odd to be giving my girlfriend money; Bobbi was very touchy about certain kinds of gifts, cash being on the forbidden list. But this was work, and Malone was the one writing up the checks; all I needed to do was to sign them. We kept it all on a professional level. It worked.

The rest of the details piled up and were either dealt with or put on the bottom of the stack depending on their importance or practicality. There was still a problem about the damned cement mixer, so the basement would go unfinished. The performers would have to make do with the few finished rooms on the main floor off the stage.

"Why is it so important to you?" Bobbi asked me after I'd groused about it one time too many. "And this time the real reason."

I swallowed back my usual answer about wanting everything to be perfect. Damn, but some nights she was a regular mind reader with me. "Okay. It's about Lena. I figure if the place is completely redone down there, maybe she will finally be laid to rest."

"Then I don't blame you, but what happened to her is all over with. You don't think she's the ghost messing with the lights, do you?"

I'd told Bobbi all about the interesting electrical games I'd witnessed. She half believed me. "No, I never thought that. Whatever is behind that is different."

"So is there another ghost in your basement?"

"No. Strictly in my head. I get pictures there and I don't like a lot of them. Changing things with cement and paint and lightbulbs will get rid of one of them." The one being the sight of Lena Ashley's spine bones sticking up out of the remnants of her red dress. The confining walls that had imprisoned her in the darkness were gone, but I had to have their marks on the floor and walls obliterated, too. Even then I wasn't sure if I'd ever feel completely at ease in that corner, but then knowing its history, who would?

Bobbi kept telling me everything would be fine. By next week, when the grand public opening took place, it would all be ready just the way I'd envisioned. This week, I'd just have to live with it.

Friday night I shot awake to the sounds of early activity. People, lots of them, were moving about, talking, joking, all quite unaware of my nearby presence.

I was not in the usual alcove at home, but on a cot with a layer of my earth that I'd installed at Lady Crymsyn. Having taken seriously Escott's suggestion about turning a section under the tier seating into a sanctuary, I'd moved in all the necessities, put a lock on the inside of the door, and allowed myself to surrender to my daylight coma with hardly a qualm. Leon and his crew were no longer needing the area for storage, and the waiters and bartenders had other places for their supplies. This spot was all mine. It was not for use every day since it wasn't fireproof, but this time I decided to take the risk.

The staff had come in before sunset to ready things, and I could hear Malone directing them. The sound of his distinctive voice, which was calm yet carrying in the big room, told me that all was going well. So far. The doors would open in less than half an hour. Had I stayed home, I'd have used up much of that meager time between my waking and the club opening just getting dressed and driving over. As it was I needed only to dress, having bathed and shaved just before coming to the club in the predawn to retire for the day.

I had a new tuxedo hanging ready for me on a convenient nail, a paper cover protecting it from stray dust. Tucking it and my shoes under one arm, I went over to remove the padlock from the inside, but changed my mind. People were working in the bar area opposite. It would require too much explanation to account for my eccentric emergence from under the seats, so I vanished to float up through the various barriers until reaching the second-floor hall. From there I floated to my empty office and went solid.

Escott and I had done a decent job of repair. The walls were whole again, the paint fumes all but gone, and the floor holes neatly covered by the rug. I tore the tux clear of its wrappings and quickly dressed. Bobbi, knowing I would be here, knocked and walked in just as I began to struggle with the cuff links.

"I thought it was about time for you to wake up," she said.

One look at her and I forgot all about the opening. She was in a spectacular white gown studded with hundreds of rhinestones that floated on her shoulders and arms like silver stars. They tapered off the lower you went on her body, whose every delicious curve was revealed by the drape of fine cloth. Silver-and-white shoes with more rhinestones caressed her feet.

She took in my expression and smiled. The special one that always sent me to the moon and back. "Well, I guess Joe James knew his stuff if this little rag makes you look like that."

"Uh . . ."

She did a slow turn. "You like it?"

"Um . . . ahh . . ."

"I guess that means yes."

"Uh." Oh, God, why did I have to waste my time opening this club tonight when I should be finding ways to get Bobbi out of that dress?

"Here, you need some help?"

"Yeah. Okay. Whatever you want, doll." Unable to think for the time being, I held my arm out so she could fix the links. Then she fussed with my collar and tie, and I thought the scent of her perfume would make my head explode. It took all my willpower to keep from dragging her down onto my desk right then and there to let her know how I felt.

"Your pants are a little tight here," she commented, her hand brushing dangerously close to a now highly sensitive and responsive area. I caught her wrists and raised them up, fiercely kissing them on the inside. The sweet pulsing of her blood teased, tempting me to linger.

"Don't make me any crazier than I am," I warned her. The white of the gown made me think of a wedding dress.

I wanted to propose to her again, even knowing that she would turn me down. It hurt to hold the question—plea?—inside, but giving it a voice would have spoiled the mood for her.

"I'm looking forward to seeing you after closing," she said. "You'll really be worked up then."

Or flattened into a state of exhaustion. "How are things downstairs?"

"Everything is going very well. I really like your Mr. Malone. He brought his little girl in today. He couldn't get a sitter for her for the afternoon. She's so precious. She sat up here and drew pictures of the building. This one's for you." Bobbi held up a pencil-and-crayon sketch on graph paper that seemed too good to have been done by a child of Norrie's age. It was very recognizably the front facade of Lady Crymsyn, right down to the diamond-shaped windowpanes in red. Off to the side stood three figures, more simply executed, all wearing smiles and waving.

"Customers?" I asked, pointing at them.

"That's you, her, and her father. She thinks he half owns the place."

"He works like he does. I'll have to give him a raise. The kid still here?" I wanted to say thank you.

"I took her home an hour ago. She's so sweet. I gave her a tour of the dressing rooms and did her nails up with polish. She was very impressed with the big girl stuff. Too bad he won't be able to marry again and give her a mother. She could use one." Bobbi knew all about Malone and had no illusions that he'd make the same mistake twice about marriage.

"Thought you didn't like kids."

"I like 'em fine—so long as they behave and they're someone else's. Hold still, your tie is crooked."

"Okay, okay, but hurry, I gotta get downstairs."

"Put your shoes on first."

"Oh. Jeez."

She watched with an indulgent expression. "Jack, stop a minute and listen to me."

I recognized that tone and did exactly that. "Yeah?"

"I've done countless opening shows, acts, reviews, you name it. I've never, ever done one that was one hundred percent perfect. So take a deep breath—whether you need it or not—and remember that you're doing this for *fun*. You are to enjoy tonight, because you will only have this kind of opening once. It won't ever come again. Relax, enjoy, and have fun so you can give yourself a good memory about the next few hours. You got that?"

There was no not-getting it with her. "Did I ever tell you you're the greatest?"

"Yes, and don't ever stop."

"Mr. Fleming, I didn't see you come in." Malone looked very dapper in his tuxedo. All that distinguished him from the arriving crowd were the white gloves he wore. The bruises on his face hadn't completely faded, but the self-possessed demeanor he'd assumed for the evening made them less noticeable.

"I snuck in. How we doing?"

Bobbi, who had come downstairs with me, patted my arm once, then went off to see to backstage things. The lobby doors were wide-open, lights blazed inside and out, and early arrivals were starting to outnumber the wait staff.

"Everything is going very well," he said, sounding similar enough in tone to Bobbi to make me think they'd rehearsed together for my benefit. "Leon told me to tell you that the cement mixer finally arrived. He put it downstairs."

"A milestone," I grumbled.

"Mm?"

"It's about time. Now they can finish that floor." I started calculating how long it would take for the cement to cure so the crew could build the dressing rooms. Even paying them extra for working the weekend and evenings, I couldn't see how they could get it all done by next Friday . . .

Made myself stop. Bobbi would have pinched me good for my getting distracted by things out of my control. I was supposed to enjoy tonight, not worry about tomorrow's labors.

"What was that?" I asked.

Malone repeated, "Lady Crymsyn is here as well."

I blinked in the direction he indicated. "Great. I see the dress got done in time."

"Indeed, and the young lady inside it is doing an excellent job." He drew me over to a delicate-looking delight of a girl with straight brows and striking hazel eyes. Her thick dark hair was swept up in a style identical to the Lady Crymsyn portrait, and she filled every inch of the blazing red costume as though it had been designed for her, not the other way around. "Miss LaBelle, this is Mr. Jack Fleming, the owner of the club. Mr. Fleming, Sherry LaBelle."

"Charmed, I'm sure," she said, her bewitching smile uncannily like the one in the picture. I had to firmly remind myself that I was not exactly available as I took her hand and gave it a brief, polite shake. In no way would I attempt to kiss it. Escott could get away with those kinds of suave Continental manners, but not this Cincinnati-born mug. I'd just slobber on her knuckles or fall over or worse.

"Everything under control?" I asked, to linger a bit longer.

"Oh, yes. You've a wonderful place here. I almost feel like I am Lady Crymsyn." She motioned toward the portrait that loomed behind her.

"You do acting the rest of the time? When you're not doing this?" Good grief, I hadn't been this tongue-tied since being in short pants.

"I try. Work is a bit thin, but it always is, so I do all that I can."

"And you can come back again next week?"

"Yes, I'd be happy to."

Malone gently led me away as a fresh group of patrons came up to meet "Lady Crymsyn." The women complimented her dress, the men reacted about the same as I to the rest of the package. Sherry LaBelle gave them all her gracious attention and answered their questions about the club as though she owned it.

"It's just as well she is able to return," Malone said. "It would be a terrible mess otherwise. We'd have to find someone who not only looked right, but she'd have to fit the dress as well."

I was glad he had such practical matters well in hand. Once out of the hypnotizing presence of Miss LaBelle I found myself better able to assume my own role as grand host. For this all I had to do was stand in the lobby and meet and greet dozens of familiar faces and the people with them. Not hard, not hard at all.

Many of them I'd met at the Nightcrawler, all come over to sample the potential delights of my place. Both clubs were alike in swank, but mine did not offer gambling in the back rooms. Gordy and I wouldn't be in any serious kind of competition for customers.

Gordy himself finally came through the double doors, filling most of the space. On his arm was the radio actress Adelle Taylor, looking very edible in a cream-and-rose gown that set off her pale skin and black hair. Behind them marched a slow parade consisting of large-shouldered guys with grim faces (Gordy's bodyguards), and another, more ordinary couple (Gordy's lawyer and his wife). I wel-

comed them all, collecting pecks on the cheek from the
ladies and handshakes from the men. The bodyguards held
apart from this, keeping their hands free should they deem
it necessary to draw forth the guns that threw off the hang
of their suits.

"Kid, it looks like you've done it after all," Gordy said,
pumping my hand and almost smiling. For him this was
really being effusive, but he relaxed a lot when in Adelle's
company.

"I hope so." It meant a lot to hear him say that.

"You'll get used to it."

"Maybe." I thought about what Bobbi had said about
this kind of night happening only once. She was absolutely
right. Better for me that I savor every moment of it and
enjoy. "I'll make a point to do so. I hope this isn't taking
anything away from your place."

"It can run itself for one night," he said. "And you're
located far enough away so I don't have to worry much."

That was a relief. I'd known it to be true, but it was
good to have it confirmed.

" 'Sides," he continued. "Wouldn't be right for me to
miss your opening. I feel like a godfather to this place."

That comment inspired a double take from me. I sin-
cerely hoped Gordy wouldn't like my club *too* much. Ah,
nuts. He was kidding. Yeah, he had to be kidding.

Malone turned up just then to escort Gordy and his party
to their specially reserved table. I'd drop by on them all
later and hope that the mantle of confident host would be
firmly in place on me by then.

More arrivals, more smiles, more handshakes, more of
a lot of good things. Everyone appeared to be in a light
mood and highly impressed with the joint. I felt a return
of that fullness of feeling that was pure pride of ownership.
It even lasted through the arrival of Booth Nevis. Rita
Robillard, his date for the evening, held his arm with one

hand and a small bunch of flowers in the other. She wore black again, a long gown with skirts composed of layers of silky stuff that swirled around her ankles like smoke as she walked. This wasn't the time or place, but I couldn't help wondering if she'd left her underwear home again. Happy as that prospect might be, there would be no wild dancing on the tables here. Not tonight, anyway.

"How are you?" I asked her.

"I'm aces," she chirped, looking happy. "This is some joint, Jack. It was nothing like this when Welsh was in charge."

"Wait'll you see the rest."

"I'm going to give her a small tour," said Nevis. "If that's okay."

"Just the public areas, if you don't mind. The dressing rooms are pretty full right now."

Rita shot him a tense, pleading look. "Booth."

He nodded at her. "Uh, Fleming, Rita would like to, well, that place in the basement . . ."

"What about it?" I was missing something.

Rita held up the flowers. "I just wanna, you know, put these there. For Lena from me and Booth. You know."

I leaned forward to peck her cheek. "Of course. I'll have Malone show you through. Take all the time you want."

"So Malone worked out for you here?" asked Nevis.

"He's doing a great job."

"I should hire him back, but I think you're paying him more. He's a good worker. Very honest."

And wasted as a bartender at Nevis's club. I kept my thoughts to myself, and called Malone over to see to things. Nevis was talking to him in a friendly way as they went into the main room. Jeez, *Nevis* was talking. After that polishing job he'd done on Coker, it was entirely possible he could persuade Malone into going back.

No, that was *not* going to happen. Nevis might win Ma-

lone over, but I'd still have the last word. I'd use hypnosis
to keep him on my payroll. Nothing quite like fighting
dirty, especially when the competition doesn't know about
it.

Time to play host again. The next wave brought in Tony
Upshaw and half a dozen leggy women, with Ruth Woodring holding his arm in a casually possessive manner. They
were all dancers if I could judge anything by their collec-
tive look. Perhaps Miss Woodring was combining business
with pleasure by showing off the best students from her
studio. I had the feeling that Upshaw would be twirling
each one of them over the floor tonight.

"Jack, you darling man," she said, forsaking Upshaw's
arm to latch on to mine. She seemed to have forgotten that
she'd been mad at me for all but openly accusing her precious Tony of murder. "I hope you'll forgive me and let
me in."

She hadn't forgotten, then. "Nothing to forgive. I was a
louse, but it's all over now." It seemed wise to play the
gallant with her in the interests of peace.

"Oh, you *are* a darling. Tony explained to me that you
had only the best of intentions."

"The only thing to pack on the road to hell." She seemed
confused, trying to work out if that was a barb or not, so
I softened things with a smile. "You're looking quite
lovely tonight, Miss Woodring. I'm glad you're here. You
will make the place beautiful."

She relaxed, but was somewhat nonplussed by the sin-
cerity of the compliment. "Why, thank you. I needed to
give this an airing." She was dressed head to foot in some
pleated gold gown that was vaguely Egyptian in design. It
ended just at her shoulders, which were decked in a wide
elaborate thing that looked like a cross between a flat collar
and a necklace. It had a lot of beads, glass, and gold thread.
Matching bracelets covered her arms halfway to the el-

bows. Her long shock of red hair was in a single braid that trailed down her front. She followed no fashion that I knew of, but everything looked good on her.

Upshaw was urbane and butter smooth, giving no sign that not too many nights back he'd been cowering on the stairs over there begging me not to hit his face. I shook his hand, welcomed him, and gestured for them to avail themselves of the main room within. It was all I could manage. I still had a very strong desire to punch that Roman nose of his around so it would stick out one of his ears.

That image put me back in a cheerful mood again.

Joe James turned up, shook my hand quite a lot, and introduced me to some theatrical types with whom he'd been staying. The woman looked like a Valkyrie minus her spear and horse; the man had a flowing black beard like a cartoon Russian. Actors in search of a stage, I thought, greeting them. They both enthusiastically dragged Joe off toward the bar. Yes, definitely actors.

Another wave of motley people hit, Escott standing out from them because of his height and manner. It wasn't something you could catch with a photograph, but tonight he looked decidedly more *English* than usual. He'd taken some trouble with his preparations: a haircut, his tux was postcard perfect, and I caught a distinct whiff of shaving lotion as he came over to shake my hand.

"Congratulations, old man. Looks like you've a real success on your hands."

His open enthusiasm really meant a lot to me. "So I've been told. I just hope the place is packed like this every night."

"Indeed. And where might I find—ah." His gaze froze in the direction of Sherry LaBelle, who was busy doing a slow turn in front of Joe James's critical eye. He seemed pleased. Considering his likes and dislikes, the approval had to be for the dress, not the girl.

Escott had a clear field. . . . and he was rooted in place, his jaw uncharacteristically dragging in a floorward direction. This was interesting; he always had something to say.

"Hey," I said.

No response. Good grief. She was a dish, but he was a big boy. He knew how to deal with beautiful women. At least I thought he did.

"Hey. Charles."

I'd heard the term *poleaxed* before, but had never actually seen it in action. He was showing all the symptoms.

"Charles. Charles—wake up before I have to stuff you with sawdust and put you in a corner."

"If it is next to that charming creature, I shouldn't mind a bit," he murmured dreamily.

He could still talk. "Come on, you've never even met her. She looks like the painting, she might not *be* like the painting, not for real."

He darted a surprised glance at me. "Yes, of course. And fish are allergic to water. Stop wasting time, man, and introduce us."

As there was a break in the line, I took advantage of it and did my social duty toward them both. Escott executed the slight bow-and-hand-kissing routine, only he made it seem like she was the only woman he'd ever tried it on. She responded with a smile, to his full-force, but under-control charm, keeping in character until I mentioned that Escott was my best friend and occasional partner in business ventures. She took this to mean he had an active interest in the club and warmed up a bit more. Knowing how I'd feel were the situation reversed, I retreated quickly from the picture so he could get on with things.

My retreat took me straight into a gaggle of reporters, and without warning at least three flashbulbs went off in my face. The scribblers then moved in, calling questions on top of one another while I dealt with temporary blindness.

Huh. I'd expected them to be here much earlier.

They were new faces, not the ones I'd put the evil eye on a week ago. The papers they represented had long been informed of the club's private opening. My plan had been to gain publicity for the club of the right kind, for them to write about the entertainment, not corpses in the basement. These guys had other ideas, though, and hammered away about Lena Ashley. I said I was satisfied that the police were doing a good job and pretended ignorance on the progress of the investigation. Not what they wanted to hear, but an invitation to a round of free drinks softened them quite a lot. After a third round was made to disappear they promised to write a glowing report about the club and mention its public grand opening next Friday. I was too smart to give them unlimited drinks for the evening; they'd have put me out of business.

That problem solved, I returned to my unofficial post by the doors to greet more people and was pleased when Shoe Coldfield turned up. His skin color brought an instant halt to most of the conversation in the lobby. It resumed again with whispers and not a few looks of horror, but they could go to hell. This was my place; all my friends were welcome.

"Good to see you," I said. More handshaking and grins.

"Well, I had to find out what the new kid on the block was doing. Charles wasn't exaggerating. This is one nice shack you've set up."

Before I could ask what Escott had said about the place, Coldfield introduced me to a stunning woman with cocoa skin and melting eyes. I didn't catch her name, only that she was a singer at his club, and I promised myself I'd come listen to her at the first opportunity. She had a deep contralto speaking voice, and I knew she'd look perfect in that blue satin dress sitting on a piano picked out by a single spotlight. Like Gordy, Coldfield had a couple of guards with him, only they'd brought dates along. It was a subtle point no doubt planned by Coldfield. A man on his own can be a target for trouble; a man with a woman along was only looking for a good time. I signed to Malone to escort them to their reserved space.

"Where's Charles?" Coldfield asked.

"He's just over—" No, he wasn't. Miss LaBelle was on her own, but positively glowing from more than what was required by her role. Good, he'd made progress with her but wasn't overdoing things. "Probably inside by now. I put him at your table. If he looks like a stunned pigeon, there's a reason for it."

"What reason?"

I nodded toward Sherry LaBelle. Coldfield looked ready to burst into laughter.

"Okay, I won't rib him too much. It's about time he discovered women again."

Some ancient history—the bad kind—had turned Escott into something of a recluse for several years. He was gradually breaking free of it.

"I'll see you later," said Coldfield, and allowed his group to be led away.

The next one through the doors was a surprise. Lieutenant Blair sauntered forward, putting out his hand. The illusion of a perpetual smile lent to him by the trim of his mustache was very pronounced. He seemed most pleased with himself.

"You've got quite a gathering here," he said. "Haven't seen so many of the wise crowd in one spot since Big Al was in town. What are you trying to do here?"

True, more than three-quarters of the people here were in the mob or connected to it. I'd have to widen my circle of friends. "Show everyone a good time. That's all."

"Of course, of course. But you'll have to excuse the men I've got outside if they note down the names of some of your customers—it's only in regard to the Ashley case," he lied.

So he wasn't here as a mere guest, but then I'd not expected that. "I thought you'd closed it."

"Not completely. I've got a new angle. We were able to take some prints off those books you gave me."

The noise around us seemed to fade as I focused my undivided attention on him. Hypnosis was unnecessary, though; he was eager to talk. "What about them?"

"We identified her. It just came in today. You probably know something about it. You were in New York at the time."

"About what?"

"Lena Ashley's real name was Helen Tielli." He gave the name an emphasis of importance.

Almost familiar, but my memory didn't toss out anything useful. "Was she an actress? With the mobs?"

"Close enough. I got some extra wire photos of the newspaper articles. Thought you'd like to see them since you've a vested interest in the case." He drew a narrow envelope from his inside pocket and gave it to me. "Consider it a thank-you for your help."

I sorted through the articles—one of them was from the paper I'd once worked at—and the general facts of the whole monstrous story came back to me. "You sure Lena was this Tielli woman?" I asked, feeling disturbed and not a little sickened.

"The general description of Lena and Helen match, same as for a thousand other women, but fingerprints don't lie."

"But how could she be? From what I heard from her friends they really liked her. Loved her, even. How could she have been that way and do something like this?" I indicated the papers, wanting him to gainsay their facts.

Blair shrugged. "I've seen enough so I know it's not impossible for someone like her to have a good side. They commit a crime that would make a mortician vomit and then forget about it ten minutes later like some animal. Except an animal has a reason for its actions. Helen Tielli had no such excuse."

I shook my head. "The world's in a toilet."

"Yes. Too bad we couldn't have caught up with her. Someone else did instead. It was a hideous way to die, but with her history . . . I'd say justice was served. And"—his teeth glinted and his eye was hard—"don't quote me on that."

"I'm not with the papers anymore. Just a humble saloon keeper, now."

Blair looked all about him, making a show of it. "You've made up a whole new meaning for the word *humble*, Fleming. Better send it in to Webster's, and quick." Blair went off to pay his respects to "Lady Crymsyn." I hoped he wouldn't be sharing his information with the now-drunk reporters. Probably not just yet. He'd more likely be checking on any men he'd posted inside.

"Where'd that dinge and his buddies come from?" a man asked, jarring me from my reading of the articles. "I didn't know you had the place that much open."

Hot flare of anger. I looked down at Gardner Pourcio. He was in a sharply cut suit, big cigar at a defiant angle between his lips. Had to let my eyes slide past for a second as an unpleasant picture flashed through my mind. Damn, I could still smell the burned flesh.

"His name is Shoe Coldfield," I said evenly.

"Oh, so *that's* him. Heard he was running things in the Bronze Belt. What are you doing mixing with the criminal element in this town I ask you? He's one tough mug."

Considering how he made a living, Pourcio had no business turning his nose up at criminal elements. "He's one of my good friends. Understand?"

"Oh, okay, I get it, takes all kinds, I guess. So, where's the action here?" He glanced around expectantly.

"I told you the club is on the up-and-up."

"Come on, no one opens a joint like this without having something on the side. Is it upstairs?"

Sighing, I fixed him with a look. "No gambling here, Pourcio. Just good booze and a great show." *Release*.

He shook his head. "Well, that's a crock. How's a guy supposed to earn a living? Saa—aay, who's the pippin in the red dress?" He craned for a look at "Lady Crymsyn."

"She's spoken for, so don't even try." He had enough wives.

"Just my luck. I better stick to cards tonight, then. You sure done a job here, though. I wouldn't a known the joint, 'cept for right over there." He pointed at the lobby bar, which was doing good business. "That's where the lady bartender got it when they croaked Welsh. Finally remembered her name—Myrna. She was a hot little pippin, too, the poor kid."

Behind him, the bar light went out. The bartender there absently turned it back on again, and took another order.

"Caught it right inna throat, boom. But it was quick, I'll say that."

Out again. This time the bartender mouthed annoyance as he slapped the toggle.

"She maybe din' know what hit her," Pourcio went on, oblivious of the show.

Out.

"You were friends with this Myrna?" I asked.

He held up crossed fingers. "Hey, me and that sweet twist were *this* close."

Now all the lobby lights went out, causing a slight stir with my guests.

I showed my teeth. "Pourcio—you are a goddamned liar."

Without hurry I went to the wall panel and flipped the switches back up once more. I stared at the bar. Nothing visible behind it except the flesh-and-blood hired help.

Pourcio followed the direction of my stare and misinterpreted. "Good idea, Fleming. Don't mind if I do." He strolled over in search of a drink.

Would that I could have one, too. A double. "Myrna?" I whispered, experimentally.

No reaction from the lights. If not for the show that had taken place while I'd been bleeding out all over the floor with a broken back, I'd have put this down to coincidence. Not anymore. Well, if there had to be a resident ghost in the club at least it—she—had a sense of humor.

16

Long after Pourcio drifted off I stood in the middle of the lobby, reading the murky copies of what had once been fresh, screaming headlines. The passage of time had not moderated the—well, what could I call it? Not a tragedy, for those are usually the result of random accident or poor decisions. Crime was too mild a descriptive. It was vile, and it was vicious, the result of the kind of stupidity and selfishness and, perhaps, insanity that is beyond any understanding; yet there was a perverse logic to Lena's—Helen's—actions.

So absorbed was I that I didn't notice when Malone came up. I started slightly upon suddenly noticing him at my shoulder. He flinched with one of those tics, and we both traded grins at this mutual show of nerves. Mine felt sickly.

"It's time for the show to start," he said, giving what seemed to be a reproachful glance at my distraction.

I pulled myself together and hastily shoved the papers away in my pocket. "Okay, let's break a leg."

He'd had enough contact with the performers to understand the theatrical version of warding off bad luck and trailed a half step behind me.

Lady Crymsyn was already in the wings waiting for her cue from me. The waiters and waitresses were busy darting around the tables, making sure everyone got well oiled. The guests were lively and talking, some circulating to greet friends, others on the dance floor. A party mood suffused the whole huge room, as it should. I noted that the air circulation was working, visibly drawing the smoky byproduct of hundreds of cigarettes and cigars upward.

One part of my mind was pleased over how smoothly things were proceeding—and they'd damned well better be smooth considering they'd been planned down to the last martini olive. Another, much more anxious part, was trying roughly to calculate how many drink sales it would take to pay for everything tonight. I consciously shoved the worrywart into a cash drawer and locked it fast. An unfortunate image, considering the fate of Lena Ashley.

Helen Tielli. I remembered the baby teeth Rita and I had found and realized who they'd really belonged to. Had they been keepsakes or souvenirs?

Wiping off a scowl before it could form, I kept moving until the smile I pasted in its place became genuine.

I was greeted a second time as I moved through the crowd—and it was a crowd—affectionately hailed by dozens feeling the effects of drinks and a good time. Some wanted to be known as friends of the owner, no doubt, but it felt immensely satisfying all the same to step up on the stage and tap the microphone to see if it worked. Filtered through the loudspeaker system, the taps turned into minor explosions, startling a few and gaining the attention of all.

Maybe I should have been nervous; I was never much for public speaking until taking a couple of debating classes in college. Those removed the terror of being the focus of an audience. Most of it, anyhow. But this was different. I was in charge, everyone was smiling and on my side, and it made me feel light yet powerful. No wonder Bobbi was so addicted to the spotlights.

The orchestra leader nodded at my cue and wound down the current song, allowing the dancers to find their seats. Several of the women were with Upshaw's party, all looking very decorative. I was curious about Upshaw's whereabouts and interested to see him seated at Booth Nevis's table. So my hypnosis had worked. Neither of them recalled any attempts to kill the other.

A sprinkling of applause brought me back to the business at hand, which was to introduce myself (more applause), compliment the audience, and thank them for being there (and more applause). Damn, but this was fun. I caught a glimpse of Bobbi shimmering in the wings. She grinned and gave me a double-thumbs-up sign.

As I didn't want the focus of the club to be on me, I'd created the mythical character of Lady Crymsyn to fill that part. She was a rare and mysterious creature deigning to share a few moments with lesser mortals. I used words to that effect as part of my introduction before finally calling her forth to present her formally to the house.

Applause. Lots of it. I wasn't sure if anyone understood the idea I was trying to get across, giving the club a personification, or if they thought she was the real owner of the place. It didn't matter. Lady Crymsyn was beautiful and gracious, and their response to her was gratifying. I slipped off the stage to allow her the freedom to get on with her Mistress of Ceremonies duties. Bobbi, having a lot of experience in the area, had written out what was required, and Sherry LaBelle flawlessly got through it all without making it seem rehearsed. She also acknowledged the orchestra, called attention to the outstanding efforts of the staff so as to encourage tipping, then introduced the first act, a local radio comedian who strongly resembled Eddie Cantor.

The spotlight shifted to him, and Lady Crymsyn faded back to the wings. I wanted to go there myself, but Bobbi had forbidden it for the sake of the performers. "They know their business," she said. "If you turn up, they'll think you don't trust them." Not willing to add to their opening night jitters, I climbed to the top tier where my reserved table was, shaking hands along the way as the comic started raking in his first laughs.

Escott was installed between Gordy's mob and Coldfield's party. Smart thinking on my part. Gordy and Coldfield did know of each other, but rarely did their worlds overlap. Escott was the perfect go-between for both. I wasn't exactly trying to form a League of Nations among the various elements of Chicago's underworld, but it wouldn't hurt for these two to socialize.

Coldfield's presence garnered continual looks, some of curiosity, others of disgust, but I made a point of shaking his hand again. He was well aware of what I was doing and played along, barely hiding his amusement at my efforts to improve race relations.

Gordy had also been briefed about who he'd be in close proximity to for the evening. If he had objections, he was canny enough not to voice them, and sometimes Escott had to lean back out of the way so the two gang leaders could exchange a comment. Escott finally gave up and excused himself so he could speak to me.

"She said she would join us later," he began, not bothering to identify which "she" in the room. It was unnecessary. "How long will she be involved with the show?"

"You'll have to be patient; she's got a full card for most of the evening."

He looked mildly disappointed. For him that was his version of having a boulder dropped on his head.

"I'll see if she can't come up and take a long break later on," I added, trying to be kindly.

A visible brightening. "Excellent. It seems we have some friends in common in the profession. She's been in a few plays with one of my old cronies. We can compare notes."

The excuse was as long as a boardinghouse reach to me, but if he was willing to use it to get to know her better, then what the hell, why not? "You're being a complete idiot, you know."

"Yes, it's quite refreshing, don't you think?" As he looked down toward the stage where Miss LaBelle lurked, there was a decided glint in his eye and a predatory cast to his face I'd never seen before.

Good grief. I had no idea about this side of him. Escott the wolf? Escott the ladies' man? On the other hand, he *was* a gentleman.

This would be interesting.

The comic ended his routine, having worked his audience up to a roomwide belly laugh. I'd heard the act before at a dress rehearsal, but it was still damned funny. He bowed out, and Lady Crymsyn returned to introduce a blues man named Jim Waters I'd discovered a couple months back. He'd been playing in a small tavern trading his songs for tips from impoverished college students and other riffraff.

At the time, Waters had not entirely believed me when I said I'd wanted him to work at my club, but all doubts were gone now. He was already seated on a tall stool, his guitar in hand, the orchestra backlit behind him. He composed his own music, and they'd done sufficient rehearsal to make it seem like they'd been playing together for years. Mindful of the legacy left him by the comic, he plunged into a fast-paced number, his grin enough to let everyone know he was having the time of his life. That got the house warmed to him. The next song (after the applause died) was more moderate, but emotionally intense. He speeded up again for his third piece. His fourth and final one for this part of the show was a slow ballad about lost love. It was his best work, deeply moving, and gave him the wistful I-want-to-comfort-you attention of every red-blooded female in the room.

The response as he took his bow was such that I knew he'd be headlining here shortly, if he wasn't snapped up by some other entrepreneur in the meantime.

Then it was Bobbi's turn. The red velvet stage curtains had been drawn shut to allow Waters to exit and the orchestra members to change their sheet music. When the curtains next opened, Bobbi was seated on the white baby grand piano, a single spot picking out all those rhinestones on her gown, making them ripple and spark. She seemed to be framed in silver fire. I heard a gleeful exclamation and single hand clap from one audience member: Joe James, who looked unconscionably pleased with himself at the effect.

Bobbi's accompanist, Marza Chevreaux, did her job with her usual expertise, making it look easy. She framed the music around Bobbi's singing, complementing rather than competing. She idolized Bobbi, but didn't much like me, though her attitude had guardedly softened over time. Bobbi and I had been together nearly a year now, and so far I'd not made her cry, something Marza had not expected.

They worked to good effect for the first few bars, then the orchestra leader gradually brought in more instruments to fill things out. I'd not been awake during the rehearsals, so the end result was a knockout to me. She was definitely the star of the show, not merely background music for the customers. No one was dancing; they were all too busy listening.

Timed down to the minute, the lights came up at the end of Bobbi's set, and the orchestra struck up a number chosen to coax people out of their applause and onto the floor. I figured it would be safe for me to venture backstage now, and did so. Escott unobtrusively tagged along.

"You'll chase her off if you're too eager," I told him out the side of my mouth.

"Nonsense. All performers appreciate congratulations from their peers."

I grinned and left him to it, hunting around for Bobbi in the backstage melee. She was busy with one of the stage crew, gesturing at the curtains, then pointing toward the lights in an authoritative way, very much in her element. I waited until she was finished to offer her my own congratulations. They had to be brief, two other people came up to claim her attention, and she had to hurry off. She did cheerfully comment that I seemed a lot more relaxed. What pleased her, pleased me. I even caught Marza looking at me with—well, if it wasn't exactly a benign expression, at least it wasn't openly hostile. Maybe in a couple of decades she might even work up to a smile.

Escott returned wearing a peculiar face, as though he had a pineapple lodged halfway down his throat, but was strangely smug about it. "She's agreed to a late-night dinner after the show."

My God. He actually had a date. "Good. Enjoy yourselves."

"There is a slight problem . . ."

"Yeah?"

"I don't know of any decent places open that late. It would be most helpful if you could recommend one."

After all this time, Bobbi and I had found several, so I named a few that might fill the bill for him. He was pathetically grateful for the information.

Back in the main room, I made more rounds and shook

more hands. As Upshaw was away on the dance floor, I paused at Nevis's table, suddenly conscious of the wire photos folded up in my pocket.

"Great show, Fleming," he said, grinning. "I think you'll make the rent this month with stuff like that to bring them in."

As tonight's party was private, I'd skipped the extra revenue of a cover charge, but my landlord didn't need to be reminded. "Did you take care of your tour all right?" I noticed the bunch of flowers Rita had brought was gone.

She nodded. "Yeah. Booth showed me where it happened and all. It's awful, not what I expected, but I donno what I thought would be there. What's that big thing like a pot?"

I made an educated guess. "A cement mixer."

"You gonna cover up the floor?"

"Yes."

"Make it like new again, huh?"

Better then new, I hoped.

Rita got a speculative look. "Jack, I was wondering . . ."

"What?"

She fiddled with the clasp on her purse. "Well, I put the flowers there 'n' all, an' I was wondering if you could leave 'em there, under the cement."

For an instant I felt a strong tug within to tell her the real name of her friend, that the monster who'd masqueraded as Lena Ashley did not deserve to be mourned. I pushed it hastily off. Rita needed her illusion and so did Nevis. "Sure. I'll have the workmen leave them alone. It's a . . . a real sweet thought, Rita."

"Thanks, Jack."

"Yeah," said Nevis. "Thanks."

Time to leave; I didn't trust my face to conceal my inner discomfort, but I'd done the right thing. It would do no good for either of them to know the truth . . .

Oh, *hell.*

I should have said something to Blair as soon as he'd told me. He might not give the news to the papers right away, even with the joint crawling with reporters, but there was always later.

Eyes peeled for him, I searched the room. He was at the bar in the lobby. Malone was helping out there, just handing him something with ice and fizz.

"Have a root beer?" Blair asked genially, still on duty.

"I gotta favor to ask, if it's not too late."

Malone, alert to the tone of my voice, did a passable job of ignoring the conversation while soaking up every word.

Blair nodded to indicate he was willing to listen.

"Do the papers know about her real name yet?"

"Not yet."

"Is there a way of keeping them from finding out?"

"Why do you want that?"

"The truth would hurt some friends of mine."

He wasn't too impressed. "How so?"

"They liked Lena; I think one of them even loved her. It would only hurt them to find out who she really was."

The name caused Malone to drop his pretense of not listening.

I spared him a glance. "You don't repeat any of this."

He gave that nervous tic. "No, sir."

"It's going to be a matter of public record in my report," said Blair. "It already is with the people who identified the prints."

"You can bury that part, make sure the papers don't get hold of it. I know how those things work."

"The public has a right to know who she was."

"Gimme one good reason why. They poured out a barrel of sympathy for 'Jane Poe' and then Lena. How do you think they'd feel knowing they'd wasted it?"

He scowled.

"Come on, Blair. The public doesn't have to know they were betrayed."

He grunted. A neutral sound.

"Besides, these are hard times. Some of them spent good money sending flowers to Lena's service. It made them feel better. You want to take that away from them?"

He rumbled now, but it was in a more positive tone. "I suppose I can fix things."

"It's not too late?"

"Just don't expect me to repeat the favor."

I had no fear of that. "You're one in a million. From now on all your root beers are on the house."

"Pah!" he said. It was the first time I'd heard him laugh.

"Mr. Fleming?" Malone. "What is it exactly I'm not supposed to repeat?"

I lowered my voice so the other staff wouldn't hear. "That we found out Lena Ashley's real name."

"Oh? Who was she then?"

It didn't seem right to exclude him since he'd probably hear me speak about it in the future, so I pulled out the wire photo reports and allowed him a quick peek.

"Oh, dear God." Even in such a truncated form the basics of the case were ugly. He looked sick.

"You keep quiet about it. I don't want Nevis or Rita hearing even a whisper. Ever."

He shook his head. "N-no, of course not."

I thanked Blair again, folded the bad news into a pocket, and went back to play host.

With the crisis out of the way, it was an easy enough job. The rest of the evening sped by so swift and effortless it worried me. I half expected the roof to fall in, things were going so well.

The second show was as successful as the first, the wait staff ran their legs off keeping up with the drink orders, and it was with a shock I realized it was nearly two and time to close the doors. The orchestra played "Good night, Sweetheart," which signaled the beginning of the end. A large number of guests had already drifted homeward after the last stage act; this took care of the rest until the only ones remaining were Gordy's party, Coldfield's, Escott, Bobbi, and Lady Crymsyn. Malone had signed out the staff once they'd cleaned the bars and put the chairs on the tables. Sometime tomorrow a janitorial crew would come in to see to the floors and rest rooms. Malone stayed behind. The cash register receipts had to be counted, and he was still educating me in his system of bookkeeping.

He resumed his bartender duties one more time, though, as we all gathered in the front lobby for a farewell drink. He opened a bottle of champagne, and I invited him to join with the rest of us in hoisting a glass as toasts were made. I participated as well, having nimbly snagged an empty glass, cupping it in my hand in such a way as to conceal its emptiness.

Miss LaBelle was at last able to break character as Lady Crymsyn to enthuse about the place and how much she'd enjoyed herself. "People acted like *I'm* the owner. I hope that's all right, Mr. Fleming."

"Call me Jack, and yes, that's exactly what I was aiming for. You did a great job."

She beamed, and Escott beamed at her. No kidding. It was the damnedest thing I'd ever seen from him. I'd have to talk to Coldfield later about this new side, just so I could stop gaping at it.

Miss LaBelle took a tiny sip of her champagne—I approved that she'd had nothing stronger than water the whole night—then regarded me seriously with a set of very intense hazel eyes. "There's one thing I want to ask . . ."

"Sure, name it."

"Has anyone died in this building?"

Conversation certainly did. There was a lengthy pause.

"Did I say something wrong?" She glanced around at our silent circle, confused.

Escott gallantly stepped into the breach. "Not at all, it was just a bit of a startlement. Have you not read the papers?"

"No, I've been too busy. What did I miss?"

In a few carefully chosen words, he explained about what had been found in the basement, making it seem like very old news. He didn't include anything about the corpse there also wearing a red dress, and rightly so.

She digested the information thoughtfully. "How horrible, but I don't think it's quite right. Was there another death?"

"Several," I said. "A gang skirmish. Some people were killed here."

"That's it, then," she said decisively.

"What's it?"

"That explains the ghost here in the lobby."

Another long pause. Bobbi and Gordy looked at me. I'd also told Escott about the business with the lights, but he was too busy looking at Miss LaBelle. No one seemed too anxious to speak first.

Except me. After I'd swallowed my surprise. "Ghost?"

"Oh, I don't expect anyone to believe me. I've had that all my life. But you've got a ghost." Her utter ingenuousness was not something any actress could have faked, no matter how talented; she was completely sincere. Escott shifted slightly, his expression frozen into a small, tight smile. Maybe he was having second thoughts about wanting to keep company with her. That, or wondering if he could overlook this eccentricity when weighed against her other obvious assets.

"Actually," I put in at last, "I do believe you."

"Oh, that's very kind. Thank you." And she seemed content to leave it at that.

"Miss LaBelle—"

"Sherry."

"Sherry, would you please tell us more about the ghost?"

"I don't know that much. She's here in the lobby, mostly by that bar."

Malone, caught between amusement and apprehension, looked around. "She's here?" he asked.

"More over that way," said Sherry, indicating a spot just to his right. He, too, put on a tight smile and moved out from behind the bar altogether.

"Er—what does she look like?" *Tic.*

Her brow puckered. "It's not like she's anything I can describe. It's really hard, like trying to explain color to a blind person. I just know that she's there, but not in a physical sense."

"Is she scary?" asked Adelle Taylor, hanging on every word.

"Not at all. She's just there. I get the impression she likes what you've done with the place, Jack."

"Thank her for me," I said in a faint voice.

"She heard you. I think she likes you a lot, too."

"Oh. Uh, that's nice."

Sherry blinked and stared at the bar area, concentrating. "She . . . she's sorry about not being able to help more when you were hurt. What does that mean?"

Gordy shot me a look. I felt my mouth drop open, and I couldn't do a damn thing about it. "Oh, jeez," he muttered.

"And she's saying something about some grenades. That she didn't know about them until it was too late or she'd have warned you."

"Oh, jeez," I echoed.

"Yes, she was pretty upset by that, but glad no one was hurt this time."

"Sherry . . . could you ask if she left the whiskey on the bar last week?"

"She heard you. Yes, she did, but she didn't know that you don't drink that. She just wanted to make friends."

"Oh, jeez." I had gooseflesh creeping on my arms. Honest-to-God gooseflesh.

"This is fascinating," Escott said. To his credit, he did appear to be fascinated. He must have made a decision about her, and it had been in her favor.

Now where had I seen that earnest, inquiring expression on him before? Then I abruptly realized his interest was genuine, beyond his current infatuation. He'd looked just like that during our first interview in his office last August after he'd swiped my home earth to ensure that I would talk to him.

"I should very much like to hear more about this gift of yours," he said.

"Just don't make fun of me for it."

"Certainly not."

Ah, what the hell. He believed in vampires, why not ghosts? Why not in a pretty young girl who talked to them?

"I wish I could see ghosts," said Adelle.

Sherry's eyes flashed at her. "No, you don't!"

"Why? Do they scare you?"

"No, but some of them can be terribly annoying."

"This is a very strange conversation," said Coldfield. His luscious date nodded cautious agreement.

Sherry giggled. "Yes, it is. I'm sorry."

My proposal for another round of champagne met with relieved agreement and worked to bring things back to normal again. At least no one suggested we try having a séance. There was a general change in the crowd as the ladies trooped off to a rest room. God knows what they would be talking about there. Escott looked at his watch.

"You can sleep in tomorrow," I reminded him.

"Hm." He'd gone a touch dubious, now, which was deadly to any budding romance.

"You don't seem to mind that she's a medium."

"She did not once mention that word, nor shall I," he said, sounding huffed.

"Sure, after all, there are more things in heaven and earth—like me for instance. Besides, she's quite a good-looker. You can talk acting, not metaphysics."

He raised an eyebrow. A warning.

I backed off with a grin, my job done. She'd ceased to be a scientific inquiry and was firmly back to being a romantic conquest.

"Heard you got a break," Gordy said. He was addressing me.

"Huh?"

"When you were talking with Blair."

"How the hell you know that?"

His mouth thinned. A smile. "I'm a medium."

I glanced over at his bodyguards, obviously the source of his information. "They look more large than medium to me."

Now his head bobbed slightly back and forth. Laughter. "So what's the story?"

Apparently Escott had been keeping Coldfield up-to-date on matters at my club. Both leaned in to hear better.

"Okay, but this stuff doesn't go past the door. I don't want Nevis and especially Rita learning about it. I made an arrangement with Blair to keep it out of the papers."

They murmured assent to my condition, then I produced the wire photo articles and delivered the news about Lena's real name. Shocked silence for a moment, then some quiet remarks of disbelief.

"How'd she end up here?" Coldfield wanted to know.

"On the run from the New York cops," said Gordy. "What I don't get is how she hooked up with Nevis. He's not on the side of the law, but he'd draw the line at this."

"Nevis couldn't have known," I said. "Same for Rita."

"I fear I am unfamiliar with this case," said Escott. "I was out of the country at the time."

As I'd read it all by now, my memory was fresh with the facts. I filled him in.

In 1923 Helen Crespi, then a sweet sixteen, married Walter Tielli. By 1929, at the ripe old age of twenty-two, she had two children and sudden widowhood when her husband was killed in a construction accident. His insurance company had crashed along with the rest of Wall Street, leaving her a worthless policy. She scrabbled along on what little she could make as a shop girl. Compared to the rest of the country she was lucky; she had a job, but the wear of working twelve hours a day selling trinkets at a five-and-dime got to her. After a few months she wanted out.

She had no close relatives to help. Her husband's relations had troubles of their own. She went to state agencies and orphanages, trying to get her children adopted out. All refused. She maintained she could no longer afford to care for them properly. No one believed her, especially when the social workers interviewed her neighbors.

Helen was by then playing house with a guy named Dixon, who ran numbers for the local mob. He sometimes contributed to the household funds, but preferred taking Helen around to the clubs. She was a pretty girl, and he liked to show her off. This was more to her taste. Dixon was willing to support her, but complained about the children interfering with their bedtime fun. This inspired Helen to continue her efforts with the orphanages.

No one was sympathetic. She was a mother; it was her

sacred duty to care for her children, not run off to dance at the clubs all night or to live in sin with a man not her husband.

Dixon was preparing to leave her; he'd already moved to a nearby hotel and cut off his money.

Then one chilly day Helen Tielli decided to take her young children on a picnic in the country. In a hamper borrowed from a neighbor, Helen packed some sandwiches, a couple bottles of pop, a butcher knife, matches, and a small can of kerosene.

Hamper in hand, she herded the boy, seven, and the girl, three, onto a northbound bus. Once clear of the city, she asked the driver to stop. The trio tramped into some woods at the side of the road until Helen found a suitable spot to camp. Cold as it was, the children had no complaints. A picnic was an unheard-of excursion for them, a treat. They ate their sandwiches and drank their pop. Helen held the youngest until the little girl fell asleep. The boy, Walter, Jr., wanted to go to the bathroom. Helen left the girl napping on the picnic blanket to follow her son deeper into the woods. She carried the butcher knife and can of kerosene; the matches were in her coat pocket. The boy asked about the knife. She said it was in case they met a bear. Trusting his mother could protect him from such a threat, he relieved himself against a tree. When he was done, she cut his throat. It didn't work too well. Blood poured out of him, but he didn't die right away as he should have, so she stabbed him several times.

The kerosene was to burn up the body, to get rid of evidence. She slopped it over him and the first match she lighted caught. Flames exploded to life; foul smoke roiled up. Only Walter, Jr. wasn't quite dead. He rolled and shrieked in agony, trying to crawl away. She looked on, not moving as he cried to her for help.

Some hunters heard his screams and came running. Helen hurried back to the little camp and stabbed her sleeping daughter, then vanished into the woods. She was found hours later trying to hitchhike home. She thought the state troopers had stopped to give her a ride.

The boy died on the spot of his burns and wounds; the girl lived to be turned over to a state orphanage. Dozens of couples stepped forward, volunteering to adopt her.

During her confession with the cops which was quoted from in a national magazine, Helen said she'd intended to set the girl on fire, but she "felt bad" about the boy and decided against it. Not once did she call the children by their names or show any further remorse. She appeared not to care about anything except when she would be allowed to go home. Her boyfriend Dixon would be waiting for her, she peevishly insisted.

"Good God," said Escott.

"She was declared insane," I went on. "They put her in a nuthouse. She spent a week there before smuggling herself out in a delivery truck. Someone got careless with their routine bed checks, and she slipped away. There was a big hunt, but no one knew what happened to her after that."

"Until she comes to Chicago as Lena Ashley and went to work for Booth Nevis," said Gordy.

"And we all know how that ended." I shook my head. Justice, it would seem, had finally caught up with Helen Tielli, imprisoning her in a death almost as ghastly as that which she'd inflicted on her own flesh and blood. "The 'Murder Mom' got hers after all."

"How alliterative," Escott said, frowning at the sheet bearing that headline.

"That's what the papers called her until some group of mothers protested that it was scaring their kids."

"What happened to Dixon?"

I shrugged. "Doesn't say. She must have paid attention to his business, maybe heard a name or two, so when she got here she could ask around for work. Nevis gave her a job. I'll have to find out from him how he met her."

"What an unholy mess," said Escott. He handed the papers back to me.

I opened my mouth to speak, then shut it. I'd felt sick before about the crime, but that was nothing compared to what swept through me now. Could they see anything of it on my face? Bobbi would instantly notice, but she was thankfully away in the rest room.

"He'll wonder why you're interested," Escott went on.

"Nevis won't remember any of it."

"I like how you operate," said Gordy.

That was the highest compliment he could pay anyone, and everyone there knew it, but I was too mentally distracted to offer an appropriate thanks. I was saved by the return of the ladies. Adelle slipped a hand under Gordy's arm.

"It's late," she stated. Her tone was cheerful rather than reproach, but unmistakably insistent. The others nodded agreement with her, and the men sensibly surrendered. Escott left with Sherry, Coldfield with his troupe, Bobbi went along with Gordy's crew so he could drop her home.

"See you later?" she asked.

How I loved that imp's smile of hers. "Soon as Malone and I get the receipts counted."

I pushed ugly suspicions out of my head and locked up, heaving a sigh of relief. No need for me to breathe regularly, but the old habit for the release of tension remained strong. I felt like a wrung-out rag, but it was a good kind of feeling for a job welldone. Maybe an army of staff and entertainers had done the real work tonight, but ultimately the success of Lady Crymsyn was my responsibility. Tomorrow I'd know whether or not it had all worked; Escott had promised to check the papers for reviews and have them waiting for me. If he had time. Ghosts or not, he still seemed most taken with Miss LaBelle . . .

The bar light was on, but then Malone was busy wash-
ing up the champagne glasses in the sink there. I offered
to help, but he said he had everything under control, so I
told him to come to the main room with the cash drawer
when he was done. He nodded absently. I made a quick
trip up to the office to get the account books and a money
bag. By the time I'd come down he'd finished and turned
off the light. I wondered how long that would last.

Passing into the main room, I paused to look up at Lady
Crymsyn's portrait. It was still beautiful even after hundreds had seen her. For some reason I thought she'd be
subtly changed for the attention as any woman might be
changed.

Not Lady Crymsyn. Me. I'd had a lifetime in a few
hours. No wonder I was weary, and even slightly dis-
jointed in mind. There was also disappointment, sadness,
and a supreme desire to avoid what I had to do next.

Putting it off, I studied the portrait. The color seemed
to overwhelm the canvas. I'd never before noticed how
many different shades of red the artist had used in the
composition. He'd been invited to the opening, but begged
off, having another engagement. I wanted him here to tell
me why the reds were suddenly so prominent, when until
now it had been the face of the woman that had dominated.
Maybe it was a sign of great art for a single piece to be
so many things at different times.

Or maybe it was my mind trying to get me to focus on
another woman in a red dress. I really did not want to; the
evening had gone so well.

Malone was at the far bar, already sorting through the
wads of cash he'd taken from the club's registers. There
was a huge pile of ones, fives, and tens, a lesser, but still
most respectable stack of twenties and fifties, and even a
lovely collection of C-notes. I was pleased by the take, but
not nearly as much as I'd have been had Lieutenant Blair
not strolled in with his news and clippings.

Seated at one of the booths, Malone and I counted through the money, recorded it, wrapped rubber bands around the paper, and sealed the coins into sturdy bank envelopes, all ready to deposit. I deemed that this would be a task for which I would never grow weary.

"That's all then," he said, folding the last one shut.

"Not really."

He gave me an inquiring look. "Have I missed something?"

I was too well aware of the vast emptiness of the place. The fans still hummed, gently circulating air, clearing out the last of the smoke. Was it also drawing away the music and laughter that had filled the room hardly more than an hour ago?

Suppressing another sigh, I pulled out the now rather crumpled wire photos and put them on the table between us. "There's some things missing here. I want you to fill in the spaces."

For a moment, as he stared without comprehension at the sheets, I had the stabbing hope that I'd been wrong. That Escott's chance comment about it being an unholy mess had triggered a false conclusion.

But only for a moment. Malone's face went utterly white, and he slumped back in the padded seat of the booth. He released a long sigh of his own that sounded alarmingly like a death rattle. He looked dead, a dead man with only his stricken gaze to show that someone was still trapped inside the unresponsive body.

17

I UNLOCKED the liquor storage, got a bottle and glass, and took them to the table. I filled the glass and slid it across to Malone.

"Drink." The old-fashioned remedies are usually the best.

Some of the frozen horror leached out of his eyes, and he made an abortive move toward the booze. His hand was shaking too much to lift it to his lips; he had to bend close to the table to prevent spillage. He sipped down a good portion, then turned away, giving in to a coughing fit. Obviously a man not used to hard spirits even if he dealt with them daily.

Tic. "Wh-what are you going to do?" he asked. It sounded like someone else was using his voice.

He'd taken it for granted that I knew everything, and this lack of denial damned him completely. I'd only had a strong certainty before, diluted slightly by the weak hope that I was wrong. "I want to hear what you have to say."

"B-but—"

"Just talk to me. I think you need to. Get some more of that into you, then tell me everything from the start."

He meekly obeyed, draining off half the glass.

"Who are you really?" I asked.

Lips trembling, but he mastered himself. He pulled out a handkerchief and blew his nose, trying to put himself in order after I'd smashed him down with a sledgehammer. "My real name is Robert Tielli. I'm—I was—Walter's older brother, Norrie's uncle."

Well, that explained his motive.

"And you did it?" No need to specify what.

"Yes."

"Go on. How'd it start?"

"God, you might well say when he married her. They were young, he was only twenty, but she was pretty and they were happy enough. I was his best man at the wedding. He did carpentry, house construction, made a good living at it. I had the store—that much of what I told you was true. He worked there between jobs. And he gambled."

"What about the hot checks?"

"True, all true. I got the blame for them. I was angry with him, disappointed, but there wasn't much I could do. He was still my brother, and if I'd shifted the blame to him, who would support his family while he was in jail?"

"You?"

He shook his head. "Helen didn't like me. She came to know about my . . . my life, and it disgusted her. Walter just ignored it. I wish to God she could have done so as well. She was afraid to leave me around the children. I know there are men out there that . . . I'm *not* one of them, but she refused to understand."

"So you took the blame for the bad checks and went to jail."

"Not gladly, but yes. I thought it better for me to go instead. If I'd only known."

"What happened?"

"Walter was killed, not in a car accident, but on the job, some falling beams. He never woke up. The prison wouldn't let me out for even one day to attend his funeral. Helen never wrote me afterward. Never told me what she was doing. If only she had just said one word."

If only. The saddest words ever put together by helpless regret.

"I would have found some way to help her, help his children. They were my blood, too, all that I had left of my brother. I loved them as though they were my own. And then she . . . she . . ."

He had to stop. To break down. To release years of grief and rage and might-have-beens. It was awful to watch, to feel. The force of all that stored-up pain rolled over the table at me like a physical thing. If he'd been a woman, I'd have known what to do; but he was a man, and we suffer alone without the comfort of touch. I found a stack of napkins behind the bar. His handkerchief was inadequate to the task of all those tears. Feeling awkward, I put them within his reach, sat, and waited him out.

Gradually his sobbing trailed off. He scrabbled in near blindness for the napkins, savagely wiping his eyes, clearing his nose. He showed no embarrassment for himself; he looked very tired, though, very old. The thin lines that defined his otherwise youthful face had deepened and stretched.

"I was in prison when she did it. It was only later I found out how she'd tried to put the children in an orphanage. There was just a month to go before my release. I would have gladly taken them in, or found another home for them. But I didn't know. Dear God, if only I'd had some hint, but she'd cut me off, and there were no other relations of mine she could turn to. She'd said I was sick, perverted. That *I* was sick."

His throat clogged. He sipped more of his drink, coughing again.

"So rather than have a sick deviant like myself care for them, or at least help support them, she preferred them dead. What went through her mind? Did she feel anything, or have even a second's remorse? Was she insane by then? By the time I was out, she was gone. All I had was speculation, the wondering why, the not knowing."

Hers was an idiot's cruelty, I thought, trying to connect her horrific actions to that bland studio portrait that had come from the cops. "We want to know the why of it, to know how anyone could do such things, but there's no way any decent soul could or should understand. If we did, we might become like her."

He puffed out a small bitter laugh. "Oh, but I do understand. I did. I turned into her. For one night."

"Did you adopt Norrie?" I asked, to keep the flow going in the right order and interrupt his staring into space. Whatever he saw there had to be ugly.

He blinked at being drawn back. "I tried. I thought I'd have a chance since I was her uncle, but they turned me down because of my jail record—and other things. She was in an orphanage. A couple was all set to adopt her. They were probably nice, kind people, but she was all I had left of Walter. I couldn't let her go to strangers, so I took her away." He grimaced. "I know it was kidnapping, and there was a terrific hue and cry. They compared it to the Lindbergh baby."

"What, you put a ladder to a window?"

"There was no need. I waited until the children were on the playground. I wore overalls like the orphanage janitors and just called to her. She knew her uncle Robert and came running over. Then I just walked out right to the train

station with her in my arms. We were miles away by the
time she was missed.

"I'd hocked or sold everything in the store I could for
travel money. I trimmed her hair and dressed her in boy's
clothing. At that age it's hard to tell a boy from a girl
except by their clothes. She still had bandaging around her
throat. The papers said she'd been stabbed, but that was
wrong. Helen had drawn the knife across just like she'd
done with . . . with . . ."

He looked ready to break down again. I refilled his
glass.

"It'll make me drunk."

"You need it."

He trembled still, but was better able to hold things in
control. This time he merely sipped, then blew his nose.
"I covered the bandages with a high-necked sweater, gave
her a teddy bear instead of a doll to play with, and no one
noticed us."

"Then you came to Chicago?"

"Not at first. I'd taken a train to Buffalo, and posted
letters to the orphanage and to my parole officer."

"Why?"

"I thought they might like to know Norrie was safe. I
gave them my reasons for taking her, and that we'd be
starting a new life, that I would treat her as my own daughter, that she would be all right. Perhaps it was foolish, but
I didn't want them thinking she was dead in a ditch somewhere."

"And a Buffalo postmark on the letter might shift their
search for you to Canada?"

Tic. "Yes. The way I wrote and worded the letters hinted
at it. I'd planned it all very carefully. It was gratifying to
read about it a few days later in the papers. We were in
Chicago by then and I had new identities for us—I learned
how to do that in prison, false birth certificates, a driver's

license. That's when we became the Malones, little Norrie and her recently widowed father. I wore a black armband. People deferred to it, were kind, and out of tact did not ask very many questions."

"Why Chicago?"

"I'd spoken to that Dixon fellow, who was from here. To give him credit, he was as horrified by what she'd done as anyone. He'd had no inkling that she would do what she—he said she sometimes asked him about Chicago, so it seemed as good a place as any to go."

"What'd you do to him?"

Malone—and I still thought of him as Malone—blinked surprise. "Why, nothing. He'd been her motive, but nothing more. He was a small, stupid man, with a small, stupid life. They had much in common for that, but her actions were quite beyond his limits."

"So you went looking for her?'

"Not realistically. I can't explain, but I had an idea, a premonition, a wish, perhaps, that it wasn't over. That she and I would meet again. Every night I prayed for it, even though God must have known what I wanted to do once I caught up with her."

"So you found a job bartending?"

"Not at first. Prohibition was still on, and if there was a raid on the speak, I'd be in danger of arrest, but there just weren't any jobs open elsewhere. I did what work I could, but never for very long. Sooner or later someone would object to me, and I'd get fired. Things got bad enough to take the risk, and I found work at the Ace. I'd been told there would be no raids there, that Nevis had influence with the police. It proved to be true." His voice dropped to a whisper. "And a lucky choice on my part."

"You found Helen was working for him, too."

"It was like God had answered my prayers. I could hardly believe it, nearly fainted on the spot. She'd changed her hair, had grown up a bit, was more sophisticated, more alive, as though she'd turned into a completely different woman. But I still knew her the instant she walked in. I'd not changed that much, so I kept out of sight. She seemed very friendly with Nevis."

"Why did you choose . . . that method to . . ."

He sighed. "All I wanted was some isolated place to take her so we could talk. I'd heard the waiters gossiping about Lennet's speak being closed up and likely to remain that way. That had only happened a month earlier. So I checked it out, and it was perfect. No one would hear her in that basement. I went to a hardware store and got an eyebolt and a hand drill, some other things. She'd have to be tied up, you see."

I nodded once.

"I called in sick that night and waited outside for her. She and Rita would often come in together, but leave separately. I didn't know what their business was with Nevis—it didn't seem a good idea to ask. Around midnight she left, heading for the El at the end of the street. I got to her before she could reach it, showed her a knife I had, told her to be quiet. She seemed too dumbfounded to react."

"And she just went along with you?"

"She did after I made her drink what I had in my flask. It kept her quiet, a little woozy, but she was able to walk. I brought her here, brought her to the basement, and tied her up to that eyebolt. After that, it was only a question of waiting until she shook off the morphine. Hours, it turned out. Gave me plenty of time to think. And it occurred to me during those hours that I would have to find a way to conceal her body. If it were found and identified, then the police might begin looking for me again. I was a man with a clear motive, after all."

"You always planned to kill her?" So far, he was leading

up to an inarguable case for premeditation, which would put his neck in a noose for certain.

"Yes, I did," he said, pulling the lever to make the trap-door drop.

I felt heavy inside, my guts all turned to lead.

"I didn't know how I would kill her, though. I had the knife, and though there was a certain justice in cutting her throat, it would be too quick. Then it came to me that all I had to do was keep her right where she was. I found loose bricks throughout the basement, not nearly enough, but they were a start so I could calculate how many more were needed. By the time she fully woke up I had it all worked out."

"What did she say to you?"

"Absolutely nothing. Just stared at me like some ox at the slaughterhouse. It was a different face than the one she showed at the club. Her eyes were . . . empty, as though her soul had gone, leaving behind only a husk. This was the face of the woman who murdered my nephew. This creature—thing—had killed him. I tried talking with it, wanting to know *why*. But she wouldn't speak. She wouldn't say one word. I spent half the day trying to—"

Easy enough to see the two of them, the dank basement, the red glitter of her evening gown being picked up by his flashlight or lantern, and him throwing questions at her, his frustration mounting in measure to her silence.

"All I got from her, *all* I got was—" He had to pause, his control in danger of slipping again. "She wanted to know when I would let her go, so she could go home. That's the only time she spoke." A truly awful grimace distorted his face as he fought more tears and rage. "She didn't seem to be aware of what was happening to her, of her situation. She didn't even seem to be afraid. I was not bloody justice come to exact terrifying retribution; I was merely an inconvenience to her schedule.

"That's what the children had been to her. A problem she had to get rid of because it interfered with her pleasures.

"She could have simply walked away from them, abandoned them. It would have been wrong, but they would have eventually been found and cared for. Instead, she chose to kill them. She *chose*. I came to see that as I faced her. She wasn't insane, she was evil."

"Did you think of turning her over to the cops?"

"No."

"Why?"

"They'd have just sent her back to that asylum, and she could have escaped again. She wasn't a smart woman, but she was very cunning, like a rat is cunning. She would have found a way out again because being locked away would inconvenience her. Besides, they might have found me and taken Norrie away. I couldn't bear that. So, I made a choice of my own.

"I saw to it she was securely tied down and gagged, then went to buy bricks and mortar. It took a few trips to bring it all in—how my arms ached—but I'd made my decision, and went through with it. Again, I don't think she really understood what I was doing. She just watched, not saying a word, but by then I was able to ignore her the same as the rats in the building ignored us. I built up the courses—Walter had taught me a bit about construction—and they went up very fast. "If just once, *once*, she had said she was sorry, said *anything*, I might have stopped."

"Might?"

"I honestly can't say I would have, but I might have if she'd shown any sign of still being human. Nothing was there, not even an animal was left, just this *thing*. You can feel sorry for an animal; all I felt toward her was fear and disgust, as one fears a disease. To let her go would be to give it a chance to kill again. I shut her away. For forever, I thought."

"Why'd you stay on with Nevis?"

"It was a good job, and it might look odd if I suddenly quit so soon upon his precious Lena's disappearance. He was fair to me, too. He could overlook certain things so long as I showed up on time and did my work well."

"Why did you come here to me? I should think after finding the body you'd have packed and left."

"I had some idea that I should be in a position where I could keep an eye on things. I never dreamed you'd give me a job like this. I actually had a hope I could give Norrie a real home, nothing fancy, but better than she'd known before. Back when I first took her away I told her that I was going to be her daddy, and we'd live happily ever after. She believes I'm her real daddy now, and sometimes I can believe it myself."

There was a world of grief and agony in his eyes. Tears threaded steadily down his cheeks. "Mr. Fleming, I shall never have children. Norrie is the closest I'll ever get to fathering my own. I love her as though she were my own daughter. She is outside of this. What I have done must not touch her. I don't care what you do to me, but for God's sake don't let her pay for it. You're a good man. Could you promise me that you will see she's protected? I've no right to ask for myself, but for her sake . . . ?"

I'd seen this coming. Had known I'd have to eventually stop listening and start doing. Didn't make it any easier.

And just as I opened my mouth to speak, every light in the place winked out.

A small amount of illumination came through the diamond-shaped windows, enough for me to see, but Malone was quite lost. He stared around, startled and blind.

Lights on. I counted to five.

Off.

Oh, shit.

I didn't know what was wrong, but instinct told me to assume the worst. At the most, I'd only look foolish, but I could live with embarrassment. Quite easily.

"Come on," I muttered. I had presence of mind to gather up the money bag.

"Where? What's going on?"

The lights stayed off. I led him from the booth down to the access door of the tier seating. He stumbled, confused in what to him was absolute blackness. I tried the door, cursing as I remembered it was locked from the inside. I thrust the money bag at him and fumbled out my key ring.

"Mr. Fleming?"

"Shuddup," I whispered fiercely just before vanishing. I could risk it in this murk. Re-forming on the other side, I opened the padlock, yanked on the door, and grabbed Malone, pulling him in.

"What is it?" he hissed, his alarm at my lunatic behavior overcoming everything else.

"Take this key, and use it on the padlock you'll find on the door. I don't know what's wrong, but it could be something serious. You stay locked in here and keep quiet, unless you want your little girl to be an orphan."

That turned the trick, instantly cutting off any further questions or protests. He made only a small worry-noise in his throat. His heartbeat seemed to fill the sheltered space with its drumming.

I closed the door softly behind, and was reassured to hear Malone following orders.

The lights came on. Hard to tell if that was a good sign or not. I hoped I was just overreacting, to find out that it was merely a problem with the fuse box. Some practical joker who'd heard about the house ghost might have come back to scare me, say, one of Gordy's or Coldfield's bodyguards.

Which didn't seem likely. Until I knew better, I'd err on the side of caution.

Floating half-visible over the floor, I was able to approach the front silently. I'd heard the snick of a shutting door there. Maybe it was Bobbi wanting to know why I'd not come over yet.

No such luck. Booth Nevis and Tony Upshaw were in my lobby, having apparently just walked in. I went solid half a second before they spotted me. The all-around surprise was almost comical. I might have laughed but for the knowledge that I'd locked those doors. Had Myrna the ghost's pranks branched out into a whole new area? Didn't seem likely, either.

"What the hell are you doing here?" I asked, not unreasonably.

"Glad we caught you," said Nevis.

My imagination, I firmly told myself, provided the extra emphasis on the word *caught*. "What's the problem?" At this hour and under these circumstances, there would always be a problem.

"Nothing we can't settle in a nice, friendly manner," he assured me, achieving the opposite effect intended. "Let's go inside, and if you invite me for a drink, I won't turn you down." He looked amiable. Both were still in their tuxedos; Upshaw sported a walking stick in imitation of Fred Astaire. What had they been talking about during the opening to bring them back to the club?

"It's late, Nevis, just put it on the table."

Nevis clearly wanted something, but I couldn't imagine what, unless this was some sort of shakedown for a percentage of tonight's receipts. If so, then he needed better muscle for the intimidation part.

He crossed the lobby to the bar, motioning for me to come along. I was aware of Upshaw hanging ominously back, but not about to let him get behind me with that stick. Nevis put an arm on the bar, leaning casually, presenting a benign face to me. "It's about that book of Lena's," he began.

"What about it?"

"Not having a club to look after for the moment, I've had plenty of free time to study. I'm pretty good with numbers, you know. Guess I'd have to be with what I do. Well, I added up all of the stuff she skimmed, and it came out to a pretty respectable sum. Just over fifty-two grand as a matter of fact."

"That's respectable, all right," I agreed, finally getting an inkling.

"Now seeing as how you had the book for a while, too, I assume you also did a little addition of your own and came up with the same number."

I gave a noncommittal shrug.

"Which leaves me with the big question of where that money might be."

"She probably spent it."

A slow grin lit his gaunt face. "I don't think so. If Lena spent that much, I'd have noticed."

I nearly suggested she'd paid blackmail, but changed my mind, picking something else that cost a lot, wanting to see where Nevis was going with this. "Gambled it away, then."

"I don't think so. Not when I had her betting on sure things. She could have easily doubled her money, tripled, on the tips she had. That wasn't it."

"Sent it home to family."

"She said she didn't have any."

That I could believe. Nevis, too, apparently.

"No, Fleming, I think she hid it. Was saving it for her old age maybe. When she first disappeared, Rita and I looked all over, searched her things for a clue as to where she'd gone. We found no bank accounts or safety deposit keys, nothing like that. She could have buried it in a hole in the ground, but that's not a wise thing to do in the city, not practical. I think she hid it and in a place Rita would be unlikely to look."

"Go on, I'm interested."

"I'm sure you are. You spent some time with Rita the other week. I'm thinking that once she was asleep you went through her flat. I know you help that Escott bird out with his little detective business; you'd have picked up the habit from him. At that time you were trying to get a handle on Lena, trying to find her killer, and I don't hold it against you."

"I'm glad," I said drily.

"But I hold that you found the money."

"Oh, I did?"

"Hm. In those old books of hers."

I tried to keep my face deadpan, well aware that it might be a futile effort. "What books?"

"The ones in that case Rita uses for a bar. I noticed a couple were missing. They used to be jammed in tight, and suddenly there's spaces between them. I pulled them out and found what you found, minus the money."

"You're saying she hid the money in books? Like between the pages?"

His eyes flickered. Was that doubt? Was I actually going to get away with a real lie for once? "Not quite."

"Then what? Come on, it's late."

The flicker was amusement. "It'll get more late, unless you come across. I know you found the money, that you took it away."

"Me? Why not Shivvey?"

"Because if he'd got hold of that much, he'd have blown town, not tried to make a grab for my club."

"Unless he was greedy and wanted both."

Hesitation. A tiny doubt. Which he squashed. "Maybe,

but before I face that calamity, I need to eliminate you from the list."

"I don't have that kind of money. I certainly don't need it."

"Everyone needs it, you especially. The cost of putting this place together must have shoved you in a very deep hole. That amount of cash would float you out of it with plenty to spare. I'm giving you a chance to return it to me."

"Return?"

"It was mine to begin with. She stole it from me. I think you're a basically honest man, Fleming. Do the right thing and give it back."

This farce had gone on too long. Bobbi was waiting for me, and I still had a hellish problem locked under the seating in the main room. I fixed Nevis with a long steady look. "I want you to listen to me . . ."

Concentration was the key—if he'd not drunk too much, if I didn't give him one of those deadly migraines by pushing too hard. But concentration went both ways when it came to eliminating small distractions. I was aware of Upshaw's close presence; I'd have to get to him next.

But the damned lights went out.

They suddenly came on again, especially the ones inside my head.

Blinding shards of brightness lancing through my closed eyes, burning holes in my brain, shuddering down the length of my body. Something hit me all over. I had the dim idea I'd lain down for a nap on the cold, hard floor.

But I don't sleep now.

"What the hell?" Nevis. "What'd you do?"

"He was acting fishy. I gave him a tap." Upshaw.

"Tap, hell, you broke his skull open."

"He'll be all right. Throw some water on him."

They threw water on me. To no effect. It neither eased

the pain nor made it worse. I had a whole world to myself, and it was all pain. Their little activities had nothing to do with me.

Something touched me, a hand at my neck. I couldn't move. Couldn't react to it.

"Tony. *You idiot!*"

"What?"

"What do you think, asshole? *Look* at him!"

"Aw, shit . . . aw, shit . . . I didn't mean to—"

Sound of a scuffle, a fist on flesh, a cry. Sound of Nevis cursing. *"You know what you cost me?"*

"I'll make it up, I promise."

More cursing. It took him a long time to wind down. None of it had to do with me, with the white-hot cocoon that held me fast and unmoving at their feet.

"Let's get outta here," Upshaw whined.

"And leave him like this for Gordy to find? Him and Fleming are in each other's suits. Gordy's got brains, and I'll make book Fleming tells him everything. He'll figure this out, and he'll come looking for me. As for you, one look and he'll know whose legs to break to get some talk."

"Then whatta we do? Hey, that plane of yours—you can take him up. You can get rid of him that way."

"No I can't. The guy at the airport won't talk for the cops, but he would for Gordy. I can't take that chance. We gotta bury him . . . we gotta . . ." He trailed off to a relieved laugh.

"What? You got something?"

"Get his feet. This will cost you a new tux, but if I hear one complaint I'll put you in the same hole with him."

Upshaw grabbed my feet. Nevis hooked iron hands under my arms and lifted. My head set up a whole new clamor of agony as it lolled back. They grunted and swung me like old laundry. No reverence for the dead here.

Just wait, some tiny voice within said, shouting thin

against the pain. *Wait it out and then you can—*

But I lost the rest as they lurched clumsily down a flight of steps. Nevis nearly dropped me as he struggled to hit the light switch.

"There, all the way to the back," he said.

More grunting, but Upshaw was in good shape from his dancing and Nevis was strong for all his leanness of frame. They made it without mishap.

"Here?" asked Upshaw.

"Yeah. Make sure his arms are over his head. It'll take up less space."

They dropped me. On something unconscionably hard. It opened up whole new frontiers of awfulness. My flaccid arms were stretched overhead like some Inquisition victim on a rack. I'd have been better off with the rack. It wouldn't have hurt so much.

"Now what?"

"Now we go to work. Get your coat off and help me drag this thing over."

"You're kidding. Are you kidding?"

"No. All the stuff we need is right here. He's planning to fill it in anyway, I heard. We just do this and they'll think he jumped the gun on the work. It'll have all weekend to set."

"But the mess—"

"I told you, one complaint and you go in next to him. You cost me fifty-two grand, you little shit, so don't think I won't. You know how much that woulda helped me getting the Ace back up and flying? So you shut up and pitch in like a good boy, and I might not break your legs myself afterward."

They left me alone. I missed their argumentative distraction. It kept me from feeling the terrible cavern of ache inside my skull.

I wandered in it, lost and alone as the two of them clattered around, doing God knows what. It was noisy and involved a lot of cursing and grunts of effort. Water splashed, then some mechanical grinding filled the room. They had to shout to each other.

"More water, another bag!" Nevis bellowed.

The grinding built in level so as to be deafening.

Belatedly, my brain came near to surfacing out of its stunned stupor. It shifted snail-like into an actual train of thought separate from the damage. It set up a number of panicked reactions for my body to go into, but for the fact that my body was inert for an unguessable time.

But that wasn't real panic. The true internal frenzy began when that first ghastly blob of wet cement slapped over my face to forever seal me in pain-suffused darkness.

18

SCREAMING, screaming, *screaming.*

I was alive. Trapped inside my body. My dead body.

Alive and aware, as cold cement oozed over it, layer upon layer, the weight crushing me into a stony trough of a grave.

Dead and unresponsive to the danger, absolutely unable to *move*.

Internal shrieks drowned out all thought. There could be no thought with such gibbering fear tearing me apart.

Caught away from my earth I had such nightmares as this, but those were softened by the innate knowledge that they were only dreams. My daylight paralysis was part of it, unavoidable but acceptable. This was different, to be fully conscious, fully sensible of every inch of my flesh smothering under the pressure.

The stuff flowed thickly, and there was no end to it. My face, then torso, it crept over and encased my raised arms, seeped under my neck, filled in the space under my back,